TIME RUMMERS

Also by Tim Robinson

A Tropical Frontier:
Pioneers and Settlers of Southeast Florida
(A comprehensive history)

A Tropical Frontier:
Tales of Old Florida

A Tropical Frontier:
The Homesteaders

A Tropical Frontier:
The Gladesman

A Tropical Frontier:
The Cow Hunters

AUTHOR'S NOTE: This is a work of fiction; however, several of the primary characters are based, in part, on actual settlers. In addition, many of the incidental and secondary characters were real, living, breathing people whose true stories are told in the history A Tropical Frontier, Pioneers and Settlers of Southeast Florida.

TIME RUMMERS

OR

HOW GNARLES AND PADDY SAVED THE DAY

TIM ROBINSON

Port Sun Publishing
PORT SALERNO, FLORIDA

ISBN-13: 978-1501002441
ISBN-10: 1501002449

Printed and bound in the USA.

Cover illustration, Jerry Fuchs
Cover design, Patrick Robinson

To Gnarles "Rick" Hawkins and Paddy "Robinson" O'Toole

Many thanks to:

Debi Murray, Pat Daum, Don Slattery, Sheila Katz,
Harold Gunn, Jerry Katz, Mom.

Are we dreaming?
Anonymous, 38 B.C.

Time Rummers

July 1890

Charlie MacLeod knew how to live. No one lived better, and no one understood better how fleeting life can be. He had, after all, wasted twenty years of his own life he would never get back. He was a fatalist at heart, though he had spent much of his life convincing himself otherwise. He told himself that if he had not tossed away that enormous part of his life, he would not – could not – be living the same life he was now.

He often wondered, if he ever had the opportunity to live his life over, if he would have the fortitude ("the cocoanuts" as he put it) to live it exactly as he had. For how could he have reached this point had he not followed the exact same path? Each turn leads to another; without the one, the second is impossible.

It was these specific, singular choices that had planted him where he was.

And he loved that place.

He thought he might like to stay a while.

"Hey, Uncle Charlie."

"What is it, Sweetpea?"

"Do you think we'll ever be able to travel through time?"

Charlie thought a moment.

"Hmmm," he said, scratching absently at his bushy, gray beard. "Can't really say, Sweetpea, but I'll tell you this: if it ever is possible, even if it's thousands of years off, then we should expect that those folks are walkin' around amongst us right now, as we speak."

He looked around suspiciously, then at her. They were sitting on the black rocks looking out to sea.

"In fact," he said. "How do I know you're not from the future?"

"Because, silly. I'm from Chicago!"

Charlie looked sideways at his youthful companion.

"Chicago of today?" he queried. "Or 1990?"

Annie giggled.

Charlie dug his toes into the deep layer of broken shells and sand at the bottom of the smooth depression in the ancient, wave-worn rocks.

"Now, why on earth would you ask such a thing, anyway?"

"Oh," she replied. "Poppa's going to be reading a book called *The Time Traveler* at his next reading."

"And I suppose you've already read it?"

"Of course," Annie giggled. "Want me to tell you how it ends?"

Charlie stuck his finger in the air.

"Let me guess," he said with a studious face. "The End."

"Right!" she exclaimed. "How did you know?!"

It was a running joke.

Charlie spent a lot of time these days pondering his lot in life, mulling over the great philosophical questions and reflecting. He wondered why he had lived such a long life when there were so many others he had loved along the way who had been deprived of the opportunity. Some had deserved it much more than he, he thought. His mind often drifted to people and places long gone, like his dear Nellie, his first love and the mother of their child. It still tore at him that she'd never had the chance to know her own daughter.

There were others who had passed from this earth; and always, each and every time, he had blamed God, shaking his fist at the sky, cursing Him and all His saints, daring the Deity to strike him dead – even denying His very existence.

Nowadays, however, he wondered. Had he been wrong to do so? Did it even matter?

He looked at Annie, red hair and freckles and happy to do nothing more than stare out to sea, just as he had been as a boy.

It seemed like only yesterday.

Chapter One

The farm wasn't much to look at – a few dried-up sprouts struggling to poke their heads above a patch of sand and weeds. The house, if it could be called that, was small as well and looked as if it might have been constructed on the side of a mountain instead of flat ground. Everything was crooked, with not a single, square corner or plumb line to be found.

It appeared as if it might fall over at any minute.

Constructed of pine plank set on edge vertically, with a cypress shingle roof, it had a fresh coat of yellow paint. Poking through the roof was a stovepipe, and on the front stoop was a single chair and small handmade table with a pile of books on top – history and literature. In the front yard was a pitcher pump and another crudely constructed table. Some distance behind the main structure was the outhouse, built along the same lines but appearing even more likely to fall over.

From behind the house came a frenzied banging, a moment of silence, then more banging. A man, covered head to toe in sweat and grime, was working over a broken grub-axe handle. It was wedged between two boards that made up the top of his workbench, which was haphazardly attached to the house. He was swinging a mallet as hard as he could, trying to knock the handle loose, cursing under his breath and growing angrier with each swing.

Then, as he had done several times that afternoon, he missed, smashing his already swollen hand. He cried out in pain and stuck the appendage under his armpit.

All of a sudden, he started beating the top of the bench with the hammer, walloping it repeatedly, as hard as he could, causing the entire structure to shudder and threaten to collapse.

He abruptly stopped and glared at the axe a moment. Then he abruptly yanked it out of the bench and flung it as hard as he could. He followed its path as it soared high, almost straight up, then came down right on top of the outhouse, crashing through the roof.

For a long while, he stared. Then he slumped against the bench, breathing hard and mumbling curses. Finally, he stumbled over to the rickety structure. Opening the door, he peered down the hole where it had landed, and, holding his breath, he reached in, fumbled around a moment, and pulled it out.

What he saw amazed him.

The axe head had miraculously come loose. Shaking excess sludge from it, he held it in his hands and stared at it.

Slowly, a smile came to his lips, then a laugh as he sputtered the words, "Ohhh! The handle comes out from the *other* end!"

* * *

Nondescript. There was nothing remarkable or even out-of-the-ordinary about Silas Hempsted. He was of average height, average build, with straight, drab hair that was thinning on top. He had undistinguished features except for a larger than normal nose, not large enough, however, to make it memorable.

He had grown up the middle child of a large family, had been an average student in school, and had gone off to the St. Louis Polytechnic Institute where he had lived up to his potential of mediocrity.

When he walked into a room, no one cared, and when he walked out no one noticed. He had lived most of his entire thirty-two years with this knowledge and had long ago conceded it to be his lot in life. He was a nobody. When he had returned home from school to Joplin, Missouri, he had worked at several jobs, first as an accountant at a local mercantile, then as a bookkeeper for a mining company, then for the railroad, and finally as a teacher in the local school. It was there that he had found some semblance of solace and competency. Unfortunately, much of Joplin was wiped out by a tornado, including the school in which he taught.

He had been teaching history to his first-through-eighth graders when the monster hit. He had done as prescribed and led his class into the cellar under the building. When he got there and took roll call, though, he discovered one was missing: Lizzie Freeman, second grade.

Panicked, he told the children to remain there while he went to find her. When he climbed out of the hole, the sky was dark, almost like night, and the wind howling. Debris was pelting the side of the small, frame building. His instincts told him to run back into the hole, to escape, but other voices told him to find the little girl. He looked out the window at the approaching monster, a quarter mile wide and moving fast. Frantically looking around the schoolroom, tossing desks aside in a fevered search, he realized she wasn't there. His eyes went to the front door. It was open.

Suddenly the windows blew out, sending shards of glass flying in every direction. Something hit him in the face. Terrified and unsure what to do, he looked back to see one of the boys peering out of the trap door that led to the cellar.

"Willie!" he shouted. "Bolt that door!"

4

Then it hit.

When he awoke, he was lying on his back in a flattened wheat field. He lay there, confused, listening to the drizzle of rain. The drops felt good on his skin, almost putting him back to sleep. He thought it a dream at first and had to force himself to stay wake. As he tried to sit up, however, he realized the school's blackboard was on top of him, the day's lesson still visible, a rough drawn map of Athens showing the Parthenon, the Acropolis, and in the top corner, Mount Olympus.

His mind reeled as he tried to wake up from the horribly life-like dream.

In his disorientation, he thought he heard voices. They seemed some distance off, first one or two at a time, growing closer, confused shouting, then screams followed by ever increasing wails of horror. A few moments later the sounds of fevered banging and boards breaking arose. He reached up and touched his head and saw blood – and it all came back to him.

Dozens had died that day, including Silas Hempsted's entire class, all of them sucked out of the cellar and tossed indiscriminately across the area.

When Silas finally stumbled up to the ghastly scene, the first question from a sobbing mother was, "Where were you?!!"

He had never tried to explain. The cellar door had been found, unlatched.

His life had been a living hell following the tornado, not only because of the question that raged in his own head – why me – but because everyone had blamed him for something that had been out of his control. Many times, he had wanted to explain himself, to say that he had told the kids to stay in the cellar with the door bolted, but every time he did, it felt as if he were making excuses – and maybe he was.

He often racked his brain, questioning his own memory.

Even his own family had abandoned him; all, that is, except his mother. She had been the only one, but even she wasn't immune to the insults and angry stares from neighbors. When Silas had told her he was leaving, she had cried, but she understood. Going into her big cedar chest, she had pulled out her grandfather's watch and coin collection. Placing them in her son's hand, she had told him to go in search of his dream.

The coins had been worth a good amount. He had enough to keep him going a while. The watch he was loath to part with, recalling the look in his mother's eyes when she had handed it to him. He was determined to keep that.

Unfortunately, the farm wasn't doing well. It seemed for every two steps forward, Silas took one back. But, he reminded himself, that was better than one forward and two back.

Now, four months after he had arrived on Lake Worth, he had a house approximately ten feet square, and nearly one acre cleared. With all the fish he could eat available for the taking, he wasn't going to starve, although he did yearn for more vegetables to go into his pot. The garden had yet to yield much more than a few underdeveloped turnips and a meager supply of sweet potatoes.

His homestead was located about a mile south of the post office and hotel, with approximately three hundred feet of lake frontage. It was 153 acres, narrow and deep, and extended nearly a mile inland, nearly to the low sandy ridge that separated it from the vast swamp to the west. Most of his property consisted of hot, sandy, dry terrain, the undesirable domain of the stubby Florida spruce, scrub oaks, saw palmetto, prickly pear cactus, Spanish bayonets, and the giant Eastern Diamondback Rattlesnake. It was only along the lake's edge, where hammock land reigned supreme, that the soil was rich, black, and fertile.

Much of the lakefront he had cleared in the four months since finishing his cabin, except for the larger oaks and gumbo-limbo trees. The first day he arrived, he had stood at their bases and looked skyward, deciding then that he would spare them. He would find out later this had left him bereft of much of the most arable soil on his property.

It had been hard work, laboring in the Florida heat, chopping, sawing, and burning all day every day. Never in his life had he worked so hard – and never had he experienced such a feeling of accomplishment. The extensive pineapple and citrus grove he envisioned remained a dream, but he was making progress.

So, as something of a reward to himself, each afternoon, after a hard day of farming, when the sun began to make its descent, he would lay down his tools and head over to the lakefront with his fishing pole and a good book. There, he had built a small dock, not more than eight feet square, which he had tied to an old, fallen, cabbage palm tree. An excellent example of his carpentry skills, the rickety structure made his house look like a professionally engineered edifice.

Sitting down in his regular spot, his back to the cabbage palm, he put a piece of dried fish from the previous day's catch on a hook and dropped it in the water. Then he picked up his copy of Herodotus's *History of the World*. Now, Silas Hempsted was doing what he enjoyed most. This was the one and only thing that had turned out exactly as he had imagined when he first headed south to the Florida frontier: balmy breezes and dangling toes.

He had been there for some time – having caught a snook, two sheepsheads, and a caravel jack and tossing all but the snook back in the water – when he heard a commotion up the Lake Trail. He knew what it was before he looked. It was his neighbors to the north, a Gnarles Hawkins and his sidekick, Paddy O'Toole.

"Must be Friday night," he mumbled to himself.

He set his book down and watched as the diminutive old codgers – one scrawny, the other portly – stripped off their clothes and jumped into the water. Silas wondered at the old men, bathing in salt water. He hated it himself, the way the salt stuck to his skin afterward, but the two geezers had explained that they had been taking salt baths for almost forty years, and they weren't about to stop now.

Gnarles and Paddy were some of the oldest settlers around, having come to Florida with the Armed Occupation Act of 1842. They had originally settled on the barrier island up on Indian River, where any fresh water had to be collected from rain or brought over from a creek on the mainland. They contended that salt-water baths were the secret to their youthful appearances – which only they could discern.

They waved. Silas waved and went back to reading.

A little while later, he noticed the shadows reaching across the water. Gathering up his things, he pulled the big fish from a washtub he had just for the purpose and started towards his house.

"Hey! Silas!"

Turning, he instantly averted his eyes from the sight before him: two ancient little men, naked and waving enthusiastically. He waved back, straining to keep his eyes averted, but they continued to wave and call.

He started towards them.

"Hi, there, fellas," he said as he approached, thankful they had pulled on their trousers. "How are you, today?"

"We're good," Gnarles, the scrawny one, said. "How you doin'?"

"Oh, fine," Silas replied, holding up his trophy for the day.

"Nice," Gnarles said. "Don't ya think, Paddy?"

Paddy, who didn't say much as a matter of course, replied in a thick, Irish brogue, "Aye. 'Tis a nice fish, for-r-r sur-r-re."

"Thanks," Silas said. "It put up a pretty good fight."

Neither man replied, so Silas said, "Would you fellas like some? I can't eat it all."

"Oh, no," Gnarles said. "We ate at the hotel. We get to eat for free there."

"Really? You get to eat for free in addition to your salaries?"

Gnarles and Paddy looked at each other as if to ask, *Salaries?*

"Never mind," Silas replied.

The two men stared.

"So," he finally said. "What's up?"

"Oh!" Gnarles said, as if he had just remembered. "We was just wonderin' if you wanted ta join us up ta the hotel t'night, you know, for readin' night."

Silas was aware that Friday evenings were "Reading Night" at the hotel. Folks from all over Port Starboard gathered around to listen to Alfred P. Humphrey read. Mr. Humphrey – who was one of the most educated men on the entire lake and had even been an actor at one time – read from current and classic novels, often acting out scenes.

The "funny little men," as they were oft described, had approached him several times before, and Silas had often thought of going, but he wasn't comfortable in social situations. He had said he was tired. In truth, he was worried that folks might not like him, that they might see through him for what he was: boring.

More than a few times over his life he had been called just that, from school days to the technical institute to most recently on the steamboat coming down Indian River to Lake Worth.

He had been sitting in the parlor, invisible as usual, when he overheard someone say the words, "Oh, him? Mr. Yawn-derson? We'd do better to play Bridge with three."

It had happened all his life, but it still hurt as much as it had the first time.

"Come on," Gnarles prodded. "We'll take *Cocoa-Nuts*. There's a nice breeze and a moon out tonight." He looked at Paddy and grinned. "We promise not ta keep ya out too late, and ya don't have ta worry about us gettin' too drunk neither. Betsy don't like us over-doin' it on the premises."

Silas wondered what the sideways grin was all about, if they had some practical joke in mind.

Yet it felt good to have someone interested in him, and he found himself replying, "Sure ... I suppose. I'll need to eat my dinner first." He looked down at himself. "And get cleaned up a little."

Gnarles punched Paddy in the arm.

"See? I told ya he'd come this time! Seventh time's a charm!"

Paddy, rubbing his arm replied, "I did'na say he would'na come."

"Yes, you did."

"Uh-uh."

Silas, not wanting to interrupt, held up the fish and pointed towards home. Then, as Gnarles and Paddy continued their discussion, he walked away. He found himself excited about his first night out since arriving at his new home.

He'd always wanted friends.

Chapter Two

Port Starboard was a growing community. By this time upwards of two dozen families were scattered over several square miles on the northwest shore of Lake Worth, a narrow, twenty-two-mile-long lagoon on Florida's southeast coast. It had not always been a lagoon. It had once been a freshwater lake complete with black bass, bream, crappies, a host of freshwater birds, and, of course, the man-eating and much maligned *Alligator Mississipiensis*.

There were many who believed this unscathed wilderness a paradise on earth, a timeless refuge, a place to escape *to* – indeed, a place to start over, as had been the case with Lake Worth's first settler.

It had been during the Civil War, twenty-seven years earlier, that a former slave and falsely accused murderer named Booker T. Hooker was cast upon her shores. He was being transported from Key West to New York where he was to get "a fair trial and be hung" when the U.S. gunship he was on, *Rappahannock*, wrecked along the coast near what the U.S. Geodetic Survey later dubbed Booker T. Rocks.

Ironically, he and another prisoner, Bobby Hackensaw – captured blockade-runner – had been the only survivors. The ship's captain had left them on board when he and crew abandoned ship. The sailors all drowned, and Booker and Bobby survived. Bobby had moved down to Biscayne Bay with his wife, Sally Hackensaw, and had years later returned to settle at Port Starboard. Booker T. had stayed and carved out a life for himself in this "Garden of Eden."

Booker's homestead was famous, described by one northern travel writer as "reminiscent of a jungle river outpost." Most who traveled down the lake stopped to look around and even venture into his extensive, lakeside, cocoanut grove. Here, hundreds of these most tropical of trees grew in magnificent profusion along his entire half-mile lakefront. Directly behind this was his farm, a showcase of possibilities available to any pioneer with a good reserve of backbone and grit.

At the southern extent of his property was Booker T. Creek – also named by the U.S. Geodetic Survey – and on the north bank was the little red schoolhouse on land Booker had donated. A few steps from the school was a colorful sight: a pink, combination post office and general store. Barely visible through a veritable jungle of cocoanut trees, glimpses of pastel yellow and lime green heralded the Hookers' home. Booker T. and Maggie had been happily married for years. They were the oldest settlers on Lake Worth.

Port Starboard wasn't like most towns. As with all the tiny settlements springing up along the many shores of coastal southeast Florida, from Indian River to Biscayne Bay, there were no roads, although there was talk of building one between Lake Worth and Biscayne Bay.

The closest thing to a road was a series of trails. In some places the Lake Trail might be a well-cleared path maintained by the owner. In other places it could be barely discernible from the jungled hammock from which it was carved. Be it on lake, bay, river, or sea – all settlement was on the water. There were no roads, no horses, no pastures. There was no place to roam, only a forested, sandy ridge overlooking the lake and the deep blue sea.

Situated in a young orange grove on the south shore of Booker T. Creek was the Port Starboard Hotel, owned and run by fellow pioneers Betsy Dawson and her husband, Major Sam Jesup. The hotel was nothing fancy, not at all like the much grander Cocoanut Grove House across the lake, but it was clean, well-maintained, and comfortable. Two stories high, with wide verandas stretching across the front, it was painted white and surrounded by a thriving hedge of red hibiscus bushes and a breezy stand of cocoanut palms.

Just to the south of the hotel was the Jesups' home. Betsy had grown up on Biscayne Bay and at the tender age of fifteen had married a much older Sam. They had spent many tumultuous years together as the owners of the St. Augustine Hotel. Several years earlier she had finally given Sam the boot and moved to Lake Worth – taking her *assistants*, Gnarles and Paddy, in tow.

There, she had taken up a homestead.

In those days there were few women willing to go off into a wilderness and start over on their own, but Betsy Dawson was no ordinary woman – as one Samuel B. Jesup eventually realized.

Major Sam Jesup had what is often termed a "checkered" past. To start with, he wasn't a major at all, though he did serve in the army for some time before he was drummed out of the corps for bedding the general's wife – and daughter. After that, he had done what came so naturally: he became a card shark and confidence man, scouring the world for lonely souls and uncompromised trust. Following the fire that destroyed their hotel in St. Augustine, he had gone back out on the road prepared to turn the world around. Things didn't work out as planned, however, there being little call for aging gamblers with memory lapses and a shaky hand.

When the old dog had run out of money and possibilities, he had returned, tail tucked, and a woebegone tale dripping from his lips.

Betsy took him back, explaining, "The old cur's like the mole on my rear end. Probably wouldn't get rid of it if I could."

From appearances, Sam had learned his lesson. He was hopelessly attached to, even in love with, his wife of over forty years: the bold, buxom Betsy Dawson. Yes, the old, card-playing, smooth-talking Lothario had finally settled down and accepted the things that matter most in life: home, hearth, and the opportunity to do as much of nothing as possible. Indeed, Sam had by this time elevated the act of sitting on the front porch – feet propped on the rail and smoking cigars all day – to nothing less than an art.

Of course, he was always available to assist Betsy, if need be.

"Sam! I need you in here!"

Sam closed his eyes and pretended to be asleep.

A few minutes later, Betsy walked out on the porch. The screen door slammed. Standing over him, hands on hips, she stared.

"I know you're awake, Sam."

Nothing.

"I always know when you're awake."

Nothing.

"Sam, my dear old dog, when you're really asleep, you drool."

"I most certainly do not!" Sam doffed his hat defiantly.

"Not all the time," Betsy replied. "Now, would you come in here? I need some help cleaning up. Everyone will be here soon, and I want to get home to spruce up a little. So, come on, big fella," she prodded. "Let's get a move on."

"But –"

"No buts. I want to get home for a minute."

"Deah Betsy," Sam implored in his deep, Virginia drawl. "You know what dishwater does to my hands."

"Yes, the same thing it does to mine."

"But what about the way it affects my card playin'? I don't want to lose my magic touch, as you know."

Betsy sighed. "Rough hands only make it harder for you to cheat. Anyway, you don't play poker anymore. You don't have any money."

"But," he mumbled. "If I did have money –"

"But you don't, so there's no need for you to perform your *magic* any longer."

"Are you sayin'," he queried, "that I do not need to perform *any* of my magic?" His eyes slowly descended to an ample, and still vibrant, bosom.

Betsy shook her head. "I can tell you this, Mr. Magic, if you don't come in here right now, you won't be layin' a hand on either one of those bunnies any time soon."

Sam scowled.

Chapter Three

It was eight o'clock Friday night at the Port Starboard Hotel. Alfred Humphrey, the former Shakespearean stage actor from Chicago, was on fire.

People were on the porch, trying to put him out.

"I'm fine! I'm fine!" He insisted, pushing helping hands away as he snuffed out one last smoldering ember. As everyone backed away, he struggled to his feet. Then he glanced downward at a very concerned, freckly face. "I'm fine, dear," he said.

The little red-haired girl heaved a big sigh, then turned to a sandy-haired boy at her side, and said, "It's all right, Benji."

"Was that part of the show?" he asked.

Annie was about to answer her little brother when Alfred announced, "Not to worry everyone! It's all part of the show!"

Alfred, a wisp of a man with a matching hairline, wondered how he might work catching himself on fire into his reading and performance of "The Time Machine."

Summer was not the best time of year for an outdoor gathering, the risk of mosquitoes being high, but with a decent breeze off the water and a good supply of skeeter switches on hand, it was proving to be a splendid evening. Even with that, smudge pots were lit and scattered throughout the cocoanut trees and around the porch.

Several lanterns were also lit in advantageous locations on the porch where Alfred had set up a small podium and several props: a fake sun and moon, a chair, and a pith helmet with wires coming out of it. Several people, including Betsy and Sam, were seated around him on the veranda. Everyone else was gathered in front of the wide steps, some in chairs, others perched on the hotel's benches; others still were sitting on blankets or leaning against palm trees. There were no lights in the small crowd, only on the porch, which allowed Alfred to see their faces.

Alfred relished the crowd more than the performance itself.

"Without an audience," he would pontificate, "acting is nothing! Taken on its own, in fact, it is nothing less than an exercise in idiocy. Insanity even! Imagine," he would scoff. "Pretending to be someone else. Pretending!" he would reiterate. "To actually insert one's self into someone else's skin and *pretend* to be them!" He would roll his eyes grandly and shake his head. "Why, it is nothing more than make believe! Like children in a school yard!"

Then he would smile and raise his finger in a very Shakespearean manner and, with a profound and righteous sigh, say, "Exactly like children."

Following an extended pause, he would continue.

"When we see an actor on stage or even read a short story or novel, what do we do but revert to a childlike state, thus *allowing* our minds to let go of our day to day existence and fly, unfettered, like a bird on the wing? We travel to another place and time, to experience and understand what it is like to be someone else. Yes," he would declare, "be he actor or author, it is you, ladies and gentlemen, dear patrons of the arts, who by your mere presence wield the power to magically transform an act of insanity into a work of art!"

"Poppa!" Annie whispered from below. She made a twirling motion with her finger, the same way her mother did to inform her long-winded husband that it was time to move along.

"Yes. Thank you, dear," Alfred said, noticing he was losing his audience. "Now, let's see," he mumbled, looking down at the open book in front of him. "Where was I?"

A blustery boom from the gallery announced, "You were catchin' yourself on fire!"

Alfred scowled and looked over his glasses at "Uncle" Charlie MacLeod.

Ignoring the droll outburst, Alfred waited for the laughter to subside. Then he returned to the book. With a curious expression, he cocked his head and sniffed the air.

He was on fire again.

*   *   *

As Alfred stomped around the stage, slapping at his pants leg, Betsy stood up, and announced, "Why don't we take a short break while *Alfred* here puts himself out!!" Then she strode off through the screen door, letting it slam behind her. "Coffee's on its way!" she yelled over her shoulder.

Those who didn't take advantage of the free coffee headed down the shore and into the woods where Gnarles and Paddy had set up their portable pub: an old ship's door laid atop a couple of cabbage palm stumps. On top of that was a jug of Gnarles and Paddy's own blend: a dark, full-bodied rum with a hint of cocoanut and eleven other herbs and spices.

With the five-minute announcement from Betsy, the pub's "doors" closed, and everyone resumed their places. Sitting in the back, down on the benches by the dock, were Gnarles and Paddy and their new friend, Silas. Across from them, on the other bench, were Charlie MacLeod and his wife, Molly Blue, and Charlie's nephew, Eddie Dawson.

Silas had never been part of such a group. He had been instructed by his parents that it wasn't proper for a good Christian boy to associate with the kind of people that drink liquor, so he never had.

But he sure was having fun tonight!

Of course, he passed on the liquor. He had witnessed what the "Devil's brew," as his mother referred to it, had done to his Uncle Ignatius. His mother had always held him up as an example of what could happen to a person susceptible to the horrors of alcoholism. He wondered about these people, though. They didn't seem at all like Uncle Iggy: when he drank, he got mean.

"Oh," Gnarles had said in reply to his query. "There's lots 'a folks just can't handle it. Me and Paddy, though, we can tell, and we only sell ta happy drunks. Me and Paddy even got beat up a couple of times, ain't we Paddy?"

"Aye," Paddy replied with a note of Irish pride.

Silas found himself enthralled with these little men, wondering what had brought them to such a state, but he didn't want to pry. He had read enough to know that most people don't question why they do what they do. They just do it.

He looked across the way at Charlie MacLeod.

According to Gnarles and Paddy, Charlie MacLeod had lived the most interesting life of anyone they knew. They referred to him as "the Old Salt." He had sailed the seven seas, and he certainly looked the part. He was old, well into his seventies, with a mass of hair on his head and a full, gray beard with traces of red remaining. On his head he wore a red bandana and, in his ear, an oversized, silver earring. Most striking of all was his peg leg, obvious to the casual observer as he wore his trousers cut off at the knee.

Fittingly, a small green parrot was perched on his shoulder.

The parrot's name was Salty, and Silas had been quick to discover that he "has a bloody mouth on 'im," as he had heard Charlie declare. Most fascinating about the old man was his wooden leg with what appeared to be a half-a-cocoanut attached to the end. He reminded Silas of Long John Silver from Robert Louis Stevenson's novel *Treasure Island.*

Charlie caught him staring at his leg.

Silas instantly turned away. A moment later he could not help but look back to see a grinning Charlie.

Silas felt himself blushing.

"It's all right, son," the old man said, revealing a hint of Scottish ancestry. "I'm used ta folks starin'. It's really somethin', huh?! Most folks get a kick out'a Ole Peg here." He laughed and stretched it out. "Best leg a man ever had!" he declared, stomping it on the ground. "Tough, too!" He nudged the woman sitting next to him.

"Ain't that right, m'darlin'?"

Silas had never met such a woman. She was younger than Charlie and statuesque; and Silas thought she might have been considered pretty when she was young. She wore a lot of makeup and a tight dress that accentuated every possible female part. He thought that if he met her on the street, he might have thought her a prostitute, or even a madam.

It occurred to him that they were the perfect pair.

Turning towards him, she smiled and, with a full, throaty voice, exactly as he would have expected from her ruby red lips, said, "Oh, it's tough, all right. That thing has been through everything you can imagine! And," she looked askance at Charlie. "It's about time you get a new one."

Charlie chuckled. "And retire Ole Peg? Why, it would be like partin' with me own other leg – the one that gives me hell, by the way." He winked at Silas. "Next thing ya know, she's gonna want a new me!"

He laughed as she leaned into him, and said, "Now what in the world would I do with a new you, Charlie MacLeod? I'm just now gettin' to like the old one!"

"Hear that, young fella?" Charlie nodded sideways. "I figured a while back that if I just planted meself on her like a barnacle, she'd get used ta me. Looks like me plan worked after all."

Charlie laughed.

"Don't worry, kid," he said. "You'll get used to us." Then he nudged Molly, "Ain't that right, sweet cheeks?"

"Oh, yes," she replied. "Me and Charlie here are like a couple of barnacles. We'll grow on you."

"That's right," Eddie said from the end of the bench. "If you're not careful, we'll all grow on you, and before you know it you'll look like the bottom of my boat."

"Hey!" Charlie suddenly barked. "Gnarles! Paddy! You gonna introduce us to your new friend here, or what?!"

"Oh," Gnarles replied. "Well, this here is Silas, and this here is Charlie MacLeod and his wife Molly and down there's Eddie."

Silas waved, astounded at his good luck. Maybe, he thought, things were going to change for him after all. Maybe a new start was all he needed, just like his mother had said.

*   *   *

A few minutes later, Alfred was back on stage, preparing to resume his performance by doing deep-breathing exercises. The assembled waited patiently, with an occasional murmur or chuckle. The only other sounds were those of skeeter switches swishing and Betsy's porch swing squeaking. Setting his glasses firmly on his nose, Alfred took one last look at the audience.

He took a moment to wink at Annie and Benji, and he raised his hand like Moses. The squeaking stopped.

"I will resume several passages back," he said; and with an affected English accent his friend Booker had labeled "positively atrocious," he began:

> *The Time Traveler said not a word, but came painfully to the table, and made a motion towards the wine. The Editor filled a glass of champagne and pushed it towards him. He drained it, and it seemed to do him good for he looked 'round the table, and the ghost of his old smile flickered across his face. 'What on earth have you been up to, man?' said the Doctor. The Time Traveler did not seem to hear. 'Don't let me disturb you,' he said, with a certain faltering articulation. 'I'm all right.' He stopped, held out his glass for more, and took it off at a draught. 'That's good,' he said. His eyes grew brighter, and a faint color came into his cheeks. His glance flickered over our faces with a certain dull approval, and then went 'round the warm and comfortable room. Then he spoke again, as if he were feeling his way among his words. 'I'm going to wash and dress, and then I'll come down and explain things ... Save me some of that mutton. I'm starving for a bit of meat.'*

The audience was clinging to every word, for no one did it like Alfred.

When he was on stage he was unstoppable, his mind suspended from reality. Under his command, barren, sterile words sprang to life, sending the characters leaping from the page. His every nuance and inflection spoke volumes, and his myriad expressions and body movements, though entirely overdone at times, brought the audience along with him; indeed, to the very shores of another time and place.

From the reaction of the assembled, Alfred was as good as ever: pompous and grandiose and in perfect harmony with the words on the page. From Alfred's perspective, however, tonight's performance was off, lacking in one very important regard. His wife, Katie, his biggest supporter and the person to whom he dedicated each and every performance of his life, was not in the audience. Instead, she had gone off to New York with two of her friends, and, though no one else noticed, it was throwing him off. But Alfred P. Humphrey was a professional, and the show, as he often declared, must go on!

'I can't argue to-night. I don't mind telling you the story, but I can't argue. I will,' he went on, 'tell you the story of what has happened to me, if you like, but you must refrain from interruptions. I want to tell it. Badly. Most of it will sound like lying. So be it! It's true—every word of it, all the same. I was in my laboratory at four o'clock, and since then ... I've lived eight days ... such days as no human being ever lived before! I'm nearly worn out, but I shan't sleep till I've told this thing over to you. Then I shall go to bed. But no interruptions! Is it agreed?'

'Agreed,' said the Editor, and the rest of us echoed 'Agreed.' And with that the Time Traveler began his story as I have set it forth. He sat back in his chair at first and spoke like a weary man. Afterwards he got more animated. In writing it down I feel with only too much keenness the inadequacy of pen and ink—and, above all, my own inadequacy—to express its quality. You read, I will suppose, attentively enough; but you cannot see the speaker's white, sincere face in the bright circle of the little lamp, nor hear the intonation of his voice. You cannot know how his expression followed the turns of his story! Most of us hearers were in shadow, for the candles in the smoking-room had not been lighted, and only the face of the Journalist and the legs of the Silent Man from the knees downward were illuminated. At first, we glanced now and again at each other. After a time, we ceased to do that and looked only at the Time Traveler's face.'

Alfred paused and looked out upon the faces staring back at him, like putty in the palm of his hand.

"Well," he said, removing his glasses. "I suppose this should be a fine spot to pause for tonight, don't you think?"

The response was more than he could have asked for – jeers, boos, catcalls, and a variety of similar grumblings.

He smiled.

"Very well, then," he announced. "I shall continue."

Following a short applause and cheers of "Jolly Good Fellow," he raised his hand, signaling silence, and started again. The best part was coming up, the scene in which he would climb into the machine – the chair – and travel through time.

Alfred picked up his pith helmet with wires and tubes protruding from it.

Chapter Four

The performance was a success. Alfred departed the stage with the crowd calling for more. The hero had been left in desperate straits, hanging on for dear life from the proverbial cliff, and it would be another week before any of them would know the outcome.

Except for Annie, of course. She was privy to everything her father read. She was resisting pleas from her little brother, Benji, to tell her what happens next.

Also pleading were Gnarles and Paddy.

Standing nearby was their new friend, Silas.

"Just a hint!" Gnarles was saying. "We gotta know now! We can't wait all the way till next week!"

Paddy nodded vigorously.

"Nope." Annie crossed her arms. "You know I can't tell what happens. Poppa would be furious."

"We just want a clue," Gnarles begged. "A little hint is all."

"Uh-uh."

Dr. Sally Hackensaw and her husband, Bobby, strolled up with one of the newer residents in town, Malcolm Geoffreys. Clearly, they had heard Annie being bombarded with begging and pleading.

"Mr. Hawkins," Sally said with a knowing grin. "Are you and Mr. O'Toole prying again?"

Everyone knew that Gnarles and Paddy had been in love with Dr. Hackensaw for years. She was the smartest, prettiest, kindest person they had ever known, they said. It was she who made sure the old geezers took good care of themselves. They didn't, of course, but she continued to try.

Sally had another distinction: that of being one of the first girls on earth to imagine she might one day become a doctor. "Unheard of" would have been a common response in the 1850s when she had attended medical school. It had been difficult being the only woman in a world of men, some of whom took it as a personal affront. *A lady doctor? Preposterous!* But she had persevered, not only by leaping the monumental hurdle of acceptance to medical school, but the more audacious feat of staying there.

She had been prepared for the reality: two years of condescending stares and tasteless remarks, but, as her father, Charlie MacLeod, had told her before she went off to school, "There's always gonna be assholes, sunshine."

It had not been her father, however, the fancy-free philosopher of the sea, who had inspired her to discover to what heights she might soar. It had been, in fact, her uncle, Will Dawson. It was he, her teacher, who had insisted from a very early age that she had the intelligence and talent to become anything she wanted.

"But," she had pointed out. "There's no such thing as a lady doctor."

Unable to argue with such ironclad logic, Will had told her in his very English way, "And what would be the shame in being the first?"

Sally loved her Uncle Will.

Now in his later years and bereft of his beloved wife, Elizabeth, he lived with Sally and Bobby up the shore where she kept a small practice. As one of only three doctors on the lake, she stayed relatively busy.

The house, a Cape Cod design, was large with all the latest conveniences, including indoor plumbing, and they had plenty of room, so when Will's cousin, Malcolm Geoffreys, had shown up unannounced several months earlier, it seemed perfectly natural that he would move in with them.

By this time, Malcolm had become a regular member of the tight-knit community. Like his uncle, he was from England. His mother was Will's cousin, but they had never met.

When he showed up one day at the Port Starboard Hotel, announcing that he was Will's cousin, everyone had been surprised – and no one more than Betsy, Will's daughter. She told everyone she had been aware that she had relatives in England, but it had never occurred to her that one of them might actually show up on her doorstep one rainy summer afternoon in all his British glory.

He had made quite the impression, the tall, dapper Englishman, a mass of blonde curls and a strong, square jawline, a sparkling smile, and the deepest, bluest eyes Betsy had ever seen. They were just like her father's, everyone noted.

Yes, when Malcolm Geoffreys arrived, the women noticed, one young lady in particular. Bonnie Blakely was Port Starboard's own lovely and unattached schoolteacher. It had been a whirlwind romance, but they were in love, each certain that they had found "the one." Everyone agreed, they were the perfect couple.

Bonnie was out of town at the moment with her two best friends, Katie Humphrey and Christiane Dawson. The three women had gone to New York City for two weeks to shop for Bonnie's wedding trousseau and to make other wedding arrangements.

"Oh, no, Sally," Gnarles pleaded. "We wasn't pryin'. We was just hopin' for a hint is all."

Sally leaned into her husband.

"They want to know pretty bad, you think?"

Bobby smiled, and said, "Looks like it." Everyone appeared confused, so Bobby continued. "What Sally is trying to say, boys, is that we've already read the book, too. You can ask us if you want."

"Really, Bobby?" Gnarles exclaimed. Then he looked around and lowered his voice. "You mean, you'll tell us what happens?"

"Sure," Bobby said, smiling broadly. He could see the excitement in Gnarles, Paddy, and Benji's eyes. "But," he added. "If I do, I've gotta tell you the whole thing."

"Okay!" Benji clapped his hands. "Tell us! Tell us!"

Paddy quickly joined in.

"Aye! We gotta knooow!"

Gnarles, on the other hand, scowled.

"Wha'd'ya mean, ya gotta tell us the *whole* thing? The ending, too?"

"Yep," Bobby said. "The WHOLE thing. Once I start a story, I can't stop."

"Never mind," Gnarles grumbled. Then he spent the next few minutes explaining to Paddy and Benji why it was a bad idea.

A little while later, Charlie, Molly, and Eddie walked up.

"How do, folks?" Charlie said, sticking his cheek out so Sally could give him a kiss. "I see you all met Silas, here."

"Oh, right!" Gnarles blurted. "This here's Silas Hempsted, our neighbor."

After everyone made their howdy-dos, Charlie said, "Well, it's nice ta finally meet ya, young man. This is the first time you've been here, if I ain't mistaken."

"Yes, sir," Silas mumbled.

When he offered nothing else, Charlie chuckled, "Well, it's about time is all I got ta say. Wha'd'ya been doin' down there anyways? Gnarles and Paddy here say you're goin' at it all day every day!"

Silas appeared put off at the familiar attitude Charlie had taken with him – as if they had known each other for years.

"Yes, sir," he replied. "I suppose I do."

"Hear that, m'darlin'?!" Charlie laughed and gave Molly a squeeze. "I'm a sir, by the burly winds that blow! Why, I suppose that makes me a gentleman to boot!" He grinned at Silas. "Now you must tell me, young fella, do I look like any kind of gentleman you've ever laid eyes on?!"

Charlie stretched his arms wide, putting himself on display.

Everyone watched with fascination as Silas stammered, "No, sir. I mean, yes, sir. I mean –"

The uproar was deafening.

Silas glanced around at all the faces focused on him, laughing. His mind reeled, taking him back to an entire lifetime of similar situations.

Charlie remained in place, arms outstretched, a cheery sheen to his rosy cheeks.

Yes, Silas Hempsted was on the verge of tears when something unprecedented happened. Instead of the usual pointing of fingers and secretive giggles that accompanied such behavior, Charlie hobbled forward and held Salty out.

"Go on," he said. "Give old Salt a scratch 'r two behind the ears."

Silas had no idea where a bird's ears were, but he reached out and scratched, then watched as the little green bird puffed out to almost twice his size, and squawked, "Son of a Sea Dog! Aarrak!"

"Look at that, everyone!" Charlie bellowed, capturing the attention of the entire gathering. "Looks like our greenhorn here's all right with Salty!"

Silas was at a loss. He wondered if it was a cruel joke.

Then he heard the words, "Oh, Charlie. Leave the poor thing alone." Molly tugged at her husband's arm. "Can't you see you're embarrassing him?"

To this, Charlie guffawed, then strode over and put his arm around Silas.

"I'm sorry, young fella," he said. "We just all been watchin' ya over there for months, livin' like some kind 'a hermit, and we wanted to give ya a hearty Port Starboard welcome is all. So, welcome ta Port Starboard!" he declared, pulling the smaller man into a giant bear hug. Then he looked at Molly, and said, "Ya know, m'darlin'. I got a good feelin' about this one. Ya see how Salty took to 'im?"

"Yes, sugar plum. Salty loves him. Now, please let go of him before his head pops right off his shoulders."

"Oh. Sorry about that, young man," Charlie replied, and he released his grip.

*   *   *

Soon after that, Gnarles and Paddy regaled Silas with tales of the old days from up on Indian River. The story, in fact, was of the Great Indian Scare of 1849, during which the entire settlement had been abandoned.

"And no one returned to their homes except for you two?" Silas asked.

"That's right," Gnarles replied, shifting his boney butt into one of several knotholes on the ancient oak tree branch.

They were sitting in their "tree house," which had been constructed twenty feet out over the water on the massive, low-sloping branch. Silas found the term tree "house" a poor descriptive as it consisted only of a variety of boards nailed together. Some of them were simply one board; others were complicated contraptions meant to give them a place to fish from or lie down for a nap. They were, at the moment, gathered around the main platform, a roughly six foot by six foot section of ship's decking situated about ten feet above the water and appearing as if it might teeter into the drink at any moment.

"Yep," Gnarles repeated. "We was the only ones ta come back … except for the Hackensaws and Dawsons. They lived across from us on the mainland," he paused and started counting on his fingers. "Then there were the Russells, and Caleb Brayton, and Captain and Mrs. Pinkham, and Old Phil and Young Phil Hermans, and Mr. Gattis." He paused again, looking curiously at his fingers.

"And Cap'n Deee-vis," Paddy said. "Dooon't for-r-rget Cap'n Deee-vis."

"Right," Gnarles replied, putting up another finger. "And Captain Davis."

"So," Silas said, filled with wonder at the two bona fide pioneers. "It was just you two – and those other people – living along this whole, entire coast with no one else around but Indians?"

"Yep," Gnarles stated proudly. "Except for a few folks down on Biscayne Bay."

"And you say the army re-activated the fort up there on Indian River?"

"For a little while," Gnarles sighed. "You should'a seen it, though. We thought with all the business goin' on, buildin' the fort back up and boats and ships comin' and goin' all the time and havin' soldiers around for pertection, that all of a sudden folks would start movin' down here in droves."

"So, what happened?"

Gnarles shook his head, and said, "Once the Indians rounded up the renegades and turned 'em over to the army, and they found out there weren't really no war at all, the soldiers over at the fort up and skee-daddled." Gnarles pursed his lips. "Then it was just us old-timers again, waitin' through the next Indian war, then the War Between the States, then another long, dry stretch before folks finally started movin' down here a few years back."

"They say it'll take a railroad before things really start to develop and grow," Silas noted.

"They been tellin' us that for-r-r years," Paddy opined. "Ya gotta wait for-r-r th' r-r-railr-r-road. Ya gotta wait for-r-r th' r-r-railr-r-road."

"Yep," Gnarles agreed, reaching for the jug. "And they won't build a railroad 'til more folks move down here." He took a slug and passed it to Paddy.

"Aye," Paddy replied. "And they won't mooove down here 'til they build a r-r-railr-r-road." He took a nip and handed it to Silas, who waved his hand.

"He already told ya, numbskull," Gnarles grouched. "He don't want none!"

"I for-r-rgot! I can'na r-r-remember everything, ya knoooow!"

"Ya can't remember *anything* is more like it," Gnarles grumbled.

Silas thought it might be a good time to change the subject.

"Don't you fellas wonder if time travel really is possible?"

"It must be," Paddy said, "accordin' ta th' story t'night anwee."

"You're so dumb," Gnarles snickered. "It's just a story. Don't ya get it? Ain't none of that stuff true." He glanced at Silas for confirmation.

"That's right," Silas replied. "That was just a story by H. G. Wells. He's a writer from England. Remember? Alfred was talking about how actors and writers just make things up and pretend?"

Surprised at the old man's *naiveté*, Silas said, "Mr. Wells published it as a work of fiction, which means it was all made up – pulled right out of his imagination."

Paddy sat with this a while, then said, "But it seemed so real."

"Well," Silas replied. "I imagine both Mr. Humphrey and Mr. Wells would be happy to hear that. It would be a great compliment."

Paddy nodded thoughtfully and, taking another swig from the jug, asked, "So, d'ya think a person c'n r-r-really travel through time?"

Gnarles laughed again, but Silas said, "I don't know. No one knows for sure, I suppose. We don't know what might be possible in the future. There's people who say that one day man will fly, or even go to the moon!"

They all three looked up at the waxing moon.

"That's crazy!" Gnarles declared. "Flying to the moon?!"

"Just remember," Silas said. "It wasn't that long ago that we didn't have electricity, or light bulbs –"

"We still don't," Gnarles mumbled.

"Or even railroads," Silas added. "Can you imagine a world without railroads?"

"Sure," Gnarles replied. "It's called right here."

Silas laughed. "I suppose you've got me there. Then again, we aren't completely without in that department. We have the little Celestial Railway right up the lake."

"Hmph," Gnarles grumbled. "Ya git on it, and eight miles later ya gotta git back on a boat again. What we need is a *real* railroad, not that little thing. One that we can just git on right here in Port Starboard and take it all the way to … wherever! Me and Paddy took a train trip all over onc't: Nashville, Louisville, Richmond, Savannah. Ain't that right, Paddy?"

"Aye. That we did."

Gnarles made a wide sweeping gesture.

"We wanna go wherever we wanna go – from right here!"

"And where would you boys like to go?"

"Inta th' fuu-ture!" Paddy blurted. "I'd like ta goo inta th' fuu-ture!"

"You're so dumb, Paddy," Gnarles said.

"Nooo, I'm not!"

"Yes, you are."

Silas rolled his eyes, then he leaned back against the branch-boards and stared at the heavens. It was nice having friends, but he was growing tired.

Chapter Five

"Oh, my Heavens!" Bonnie declared like the Southern belle she was. "I am simply going to melt right away to nothing. Have you ever seen it so hot in all your life?!"

The three women were standing in the shade of a small, covered area on the Titusville dock, their eyes fixed, staring southward, scanning for a puff of smoke.

"If I have," Katie replied. "I certainly don't remember, and I grew up down here."

"Oh," Christiane announced in a cultured French accent. "When I go on board, I am going straight to the hurricane deck, and I will remain there until we have traveled all the way to Jupiter."

"A breeze would be nice," Katie said.

"A breeze would be glorious," Bonnie added.

All three women were dressed for traveling in full-length, white and light-colored cotton and lace frocks with recently purchased, fashionably feathered hats. They each had fan in hand and were vigorously utilizing them.

From the end of the steamer wharf, the entire town and waterfront of Titusville could be observed. The old docks to the north were a mishmash of worn boards and pilings, bent and twisted by sun, wind, and rain. In some places a dock started and ended out in the middle of nowhere as if it had sprung from the water by itself. Many of them were completely stripped of their decking by the forces of nature, leaving only the rotting pilings and sagging stringers to remind one that in the end, everything belongs to Mother Nature – and that it is best to know the extreme high tide mark before building a dock.

To the east, a mile and a half across the northern extent of the one-hundred-and-fifty-mile-long Indian River, was Merritt Island where Captain Dummett kept his world famous orange grove. Beyond that were Cape Canaveral and the Atlantic Ocean. To the south was nothing but river – wide and flat, separated from the sea by a low, narrow, strip of land. The farther the eyes traveled southward, the more the river blended into the scrubby growth of the shoreline until there was no differentiating between the two at all.

A haze of humidity shimmered off the water.

"Remember how cool it was coming through the foothills?" Katie sighed.

"Oh," Christiane agreed with an even bigger sigh. "It was *so* wonderful. I wish we could have brought it with us."

"Well," Katie said. "It certainly was cool, but I am so glad to be off of that train!" She looked down at her dress and brushed at a smudge. "There's really no escaping all that smoke. This is the first time in days that I've actually been able to breathe." Taking a deep breath, she made a face.

Christiane and Bonnie giggled.

"It sure doesn't *smell* like home sweet home yet," Bonnie noted. "They really ought to do something about that." She looked towards the docks and several fish and oyster houses. "When I said earlier that I was excited about smelling the salt air again, I didn't mean this!"

"The man at the ticket booth said you get used to it."

"Oh," Christiane stated. "I would never get used to such a thing. It is, how do you say, steeenky."

Katie and Bonnie giggled at her use of the vernacular. They always found it amusing when she tried to sound American. Though a recent transplant, Christiane Dawson was well on the way to her ultimate conversion from French nobility to regular American girl, which they knew was her dream.

"Oh, I cannot wait for the wedding!" Christiane said excitedly.

It had been the primary topic of conversation for the past month, and beyond – ever since Malcolm Geoffreys had proposed to Bonnie. Over the past weeks, while the women had been on their shopping spree in New York, the subject of matrimony had rarely been but a few syllables away.

And so it continued.

"You will make such a beautiful bride," Christiane gushed. "Oh, and what a gown!" she sighed. "It is a beautiful dress."

"I cannot believe that dress!" Katie agreed. "And what a deal! Can you believe the deal Maggie got for us?"

Bonnie replied, "It just goes to show that it pays to know people in the right places."

"Yes," Christiane said. "And Maggie certainly was the right person in the right place. No?"

"No," Katie replied. "I mean, yes. Oh, Bonnie! I cannot believe you actually had your dress designed by one of the biggest costume designers on Broadway! Can you imagine? Broadway!!"

It had been a magical trip for the three women.

When they had departed Port Starboard to shop and see their best friend, Maggie, they had never imagined it would turn out as it did. Maggie had told them through a series of letters that she was indeed singing on Broadway, but not that she had become "A SENSATION!"

The girls had been floored when they laid eyes on the apartment where she and Booker T. lived, but that was nothing compared to seeing her on stage, belting out a series of Negro spirituals. Katie's first thought had been of Alfred and how proud he would be of Maggie, and maybe a little jealous. She had also thought of Alfred, however, when she saw how miserable his best friend, Booker T., was, living in the big city, his beloved farm fifteen hundred miles away. To his credit Booker T. put on a good face, getting out there and mingling with the upper crust, wearing formal dinner attire, taking it all in stride.

The girls had once again been astounded when Maggie told them that she would be giving up the stage after this, her first season. How, they wondered, could she give up the limelight. She was a celebrated member of "the stage" for goodness sake! A diva! Their Maggie was A BROADWAY DIVA!!

But they knew she was right. Booker's misery was hers. It was in her make up.

"Anyway," she had told them, "I miss home, and I miss my friends."

They had all cried.

Maggie told them she had not wanted to go to New York at all. Of course, she had *wanted* to go, but when she received the much-anticipated invitation from a Broadway producer to come to New York for an audition, her first thought was of her husband. There was no force on earth that could compel Maggie to even consider asking Booker to leave his farm for the summer and travel to New York – except for Booker himself.

No woman was ever loved or adored more than Maggie Hooker. It was an amazing thing, their devotion. They did argue like most couples, but theirs usually revolved around pleasing the other: "Whatever you want, sugar"; "No, whatever you want, sweetie."

It could be nauseating, Katie thought.

Everyone knew an argument had ensued, lasting for days: "No, sweetie. I won't take you from your farm"; "No, sugar. You can't pass up an opportunity like this."

It went on and on, eventually dragging the entire community into the fray. Everyone, however – to the man, woman, and child – had sided with Booker.

"Go on!" they had decreed. "Have fun!"

The neighbors were excited for Maggie to be sure, but mostly everyone wanted to imagine the "big man of the earth" in top hat and tails. If it had ever come into question before, it was now apparent to all that Booker T. Hooker was indeed a man of courage, strength, and valor.

"Oh, I'm so glad you decided to let someone else make the dress for you," Katie said. She crossed her arms. "A bride can *not* make her own dress. It's just not right."

"And," Bonnie replied. "I'm so glad you convinced me not to. I don't think I've ever had so much fun as we did buying that dress! It was nice to be on the other side of the sewing machine, that's for sure. You know, I really think I could get used to being pampered and fretted over."

"It is not as wonderful as you might imagine," Christiane replied, "when it is all you know."

"I'll take your word on that," Bonnie said, "but I still wouldn't mind finding out for myself what it's like to have servants waiting on me."

"You might be able to do that before you know it," Katie replied. "You'll be a millionairess yourself soon."

"Yes," Bonnie sighed. "And not a moment too soon."

"You are, how do you say, cutting it close. No?" Christiane said.

"Well," Bonnie stated flatly. "You both know I was willing to give up the entire inheritance if I hadn't found the right man."

"Oh," Katie replied. "I think you've found a good one this time. Malcolm is a wonderful man: kind and thoughtful and," she sighed, "absolutely gorgeous!"

Stars filled Bonnie's eyes.

"He really is wonderful. I know it sounds kind of crazy, but I almost feel blessed to have had such bad luck with men all my life. If I hadn't, I might have married someone else and never met Malcolm."

"Fate can be a strange thing," Katie giggled. "Alfred can't tolerate even the thought of it."

"And why is that?" Christiane asked.

"Ohhh," Katie waved her hand. "He says that if fate is real, then we must all be like puppets on a string and our destinies are in the hands of 'the great puppeteer.'" She shrugged. "He's quite the romantic, my man."

"But," Christiane said. "We know that Alfred is not completely without romance. As you have told us, you ask for something and he makes it appear. I cannot think of anything more romantic than a man who brings you whatever you desire."

Katie smiled and looked southward.

"I do miss my little man."

"And I imagine he's missing you right about now," Bonnie laughed. "He was stomping around for weeks before we left. Remember? Just walking around grumbling about the 'apocalypse' to come?"

"Oh, he misses me all right," Katie replied. "I do *not* want to see that house when I get home." She giggled. "I swear, all I see when I think of Alfred is the look on his face when we sailed away on that steamer."

Bonnie almost doubled over.

"All three of them!" she howled. "They all looked the same! Standing there on that dock with their hats in their hands!"

"It's true!" Katie giggled, "They all looked so –"

"Pathetic," Christiane suggested. "No?"

Bonnie and Katie looked at each other and burst out laughing, prompting the people at the foot of the dock and some men at the nearest fish house to stop what they were doing and stare.

"Oh!" Katie exclaimed, catching her breath. "You hit that nail on the head, Christiane. Those three men," she tried to keep from laughing, "standing all in a row, tallest to shortest, Eddie dressed in his "usual," and on either side of him the two best-dressed men in Port Starboard, all three of them looking as if they had just lost their puppies. Oh!" she cried. "It was *so* funny!"

Wiping at tears with hankies, the women re-composed themselves.

A moment later, Christiane sighed heavily and, pushing a wisp of raven hair from her eyes, said, "I meeess my Ed-die."

"It's all right, Christiane." Katie put her arm around her. "We'll be home tomorrow, and there is nothing more fun than coming home. Going is great, and being there is better, but, as my Granny always said, there's nothing finer than coming home to a man who loves you – or vice versa."

Looking southward, she sighed.

"I can't believe we're going to steam right past home and I'm not stopping in." Noticing the looks on the girls' faces, she waved her hand. "Oh, don't worry. I wouldn't get out of there for a week! Everyone would come over to Aunt Abigail's, or we'd go over there to Momma and Poppa's place. Of course, they'd have to ride out to get Little Joe and Daisy and all theirs –" Her voice trailed off. "I was wrong. It would be a *month* before I'd get out of there."

A moment passed, then Bonnie said, "I really do envy you, Katie. It must be so wonderful to have such a big family."

"Oh, yes," Christiane chimed in. "You and Ed-die have such a wonderful family. I feel very lucky to be a part of it. I would love to stop in at their dock, but," she shrugged her delicate shoulders, "I am like you. I would not want to leave." Then she sighed and looked southward. "I meeess my Ed-die. He is so down to dirt."

The ensuing laughter caused people from across the docks to stop what they were doing and stare.

Chapter Six

Eddie missed Christiane, but at the moment he was missing Maggie even more. He hated being the interim Port Starboard General Store and Post Office manager.

Upon her departure for New York several months earlier, Maggie had laughed when he said, "But what if they like you and you're gone for months, or even years?!"

It was Maggie who got the bigger surprise when the producers hired her on the spot for the role in question – a short, fat, black woman with the voice of an angel. She had written Eddie a heartfelt letter in which she had apologized for leaving him in the position and even offered to turn down the role and return home.

What could he do?

He had replied that it was not a problem; he and Annie and Gnarles and Paddy had everything well in hand, running the store and post office. He had even told her they were having fun. Christiane had insisted on his doing so: there was no need to make Maggie feel guilty.

Eddie missed Christiane terribly, much more than he did Maggie, especially since the housekeeper Christiane had hired had quit in a huff, mumbling something in French about "feelthy Amereecans." He had spent the past three nights cleaning up the accumulated mess in anticipation of his bride's arrival back home to his loving and contrite arms.

He was sitting on the stool behind the counter at the Port Starboard General Store and Post Office. At the other end of the counter, on their respective stools, were Gnarles and Paddy. Sitting at the desk behind them was little Annie Humphrey, who was making some final notations in the sales ledger. Snoring at her feet was her pet raccoon, Copernicus.

"Mrs. Guildersleeve is almost up to her limit again."

Eddie didn't hear.

"Did you hear me?" Annie asked.

"Huh?" Eddie snapped out of a daydream.

"It's Mrs. Guildersleeve."

He scowled. "All right. I'll talk to her."

Although Eddie was in charge of the store and post office, Annie actually ran the place. Eddie was merely a figurehead – a figurehead that had to be there every day, day after day, week after week, instead of sailing hither and yon, which was his real job. For years he had run a small freighter service between Lake Worth and anywhere else – until lately. He found it strange that when hardly anyone lived on the lake, business was nonstop, but now that folks were arriving in earnest, business had dropped off – at least the business he preferred.

In the past it had been long, salty voyages out on the high seas to St. Augustine, Savanna, or Charleston. Lately, though, ever since the railroad had arrived at Titusville, it was short jaunts up the coast to Jupiter or Fort Pierce, and then a long, drawn-out, soul stifling slog up the river to Titusville. Eddie was growing to hate the Indian River – not nearly as much, however, as he did the Port Starboard General Store and Post Office.

Of course, if he were to lower his rates, as Christiane had suggested, he might get more business. Eddie had been incredulous.

"What?! I charge more than anyone else because me and *Hasta La Vista* are the best, the fastest, most dependable freight service on the entire lower east coast!"

Christiane had been kind enough not to add, "Except for the railroad." She had smiled and touched Eddie's cheek. Then, reaching behind his head, she had grabbed a handful of black curls and squeezed, pulling him close.

That's where Eddie was at the moment, staring into black, bewitching eyes, pulling his wife close, reveling in her aroma and fondness.

"Did you hear me, Eddie?"

It was Annie again – pigtails and oversized incisors.

He sighed. "I think we need to order more turpentine. Maggie says we should stock up on winter supplies way ahead of time."

Eddie waved his hand and stared out the window.

"How much should we get?" Annie asked.

"I'm going out to sit on the dock a while," Eddie replied, and he was out the door.

*　　*　　*

Annie looked at Gnarles and Paddy and shrugged.

"I'll just see what Maggie ordered last year."

"That's good thinkin', Annie," Gnarles replied.

"D' ya think we c'n have a pickle yet?" Paddy added.

Annie looked at the clock.

"I suppose, but take them out front." Then she got up from the desk and took her perch on the official Postmaster's stool.

As they were heading out the door, in walked Malcolm Geoffreys. Gnarles stopped short, causing Paddy to bump into him. Paddy made a face and checked his pickle for damage.

"Top of the day, fellows," the tall, dapper Englishman said as he removed his bowler hat. A mass of blonde hair spilled out. "How are you chaps this fine day?"

"Oh, fine," Gnarles said. "How are you?"

"Jolly well, thank you," Geoffrey replied, then he looked past Gnarles. "And how are you today, Paddy, old chap?"

Paddy looked away bashfully. It was clear that he liked Malcolm because he always asked him how he was doing and called him "old chap." Paddy, who rarely answered with more than a mumble, smiled and looked at the ground.

As Gnarles and Paddy shuffled out the door, Malcolm turned.

To Annie, Mr. Geoffrey's smile was comparable only to that of her Uncle Bobby Hackensaw. She could sit there on that stool and stare at him for hours on end. And soon he would be marrying one of Annie's favorite people on earth! Her teacher! Bonnie Blakely! The most beautiful woman in the world!

Except for maybe Christiane.

"And a jolly good afternoon to you, young lady!" Malcolm said, eyes sparkling, his complete attention at her disposal.

"Hello, Mr. Geoffreys," she gushed. "I have your mail ready!"

He stepped up to the counter and set his hat down; then he ran his fingers through golden tresses, and said, "Why, thank you, Annie. It's quite the boiler room out there today, don't you think?"

"Oh, yes!" Annie replied. "It sure, I mean, it most certainly is. I don't remember it ever being so *sultry*." She handed him the latest copy of the *London Times* and a single letter. He looked at it and smiled.

"Well," he said. "It certainly isn't damp, musty old England, but I am most definitely looking forward to this winter. I hear the most equable weather on earth is here on Lake Worth, the Riviera of America as they're now calling it."

"Oh," Annie replied. "It's much more pleasant during the winter; that's when we get most of our visitors. It gets cold sometimes at night, but it warms up by noontime."

"So I hear," he replied. He smiled at Annie, and she sat up straight, hanging onto every word. "I suppose you're excited about your mother coming home tomorrow," he said.

"Oh, yes! We can't wait!" Annie paused, then added, "And I suppose you're excited about your fiancée's return?" Whenever she talked to Malcolm, she spoke better, more like an educated person from England. She was completely entranced with the way he spoke – kind of like Uncle Will, but *so* much better.

"Why, yes," Malcolm chuckled, his eyes dancing. "I am. And will you be going up to meet her at Jupiter? According to the telegraph we received yesterday, they'll be here on the *St. Lucie* tomorrow afternoon."

"Oh, yes!" Annie replied excitedly. "I can't wait!"

"Yes, and I imagine you must be excited about the train trip as well."

Annie squirmed in her seat. There was little she enjoyed more than a ride on the diminutive Celestial Railway.

"Oh, yes!" she said. "Poppa said we're going to take the first train in the morning so we can spend the day with the Carlins and maybe go over to visit the Armours at the lighthouse. He said we might even go swimming at the big rope swing!"

"Ahhh, yes," Malcolm said. "The rope swing. I imagine your little brother must be excited as well."

"Yep," Annie said. "I mean, yes. Benji certainly is." Following a short pause while she gazed into sapphire eyes, she asked, "Is there something else I can get you today, Mr. Geoffreys?"

Malcolm smiled engagingly, and replied, "I don't think so, Annie. But," he looked down at the papers in his hand, "I must commend you for doing such a good job here in Maggie's absence. She's lucky to have an assistant like you."

"Well, thank you," she stammered. "You're so kind."

Appearing to swallow a chuckle, Malcolm picked up his hat

Then he nodded in a very European way, and responded, "As are you, young lady." Turning to go, he paused. "I'm looking forward to our train trip tomorrow. Maybe we can sit together. You can point out landmarks along the way." Then he smiled, tipped his hat, and strolled out the door.

Annie, chin resting in hands, sighed.

*   *   *

Malcolm Geoffreys was aware of his powers over the opposite sex. He had a way of making women, and men for that matter, feel comfortable, to instantly accept him as one of their own. He possessed an uncanny ability to make them feel important, as if he were really listening.

And he was. It was a skill he had learned at a very early age while enrolled at the Wellington House Academy for Boys, that most people want to talk mostly about themselves.

He hadn't been particularly popular at school, though he had done well at making friends. Yet something, a constant nagging from deep inside, had told him he must be better, more popular. Always more popular. Everyone must like him: fellow students, teachers, and staff. To him it had become a never-ending quest, especially after some of the older boys spurned his attempts to become friends. It had cut him to the core: the thought that someone might think him less a person than they, when it was, as another voice declared, the exact opposite.

His mother had told him as much from a very early age: that there was no one more special, not in the world, not in their little town of Coventry, not even in their family. Geoffrey had always been her favorite; it was obvious to one and all, including his sisters and brother, but especially to his father. His father had been a weak man. At least that was what his mother had ingrained in him from a very young age – that his father was merely a means to an end. She had never said anything about his siblings in that regard, that they weren't as good and pure as her "sweet boy," but she did take his side in any and all disputes.

He recalled lying in her arms at night, his father in the room next to hers, his siblings all tucked away in bed. She would sing to him and whisper in his ear, telling him of all the great things he would do and become: the mountains he would scale, the valleys he would traverse, the oceans he would cross. In her mind, nothing was impossible for her special little boy.

Then she died, and he was sent off to boarding school, rarely to return home, even over the holidays. He had told himself he didn't care; he hated home. It meant nothing that his family despised him, or worse, had no feelings for him. Sometimes he would wake up in his bed in the dormitory – the other boys lined up side-by-side, mere feet away – his sheets soaked with tears.

It was during this period that he had made his discovery that the path to people's affections was through their own sense of vanity. He had uncovered the secret to making people like him, and, from that point forward, his first and only goal in life was to ensure that he was loved.

Unfortunately, he had never attained that lofty goal. He had never, not once since his mother died, felt loved. Instead, he had spent his entire life observing people and their relationships, particularly those in love and in close friendships. And never, nor once, had he felt like he thought they must feel.

So, in keeping with this innate talent for adaptation, Malcolm had learned to fake it.

*   *   *

There was nothing in life that thrilled Annie Humphrey more than a train ride. The Celestial Railroad – as many were now referring to the Jupiter to Juno link of the Jacksonville, Tampa, and Key West Railway – was barely there at all. The entire trip took a half hour at most, but it was something to experience. On the east side, the Atlantic filled the vista, waves washing over the beach, nearly to the escarpment upon which the tracks of the roadway lay. Off to the west rolled swelling dunes covered with saw palmetto and Spanish bayonets, topped here or there with a cabbage palm or a towering pine tree. At the feet of all of this was sand.

White, hot, sun-beating-down-and-reflecting-and-blinding, sugar sand.

Diminutive in every way, the Celestial Railway was eight miles long and a so-called, narrow-gauge line. The engine and cars were narrower than a standard-sized train. There were the same number of seats, but they were smaller and less comfortable, and quite cramped – but that didn't bother Annie one bit.

There was something terribly exciting and romantic about the experience of riding the rails. She wondered: was it the rumble of the heavy metal wheels on the tracks, or maybe the steady clickity-clack, clickity-clack? Or was it the friendly toot of the train's whistle as it rolled into the station, or even when Mr. Rice, the engineer, tooted out the tune "Dixie"? Maybe it was the idea that directly under her the ground was rushing past at a blinding pace, and the accompanying knowledge that at any moment the train could potentially go right off the tracks into the hot, blinding sand!

"It can make you dizzy."

Annie blinked and looked up at Malcolm. She and Benji were standing between him, Eddie, and her father on the back platform, looking downward, watching the railroad ties blur past.

"It certainly can," she replied.

They had just stopped at Mars, where old man Wells lived with his cats, to drop off several mason jars of pickled mullet. The widow Marcinski made these up for him every week and sent them by way of the conductor, Captain Matheson. She was hoping at some point the old man might ask her to marry him. Everyone knew that Betsy had told her some time back that she would probably do better to stop sending him jars every week in order to make him miss her.

"But he so adores my pickled mullet," Mrs. Marcinski had said.

"I wonder if I could run this fast," Annie said.

"I guess there's one way to find out," Eddie replied thoughtfully. "What do you think, Malcolm? We could tie Annie to the rail here. That way if she can't keep up, we'll just reel her in." He grinned. "Like a big fish."

"Oh," Annie replied. "You're not gonna tie *me* to a rope!" She looked up at Malcolm for affirmation, but he seemed deep in thought.

"You know," he mumbled. "I took some engineering classes in school, and I think it would be quite possible." Malcolm stroked his dimpled chin and looked down at Annie. "But," he quickly amended. "I believe that only works with boys."

"I'm a boy!" Benji declared. "You can tie me to the train! I bet I can run that fast!"

"And I'd be willing to wager you could," Malcolm replied, "but I don't think Captain Matheson would appreciate us tying a boy to the back of his train."

Everyone grew silent as they came into view of the ocean. Merely the sight of the cool blues of sky and water seemed to lower the temperature.

A moment later, Annie said, "I can't wait for the ride home. I'm going to try to get Miss Bonnie out here." She giggled. "She comes out here for the ride up to Jupiter because we're at the back of the train, but on the way home this is the *front* of the train! She says it's too scary."

"Uh-huh," Benji added. "It's a lot more fun when the train's going backwards!"

Malcolm tugged at his collar and replied, "As hot as it is, I wouldn't be surprised if we might get Bonnie out here for a moment or two. Even with the windows open it is nothing less than paralyzing in there."

They hadn't noticed it on the train as much, but when they got to Jupiter it hit them like a brick wall.

Not a breeze. Muggy.

A little while later, the welcoming party was gathered under a stand of cocoanut palms the railroad company had planted next to the wharf. Nearby, the train's engine was hissing steam.

Wiping sweat from his brow, Eddie said, "I don't know about you folks, but I'm headin' over to the Carlins' to borrow a boat."

Annie and Benji clapped their hands and jumped up and down.

"Can we go, Poppa?!" Annie begged. "Can we go with Eddie over to the rope swing?!"

Dabbing at his upper lip with a handkerchief, Alfred took out his watch, and said, "I can think of nothing better myself. We'll borrow some swimming togs at the Carlins'."

*   *   *

People were staring again.

The women were standing on the forecastle of the *St. Lucie*, Indian River's newest and most advanced steamer; and once again they were hysterical, holding their sides, and feverishly dabbing at eyes and noses with hankies.

They had just passed the expansive mouth of the St. Lucie River and entered the Jupiter Narrows, a natural maze of mangrove islands. Here the steamboat company had carved out and dug a channel through much of this watery jungle. In some places passengers could reach out and touch the shiny, leathery leaves as they passed through.

Fellow passengers watched with looks of wonderment on their faces. It had been like this for the past day and a half. Of course, Katie thought, they might behave similarly if they had just come back from a trip to New York City in which they shopped – and shopped – and saw all the sights, and attended a flurry of Broadway shows, went backstage at all of them and met a never-ending procession of producers, actors, and directors. That was not to mention a host of rich, influential people, all of whom were interested in them simply because they were friends of Maggie Hooker.

The newest Broadway sensation!

"Oh," Katie giggled. "I would give anything to have been there to see Booker T. the first time he put on a waist coat and tails!"

Bonnie dabbed at her eyes, and said, "I know! Maggie said she thought he was going to faint dead away and even ran over to push a chair behind him!"

"But," Christiane noted. "Mister Booker T. looks very splendid in a dinner suit, yes?"

"Absolutely!" Bonnie said. "My eyes almost popped out! I couldn't believe it was our Booker T.! In black tie!"

"With top hat!" Katie added. "Oh, if only Alfred could have seen it!"

"But he will, no?"

"Yes, he will," Katie said. "In fact, the photographs could already be there when we get home."

Bonnie said, "I simply cannot wait for everyone to see them. The toast of the town! And it's not just Booker T.'s *appearance*. I can't wait for him to come home so we can have long involved talks about literature. I don't think I've enjoyed talking books as much as I did with him. He was so *excited* about it!"

"Poor thing," Katie sighed. "When he got there, all he had to do all day, every day while Maggie was at practice was sit around that big old apartment with nothing but that giant bookshelf filled with all the greatest works." She giggled. "Alfred would be jealous."

"Oh," Christiane said. "And it was not easy getting him out of that apartment."

Katie nodded. "It's true. That man only moves when Maggie says move; otherwise I think he would become part of that sofa with a book glued to his hand. And you know he must simply hate doing all those social engagements." She sighed. "How the poor man must miss his farm."

"Well," Bonnie agreed. "I hope he doesn't stop reading when he comes home."

"Are you kidding?" Katie said. "The man is obsessed! I'm more worried he'll forget all about his farm! I'm picturing him lying in a hammock all day, eating bonbons with his nose buried in a book." She paused a moment, then giggled, "Never mind. That's crazy talk!"

A little while later the *St. Lucie* slipped out of the Narrows and onto the wide, shallow expanse of Hobe Sound. In the distance was the unmistakable red tower of Jupiter Lighthouse. In contrast, the water was suddenly as blue as the sky, blending into greens and a myriad of vibrant hues where the oyster bars flourished along either shore. Occasional glimpses of the Atlantic were visible through the growth along the beach.

Then, as if by magic, a light breeze arose off the ocean. The fresh, salty air spurred all three women to take in a deep breath.

It smelled like home.

Chapter Seven

A week later

"All aboard, matey!"

Copernicus the raccoon scampered onto Annie's little catboat, *Miss Kitty,* and up to the prow.

"Prepare to set sail, Lieutenant Mudge!" Annie cried out in her best John Paul Jones voice.

Copernicus yammered fitfully and crossed his arms.

Several nights earlier, Annie and Benji had persuaded their mother, who had grown up on the Florida Prairie, to tell them a story about the great cow dog, Mudge. Of all Katie's stories about the frontier, it was the Mudge stories that most enthralled her children.

"All right. Which one?"

"The one about the alligator!" Benji's voice rang out.

Katie sighed, then reached over and pinched a rosy cheek.

"Okay," she said. "Which one?"

Two voices. "The one with Goliath!"

She rolled her eyes.

"All right. Which one?"

"The one where Mudge saves Goliath!"

"And, which one would that be?"

"The one where he bites off the alligator's foot!" Benji had begged.

"No!" Annie pleaded. "The one where he tows the cow upstream with Goliath on his back!"

"No! The one with the foot!"

"All right!" Mom finally conceded. "I'll tell both!"

Whining had prevailed; kids cheered.

Now, several days later, *Captain* Annie was barking out orders.

"Lieutenant Mudge!" she cried. "Name your heading!"

Copernicus was ignoring her. Ever since Annie had started calling him that, he had been on strike. He hated being Lieutenant Mudge.

What kind of name is that for a raccoon? Raccoons have names like Aristophanes, Shakespeare, and DaVinci.

"What's wrong with you, Lieutenant?" Annie adjusted her sails. "How come you won't look into the wind today?"

Across Lake Worth on the barrier island, was "The Castle," as the locals called it, where Charlie and Molly lived. That's where Annie went every day, weather permitting, after stopping in to check on Eddie, Gnarles, and Paddy.

She rarely missed a day. He had Molly to take care of him now, but Annie still felt the need to check on the old mariner. After all, it was she who, several years earlier, had managed to extract the old crab from his crusty shell. It was his little "Sweetpea" who by sheer force of cuteness and bold-faced cajolery had compelled him to take a good look at himself, to rejoin the human race, and, most important, to get up the gumption to "rustle up some Molly" – as he had put it.

Annie knew that many years earlier he and Molly had been best of friends, bosom buddies, confidants even. Back in the day, Charlie told her, when he was the boldest, blusteriest, barnacle-bellied, sea dog to ever sail the briny deep – whenever he happened in at the friendly little port known as the Happy Clam in Key West, he and Molly were like two sides of a coin, joined at the hip and melding together as naturally as salt and water.

He said he had thought of her often over the years, but it wasn't until Annie had performed her magic that he had decided to go off and look up Molly. When he did, lo and behold he discovered that she had made, on a tip from one of her clients, an especially profitable investment in the Pennsylvania Rock Oil Company and was worth a veritable fortune. Now they were happily married, and the "crazy old hermit," Charlie MacLeod, who once lived in a tiny, bug-infested, palmetto shack, had taken up residence in a grand mansion overlooking the sea.

Sort of.

Lake Worth here was wide, almost one mile. On a day like today, with a breeze out of the east following a strong summer storm, Annie could make the southeast crossing, around the sand banks of Little Pelican Island, in less than fifteen minutes. If the wind wasn't right, it could take much longer. Then there were times when there was no wind at all, and it was best to just pick up the oars and row – or not go at all.

Uncle Charlie understood.

It was a sight to see, especially for people traveling down the lake for the first time: a large, Victorian, stone and brick edifice. For travelers headed south it was the first building of its size since the Rockledge Hotel, a hundred miles to the north. On each end rose a high, square tower with spires on every peak and corner, making it resemble a fairytale castle befitting a storybook king and queen. The building towered over the trees surrounding it, many of which had been spared from the lumberman's axe. To the south, along the ocean beach for several hundred yards, was "Booker T. Rocks" and beyond that the inlet. This is where Charlie MacLeod could most often be found.

Otherwise, he was at home. Not in The Castle, however.

After Molly had built the house of which she had always dreamed, she realized Charlie was miserable, so they had moved into the caretaker's cottage just north of the house – where they had lived while the main house was being built. Molly retained the servants, Willie and Millie Melton, who now resided in The Castle by themselves.

Molly was nothing like anyone Annie had ever known. Until she had moved to Port Starboard, it had been Betsy Dawson who was "the sauciest gal around," as Mr. Booker T. put it. But when Molly came to town, Aunt Betsy suddenly became "rather tame," as her father put it. Uncle Charlie would constantly remind Molly to watch her mouth. Annie would giggle – and learn an awful lot.

But Molly was real nice, and she sure did love Uncle Charlie, though there had been a few instances that made Annie wonder: like the time she had caught Molly fumbling around in Charlie's pants, and she had explained that he had somehow gotten a splinter up there. It seemed to Annie that Molly spent a lot of time thinking about Uncle Charlie's trousers.

But she sure did make him happy!

As they pulled up to the dock, Copernicus put his tiny, human-like hands up to his ears just as Annie screamed, "HEY, UNCLE CHARLIE!! WE'RE HERE!!!"

Uncle Charlie had told her it was always best to announce herself – several times.

"HEY, UNCLE CHARLIE!!!"

All the way up to the house.

The entire lakeshore directly in front of the mansion was cleared and covered in a lush carpet of Bermuda grass. Near the south portico were several curvy, fully-grown, cocoanut palms planted haphazardly in bunches around an expansive, circular terrace. In the center of this was a large ornate fountain with three dolphins spouting water from their mouths at Poseidon, Lord of the Deep. On the north end were eight massive, perfectly straight, royal palms placed uniformly along the wide, limestone-paved walkway that led from the main entrance to the dock and boathouse.

The dock was big enough to accommodate a large yacht, but was home only to Charlie's little sailing skiff, *Dolly Varden,* a chunky little cutter he had found washed up on the beach several years earlier with the moniker *Bertha Belle* painted on her plump but attractive transom. Charlie had indignantly stuck his finger in the air and declared that "any *indolent oaf* with the *temerity* to give such a pretty little craft such a *hideous* name should not be allowed to own a boat – not to name one anyway."

Splitting off from the main walkway was a similar but smaller pathway that disappeared into a breezy, shadowy forest of cocoanut palms. Molly had planted them, fully grown trees, everywhere there wasn't already something else "big" growing. This "grove" extended all the way to the inlet on the south and just beyond the servant's cottage to the north. It was, as Molly had always dreamed, her "tropical kingdom by the sea."

And Charlie was her king.

She had made the mistake of mentioning that to Charlie and Annie one day, and they now – both of them – regularly referred to him as *King Charlie, His Highness, His Majesty*, or a host of other noble sobriquets.

Molly would roll her eyes and say, "Here, King!"

Annie would giggle.

Now, Annie followed Copernicus up the winding trail towards the tiny cottage by the sea. The ocean was announcing itself that day with thunderous waves and salt-saturated air. Annie breathed deeply as she scampered through a sward of mother-in-law tongues that had taken hold and sprung up like weeds around the tiny abode.

She screamed again, and waited. No answer. Then she ran over the dune line and through the swath of sea oats, beach morning glories, and beach sunflowers. When she emerged onto the shore's expanse, she looked southward, screamed again, and listened. A few moments later she grinned at the sound of barking. Then a small, white dog with floppy ears burst over the berm and came galloping towards them.

Floppy stopped to give Annie a heartfelt greeting, then dog and raccoon took off down the beach in the direction of the inlet. As Annie made her way after them, she stared in awe at The Castle, once again wondering why anyone would prefer a tiny, one-bedroom cottage to such a fabulous dwelling. Then again, she reminded herself, it was Uncle Charlie. To him, the cottage *was* a castle.

She had just passed Booker T. Rocks and was in the midst of chasing some sandpipers when she heard a gravelly voice call out. "Well, there's my Sweetpea!" Then Charlie yelled over his shoulder, "Looks like a ray of sunshine just landed on our shores, m'darlin'!"

He was dressed in nothing but knee length britches, with a red bandana tied around his head. In his hand was a gnarled piece of driftwood devoted especially to the purpose of keeping him upright. Finding it a handy implement in a variety of situations, he was rarely without the weathered staff anymore.

Standing with hands on hips, he let out a belly laugh. Then he looked skyward at approaching clouds and held his hands out, palms up.

"Didn't think we'd be seein' ya today, kiddo, the weather and all. But," he quickly added. "It sure is a fine and dandy surprise!" He turned and yelled, "Ain't that right, m'darlin?"

A muffled response.

Annie gave him a hug, then put her finger out for Salty.

"Sweetpea's here!" the little bird squawked. "Hurry up! Hurry up!"

This narrow point of land was where Charlie and Molly spent most of their days. From where the "beach hut" was situated on the ocean side of the inlet, they had an almost three hundred sixty-degree, panoramic view. It included the entire coastline north and south around to Port Starboard and settlements south of there on the opposite side of the lake.

The breezy sanctuary was a rambling amalgamation of palmetto shack, palmetto chickee, and palmetto, open-air veranda. The floor in most places was constructed from the deck of a wrecked ship; otherwise it was sand. Nailed to a post supporting the veranda roof was a hand-painted sign that read, "The Last Resort – No Lollygagging!" There were two hammocks hanging from other posts, and in the chickee was everything necessary to ride out an afternoon storm. To Annie's knowledge, all they did all day was sit around and read, and watch sunrises and sunsets, and fish, and go swimming, and relax, and read some more – and, of course, ride out the perfunctory afternoon storm.

"Come on, kid," he said. "Me and Molly was just gettin' ready to boil up an afternoon snackeroo."

"Oooo," Annie said. She pursed her lips. "I'm not supposed to. Momma says it might ruin my appetite for dinner."

"I know," Charlie replied. "That's exactly what mothers are for, and that's why we're only havin' one lobster between us." He yelled over his shoulder. "Right, m'darlin'?"

"That's right, Charlie," Molly's voice replied. "One lobster." The flap on the chickee opened, and she climbed out, rear end first. Standing up straight, she looked down at herself, adjusted her skirt a little, and grinned broadly. "Well, hi there, sweetie," she said. "How you doin' today?"

"Oh, fine, Molly," Annie replied (Molly insisted that Annie call her Molly, not Aunt Molly), and after another round of hugs, Annie sat down on a large ship's timber next to Charlie in front of a boiling pot of water. He had just taken a fresh lobster out of another pot filled with saltwater and was speaking to it, asking forgiveness; then he deftly popped the little fellow in the pot and averted his eyes.

Annie cringed. She hated this part – but she loved lobster. Uncle Charlie had told her that sometimes in life it's perfectly fine to rationalize things away, and lobster was one of those times.

"The Deity would understand," he would say. "It's lobster, after all!"

As they stared into the vat of death, their mouths watered.

"So," Charlie said as he pulled out the tasty morsel and laid it on a rough-hewn table for final preparation into *hors devours* befitting true, blue-blood royalty. "How's things goin' over at the post office?"

"Okay." She fidgeted. "I mean, I just wish Eddie would write more stuff down. He always thinks he's going to remember, but all he ever remembers is that he has something to remember."

Charlie and Molly laughed.

"So what else is goin' on over there?" he asked, bending into his task. "Would ya hand me a couple of those limes, m'darlin?"

Molly reached over from where she was reclining in a giant, whale-backbone chair, and said, "Heads up!" She tossed them in the air, one at a time.

Charlie snatched them, one at a time, and started slicing them.

"Not much," Annie sighed. "Just the regular. Oh!" she said excitedly. "Miss Bonnie got her wedding dress in the mail today! You should have seen it!" Annie took herself in her arms and hugged. "She's going to be the most beautiful bride ever!"

Molly looked up from her nails.

"Really? You saw her in it?"

"Well, no." Annie made a pouty face. "She just held it up so we could all see it, but," she brightened, "she said she'd put it on for all us girls later on! She's going to be soooo beautiful."

"There ain't much doubt about that," Molly said thoughtfully. "She really is something. I suppose young Malcolm is getting pretty excited himself. Bonnie is quite the catch."

"Oh," Annie giggled. "He's always so calm and collected, but I can tell by the look on his face whenever she walks into the room that he's just about to pop with excitement! His eyes get real wide, and then he reaches up and straightens his tie. Every time!" she added. "It's funny. Momma and I were watching him the other day when he didn't know, and he can stare at her a *real* long time! Without ever blinking!" She laughed out loud. "You should have seen him when he caught us staring! He got all embarrassed and turned red around his ears." Annie paused a moment, gazing at the horizon, and added, "He is soooo handsome!"

Charlie started to laugh, but Molly made a face.

"Yes," she said. "Mr. Geoffreys is a very handsome man. I'd say Bonnie is a lucky lady as well, don't you think, Charlie?"

"Absolutely, my dear. They are both extremely lucky people."

"And they do seem a good match," Molly added.

"They sure are!" Annie said as Charlie motioned for her to help herself to a platter of steamy, buttery lobster. He handed a smaller plate to Molly while he and Salty and Annie dug in. "I don't know of anyone who's a better match, except for maybe you," she said, licking her fingers. "My Momma says you two were made for each other, and Poppa says it's almost like you came out of the same mold!"

Molly and Charlie locked eyes. Molly reached out and patted Charlie's stumpy leg, and said, "Yes. It has taken a long time, but it has been worth it. It is almost like we were made for each other."

Charlie grinned and, popping a morsel into his mouth, took her hand in his and squeezed.

"I don't know how I could possibly argue with that, m'darlin'," he said, "seein' as how no one else on earth would have me."

"Oh, contraire," Molly replied. "You, Charlie MacLeod, are still a very desirable man, and who would know better than me, an expert in the field."

As the old lovers gazed into faded, wizened eyes, Annie asked curiously, "Really, Molly?! You're an expert in the field?! Of desirable men?!"

Charlie and Molly looked at each other, then changed the subject.

A little while later Charlie was lying in one hammock, Annie in the other. He was starting to nod a bit, his pipe hanging haphazardly from the corner of his mouth. Molly was relaxing in her strangely comfortable, whale-bone chair, trying her hand at knitting.

"Oh, Annie," she said. "How is your Uncle Will doing? You said he's been feeling under the weather."

"Uh-huh," Annie replied, pinching Salty's neck feathers. "That's what Aunt Sally said yesterday, but I haven't heard anything else. She said she thought he had some kind of sinus condition or something. Probably nothing serious."

"He's such a wonderful man," Molly said, doing mortal combat with a particularly stubborn knot. She picked up her scissors, cut it off, and started over. "I don't remember knowing anyone so thoughtful. He could be on death's doorstep, and he'd be more concerned over someone else's ingrown toenail."

"Yep," Charlie snorted awake. "Ain't nobody I'd want in my corner more than Will Dawson – at sea or on land! I'll never forget the day Elizabeth and I found him, near death, washed up on our beach. I must 'a been about your age, Sweetpea. Their ship went ashore right off our island. Every soul on the vessel drowned except for him. Talk about great love stories," he sighed nostalgically. "Ya ain't gonna find one better'n that. Girl finds shipwrecked sailor on beach, marries him, and they live happily ever after. It was odd. I don't know if I ever saw those two so much as wrinkle a brow at the other."

"That's so romantic," Annie sighed, looking out to sea. "I wonder how I'll meet my husband."

"Oh," Molly said with a sly smile. "You won't know that until it happens, but you can bet it will be at a most unexpected time and place. Then, if you're lucky, you can be like me and Charlie and grow old together."

"Don't know about that, m'darlin'," Charlie said, stretching grandly. "There's only one of us gettin' old, and it ain't you." He stood and bent over to kiss her on the forehead. "You, m'darlin' are as young and vibrant as the day I met you, what," he said "forty some odd years ago?"

"And I love you too, babycakes, but the fact that we've known each other that long would seem to disqualify me as young or vibrant."

"Well," Charlie insisted. "Ya are to me!"

Watching the two old lovebirds prattle on made Annie sigh.

"I sure hope I can have a great love story, too. Just like you two, and Uncle Will and Aunt Elizabeth." She looked seaward as if she might spot a castaway cabin boy floating by on a raft.

"I know what'll make Will feel better!" Charlie declared, sticking his finger in the air like Isaac Newton. "Broiled pompano! It's his favorite! And nothin's better for what ails ya! Come on, Sweetpea! Let's go scoop up some sandflies and rustle up a special dinner for our favorite ancient mariner."

As they ambled off towards the rocks, a happily oddball pair, Molly yelled out, "Make sure you bring enough for Willie and Millie!"

Chapter Eight

Annie pulled up to the Hackensaw dock. Soon she was in Bobby's boat shop. She'd had a crush on her Uncle Bobby forever. He was married to Charlie's daughter, Dr. Sally Hackensaw, and it had always been rooted in her mind that she might go off to medical school one day, like Sally, and end up marrying someone just like Bobby.

"Well, hello there, young lady!" he called out, drying his hands. "I was just finishing up."

"How's your new boat coming?" she asked him.

"Oh, good," Bobby answered. He shook his head, concentrating on a certain misalignment of boards. "I've never been the craftsman Uncle Will is, but it's coming along." He smiled.

No one had a prettier smile – except for Mr. Geoffreys. Annie thought of him like a younger Bobby, but not as funny. Uncle Bobby had a gift for making a funny joke but keeping a straight face so you're not sure if it was a joke at all.

"What have we here?" Bobby asked, looking at her stringer of fresh pompano. "A gift from the old sea dog himself?"

"Yep," Annie grinned. "No, Copernicus," she scolded. "You have to wait."

Copernicus crossed his arms.

Bobby laughed. "I swear, if I didn't know better, I'd say that raccoon is half human."

Annie giggled. "Poppa says he *is* part human: the ornery part."

"Let me guess," Bobby said, holding up the mess of fish. "Pompano is just what Uncle Will needs."

"Yep," Annie replied. "For whatever ails ya!"

Bobby grinned. "Ahhh, the hermit philosopher. You know, your Uncle Charlie knows how to live."

"He sure does," Annie replied as they headed up the sandy path to the house.

Bobby and Sally's house was one of the nicest on the entire lakeshore. A large, Cape Cod design, it had porches all around and balconies on the two main upstairs bedrooms. A widow's walk crowned the upper floor and, like a handful of homes on the lake at this time, the house had running water and built-in bathrooms.

Annie skipped ahead of Bobby to where, out front, near the dock, there was an open-air, Seminole chickee-style hut. Shading the entire area was a magnificent Royal Poinciana tree in full bloom, the flamboyant flowers engulfing the mushroom-shaped canopy. Underneath were a hammock, several chairs of varying design, and a picnic table.

This was where Will Dawson, the patriarch of the MacLeod-Dawson-Hackensaw clan, spent most of his days. From this shady observatory, a crow's nest of a sort, the old mariner watched the days sail by from the confines of a wheelchair. He had expressed to Annie and the others that he was grateful for that wheelchair. It got him out of the house and into the balmy, salty air, allowing him to breathe in the sights and smells of life. It was becoming clear to everyone, though, that this wondrous ability to breathe, sadly, had become more difficult of late as he found it ever more trying to put forth any physical exertion.

He also said he felt cold all the time.

Annie said, "I thought Uncle Will would still be out. It hardly rained at all."

Bobby shook his head.

"He wasn't feeling real good earlier. Sally had me take him in before the storm rolled over."

Annie stopped at the porch steps, turned around, and with a serious expression, asked, "Do you really think it's allergies making Uncle Will so sick lately?"

Bobby leaned against the rail and sighed. He pursed his lips.

"Annie," he said, "Sally didn't want to worry you, but Uncle Will might not be getting a whole lot better."

"You mean, he might … die?"

Bobby took a deep breath.

"The fact is, we don't really know. Sally says he might get better, but he's never going to be, I don't know, a *whole* lot better. You see, Annie," he said. "We just don't know. It's possible Uncle Will could live years still, but it's very likely that he only has a short amount of time left."

Annie stared at the ground.

"How short?" she asked.

"Only God knows that, I suppose."

Following a pause, Annie said, "I'm gonna pray for him tonight. I'm gonna pray for him tonight and every night, that he'll live a really, really long time."

Bobby patted her on the shoulder.

"That might just be the best thing you can do, young lady. Now, come on. Let's see if Uncle Charlie's right about this fish."

As Annie and Bobby stepped onto the porch, Sally walked out.

"Oh! Hello there, Annie," she said. She was holding a pot in her hands. "I was just coming out to snap some beans. Would you like to help?"

"Sure!" Annie replied, and she followed her to the end of the porch.

Sally looked at her husband, holding up a mess of pompano, a big grin on his face.

"I suppose I'll be changing the menu for tonight?"

"Looks like it."

"Let me guess," she said, sitting in a rocking chair. "It's for what ails ya?"

"Yep!" Annie giggled.

"My father," she sighed, and she handed Annie a handful of beans. "So, how are those two today?"

"Oh, fine," Annie replied. "I mean, Uncle Charlie had his trousers on inside out again, but they're both fine."

"And he's taking his medicine?"

"Yep," Annie replied confidently. "Molly always mentions the fight he put up over it that day."

"My father," Sally reflected, "must be the worst patient ever. He thinks he's immortal or something. I suppose he's my comeuppance for having such a good patient as your Uncle Will all these years.

"He's always been like that," Bobby said. "I remember after Will had his first heart attack back, during the war; he was laying in bed, all pale and looking like he might die at any minute. He barely had the strength to lift a finger, and *he* was reminding *you* of the proper mixtures for his medications."

"I know," Sally replied. "To this day, he remembers everything." She sighed. "Oh, how I wish his body was only half as strong as his mind."

"Uncle Will's been sick a long time," Annie stated matter-of-factly.

"Yes, he has," Sally replied.

"I told Annie about … you know," Bobby said.

"Oh." Sally placed her hand on Annie's knee. "I know it makes you sad, sweetheart, but you're old enough to understand; your Uncle Will seems to be losing a little bit of ground lately. But we just don't know at this point. He has made remarkable recoveries in the past."

"That's for sure," Bobby replied. "And if you ask me, I think he's on the verge of another one right now!"

"I hope so," Sally said.

Annie could tell Sally didn't believe it. A lump rose in her throat, and she felt like crying. She snapped a few beans, tossing them into a basket at their feet.

"I can't stay long," she said. "Do you think Uncle Will's up from his nap yet?"

"Most likely," Sally said, looking in the window at the grandfather clock. "Bobby? Would you put those fish out back for me and see if Uncle Will's awake?"

48

"Sure. You want me to clean these first? Won't take any time at all."

"Oh, thank you, darling," she replied. "Just leave them in the pan on the back porch. I'll be there in a minute."

As Bobby walked around the corner, Sally called out, "And let us know when Uncle Will's ready! Annie will want to wheel him out! Don't you, dear?"

"Sure!"

A little while later everyone was sitting on the porch when up the Lake Trail strode Malcolm Geoffreys, a spring in his step as usual.

"Oh, good!" Sally said. Bobby, Sally, and Will had told Annie they truly enjoyed having Malcolm with them. He was not only friendly, genial, and easy to get along with, but a big help around the house as well, even helping Sally in the kitchen at times.

Since his arrival, not only were they all eating better, and on time, they were eating more. As it turned out, Malcolm was quite skilled in the kitchen, having been assigned to assist the school's cook, who happened to be a formally-trained, French chef, when he was a lad.

Sally had told Annie that she had already communicated to Bonnie that she would be a fool to let this one get away. In fact, she said, most everyone in town, for one reason or another, had made these same sentiments known to the blushing bride-to-be.

"Well, good afternoon, my fine lads … and ladies," Malcolm added, doffing his hat and bowing to Sally and Annie. "How are we this fine day?"

Sally smiled.

Annie grinned.

"And how are you feeling today, Cousin Will?" Malcolm asked. "You certainly look hale and hearty!"

Will, who was sitting in his wheelchair next to Annie, nodded, and said, "On top of the world, actually, thanks to my lovely and attentive nurse here." He smiled at Annie, his soft eyes making her feel both comforted and sad. "Not to mention," he added. "I hear the old sea dog sent us a smattering of pompano for dinner."

"You know," Geoffrey said, a smile coming to his lips. "I have a magnificent recipe for *Sole Meuniere*. If you don't mind my being so forward, I would love to assist in the kitchen tonight."

Annie could sit and listen to Will and Malcolm talk all day long. It didn't matter what they said; it was the way they said it. Not at all like Mr. Wimbly, down the lake. He was English, too, but she could hardly understand a word he said. Her father told her it was Cockney, like the characters spoke in Charles Dickens's novels – but worse.

His accent wasn't anything like Uncle Will and Mr. Geoffreys's. Theirs were beautiful. She had been practicing in front of the mirror at night. The problem was, of late, when she was around either of them, she would suddenly start speaking like them. They would all laugh, then she would be embarrassed.

"Go on," Malcolm prodded. "Give us a bit of the King's English."

Will grinned ear to ear.

"You do have a knack for accents, young lady. You'll have to get with our good friend, Booker T., when he gets back from the big city." He laughed. "I can't get enough of his sendup of me."

"Oh," Annie said in a deep voice, tucking her chin low, crossing her arms, and spreading her feet apart. "You folks talkin' 'bout me? Booker T. Hooker?"

She then rolled right into her impression of her father, pointing her finger in the air and wrinkling her brow in a very scholarly fashion.

"Of course, they are, my good man, Booker T. I have deduced this through a series of scientific and mathematical channels."

Back to Booker, legs apart, arms crossed, Annie rolled her eyes grandly.

"Good thinkin', Alfie," she said, chin tucked, deep voice, "Good thing you were here or who knows what could'a happened!"

Will couldn't stop laughing. Then he started to cough; then it turned to wheezing and gasping for air. Everyone stopped laughing, but Will waved them on.

Sally bent over him, her hand on his shoulder.

"Slow down," she said, "Breathe slowly," she said. "Nice and slow."

Will had been ill for years, but following the death of his wife Elizabeth three years earlier, he had declined.

Annie was horrified that she might have been the cause of this latest episode.

As soon as he was able to breathe again, he smiled at her, and said, "It's not your fault, dear." Taking her hand in his, he said, "You remind me of Sally when she was your age. She used to make us all laugh." He patted Sally's hand. "Remember, dear? Our home was always filled with laughter."

"I do remember, Uncle Will," she replied. "We really did have a happy home."

"And you do still," he replied, "and one of those reasons is Annie here, don't you all agree?"

Annie thought she might cry.

"Annie," Will explained. "I would never want you to stop making me, or anyone else, laugh. We need laughter. In fact, I believe it is impossible to be truly happy without it, and what's the point of life if we can't be happy?!"

Annie shrugged. "I guess there isn't any."

"That's right," he said, patting her hand. "So, don't you worry about me. I don't think I could live without your sendups of your father and Booker T., and," he added, "Charlie and Molly."

"You mean," Annie said, trying not to be *too* funny, "the one where Uncle Charlie forgets to put his half-a-cocoanut on his peg leg before he walks out onto the beach?"

Just the mention set everyone to laughing again.

"Or," Annie went on. "How about the time when you and Charlie and Jimmy discovered gold on the beach!" Annie giggled, doing Will's impression of Charlie – eyes popping, mouth in a perfectly round circle.

It grew suddenly quiet.

It was not a subject the family talked about except amongst themselves. It wasn't really a secret. Most people knew, or had heard the rumor, that Will and Charlie had gold buried somewhere up on Indian River.

A quizzical look appeared on Malcolm's face.

"So … it's true?"

Will nodded.

"I take it you've heard the rumors?"

"Yes," Malcolm replied. "Back in England, actually. The family often mentions it. Most think it has been blown out of proportion, actually."

"It probably has," Will replied.

A long, remarkable pause.

"So," Malcolm queried. "Is it true? Or, should I not ask?"

Annie was chomping at the bit as well. There was nothing she liked better than a story of the old days, but when it came to this subject, both Charlie and Will could be vague, evasive even.

Annie had heard several renditions, all set in different locations, a couple more from Uncle Jimmy. Other than the location, however, the tale was mostly the same.

They had been coming home to Biscayne Bay from St. Augustine in 1833. Charlie was twenty-three, Will thirty-two, and Jimmy, eight. Seas had picked up, so they had run for cover inside Gilbert's Bar Inlet.

While there, sitting out the northeaster, they had discovered gold, Spanish doubloons, washed up on the beach. From that point, the tale would become unreliable again. In one version Charlie once told, there were three wagon loads that included the crown jewels of Cleopatra – and the Queen of Sheba.

Will patted Annie's hand again.

"It's perfectly fine to ask, Malcolm, my boy, and maybe next time Annie's here, I'll tell it again. It's a long story, though, and you, young lady, should be getting home. You know how your father worries once the sun gets low."

Annie looked out towards the lake – shadow time.

"How about," Will said. "I tell the whole story next time you come for a visit?"

Annie, grinning pigtail to pigtail, asked, "You mean the real one? The really, really, reee-ally real one?"

Will cocked his head thoughtfully, and replied, "That, young lady, is a definite maybe."

"Uncle Will!!"

Chapter Nine

Often times on a Sunday, Charlie and Molly would show up at the Hackensaw place with a load of fish. The old mariner would hobble onto their dock and announce at the top of his lungs, "Fish fry!"

The Humphreys would join them, along with Maggie and Booker, when they were in town, sometimes Eddie and Christiane, and pretty much anyone who happened to show up or pass by.

They would make an afternoon of it.

As soon as Charlie got there, without any notice but the big shout, he would start a fire in the pit, then hobble off to the end of the dock where there was a cleaning bench and a couple of buckets, and he would start cleaning fish, or conchs, or whatever – like he owned the place.

"You there! You think you own the place?!"

Without turning from his messy task, Charlie replied, "What's yours is mine, oh former good and true sailing partner! Now, get on over here and dip me a bucket 'a water! We got a mess 'a fish ta fry!"

Bobby grinned and slapped Charlie on the back, then, taking a pail on a short length of rope, he dipped out a bucketful. He held it up so Charlie could rinse his hands, then Charlie stood back while he sloshed it over the table.

"That's better," Charlie said, and he went back to scaling, gutting, and filleting, one at a time, then closely inspecting each one before tossing it in another bucket filled with saltwater.

"I see the blues are still running," Bobby said.

"Yep. Got a few squid and shrimp, too. Appetizers."

"Gotta tell you, Uncle Charlie. Haven't really noticed you lacking for appetite."

The hollow note of a conch shell filled the air, and both men looked northward. Annie and Benji were standing on their dock, waving and jumping up and down.

"COME ON!" Charlie yelled at the top of his lungs, accentuating it with an exaggerated wave.

They watched as the kids jumped up and down a couple more times, then ran off towards the house.

Charlie smiled, and said, "Old woman's gonna be mad."

"You mean Katie?"

Charlie gave his nephew a look.

"No. That would be silly … and dangerous. The mother-in-law."

They both glanced over at Molly. She was getting comfortable in one of several chairs, settling in for an afternoon of food, fun, and entertainment.

She put her hands to her mouth, and yelled, "Are you boys gonna break out the badminton net today?!"

Charlie shot her a look.

"I suppose," he shouted. "If we can get Alfred to set it up. The *Fry Master* cannot be deterred from the commission of his duties!"

Molly smiled. Bobby knew she loved watching Charlie interact with his family – almost as much as she enjoyed watching him play badminton.

"I'm sure Bobby doesn't mind helping," she called out.

"Not at all," Bobby replied. "If Simon Legree here can spare me a few moments."

"Water!" Charlie shouted, extending his hands like a surgeon.

Bobby rolled his eyes and, looking back at Molly, winked.

Bobby and Molly had been good friends for years, from before the war even, their common bond, one Charlie MacLeod.

Bobby had been fifteen years old when he started sailing with Charlie. Back then they covered much of the eastern seaboard, from New York City to the Bahamas and Havana, transporting anything they could fit in the hold of the light schooner *Miss Betsy*. They had sailed together until the mid-fifties, when *Miss Betsy* became sanded in at Jupiter Inlet through a string of unlikely circumstances. Bobby had gone on to captain his own small freighter, *Abigail,* but Charlie had remained right where fate had landed him, living in a palmetto cabin for several years, perfectly happy to do nothing at all but comb the beach, just him and Salty. Then, when the Civil War appeared on the horizon, Bobby had talked his free-spirited uncle into joining him in running the Union blockade.

Throughout these many years of fun and adventure, Bobby knew Molly had been one of the constants in Charlie's life. Her fair enterprise, The Happy Clam, had been a typical establishment unique to the wharves of the world, a place that catered exclusively to an interesting and diverse amalgamation of thirsty, lusty seafarers.

In those days, Key West was Charlie's second home, and to there he invariably returned, to where he had met and married his good, sweet Nellie, Sally's mother. It was their home port, and The Happy Clam had been their home away from home.

And there was Molly.

It had taken a few decades, but the two old lovers finally connected when Charlie decided that what he needed was "a little bit of Molly."

Now he had the whole thing.

And Bobby couldn't be happier. During those twenty years that Charlie had isolated himself from society, it had been hard on those he loved, something Bobby knew better than most. It was he who had witnessed the heartache it caused Sally to see her father, the bold, blustery, jolly sailor, transform into a sad, miserable hermit after the death of his second wife and child.

Yes, there were many people thankful for the "reconstituted" Charlie MacLeod, and all of them gave full and deserved credit to the little, red-haired girl, the one sailing towards them in her skiff, *Miss Kitty*.

Copernicus stood on the prow looking very much like a short, furry George Washington.

They watched a moment, then Charlie said, "Did you say that alligator pear tree is bearing?"

"Yep," Bobby replied. "We have avocados. And mangos, too, before you ask."

"Bananas?"

"Nope."

Charlie waved his arms at the little boat and yelled, "BANANAS!"

Annie held up her arms, indicating she couldn't hear, so Charlie stood back, hunched his shoulders, and hopped up and down like a monkey.

Annie signaled she understood and turned *Miss Kitty* around.

"I see you haven't lost your knack for Indian sign language."

"Ya never know when it might come in handy." Charlie turned to grin at his wife, who seemed to approve.

"Oh, Father!"

They turned to see Sally standing on the porch, arms crossed.

"Yes, m'darlin'!"

"It's nice to see you're setting a good example for the kids!"

Charlie bowed. "Not a problem, m'dear, lass!" And with that, he cried, "Water!!"

Katie and Alfred Humphrey arrived. Sally and Katie were best of friends. They visited often, their houses separated only by the church and about a quarter mile of white sand beach.

And Molly made three.

They all got along well. Of course, if Molly was there Mother Humphrey would contract some sort of malady and be unable to attend.

Molly was a very welcome addition indeed.

It had taken a little getting used to, her former profession, but she made Charlie so undeniably happy that it was impossible not to accept her with open arms as a valued member of the family. She still didn't quite blend in, her choice of clothing tending more towards the flamboyant and risqué; but Charlie seemed to like it, so who was anyone else to say?

But there were others without such tact.

"How come I can always see so much of your bosomses?"

It was Benji.

"Benji!" Katie gasped.

Annie and Bobby giggled.

"You cannot ask such personal questions!" Katie admonished her youngest. "It's not polite!" She smiled sheepishly at Molly.

They were all sitting around the chickee, enjoying the last vestiges of a sunset sky. Will was managing to contain his amusement; Charlie and Bobby weren't doing so well.

Dinner had been delicious. It had lasted well over two hours.

From the time the first fritter hit the frying pan, there had been a steady stream of seafood, along with several side dishes and a healthy batch of hushpuppies. Charlie sat over the skillet, moving food left to right, taking bites in between, eating more than anyone else in a ballet of gluttonous joy. He appeared to be savoring the food almost as much as he did the satisfied faces and bulging cheeks on display before him.

Now, as light began to fade, Molly took little Benji's shiny face in her hands, and said, "You, Mister Humphrey, are a scamp, aren't you?! Well," she sat back. "I suppose I wear dresses like this because … I'm hot-natured." She looked at her husband. "Isn't that so, Charlie?"

"Oh, yes," he replied with confidence. "She gets real hot up there."

Benji stared a moment longer, then said, "Oh."

A little while later Benji was in the house, sleeping peacefully on Sally's sofa. The smudges were lit, and the muted light gave a soft glow to the tropical scene. Annie had waited patiently for Benji to grow sleepy-eyed.

"So, Uncle Will," she said. "Remember you said you'd tell the whole story of the buried treasure next time I came over?"

"Why, yes, I do."

"The real story?" she asked, glancing over at Charlie.

"What're you lookin' at me for?!"

"Because," Annie giggled. "Every time you tell the story, both the treasure and the story get bigger and bigger! Last time you said you were captured by Blackbeard and had to save a harem of fair maidens from him and Attila the Hun, and then the Sultan of Arabia gave you a king's ransom in return for saving his daughter, and then your friend the Pharaoh of Egypt built a pyramid for you to store it all in!"

Charlie shrugged and stated plainly, "It was a fine story."

"It was a great story!" Annie replied, setting Salty on her shoulder. "But I just want the regular one."

"Oh," Charlie said. "You mean the *real* one."

"Yes!"

Charlie scowled. "It's not as good. Doesn't even have a troll in it."

Annie punched her old uncle in the arm.

"Uncle Charlie!"

He shrugged. "All right. I suppose if you want the *real* story, you'll have to get that from your Uncle Will." He paused and, with a perplexed look, said, "Now that I think about it, I should hear that one again meself."

Will had been waiting patiently, the look on his face saying that he knew his brother-in-law well enough to know this moment would come.

Charlie sat back and shut his mouth.

"Well," Will began. "Keep in mind this tale is for family only."

"I know," Annie giggled, squirming in her seat.

"Let's see," he began. "It was back in '33, I believe. We were returning to Biscayne Bay from St. Augustine. Charlie was at the helm and noticed the wind shifting to the west. By the time I woke up early next morning, the wind was blowing at thirty knots from the north, it was raining, and there was a distinct chill in the air. The waves were growing large enough to cause us concern, so we decided to run for cover at Gilbert's Bar. When we came upon the inlet, we found deep water over the bar, the tide high and rising, so we lowered all but one sail and brought *Mary Ann* around. Then we timed our run to coincide with the smaller waves.

"Easier said than done, as you can imagine," Will said, glancing at Alfred, who was devouring his words with relish, for everyone knew he loved nothing more than a good sea story. "Well, we crossed the bar just as a rogue wave rose up, amassing an enormous amount of water that came crashing down on our stern. The cockpit was completely flooded. I don't know how we managed to hold on, do you, Charlie?"

Charlie shook his head.

"Regardless, we made it safely over the bar and sailed onto the river. We could see it narrowed to the south and widened to the north, so we sailed up river until we found a sandy beach on the east shore. You all know the location, the St. Lucie Rocks, where the House of Refuge is now."

"Oh!" Annie exclaimed, as if realizing he had just given her a clue. "Sorry. Go on."

"As you know, it's only a narrow strip of sand and a large outcropping of rock that separated us from the ocean. I remember directly across from us at the mouth of the St. Lucie River there was an absolute hoard of ducks and other water fowl. Remember, Charlie?"

"I don't think I've ever seen more ducks gathered, there or anywhere else," Charlie stated.

"Yep," Will replied. "There were literally thousands, tens of thousands, of ducks within our view. Bringing *Mary Ann* as close to shore as possible, we dropped *Squirt* in the water –"

"Good old *Squirt*," Charlie sighed.

Will continued. "The next morning we were up early, and I thought it a good idea to scrape the barnacles and other growth from the bottom of *Mary Ann* while we were there."

"Ugh," Charlie moaned. "I hate scraping barnacles."

"Anyway," Will continued. "Jimmy asked if he could go over to the beach, and the next thing I know he comes running back screaming at the top of his lungs, something about finding gold!"

Charlie chuckled. "The way he came over that berm, I thought his pants were on fire."

"He was pretty excited," Will agreed. "Well, I looked, and in his hand was a gold doubloon. I remember you two wanted to go treasure hunting right away."

"That's right," Charlie grumbled. "But you told us we had to finish the boat first."

Will laughed. "I don't think I've ever seen our Charlie tackle physical labor with such enthusiasm, and all it took to get him moving was the prospect of a yellow-colored metal!"

Everyone giggled.

"On the way up the beach, I told them everything I knew about the Great Armada of 1715, how the entire fleet had been destroyed in a hurricane, scattering treasure all along this part of the coast. When we got over to the beach, Jimmy showed us where he had found it, sticking right out of the escarpment.

"By this point I had the fever as well, and we spent the remainder of that day traipsing the beach. We covered several miles that day and found dozens of doubloons. The next morning, we went south as far as the inlet and found a few, but after sailing *Mary Ann* several miles up Indian River that afternoon and crossing over to the beach, we found even more than we had the previous day. The third day we sailed even farther north, but only found a few, so we concentrated on the area just north of us for the rest of that day. The next day I decided – against the objections of my crew, I might add – that we should head home while the seas were smooth.

"That last night, after Jimmy went to bed, Charlie and I discussed things. He wanted to take it all with us, but I pointed out that there are people who would literally kill us if they could get their hands on what we had, and I told him people don't usually walk into a bank to make a deposit with twenty-five pounds of gold doubloons; people would ask all kinds of questions."

Annie mouthed the words, "Twenty-five pounds."

"About that," Will said. "Anyway, I thought it a bad idea to keep it at home. It could put our family in danger if anyone got wind of it, and I pointed out that large amounts of money rarely bring people the happiness they expect." He chuckled. "I don't think Charlie or Jimmy bought that argument. I remember Charlie asked what I thought we should do with it, and I suggested burying it in the rocks nearby. I explained that those rocks would make a first-rate vault. The gold could not be removed unless someone actually moved it."

"I couldn't believe what I was hearin'!" Charlie blurted. "He just wanted to leave it there!"

Will laughed. "No, you couldn't. But I talked you into it, and you later told me it was the best decision we could have made."

"That's true," Charlie said.

"So, we each took a doubloon for ourselves and Charlie the necklace he had found for Nellie; then we made up a rhyme so we would remember where it was, but," he smiled, "I'm afraid I'm not at liberty to divulge that, not without Jimmy here."

Annie was mesmerized. "And it's still there?!"

"Last time Charlie looked," Will said. "Right, Charlie?"

"YYYYep."

A few minutes later, they heard the familiar splash of oars meeting water and a row boat came into view.

"Ahoy there!" Malcolm called out. "No one made mention of a shindy going on."

Sally answered, "Oh, you know my father. Always full of surprises."

He pulled the skiff onshore and walked over.

"So, did I miss anything?"

Before anyone else could answer, Will said, "Not much. Just salty old tales."

59

Chapter Ten

Several days later

"Oh, my Lord!" Bonnie Blakely cried as the front door of the Port Starboard General Store and Post Office slammed open. As wind and rain howled, she put her back to it and pushed with all her might. The latch clicked.

"Whoo!" she said, looking down at herself and shaking out her dress. "That is some kind of storm!"

Four faces stared back at her – five, counting Copernicus.

"Guess you didn't make it in time," Gnarles observed.

"Not quite."

The storm had come up early that afternoon, and with unusual force. The rumbling of thunder was ceaseless. Sudden and violent cracks of lightning pounded the coastline, causing the building to shake and the hair to rise on the backs of necks.

"I think I might have if I hadn't stopped at the schoolhouse." She closed her umbrella and hung it on the side of the pickle barrel. Then she looked out towards the lake, nearly invisible through the deluge. "I hope it doesn't last too long," she sighed. "Betsy is expecting me to help with dinner."

"No telling," Eddie replied, handing a towel over the counter. "But usually the worse the storm, the faster it goes by."

"Not always," Annie said.

"I said usually."

Bonnie giggled as she dabbed at her face and arms.

"I do declare. Sometimes you two sound like an old married couple."

Eddie and Annie made faces at each other.

"Well," Bonnie said, pulling up a chair at a small table near the front window. "I suppose I might as well get comfortable." A few minutes later, she said, "Now, who in the world is that?!"

It was hard to see, but someone was tying a boat to the dock. They watched as the figure dashed up the dock towards the store. When the person arrived, Eddie was ready and opened the door just as a drenched form barreled through.

Silas pressed his weight against the door, as if fending off a pack of hungry wolves instead of the usual summer storm. Eddie handed Silas a towel.

"Are you all right?" he asked, concerned at how pale Silas looked. Bonnie took the towel from Eddie.

"Oh, Silas!" she exclaimed in alarm. "You're white as a ghost! Come over here and sit down." Wrapping the towel over his shoulders, she said, "Why, you're shaking like a leaf! You poor man! Annie, do you have another towel, or a blanket?"

"Sure," Annie replied, and she ran off to the back room, returning with a heavy, gray, wool blanket.

"I'll get some coffee going," Eddie said.

"Maybe we should light the stove," Bonnie suggested.

"No," Silas finally spoke. "I'll … be okay," but his teeth were chattering so hard they sounded like they might shatter.

"You just relax right here," Bonnie said, and she nodded to Gnarles and Paddy to go ahead and light the potbelly stove.

A little while later, as Silas started coming around, he said, "I think … I was struck … by lightning."

"Oh, my Lord!" Bonnie said, handing him a hot mug. "Drink this. Slowly."

As Silas took it, he gazed for what seemed to Eddie a long time into Bonnie's bottomless, blue, beautiful eyes.

"Thank you, ma'am," Silas stammered. "You're awful kind."

"Oh, it's nothing," she replied, patting his hand.

Silas simply stared, as if he had just fallen in love, Eddie thought, not at all an unusual effect when it came to the pretty, kindly schoolmistress.

*   *   *

Bonnie Blakely had arrived in Port Starboard two years previous expressly to take the job as the first school mistress. She adored her job of imparting knowledge of the world to young, porous minds. She had always been a good student herself, interested in and even enthusiastic about almost any subject: from mathematics to history, English to Latin.

Of course, teaching was most often a temporary pursuit for women. Men could make a career of it, but once a woman married she was expected to give up her position and tend to the duties of home and hearth. Yet Bonnie had always dreamed of being a teacher. She had truly adored many of her own mentors and had thought of doing little else since graduating, near the top of her class, from Daughter's College in Harrodsburg, Kentucky.

She had not, however, been remiss in scouring the debutante balls and promenade halls of Lexington for a suitable mate. In fact, a great many of Lexington's most eligible bachelors had, at one time or another, vied for the hand of one Bonnie Blakely, the soul heiress to the fabled Blakely fortune. It wasn't the fortune, necessarily, that drew these well-heeled, young men to her like the proverbial bees to honey. It was, in fact, Bonnie herself. She was fun to be around: attentive, curious, and trusting – to a fault.

From appearances, it was her one and only character flaw.

There was a long list of bounders, scoundrels, rapscallions, and con men, one of whom had actually gotten her to the altar before the facts, miraculously, had come to light. In addition, another two weddings had been cancelled, not counting the one in which she had nearly eloped after the cad had skillfully and connivingly plied her with chocolate bonbons and mint juleps.

Then she had met Malcolm.

Unlike the many other times she had been in love, this time everyone was in solid agreement: Bonnie had finally found a man who loved her and wasn't interested in her money.

It was apparent from Malcolm's dress, manner, and education that he had come from money. As he had explained, he had come to America for many reasons, but most of all for the freedoms it afforded the investor and entrepreneur. He had already secured several backers for his plans to build a "magnificent" hotel and resort on the lake and was currently in the process of selecting and acquiring a most suitable location.

Bonnie had never known a man so attuned to her needs. She wondered at a man so attached and devoted, so connected to her own wants and desires, just as she was certain that this time would be the last. It was merely coincidence that she would be marrying mere days before her thirty-first birthday, her last opportunity to claim her inheritance.

Not that she was concerned.

When she said, as she always had, that she would not marry for the wrong reasons, that she would rather give up the family fortune than marry a man whom she did not adore and respect, she meant it. In her mind, she was resolved. She would not marry until she found the man of her dreams.

Finally, she had.

*   *   *

Silas's nose had turned all red and grown one or two sizes. He was holding a handkerchief to it and blowing.

"I guess I got cold out there," he honked. He used the corner of the hanky to wipe at his eyes.

It was still raining steadily. Gnarles, Paddy, and Eddie were sitting on their stools, all in some stage of nodding off. Silas, Bonnie, and Annie were at the table, talking about books.

"Oh!" Annie sighed. "And what about the part when Mr. Rochester kisses Jane for the first time?!"

"Oh!" Bonnie put her hands to her heart. "That was so touching."

Honking again, Silas added, "I really think she's one of my favorite writers." He thought a moment, then added, "I feel so ... connected to her characters, like I know them personally."

"I know!" Bonnie exclaimed. "She has a way of *making* you like them," she paused, "or really hate them. Just like Dickens ... or MacLeod!"

Annie giggled. "Uncle Charlie loves it that Maggie uses his name as her pen name. He walks around talking about his most recent 'work.'"

"Sometimes," Silas went on, "her writing reminds me of Dickens, I don't really know why. Her character, Mr. Patch, kind of reminds me of Bill Sykes."

"Oh," Annie said. "I was afraid to go to sleep for a week after I finished *Oliver Twist*. I dreamed Bill Sykes was coming after me. I've never been so scared in my whole, entire life!"

Bonnie replied, "I cannot imagine being in an orphanage – any orphanage."

"Well," Silas noted. "That was actually a workhouse. They were more like prisoners. Not all orphanages are like that one, I hope."

"As do I," Bonnie said, staring out at the rain coming down.

"Me, too," Annie agreed. "I really feel sorry for orphans. First you lose your mother and father, then you have to go to a workhouse and work all day with hardly anything to eat and awful, mean people telling you what to do all the time."

"I suppose we should be glad there are orphanages, though," Silas said, "or where would children without parents go? Just live on the streets? That could be worse."

"Worse than a workhouse?!"

Silas thought a moment.

"I don't know," he said. "Either one sounds pretty bad to me."

"Not me," Annie replied. "I'd rather live on the street without any food, or blankets, or *anything* than live in that place!" She paused, then said, "I'd rather die! Wouldn't you, Miss Bonnie? ... Miss Bonnie?"

"I'm sorry," Bonnie replied. "My mind was drifting. What did you say, sweetheart?"

"I said, I'd rather *die* than go to a workhouse!"

Bonnie patted her hand.

"Oh, you don't mean that. And you shouldn't say it either." She looked out the window. "The rain is slowing down. I think I'll make a run for it." Then she stood, prompting Silas to leap to his feet, almost knocking over the table.

"Well," she said. "I had fun, just the three of us, talking about books. We should do it again sometime."

"Really?" Silas said. "The three of us?"

"Sure," she replied, glancing at the clock. "Oh, I cannot believe where the time went!"

"Hey!" Annie exclaimed. "Why don't we start a book club!"

"Oooo," Paddy exclaimed. "Can we be in the club, too?"

"I don't see why not," Bonnie said. "You'd have to read the books we read, though."

"Oh."

Bonnie smiled. "But that is a wonderful idea, Annie. Oh, and wait until Maggie gets back. And Booker T.! Oh! I know Booker's going to want to be in the club. Annie, this is a wonderful idea! Don't you think, Silas?"

"Uh, sure," he stammered. "That would be great." He instinctively wondered if it was some kind of joke.

As Bonnie picked up her umbrella, she turned, and said, "I really enjoyed myself, Silas. You're a very interesting and insightful man." With that, she turned, opened the door, and strolled out, unaware of Silas' addled expression or that she had made a human being feel worthy for the first time in his life.

Chapter Eleven

Gnarles and Paddy were up bright and early the next day; it was their first opportunity to go salvaging in months. Summer could be feast or famine in the business. Of course, summers produce hurricanes, but it wasn't steady like winter, with the constant series of northeasters sweeping down the coast. Some years, hurricanes would come roaring though like freight trains, as if on schedule. Other years there would be nothing at all.

It was a fact of summer: without hurricanes, pickin's were slim.

The hurricane doesn't have to actually hit Florida or anywhere nearby in order to send rafts of goodies floating to her shores. Hurricanes as far away as Mexico and South America regularly conspire with the trade winds that steer them, exploiting the currents that feed them, and delivering untold treasures to the ever vigilant and patient salvager. To live along her shores is to understand that Mother Ocean rarely plays favorites, for as she delivers, she also takes away.

Today, however, she would be delivering.

Gnarles and Paddy had been aware of this fact before they even got up that morning, because the storm of the previous day had turned out to be more than just the garden variety, summer squall. They had noticed the barometer falling – not fast, but steadily – and by the time they had left the store for home, word was out all over the lake that a hurricane was on its way.

They had prepared as much as possible at the store and hotel, but with night coming on there had been little time to do much: bring in some of the smaller things, make sure the shutters were latched, tie any boats securely to docks – or in a few cases, such as with Gnarles and Paddy, cram *Cocoa-Nuts* as far into the mangroves as possible.

Nothing weathers a storm like mangrove.

Betsy had urged them to stay at the hotel, but that wasn't likely. Of all the hurricanes they had ridden out over the years, they had never deemed one severe enough to cause them to leave their still behind, even the time it actually floated away, taking them with it, hanging on for dear life and refusing any attempt at rescue unless the still was saved first.

Overnight, the winds had picked up steadily, first out of the southwest, then swinging to the north as it passed through. Gnarles and Paddy had spent the night in their "hurricane hut," a tiny, roughly built but nearly impregnable fortress. Constructed completely of 4x12 inch timbers set on end and buried three feet in the ground, it was rectangular in shape with six walls, each two feet longer than the last, mazelike, creating a passageway leading inward. It had, in fact, been designed by none other than the Old Sage himself, Charlie MacLeod.

Over the "front" wall was a hole in the roof so smoke from the fire could escape. The roof sloped towards the back and was of the same lumber as the walls – notched, lashed, and spiked. On top of that was a layer of palmetto fronds to keep it from leaking. It was big enough to hold Gnarles and Paddy and the still with a fire going under it. There were benches built into either side, and along the back wall was everything needed, including all the ingredients and utensils necessary for the creation of the most magnificent brew on earth, the one and only "Cocorum."

There were also a few cans of food and a keg of water.

Wind and rain could penetrate the gaps along the sides, but it was strong – though it had yet to be tested. For two years now they had been hoping for a monster to barrel through, but by midnight they had determined this would not be it.

First thing the next morning, they pulled *Cocoa-Nuts* out of the mangroves, cleaned her out, packed a few belongings, and headed for the inlet. This was not to "go-a-salvaging," but to see what the seas looked like. The waves could be heard crashing on shore from all the way across the lake, one right after the other, in perfect, natural time.

They set their heading for Charlie's.

It is an ingrained, inborn tradition with coastal dwellers to migrate to the beach to watch the ocean at work following a hurricane. When Gnarles and Paddy arrived, the Humphreys were all there, with Annie, Copernicus, and Benji leading the way. As they were pulling up to shore, they noticed the sails go up on Bobby's sloop, *Nonesuch.*

There was a chop on the lake, still a good stiff breeze but not enough to reef any sails. It was fine sailing weather, actually.

Out on the ocean was a different story.

When Gnarles and Paddy came over the berm, they could see Charlie and Molly and the Humphreys out near the rocks, watching the waves crash into them, shooting plumes of water thirty feet in the air and causing the ground to tremble. It was a sight to behold, especially up close. For Gnarles and Paddy, however, it wasn't about the power and grandeur at all, but the aftermath.

There was nothing on earth they enjoyed more than collecting stuff off the beach, or better yet, wrecking. It had been a long time since they had come across a good, old-fashioned wreck. To Gnarles and Paddy, wrecks were much more than a treasure trove. To them, there was something transcendental and mystical about an abandoned hulk.

Neither could explain it – neither really thought about it – but whenever they came upon a ship, or even a boat, that retained much of its former shape, they couldn't help but celebrate by tying one on. They would imagine and make up stories of what might have transpired on the vessel during its last moments, or what had happened to the crew – indeed, if they had survived the wreck. Then they would drink to the sailors of the ship, or just sailors in general, and to their own good luck at finding such a prize.

"How do, everyone?!" Gnarles said as they ambled over the berm.

"Well, hey there, boys!" Charlie shouted. "I was expectin' you here before the sun come up!"

"We was up, but we had ta get *Cocoa-Nuts* out'a the trees first."

"Wasn't as bad as it could have been," Charlie said.

"Nope." Gnarles looked down the beach.

"Hurricane hut hold up all right?"

"Yep." Gnarles looked up the beach.

"Lost a bit of beach." Charlie pointed northward.

"Yep," Gnarles replied absently.

Charlie suddenly guffawed, slapping Gnarles on his boney back.

"You boys just can't stand it, can ya?!"

"That's right!" Annie giggled. "Uncle Charlie said you two would be so excited that he wondered if you had already headed out last night!"

Gnarles shook his head.

"We ain't in *that* big a hurry. Ain't that right, Paddy?"

"Aye," the portly man replied. "Ya wooon't find me out there, not in a Doooblin moon, ya wooon't."

"What the heck is a Dublin moon, anyway?" Charlie asked.

Paddy shrugged. "I dooon't knooow, but that's what m' dear old Nanna'd seyyy."

Before the sun cleared the horizon the following morning, Gnarles, Paddy, and *Cocoa-Nuts* were out the inlet and bounding over the rolling waves. They had spotted Charlie and Molly taking their morning swim as they sailed by, both half-heartedly shielding their eyes from a view of Molly's unmistakable assets – and grateful for her lack of modesty.

The waves had continued to roll in but were beginning to wane. Once across the bar, it was smooth, easy sailing. They had decided which direction to sail by tossing a coin in the air, taking a drink real fast, then spending several minutes trying to find it in the bottom of the boat. It had come up heads, so they had steered northward.

The storm had done some damage. There were pieces of boats and ships scattered all over the beaches in addition to the cargo they had been carrying: the treasure!

They had been making notes of what they saw and where they saw it, but it was difficult with the waves running three to five feet. They couldn't come more than a quarter mile in without being in danger of a rogue wave breaking over their seaward side and capsizing them, and with the wind steady out of the southeast, they had to be careful not to push their luck. They could end up on the beach before they knew it – or worse, drowned.

Normally, the first and most important thing to watch out for was liquor: kegs, hogsheads, casks, jugs, or bottles: it didn't matter whether it was wine, whiskey, rum, or tequila. It made no difference to them. If they spotted anything that even looked promising, they logged it on a special map set aside explicitly for the purpose.

"I thought you said you were positive." Gnarles was speaking.

"Nooo," Paddy argued. "I said meeeybe. Meeeybe!"

"Dang it," Gnarles grumbled. "Now I gotta erase."

Paddy shrugged. "Dooon't let gooo th' rudder."

Gnarles glared.

Paddy was upset because Gnarles was taking notes. That had always been his job, but that was before Gnarles had learned how to read and write. Paddy had liked it better then, when he was the only one who could do such things. It had made him feel good, knowing he was better than Gnarles at something. Now all he was better at than Gnarles was tending the sails. He knew he was better at that because Gnarles had never done it. Of course, Paddy had never steered before.

It was something he dreamed about at night, to someday be the helmsman. The captain of the vessel: Cap'n Paddy.

"Hey, Paddy, you dolt! What're ya doin'?! We're losin' steam here!"

"Huh?!" Paddy took in the main sheet. "Sorry."

They were a few miles north of Jupiter, near old Gilbert's Bar. The high, sandy cliffs of Hobe Sound were visible over the low growth along the beach.

"What's that up there?" Gnarles pointed.

Paddy squinted and grew suddenly animated.

There was something large, several hundred feet offshore, outside the line of breakers.

They pulled out their telescopes. They used to carry only one, but it had gone overboard during an especially raucous exchange over whose turn it was.

"Hmmm," Gnarles said.

"Hmmm," Paddy echoed.

"Is that what I think it is?"

Paddy squirmed. "I hooope sooo!"

The nearer they grew, the more excited they became. A wrecked ship! Not a big one, but enough to kick off the celebration.

Out from under the seat came the bottle of brandy.

It was a three-masted schooner, seventy feet, maybe as many tons. The name on the stern identified her as the *Julia B. Ware*, out of New Brunswick. It appeared the crew had attempted to save her by jettisoning most of the cargo, stripping her of sails, and running "bare poles a'fore the wind." There was still plenty to salvage, however, in fittings, spare sails, galley equipment, a steam-powered, auxiliary engine, and a variety of other items.

Gnarles and Paddy assumed the vessel had been abandoned somewhere south of here or even along the Bahama Banks. By the positioning of the davits, the crew had abandoned the vessel, and the captain's charts and navigation equipment were missing. The forward hold was stove in, and there appeared to be substantial damage to the starboard rail, as if the ship had been dragged against the bottom at one point. It was listing heavily, and they wondered if captain and crew had survived, and if they would have abandoned the vessel had they known it wasn't destined to sink at all.

The first thing they had done was to claim the wreck, assuming their rightful roles as "Wreckmasters." The mere word, "Wreckmaster," summoned forth visions of stalwart men of the sea, men of distinction and consequence.

"I hereby dub thee, Sir Gnarles, Wreckmaster of the good ship *Julia B. Ware*!" Paddy declared, touching Gnarles' shoulders one at a time with a rusty old cutlass they kept on board just for the purpose.

"And I hereby dub thee, Sir Paddy, the other Wreckmaster of the *Julia B. Ware*!"

It was maritime law. If anyone else showed up and wanted a piece of the action, they could agree to be employed to work for "The Wreckmasters" – or go find their own wreck.

They proceeded to raise several toasts to themselves, drinking to the ill-fated ship and crew, then a few more to whatever came to mind, including Mother Ocean herself. Then they got to work, first by exploring the vessel and deciding in what order things were to be evacuated to shore. As usual, they started with the ship's store of alcohol, primarily rum and beer, and the Captain's personal cache – in this case, two bottles of French brandy and a half case of Spanish claret. All this they brought up on deck, loaded in *Cocoa-Nuts,* and sailed to shore, grateful that the seas had continued to decrease throughout the day.

Things were working out perfectly. They made another toast.

Several hours later they were sitting in bilge water, peering through a knothole into the aft hold. The ship had buckled at the aft mast, and they reasoned it was this that had spurred the crew to abandon her.

It wasn't much, hardly noticeable from the port side, but the entire bulkhead had shifted, making it impossible to get through the hatch. The two men could have accomplished much more had they not spent so much time trying to get into that particular compartment. But what could they do? They had never come across something like this in all their years of salvaging, something so tempting and tantalizing that there was no option but to put all their efforts into the one job: to gain access to the *Julia B. Ware*'s aft hold.

Five hours earlier, Paddy had been busy removing the ship's gimbaled compass when Gnarles exclaimed from below, "Holy Constantinopl-ee!!"

In a flash, Paddy was down the curiously tilted ladder, thumping and bumping all the way.

"What is it?!" he had cried.

Gnarles had turned from the knothole, his face like a ghost, and mumbled, "Ain't never seen nothin' like it."

"What?! What?!!"

"It's … ginger ale, Paddy. Tons of it!"

Paddy's eyes grew wide, then he repeated the words with unaffected reverence: "Ginger … ale?" It was their favorite. "Tons of it?"

"From deck to overhead."

"Ooooooooooo!" Paddy had cried. "Let me see! Let me see!"

Now, they were still at it. They had given up trying to open the hatch and were taking turns, sitting in putrid water, sawing.

As soon as they had a hole big enough to reach in for a bottle, they had begun drinking and hadn't stopped since. Both were bloated, belching exuberantly, and talking a mile a minute as one after the other got in position and started sawing.

They were almost there.

Neither man had noticed the waves picking up again, nor that the sky was growing dark.

Nor that the *Julia B. Ware* had begun to drift.

Chapter Twelve

Several miles to the south, Charlie and Molly were relaxing, waiting for the moon to rise. She was sitting in a chair placed in a tidal pool that routinely formed south of the rocks. Charlie was propped on his elbows, lying next to her in the pool, smoking his pipe, not a stitch on.

He tossed a stick for Floppy.

"I can't see enough to read anymore," Molly grumbled, and she set her book down.

"Come on, m'darlin'," Charlie said. "It's warm tonight and with this breeze there won't be any sand flies out. Why don't ya join me in here a while."

Molly tossed the book a few feet up the beach onto a blanket.

"Don't you ever get enough, Charles MacLeod?"

"Enough of what, m'darlin'? Relaxin' and enjoyin' God's creation?"

Unbuttoning her dress, she replied, "Enough of whatever it is you're callin' God's creation."

A little while later they were relaxing once again. A storm raged far out over the ocean, sporadically lighting up the sky. They had moved farther up the beach to a small chickee, just big enough for stretching out underneath.

Molly dug her feet into the sand.

"I simply cannot believe that the President of the United States went to see Maggie sing!"

"Well," Charlie replied, "I don't know if he went there specifically to see Maggie, but he was there, and I'm bettin' he got himself an earful. That girl can belt it out, I tell ya!"

"Ain't that the truth," Molly sighed. "That girl almost makes it worth goin' to church on Sundays."

"Almost," Charlie agreed. "That girl's voice has the power to turn the most crotchety old atheist into a gentle lamb of God. I cannot believe it," he laughed. "That girl, that little waif me and Bobby met back during the war, the same one who hardly uttered so much as a peep, has turned out to be one of the most talented women I've ever known."

"You don't have to tell me," Molly said, reaching over to pick up a magazine lying nearby. "Have you read her latest story in the *Saturday Evening Post*?"

"You mean the latest story by me? Charles MacLeod?"

"Yes," Molly slapped him. "YOUR latest story."

Standing up and putting his shirt on, Charlie replied, "Well, since you've read it to me at least three times, I gonna sayyy … yes?"

"Smart ass," Molly said, throwing a shell at him. "I mean, have you really taken the time to listen to her words." She sighed. "It's almost as if she's speaking directly to me. I don't know how she can put it all into words."

"Put what into words, m'darlin'?"

"I don't know," she said, looking off towards the rising moon. "I guess, how it feels to be human. How can she look into her own heart and by doing so see a little bit into so many others' hearts?"

Charlie scowled. "I don't know, m'darlin', but it could be you're a'cogitatin' a tad too much. I just think it's a great story."

A moment later, Molly sighed, "I would simply love to see her on stage. Annie seems to think it's pretty certain she's not going back for another season."

"Ohhh," Charlie waved his hand as he picked up his fishing pole and hobbled the few feet to the water. "She's just a little homesick is all. I'm thinkin' she'll have a change of heart."

"Poor Booker T.," Molly said.

Charlie chuckled. "That man's gotta be miserable, and there's nothin' Maggie can't stand more than seein' that man in misery. Remember when he got the shingles last year?"

Following an extended pause, Molly said, "Charlie –"

He raised his hand, signaling he had a bite. A moment later, he was reeling with all his might, letting loose with a series of heartfelt grunts. Without knowing what was on the line, he declared, "Wha'd'ya say to seared kingfish with spicy mango sauce for dinner t'night, m'darlin'?!"

"No one makes it like you do, m'darlin'!" she called back.

"That is true," he replied.

A moment later, Molly said, "I wonder who that is."

Charlie looked out to sea, and bounding over the rising phosphorescence was a small, sloop-rigged sailboat.

"Hmmm," he said, letting the fish run a bit. "I have no idea. Some kind 'a maniac I reckon, out in that little thing with these seas runnin' like they are. Must be tryin' to make Jupiter before low tide." He chuckled. "Looks like somethin' I might 'a tried back in the day." Studying the lines of the tiny craft, Charlie mumbled, "That little skimming dish sure does look familiar, though."

When he had the fish to shore, a kingfish, Charlie turned and, holding it up proudly, declared, "And how about, m'darlin', if you and me catch a steamer tomorrow for Titusville ... then a train to New York City?"

* * *

Gnarles and Paddy had finally managed to get into the aft hold, and, following a moment to celebrate with a couple of ginger ales, they started hauling case after case out of the compartment – 134 cases in all. It was then, when they climbed out of the hold, that they discovered the sun had gone down, and light was fading from the sky.

The fresh breeze felt good on their skin.

"Gee," Gnarles exclaimed. "It's already gettin' dark."

"So, what should we dooo?" Paddy asked. "I'm tired."

"Me, too," Gnarles replied. He looked around. "Holy Mackerel! Look at the size of the waves!"

Paddy looked worried.

"I noooticed th' boat was r-r-rockin', but I didn't knooow it was this bad! And, look!" he said, pointing towards shore. "It loooks like we're a'driftin'."

"Dang it!" Gnarles complained. "You didn't set the anchors when we got here?"

"Ya did'na tell me toooo! We was celebr-r-ratin'."

Gnarles remained calm.

Scratching his grizzled face, he said, "Well, we can go for Jupiter and hope to make it over the bar," he gulped, "or we can try to ride it out right here."

"I d'na like either one 'a those!" Paddy protested. "I wanna gooo hooome."

"We can't go home, Paddy!" Gnarles growled. "We gotta do like Charlie or Will. First thing we'll do is load up a few cases on *Cocoa-Nuts*, then we'll set the anchors and sail for Jupiter."

"But the tide's low. What if we can'a get in there?"

"Look, Paddy! We gotta do somethin', all right?!"

Paddy lowered his oversized, round head.

"All r-r-right."

It didn't take but a few minutes for the two men to bring up several cases and set them on deck.

"All right," Gnarles said, walking over to the port side, "Let's get these load...ed. Hey, Paddy," he said, his voice cracking. "Didn't we tie off *Cocoa-Nuts* to the port side?"

He looked forward.

"Where's the boat?!" he cried, running over to the other side.

73

Both men scurried back and forth across the deck. *Cocoa-Nuts* was gone, nowhere in sight. And Paddy was starting to cry.

"Paddy," Gnarles said, taking him by the shoulders. "It's all right. We'll just set the anchors and ride it out. Everything will be fine."

The men hurried up to the foredeck, only to discover a pair of frayed anchor lines. Paddy was losing it, but Gnarles remained composed.

"Like Charlie and Will," he repeated. "Like Charlie and Will."

He was still hanging in there when Paddy abruptly stopped crying, and said, "That's funny. Are we sinking?"

Chapter Thirteen

The *Julia B. Ware* was sinking. Only her foredeck remained above water. The seas were building by the minute and it was growing dark, the moon having yet to rise. Gnarles and Paddy were perched on the bowsprit, clinging to each other, hoping against hope that the tide would change and push the vessel landward. It was their only hope.

Paddy was sobbing; Gnarles, griping.

"I wish we didn't take that keg 'a rum ta shore. We could'a emptied it and used it ta float on."

Through tears, Paddy sniffed, "You mean, just dump it out?"

"Yes, you idiot! The rum won't do us any good if we're dead!"

"I dooon't s'pooose," Paddy sighed mournfully.

"Well, I ain't just gonna sit around doin' nothin'," Gnarles declared. "That's not what Charlie and Will would do."

"So, what're we gonna dooo?" Paddy sniveled.

"We're gonna make a raft," Gnarles declared, scooting down the bowsprit and sliding onto the deck and into the forward hold. "There's gotta be somethin' in here we can use," he said, slipping into the water and feeling around for anything that floated.

"Hey!" he cried. "What's this?!"

"What's what?" Paddy said, scooting down the bowsprit, careful not to let go of the lines.

"It's a keg!" Gnarles exclaimed. "Hey Paddy! I found a keg of something."

Pulling it up on deck, he let it roll down to the gunnel, then climbed out and started prying at the stopper. When he got it open, he dumped some out.

"It's water! Come on, Paddy," he said. "We'll drink as much as we can, then if the boat goes under, we'll dump it out and hold onto it. The waves will take us to shore when the tide changes and we'll be just fine."

Paddy wiped at tears.

"Really? We'll be fine?"

"Are you kiddin'? This is gonna make one *hell* of a story! Just think of it. It'll be almost as good as the one of Charlie and Ole Peg floatin' him and Salty to shore that time. Remember?" Gnarles propped his head under the keg and guzzled.

"Sure," Paddy said. "I love that story. R-r-remember? Charlie was r-r-rescued by an Indian princess. Maybe," he said, excitement building in his voice, "we'll be r-r-rescued by some Indian princesses, too!"

Wiping his mouth with his forearm, Gnarles replied, "No tellin'. Now come on! Drink as much as ya can."

Two hours later the moon was up, nearly full, casting a welcome luminescence over the large, lazy swells surging landward. Gnarles, Paddy, and their barrel were just a tiny speck floating on the dark expanse, rising and falling over the ever-increasing depths. The two men clung to the water keg and watched in silence as storm clouds rose from the east. Lightning bolts lay bare the massive thunderheads, towering thousands of feet and threatening to block out the moon.

Gnarles didn't want to alarm Paddy, but he was certain the keg had a leak. He had been trying to push the bung tighter, hoping that was the cause – but it was only a matter of time.

As the storm swept closer, the wind whipped across the water's surface, stirring the sea into a frenzy. The clouds blotted out the moon and the rains came – spurts at first, then torrents. The waves transformed from rolling to unrelenting, and within a matter of minutes all became completely black. Neither man could see the other, though they were only inches apart. It was becoming ever more difficult to hold on to the keg. Their fingers were numb with cold.

There was little conversation, each man grappling with his own fate in his own way. Paddy had stopped crying and started praying, promising anything, that he would quit drinking and become a preacher just like his mother had wanted, if God would only spare them.

Paddy whimpered, "We're gonna die, aren't we, Gnarles?"

"Don't be stupid," Gnarles replied. "We ain't gonna die."

A little while later, Gnarles spoke into the blackness. "I love you, Paddy ... in a manly way, of course."

A moment later, Paddy choked, "I love you, too."

Lightning bolts seared the sky, lighting up miles of nothing, nothing but dark monsters rising all about them, capping and breaking, and exposing their faces for the other to see the terror, the despair, of knowing their fate.

Then an amazing thing happened.

Gnarles waited for another flash to light up Paddy's face, then he said, "You hold on, Paddy. Maybe one of us can make it to shore." With that, he released his grip, pushed himself away, and said, "Tell everyone back home that Gnarles says 'Hey!'"

Chapter Fourteen

The storm passed, moving inland and dissipating over the headwaters of the Loxahatchee River and the spongy expanse beyond, known as Allapattah Flats. The winds continued to howl, blowing Paddy ever shoreward. Both tide and wind were in his favor, but the keg continued to take on water, and he was losing strength.

It was the darkness that terrified him most. When he noticed the cloud cover thinning, then breaking up, he found a glimmer of hope that the benevolent orb in the sky might finally reveal itself. When it did, Paddy found new strength and, turning westward, he started kicking his feet.

He was talking to himself, to Gnarles actually, apologizing for not tying off the boat. It had been his job. It had always been his job.

Whenever they went anywhere, Gnarles would say, "Tie off the boat, Paddy," and Paddy would reply, "How come I gotta dooo it?" "Because, knucklehead," Gnarles would snarl. "If you don't, it'll float away!"

"I'm sorry, Gnarles," Paddy sniffed now. "It's all my fault, and you didn't even yell at me." He wiped at his eyes, and added, "Maybe a little." He flopped his feet impotently, telling himself that everything would be fine, reminding himself that at least he could see now, a blessing in its own right.

Then he saw it: a large, gray triangle sliding through the water. The moon's glow reflected off the waves, illuminating the unspeakable. It was his worst nightmare, only much worse.

As the fear of drowning became infinitely more tolerable, Paddy realized there was a way out.

The prospect of drowning is a common topic amongst sailors, the question being: "Does it hurt?"

Charlie and Will agreed that drowning was physically painless, and each of them had been to the point where they had been forced to consider the possibility. They had concluded it would best simply to lie back, relax, think about something beloved, expel air, and take in a deep breath of seawater. What could be easier?

What could be more terrifying?

Paddy remembered his pocket knife and reached into his pocket to pull it out, then he dropped it. He almost started sobbing again, but instead said to himself, "Gotta do like Charlie and Will … and Gnarles," he added, which brought on another river of tears.

The shark continued to circle, silently and concentrically closer, ever closer.

The fin slowly disappeared under the surface. Horror-struck, Paddy looked around feverishly, clawing desperately at the cask and going under with it. Something hit him violently, sending shockwaves through his body. He resurfaced, gasping for air and realizing he had not been bitten.

But it was only a matter of time.

Sobs filled the brisk night air, but there was no one to hear.

The fin slowly rose again, circling even closer now, and Paddy realized he was about to be eaten alive by a real-life monster. So, taking several deep breaths, his last, he closed his eyes and thought about his childhood dog, Blarney, and about Gnarles, imagining his beautiful, grizzled, smiling face. Then he released his grip on the cask and expelled all his air.

"Paddy! Hey! Paddy!"

Paddy imagined that Gnarles had come to save him. He was in a boat and was reaching over the rail for him.

"Hey, ya big lummox! Give us a hand here!"

"Huh?!" Paddy snorted, spitting out saltwater. The plump, little man moved like a cat, and in no time he was safely in the boat, his feet clearing the rail just as Mr. Shark was going for a fat, juicy drumstick.

Splayed across the bilge of the small vessel, Paddy alternately gasped for air and tried to hug Gnarles.

"Cut it out, Paddy!" Gnarles said, pushing him away. "You're fine now! We're both fine, all right?!" But Paddy carried on, desperately clinging to Gnarles and sobbing uncontrollably. "Ya big old sissy!" Gnarles said, then he gave him a brief hug and extricated himself.

"I knew you'd come for me!" Paddy cried. "I knew you'd come back!"

"Don't thank me!" Gnarles said. "Thank *Señor* Salvatore here! He's the one saved both of us!"

Paddy wiped tears and seawater from his eyes and looked up to see a small, olive-skinned man with an expansive grin.

"Excuse me if I do not hug you, *Señor* Paddy!" he said with a heavy Spanish accent. "But the seas insist that I keep my hands on the tiller."

Pushing himself into a sitting position, Paddy stared.

The little man looked out from under a broad straw hat and smiled.

"It is good to meet you, *Señor* Paddy. *Señor* Gnarles here was very worried about you."

"I knew you'd come back for me!" Paddy slobbered. "I love you, Gnarles," and he tried to hug him again.

"Cut it out, ya big baby!"

"I'm not bein' a baby!" Paddy sniffed. "I just love you so much!"

As Paddy calmed down, *Señor* Salvatore laughed heartily, and said, "It appears to me that you fine gentlemen might like something to smoke, to warm your bones."

"Sure would," Gnarles replied. "But we lost our pipes and everything in *Cocoa-Nuts*."

"It is not a problem," the little fellow said, and he pulled two pipes from his pocket and handed one to each of the astounded men.

"You carry extra pipes?" Gnarles asked curiously. "Like you was expectin' us?"

Señor Salvatore laughed again, jolly and genuine.

"But I was! There is always someone in need on a night like tonight, *si*?"

"I s'pose," Gnarles replied, looking at him curiously.

Lighting a match, *Señor* Salvatore held it out and lit both pipes, one after the other.

Taking hearty puffs, Gnarles and Paddy both coughed.

Then Gnarles looked at his pipe curiously, and said, "What the heck kind 'a t'bacca is this anyway?"

"The very best kind!" *Señor* Salvatore replied. "The kind we grow in my beautiful homeland of Puerto Rico!" He uttered the words with pride. Then he looked at Gnarles, and said, "You have done a very brave thing tonight, when you surrendered your own chance at life to give it to your friend."

"How'd you know that?" Gnarles asked suspiciously.

"It is obvious," *Señor* Salvatore shrugged. "When you climbed aboard my fine little vessel, *Angelica*, you said that you had left your friend out upon the ocean holding onto a cask. Why else would you have left him there but to give him a chance, to unselfishly save his life."

Gnarles shook his head and looked at his pipe.

"What the hell kind 'a t'bacca'd you say this is?"

"The very best kind," *Señor* Salvatore replied.

Gnarles looked at Paddy, who was nodding off. Through his own drowsiness, Paddy saw that Gnarles was growing tired as well. Gnarles propped himself up, then foggily watched *Señor* Salvatore dig into a small, purple, velvet satchel tied to his waist.

"*Señor* Gnarles," he asked. "Do you believe in magic?"

Gnarles shook his head groggily.

"Uh-uh."

"Oh, but you should, my friend. Look!" he said, holding out his hand.

Gnarles, his eyelids barely open, answered, "Wha'cha got there? Beans?"

"Not just any beans, my friend, but *magic* beans!"

"Hmph," Gnarles replied. "They look like regular old beans ta me!"

"Oh, no, my friend! These are magic beans!"

"What kind 'a magic?" Gnarles slurred, pushing himself into a sitting position. He took a long drag from his pipe.

"Why, whatever it is you wish them to be, my friend. Whatever it is you dream of at night, it will come true." With that, he handed the beans to Gnarles, and added, "But remember, magic is fleeting; it never lasts."

"Hmph," Gnarles replied, waving his hand weakly, then he fell fast asleep.

Chapter Fifteen

Early the next morning, Charlie MacLeod could be seen heading across the lake to the Humphrey's house. He was in his fat little boat, *Dolly Varden*, with Salty and Floppy aboard.

Alfred, who was sitting on the front porch reading a two-week-old edition of the *Chicago Tribune*, noticed the approaching sail and, calling to Katie, headed down to the dock. Annie, Benji, and Copernicus followed.

As Alfred assisted the old, one-legged man onto the dock, Annie giggled.

Charlie gave her a sour look, then said, "I know."

"Uh-huh," Annie snickered. "Your beard is all trimmed nice and neat. You look really super handsome, Uncle Charlie!"

He gave her a hug, then tousled Benji's hair and shook Alfred's hand.

"You certainly do!" Katie's voice sang out from up the walk.

Charlie grinned broadly.

"How are ya, lassie?" he said, then he enveloped her in a bear hug and happily accepted a kiss on the cheek.

"Is everything all right?" she asked. "I don't think we've ever seen you over here so early!"

"Oh," he said. "Everything's fine. I suppose I'm here ta ask a favor is all."

The Humphreys looked at the old salt curiously.

Getting comfortable against a piling, he handed an impatient Salty to Annie, and said, "Turns out the missus has a hankerin' ta see Maggie sing."

"Really?!" Katie said excitedly. "You're taking Molly to New York?!"

"Looks like it."

Everyone knew what he was thinking, but it was Annie who said it. She clapped her hands and jumped up and down.

"So, you're gonna wear a suit, Uncle Charlie?"

Charlie sighed. "Yes, Sweetpea. Your old uncle's gotta wear a suit – again."

"Oh," Katie said, playfully slapping him on the shoulder. "It's been what, three years since you got married? I think it's time you get all dressed up again. Oh!" she said, clasping her hands to her chest. "Molly must be so excited!"

"She's excited all right," Charlie replied. "About to go crazy is more like it, gettin' everything packed and all. It's been a madhouse ever since last night."

"You mean," Katie asked, "you're leaving soon?"

"Today." He shrugged. "Maggie's only gonna be on stage a couple more weeks. Anyway, you know me. I ain't one for sittin' 'round waitin'."

"No, you're not, Uncle Charlie. So, what is it we can do for you?"

Charlie nodded at Copernicus and Floppy happily digging in the sand down by the mangroves.

"Do you mind?" he said. "Can't very well take Floppy on the train with us."

"Or to the Broadway shows," Katie reminded him.

"Or to the Broadway shows," Charlie droned.

"Oh, you'll have fun," Katie patted his broad chest. "And yes, you're perfectly welcome to leave her with us."

"And what about," he nodded towards the house, "you know who?"

"Mother Humphrey?" Katie replied. "Oh, she won't mind, will she, Alfred?"

Alfred shrugged.

"All rightee, then. I sure do appreciate it." Charlie clasped his hands together. "There is, however, one more thing." He glanced at Salty, sitting on Annie's finger.

Annie's eyes grew wide.

"Really, Uncle Charlie? You're gonna leave Salty with us?!"

"With *you*," Charlie corrected, looking hopefully at Katie and Alfred. Alfred knew there was only one thing Mother Humphrey disliked more than dogs, and that was birds, in particular, that one.

The feeling was mutual, and, whenever in her presence, Salty let it be known in a very loud, very salty manner. No one could deliver a wider variety of curse words, or in quicker succession, than the old Son of a Sea Dog himself.

"Of course, you can leave Salty with us," Katie replied, ignoring Alfred's sour look. "He is part of the family after all."

"You mean you're gonna leave him with us? Right now?" Annie asked.

"Yep," Charlie replied. "We'll be flaggin' down Harlan and Fred when they come by later on, so we won't be seein' ya again 'til we get back."

"So, how long will you be gone?" Katie asked.

"I suppose until whenever my lovely wife says it's time to come home."

"Oh, that's wonderful," Katie said dreamily. "An open-ended vacation."

Removing himself from his perch on the piling, Charlie mumbled, "I just hope I fit into that old suit 'a mine." He rubbed his healthy belly and gave Salty one last scratch behind the ears.

Then he turned to climb into *Dolly Varden,* and said, "You be a good bird for Mrs. Humphrey now."

"Bloody battle axe!" Salty squawked.

Charlie smiled sheepishly and shrugged.

"Sorry."

"You sure it's all right?" Charlie asked again.

"Of course," Katie replied. "It's nothing he wouldn't hear in a shipyard. Anyway," she continued. "You just go on and have fun. We'll take good care of Salty and Floppy."

As he was climbing into his chubby craft, Katie announced, "Oh, Uncle Charlie, there is one thing you could do for me."

"And what's that, lass?"

Katie smiled. "If Mr. Dye has time, would you ask him if he'll stop by here on the way to Juno?"

"Sure," Charlie said. "What for?"

"Well," Katie said hesitantly. "I want Alfred to get his camera out and take a photograph of you and Molly." She paused. "You know. In your suit?"

Charlie scowled, then said, "For you, m'darlin'? Anything!" With that, he cast off and sailed away.

Alfred grumbled, "The lighting won't be right."

Katie kissed her husband on the cheek.

"I'm sure you'll do wonderfully, sweetheart."

Chapter Sixteen

Paddy was soaring high over the clouds, the ground far below. People looked like ants. It was many years in the future when men could fly. He was sitting in a chair on the back of a giant pelican. Scientists had long ago discovered how to grow birds large enough to carry people.

He was flying over his childhood home in Ireland, just up the road from the old shillelagh factory. Down below was his mother, hanging clothes on the line. She waved and blew him a kiss. He waved back and turned the "peliplane," as they would be called, for Florida. After only a few minutes over the ocean, they were there.

Paddy nosed the peliplane downward when he saw land and swooped over a small boat sailing down the coast near Cape Canaveral.

"Hey, Gnarles!" he shouted. "Ya wanna go for a ride?"

Gnarles looked up from *Cocoa-Nuts,* and yelled back, "No thanks, Paddy! You know I'm afraid to fly on a peliplane!"

"Are ya sure?!" Paddy asked. "It's perfectly safe, ya knooow!"

"That's all right," Gnarles called back. "I'll just stay down here."

"Okay!" Paddy shouted back. "I'll see ya later then!" and he soared off towards home.

Suddenly, he heard a call for help. Using his new, future "super-ear," he turned his head so the giant ear-shaped device could pick up where it was coming from.

"It's Bonnie Blakely! She's in trouble!"

Without hesitation, Paddy directed his loyal peliplane, Danger Dan, forward to Port Starboard. Coming up on the magnificent city, ablaze with electrical lights, he spotted her with his giant, eye-shaped device and zoomed over to where she was being held captive by a giant gorilla hanging from the side of the tallest building in the world – ten stories high! Before the giant ape knew what was happening, Danger Dan swooped down as Paddy reached out with a giant, arm-shaped device and scooped her right out of the mighty beast's grip. The gorilla shook his fist at Paddy, who laughed and kissed Bonnie Blakely – right on the lips!

Holding on tight, Bonnie exclaimed, "Oh, Paddy, you're so brave!" Then she squeezed his arm, and said, "Oooo! Muscles!" Paddy raised an eyebrow and casually brushed his hair out of his eyes.

"Look," he said, pointing. "What is that tied to the Celestial Railway tracks?"

"It looks like a baby!" Bonnie cried. "Someone has tied him to the railroad tracks! And a train is coming!!"

"Plenty of time," Paddy said, and he sent the peliplane into a steep dive.

As Danger Dan swooped past, Paddy pulled out his giant, arm-shaped, scooping device and snatched up the bundle of joy just before the colossal mass of fire and steel rumbled past.

"A little closer than I thought," Paddy said as they sailed high over Jupiter Inlet. They waved at the Carlins who were out on their dock, then at the Armour kids over at the rope swing.

Up river was the *St. Lucie,* steaming for Jupiter Narrows. Flying over, they could see everyone gathered on deck, waving and pointing and cheering.

Captain Bravo stepped from the pilot house and called out, "Hey, Paddy! Thanks for saving the day! You're the best!" Then he went back inside and started blowing the steamer's big whistle.

Toot! Tooooot!

Everyone cheered.

Toot! Tooooot!

Paddy awoke with a start.

He looked around. He was lying next to Gnarles on a large tarpaulin under a dense canopy of seagrape. Gnarles was talking in his sleep, something about Earth having plenty of cheese.

Toot! Toooooot!

Paddy sat up, wondering where he was and how he'd gotten there. They were on the beach somewhere, and by the sound of the steamer's whistle, the Indian River was just over the dune line through a dense thicket of mangrove. He was wondering if the steamer was heading south or north when the previous night smacked him in the face. Instantly, he no longer cared where he was or how he got there, only that he was alive. Looking down, he poked himself in the belly.

The last thing he remembered was being pulled onto a sailboat by Gnarles and a little Spanish fellow. He vaguely recalled him offering them pipes to smoke.

"Hey! Gnarles!" he said, trying to peer beyond the facade of greenery. "Where are we?!"

"Grumphumphph."

"Hey, Gnarles!" Paddy shook him. "What happened?! Where are we?!"

Suddenly, Gnarles was wide awake, sitting up and looking around.

"Where are we?!" He rubbed sleep from his eyes. Without waiting for an answer, he scurried on hands and knees out from under the seagrapes.

"It's *Cocoa-Nuts!*" he cried as Paddy bumped into him from behind.

The two men scrambled to their feet, astonishment written on their faces. *Cocoa-Nuts* was pulled high on shore, away from the encroaching waves. Astonishment turned to flabbergast, however, when they looked up the beach to see 134 cases of ginger ale, neatly stacked.

The men stared in wonder, trying to make sense of it all.

Finally, Gnarles spoke.

"It must 'a been *Señor* Salvatore done it," he mumbled. He scanned the horizon. "I wonder where he went."

Starting forward on wobbly knees, the men walked down to *Cocoa-Nuts*. It was as if she had never been lost at all; everything was exactly as they had left it. Gnarles didn't waste any time reaching under the boat's seat for the bottle of brandy. Staring at it, he popped the cork and took a long, satisfying drink.

He handed it to Paddy.

Paddy shook his head. "Uh-uh," he said. "I d'na dr-r-rink n'mooore."

"Wha'd'ya mean, ya don't drink no more?!"

Paddy shrugged. "I mean, I d'na dr-r-rink n'mooore. God saved me and I promised 'im I wooon't dr-r-rink n'mooore."

"God didn't save us, you moron. *Señor* Salvatore did!"

"Dooon't ya see?" Paddy replied. "*Señor* Salvatore is an angel sent from abooove. Dooon't ya r'member? Reverend Wickman said it at church that time. 'The Lord moves in mysterious ways.' That's what he said."

Gnarles laughed. "You're crazy, Paddy! *Señor* Salvatore ain't no angel. Angels are beautiful with long hair and wings. Anyway," he said, shaking his head. "You can't quit drinkin'. It's ... what we do!" He handed him the bottle.

"Nooope!" He crossed his arms. "I d'na want it."

"It's brandy!" Gnarles drove it home. "Your favorite!"

"No," Paddy replied steadfastly. "I'll just stick with ginger ale from now on." He took on a ponderous expression. "D'ya knooow how ta make ginger ale?"

"No," Gnarles grouched. "I don't." Then he crossed his arms. "And I won't neither, so just forget it!"

"Then I'll just sell my half of the Coco-rum and buy ginger ale," Paddy said, and he started up the beach towards the wondrous sight.

"Oh, no, you won't," Gnarles shot back, stomping alongside. "You don't own half the rum anyway. I'm the one that knows how ta make it."

"I knooow how ta make it, too!" Paddy asserted.

"Sure," Gnarles replied. "Because I showed ya."

"And I dooo just as much work as you. More than you, if ya count mashin' th' corn with me toes."

"But you like doing that," Gnarles countered, "and if you like it, it ain't work."

"Yes, it is," Paddy insisted. "Anyway, dooon't ya r'member th' time Betsy said we were even partners? She said *Even Stephen*, and you didn't say nothin'. That's b'cause we're *Even Stephen!*"

Gnarles looked at the bottle of fine French brandy, and said, "Fine. More for me!" and he put it to his lips and tilted it upwards.

Paddy glared at him for several moments as he smacked his lips, wiped a stream of the precious liquid from his chin, and turned it up to finish it off.

Setting his hands firmly on his hips, Paddy declared, "And I'm gonna be a preacher, toooo!" causing Gnarles to spew his last mouthful of brandy all over him.

They remained as they were, standing in front of the stack of ginger ale, evaluating this most recent development, when Paddy said, "Hey! How did *Señor* Salvatore get all that ginger ale up here?"

"You numbskull," Gnarles replied. "He carried it, of course."

"Then how come ther-r-re's no tracks leadin' up here from th' water?"

"Huh?!"

The two men walked around the stack, scanning the area, then looked down to the water.

"That's funny," Gnarles mumbled. "There ain't so much as a toe-print."

"I tooold ya," Paddy exclaimed. "*Señor* Salvatore is an angel!"

"He is not," Gnarles insisted, scratching his stubbly chin. "Come on," he said, grabbing a case. "Let's get *Cocoa-Nuts* loaded up. We can have two loads home by t'night."

Paddy dutifully picked up a case and followed Gnarles, staring down at the sand, now covered with footprints, but only theirs.

"Yooour'e r-r-right about that bein' queer and all," Paddy said, gingerly placing a case in the boat.

"Yep. Queer," Gnarles agreed. "Now, come on! We got a lot to do!"

Paddy hastened his waddle.

"It's like a sign from heaven," he mumbled.

Gnarles rolled his eyes.

Paddy picked up another case.

"I mean," he went on, "*Señor* Salvatore showin' up like he did, r-r-right when we was boooth about ta … you know, then boooth of us wakin' up on the beach under the seagrapes, and not rememberin' nothin'."

Gnarles snorted, "That's probably 'cause of that wacky t'bacca he gave us ta smoke; did somethin' strange ta us is all."

"Aye," Paddy agreed. "Strange. Like th' dream I had."

"Dream?" Gnarles said, setting a case in the boat. "What kind 'a dream?"

"Well," Paddy said, trying to keep up with his spry friend. "First I was in the future."

Gnarles stopped in his tracks. "Really?"

"Uh-huh, and I was flyin' around on a giant pelican and I was all th' way over ta me dear old Ir-r-reland and then I was all of a sudden across the ooocean and then I heard screaming and it turned out to be Miss Bonnie! And a giant gorilla was hangin' from a tall building and I swooped down on Danger Dan –"

"Danger Dan?"

"Uh-huh," Paddy nodded. "Anywee, we grabbed 'er right out'a his hands and Miss Bonnie kissed me – right on the lips! Then we was flyin' ooover the r-r-railroad and a baby was tied ta th' tracks b'looow!"

"A baby?! Tied to the tracks?!"

"Aye!" Paddy said excitedly. "Then we swooped down again and saved th' baby with this giant scooper-upper thing, and we flew over th' steamboat and," he sighed, "everyone cheered."

Paddy gazed dreamily into the clouds.

"That's funny," Gnarles said. "'Cause I had a strange dream, too."

"Really?"

"Yep," Gnarles said. "I dreamed I was with *Señor* Salvatore. And," he said, almost in a whisper, "we were in the future."

"Oooooo," Paddy said, a chill running down his spine. "Really, Gnarles? For real?"

"Uh-huh," he replied, then he scratched his head. "Somethin' funny is goin' on around here."

"I tooold ya!" Paddy said excitedly. "I tooold ya somethin' was goin' on!"

"No," Gnarles corrected. "You said 'an angel'; I just said 'somethin',' and I don't know what."

"Right," Paddy said, looking around suspiciously. "What?"

"Anyway," Gnarles continued. "We was flyin', too, except we was flyin' with our own arms, like birds, but not flappin' 'em, just soarin' like. Then I looked over and it wasn't *Señor* Salvatore at all! He had turned into *you*!! And then we went all the way to the moon!!!"

Paddy's eyes almost popped out of his head.

"And when we got there, Charlie and Molly was there!"

"Charlie and Molly?!"

"Yep, and they was real happy ta see us, and Salty and Floppy was there, and they had their little chickee set up like they do on the beach, and they was eatin' cheese! They told us the whole moon was made of cheese! Cheese, Paddy!! All kinds of cheese!!!"

"Cheese." Paddy mouthed the words with reverence.

"That's right, and when we asked 'em if they wanted ta come back with us ta Earth, they said, 'No thanks.'"

Paddy looked at Gnarles in wonder, his round, shiny face belying the burst of activity inside his head.

A moment later he mumbled, "All kinds of cheese?"

Chapter Seventeen

Sam Jesup was in his most usual and favorite position: reclining in a rocking chair on the front porch of the Port Starboard Hotel, top hat pulled over his eyes, feet propped lazily on the rail. A cigar smoldered next to him. He was lightly snoring.

Across the way, on the other side of the front door, was Malcolm Geoffreys, in a similar position but with a bowler hat.

The screen door slammed, and both men startled awake.

"How you boys doin' out here?" Betsy asked.

Malcolm stood, followed by Sam.

"Cracking good, actually," Malcolm said, hat in hand and bowing slightly.

Betsy smiled. "It's nice you two have so much in common. Like father-in-law, like son-in-law."

The men looked at each other.

"I hate to disturb you two, but I'll be starting dinner soon, and if you want a cup of coffee or some of those cookies Mrs. Sebastian made today, you gotta have 'em now."

"Yes, deah Betsy," Sam said in his soothing Virginia drawl, "that would be delightful."

Malcolm flashed a winning smile and, in his King's best English, replied, "It would be nothing less than smashing! Shall I assist?"

Betsy looked askance at her husband, and replied, "Why, yes, Malcolm. That's very *thoughtful* of you. I already have coffee on. I'll just need you to bring it out, if you don't mind."

"Nothing would please me more." He smiled generously.

Betsy smiled at him, then made a face at Sam as Malcolm opened the door for her.

Sam scowled, then sat back down and got comfortable. He picked up his cigar and took a few puffs. Looking out at the water, he thought about his future. It was often in the forefront of his mind these days.

Of course, it wasn't going to be *his* money. It was Bonnie's inheritance. But with him being the father, well, he was certain that there would be a few crumbs left over, she being the generous and compassionate daughter she was.

An allowance would be nice, he thought.

Sam was not the average, run-of-the-mill "Dad." In fact, he'd never even known he had a daughter until a couple years back. Years earlier, shortly after his dalliance with a sweet young thing from Lexington, Kentucky, the expectant mother had sent Sam a letter informing him of the forthcoming birth of what turned out to be a bouncing baby girl.

He had never replied.

Years later, when Sam had been off on one of his "exploits" – his last – Betsy had discovered the decades-old letter in his things. After he had returned, tail tucked, she had been furious, and a little bit curious, and had taken it upon herself to look up the long-lost child.

Betsy had been shocked – and thrilled – to discover that Bonnie just happened to be a school teacher in search of a new start following a messy break-up. And Port Starboard just happened to be in need of a new school teacher.

Fate? Chance? Who knew? But Bonnie was hired and moved to Lake Worth, and soon after that it came to Sam's attention that she was indeed his daughter. It had quite an effect on the self-proclaimed "Gambler and Troubadour of Love." In fact, he now defined himself instead as "Devoted Husband and Father."

To anyone who would listen, he would go on about what a lucky man he was to have such a patient, attentive wife and such a lovely, talented daughter. He also considered himself fortunate that she happened to be the heiress to a fortune – if she were to meet the criteria set forth in her grandfather's will that she be married by her thirty-first birthday, which was approaching at a precipitous rate.

Thus, Sam's acceptance of the young Englishman, Malcolm Geoffreys, was unencumbered.

"Here we are," Malcolm announced as the screen door squeaked open and slammed shut. "Two coffees, both black, and some truly amazing cookies." He set Sam's down in front of him, and added, "You must forgive me, but I sampled one on the way out."

Taking one of the morsels from the plate, Sam replied, "And how could you not?"

Following an extended silence, as each man munched and sipped, occasionally pausing to study texture and form, Major Jesup said, "These, suh, are delightful!"

"Mmmm," Malcolm agreed. "Most definitely well versed in her craft, Mrs. Sebastian."

"No doubt," Sam agreed, licking his fingers. A moment later, he commented, "That'll be the hardest thing about runnin' a resort of the sort you're plannin'. Consistency." He paused to inspect another cookie. "Getting everything right and doing it that way every time. Next month. Next year. It's difficult enough here in our little establishment, especially with such unreliable transportation in and out."

"But it is getting better," Malcolm replied. "And it's only a matter of time before Flagler brings his rails this far south. He has to! The man is never satisfied! There are rumors, in fact, that he's already been buying up tracts of land along the coast under fictitious company names. Can you imagine what these landowners would think if they knew it was him? What they would be asking? No, demanding!"

"Yes," Sam replied, leaning back and propping his feet. "I can only imagine." He cocked his head. "How are things goin' on that front? You don't want to sit on your hands too long if what you say is true, that the Florida East Coast is preparing to bring her rails this far south. Once word gets out, the price of land will soar."

"Yes," Malcolm replied. "I am in negotiations at present, as you know, and I've had George Lainhart out to survey a couple of tracts, but I must find the perfect location." He looked out towards the inlet. "I need deep water, easy access to the ocean, and high ground. And I would prefer a gathering of large, mature trees already on site."

Sam selected another cookie.

"Sounds like you're describin' Eddie's place, which is NOT for sale –"

"No."

"Or Gnarles and Paddy's, which is also NOT for sale."

"No," Malcolm concurred.

"Which leaves you –"

"Yes. Silas Hempsted."

"Mm-hmm."

"It is the perfect location."

"Yes," Sam agreed. "It is."

Sam Jesup had always dreamed of being the owner of an opulent resort for the rich and well-heeled. Ever since his days back at the St. Augustine Hotel, he had imagined himself in charge of a palatial inn, catering to only the best, the richest.

When he had heard Malcolm had the same dream, he was all on board.

He hadn't mentioned it directly, but he was certain Malcolm would find a place for him. He thought "Chief Greeter" would be fine. He could work his own hours, show up for the most exclusive affairs, rub some elbows – maybe land himself in a few card games.

Malcolm said, "I'd gladly give up the deposit I made on Mr. Gale's land if that farmer would just give in and sell."

"And you've mentioned it to Bonnie? Those two have become quite the pair, you know."

"Yes," Malcolm frowned, staring into his mug. "They have." Following a pause, he said, "I must stress to Bonnie that I would be happy to let him keep the entire area back from the lakeshore and give him free and clear access to the lake."

"Mm-hmm," Sam agreed. "If you want that piece of land, you'll have to do some serious negotiating, and not with Silas but with your future bride. She's the key. And," Sam added. "I don't think she's the type to twist arms, if you know what I mean."

Malcolm nodded.

"Speak of the devil," Sam said.

The two men watched as the tiny sailboat passed, then changed its tack for the Hooker's dock.

"Might as well get comfortable," Malcolm yawned, and he propped his feet. "Bonnie will be a while at her little meeting."

"They do seem to enjoy it," Sam mentioned. "We can hear laughter all the way over here sometimes."

"Yes," Malcolm replied, deep in thought.

"It's buried treasure," Sam noted.

"Say again?"

"Buried treasure," he repeated. "They've been reading *Treasure Island* this week."

"Ah, yes. Robert Louis Stevenson, I believe. You know," Malcolm said, "I hear it's true about cousin Will having buried treasure up on Indian River."

"You know about that?" Sam was surprised.

"Not really," Malcolm answered casually. "They brought it up the other night while little Annie Humphrey was there."

"Really." Sam's brow furrowed.

Sam was one of only a few people who knew the location of the gold. He had discovered it through questionable means several years back and had actually dug it up and stolen it. However, when he finally had it in his possession, he realized he was miserable without Betsy and returned the gold and crawled home on hands and knees.

"I'm surprised they brought it up in your presence," Sam stated. "Will, especially, doesn't like to talk about it. He says only that it's there if he ever needs it, and he's never needed it."

"Actually," Malcolm said. "It was Annie who brought it up. I could tell they didn't really want to talk about it, so I didn't pry." He paused. "I can't help but wonder, though, with all the rumors that swirl about." He glanced over at Sam. "You know. How much there is. Where it is."

93

Sam studied the plate of cookies, then selected one.

*   *   *

The Port Starboard School was located on the opposite side of Booker T. Creek from the hotel's orange grove. It was a hundred feet south of the store/post office at the end of a meandering boardwalk. Situated in a lush grove of cocoanut palms, it was painted red with white trim and had a steeple. The structure had originally housed the Port Starboard Community Church, but when Charlie MacLeod donated a much larger church building, they had placed the smaller building on a barge and moved it to its present location.

It was large enough for the twelve pupils currently enrolled, and several more.

There were two picnic tables placed nearby, one directly in front of the building, near the boardwalk, and another out on the point, by the water. This was the more used table, and it was there the Port Starboard Book Club held its meetings, weather permitting. This would be the third gathering. So far it was just Bonnie, Annie, and Silas, which was perfectly fine with him.

In only a short amount of time, Wednesday afternoons had become his favorite part of the week – indeed, of life itself. He was deeply in love with Bonnie, but that could be said for most of the men of Port Starboard. Sweet, attentive, intelligent – and a little naïve – she was the perfect woman.

He had no delusions that anything would ever come of this one-sided love, but he did have more than his share of daydreams, all of which ended with Bonnie falling into his arms.

The meetings were scheduled for three o'clock, giving Bonnie a few minutes to relax after school before the rest of the book club showed up – Silas. Annie was already there.

As he sailed by, Bonnie waved, and his heart went aflutter. Annie waved, too.

Silas could not believe his good fortune. Maybe his mother was right. Maybe all he needed was a change of scenery, a fresh start.

He grew increasingly nervous as he approached the Hookers' dock. He was becoming relatively proficient with the sailboat as long as he was nowhere near a dock. He wasn't worried about damaging his own boat, *Bonnie Blue*, but someone else's. He had already bumped both *Miss Kitty* and *Daizily*, Booker T.'s boat, and dinged *Arthur*, the mail boat. He had put a substantial dent in Alfred Humphrey's cranky sloop, *Socrates' Revenge*, too. This had prompted Alfred to declare himself no longer the worst sailor on Lake Worth.

Others present had disagreed.

As Silas drew near, he did as he had begun of late and dropped the sail, pulled out the oars, and rowed the rest of the way. It was degrading, but not as bad as destroying other people's property.

Hopping out and tying off the craft, he glanced southward. He could make out Bonnie and Annie through the gently swaying palms. He checked himself, tucked his shirt, and taking his books he headed up the dock, a hesitant spring in his step. As he passed the store, he poked his head in.

"Hey, Eddie!"

Eddie raised his head from the counter and mumbled something.

Pulling his watch from his pocket, Silas checked the time. A little early.

"Darn it," he grumbled.

When he strolled up to the table, his heart leaped. He had never thought it possible that anyone could be so beautiful. She was standing with Annie and Copernicus out on the sand bar, barefoot, dress hiked with one hand. In the other she was holding a jar up to the light. Inside was a sea cucumber. Her angelic voice rang out, sounding much like heaven's bells themselves.

"Ewwww!"

"I know," Annie giggled. "Isn't it disgusting?!"

A little while later, the conversation was fully engaged: Pirates! Buccaneers! Swashbucklers!

The Spanish Main.

There is little in life more intriguing. From time immemorial, men would return from the sea, thrilling those left behind with amazing and unbelievable tales of adventure, peril, and survival. They would evoke images of windswept ships and towering waves, visions of scantily-clad, island girls and exotic ports of call; memories of recently lost comrades or those who had returned to Mother Ocean's bosom long ago. These stories spilled forth from their lips, growing larger and bolder with each and every telling – the waves were bigger; the winds fiercer; the girls were prettier; the living better – and always, to a rapt audience.

Boys, especially, would listen with eyes wide.

One of those boys was Robert Louis Stevenson, and from those many, lofty yarns he had heard over the years, he created one that would live on in perpetuity: a masterful tale of greed, lust, and glory, a gift to the ages.

Silas had Bonnie and Annie in stitches. He was doing his pirate impression, closing one eye, scrunching up his face, and speaking out of the side of his mouth.

"Aaarrrgh, me hearties!"

They had been talking about Long John Silver, and Silas had happened to say, "Where can a pi-rate with two wooden legs go? Not very faaarrrgh!"

He had been surprised at the reaction; then he couldn't stop himself.

He was incredulous. He had always wanted to make people laugh but had been much too afraid they might be laughing at him. So, all his life he had rarely uttered anything but the most mundane of small talk, fearful that someone might call him goofy. That's what little Billy Swires had called him in third grade. It had horrified him, all the other kids laughing and calling him goofy. For nearly thirty years he had muzzled every amusing thought that came to mind. Instead of letting loose, allowing his wit to wander, he would suppress, say nothing, and hold it all in, left to speculate if what he was thinking was indeed of interest to anyone or not.

He wondered if Bonnie and Annie were humoring him. The thought terrified him, and he felt the urge to stifle himself.

Instead, he said in his best pirate voice, "How d'ya know if you're a pi-rate?"

"I don't know," Annie replied in her own pirate voice. "How do ya know if you're a pi-rate?"

"Ya don't," Silas replied. "Ya just aaarrrgh!"

Bonnie was holding her sides.

"Oh, stop it, Silas!" she cried. But her eyes said otherwise.

"Okay," Silas replied. "But then I can't tell you what a pi-rate's favorite booty is."

Dabbing at her nose with her hanky, Bonnie surrendered.

"All right," she asked. "What's a pi-rate's favorite booty?"

"Aaaarrrt."

Bonnie was waving her hand, gasping for air, but a flurry of ideas were coming fast and furious, prompting Silas to ask, "Okay, what did the doctor say to the pi-rate?"

Bonnie couldn't speak, so Annie took over.

"I don't know. What did the doctor say to the pi-rate?"

"Open wide and say, 'Aaarrrgh!'"

With Bonnie turning purple, Silas was growing concerned he might hurt her, so he forced himself to change the subject.

"Anyway," he finally answered Annie's original query. "I think the reason pirates look the way they do is because they're outcasts of society."

"If you ask me," Bonnie replied, finally composing herself, "I think they just want to scare people."

"Well, they sure scare me," Annie said. "I remember the first time I met Uncle Charlie. I thought *he* was a pirate!"

Bonnie nodded. "He does look a little like a pirate, doesn't he?"

"Sure," Silas agreed. "He's got a wooden leg, and an earring –"

"And Salty!" Annie exclaimed.

"Yes," Bonnie said. "I suppose all he's missing is a hook and a patch over his eye."

Annie pondered this a moment, then said, "How come pirates always have hooks and patches anyway?"

"Well," Silas suggested. "I can't say why so many pirates have hooks, but I know why so many of them have patches."

"Really?"

"Sure," Silas dared to say. "Imagine all those pirates waking up the first morning with their new hook and they go to wipe the sleep from their eyes."

Once again, the conversation had turned.

Bonnie and Annie were laughing hysterically when a voice said, "So, this is what goes on in a book club. Maybe I should join myself."

Malcolm was standing at the foot of the cypress log bridge with an amused expression.

"Oh, Malcolm!" Bonnie exclaimed, hopping up from the table and running over. "How long have you been here?"

He took her in his arms and kissed her.

"Not long."

Annie watched intently, with a big sigh.

Silas, suddenly self-conscious, looked away as Malcolm's eyes met his.

"Hello, Silas," he said, and he bowed slightly. "And Annie."

"Hello, Mr. Geoffreys!" Annie gushed.

Malcolm walked over, his hand extended.

"Nice to see you again, Silas."

Silas took his hand and immediately wished he had squeezed harder.

"Nice to see you, too," he replied.

He liked Malcolm. He seemed kind, interested in his farm, but there was something about the man that Silas found utterly intimidating, so much so that he clammed up every time he came around. He was naturally shy, of course, but with Malcolm it was different, something he could not put his finger on. He assumed it was because he was so English, and so tall and handsome, and a smooth talker. He was also the man that Bonnie adored.

Everything Silas wished he was.

Malcolm chuckled. "We could hear your laughter all the way over at the hotel. What on earth could have you so tickled?"

"Oh," Bonnie said, "Silas here is so funny! He was going on with pirate jokes, one right after the other."

"Really," Malcolm smiled. "Like what?" He looked to Silas.

"Oh, it was nothing really, just a couple of puns is all."

"Go on," Bonnie prodded. "Tell one."

"Yes!" Annie said excitedly. "Tell one!"

Silas suddenly didn't feel very funny.

"I don't know," he squirmed.

"Come now," Malcolm pressed. "You have my curiosity piqued. I won't be able to sleep a wink tonight if I don't hear at least one of your quips."

Silas looked around nervously then mumbled with almost no pirate flair, "Where does a pirate put his gold?"

"I don't know," Malcolm replied, squeezing Bonnie. "Where does a pirate put his gold?"

"In a jaaar."

Something was terribly different. Timing? Delivery? Content? No one could say, but the silence was crushing.

Malcolm forced a chuckle.

"Yes," he said. "That was a good one, Silas." Then he glanced at Bonnie with an expression that propelled Silas all the way back in time to the third grade.

* * *

Later that evening, everyone had gone off to bed and the young lovers had the porch to themselves. Malcolm had considered moving into the hotel so he could spend more time with Bonnie, but that wouldn't be appropriate, they being betrothed and living under the same roof. If he wanted time alone with her, he'd just have to pay the price, and that turned out to be a long row there and back.

It was worth it, though, for there was nothing he enjoyed more in life than spending time with Bonnie. He truly believed he was in love with her, and in some strange way, she reminded him of his mother. He'd been through several relationships by this time, and it had never been quite like this.

She was so agreeable.

When she wasn't, she was easily persuaded – a kiss here, a flirtatious nudge there. Puppy dog eyes. Yes, even the English have the capacity for unabashed cajolery.

"Oh, Malcolm. You're so funny."

They were sitting on the porch swing, perilously close, the lamp on the wall turned down, with only the sporadic glimmer from a half moon sneaking through a patchwork of clouds. A crisp breeze puffed off the ocean.

"Really?" He raised an eyebrow. "As funny as … Silas?"

"Oh, yes," Bonnie replied. "Absolutely!"

"Is that so?" he asked. "Because I don't ever recall bringing on such laughter before. You were positively rollicking."

"Oh, Malcolm," Bonnie said, looking away. "Of course, I find you funny. It's just different, that's all."

"Is that so?" Malcolm pulled her close and looked off towards The Castle – a light was on. "Tell me then. What is the difference?"

"Well." Bonnie appeared deep in thought. "With you, it's more ... hmmm. I guess your sense of humor is more ... down to earth. I think yours is more ... subtle. Understated," she concluded. "Yes, yours isn't so –"

"Goofy?" Malcolm suggested.

"Well, no. I wouldn't say goofy. Silas's is more ... ummm ... out there!" she finally capitulated, waving her arm towards the beyond.

When she turned, he was staring at her

"That's a strange expression," she said. "Did I say something wrong, or hurt your feelings somehow, making you feel I like Silas's sense of humor more than yours?"

Malcolm smiled and protested, "No, no. From what I heard this afternoon, his sense of humor is ... indeed 'out there'."

"Oh, Malcolm!" She changed the subject. "Speaking of our meeting today. Oh, I am so excited!"

"Oh? A pirate joke I might have missed?"

"No, silly," she nudged him playfully and took his arm. "As you know we were talking a couple of weeks ago about Dickens's *Oliver Twist*, and how bad those orphanages can be, even today. Right here in America!"

"Yes. I have heard, but things are getting better; slowly but certainly."

"That's true," Bonnie said. "But it can be simply awful for these poor, orphaned children. Some of these places still use them for labor! Children!!" she asserted, her voice rising.

"It is terrible," Malcolm agreed. "But what can we do other than elect politicians who support laws designed to end such practices?"

"Well," Bonnie said, about to burst. "We were talking about it today." She took a deep breath. "And I think I've decided to use my inheritance to ... start an orphanage!" She squeezed his arm with both hands, her eyes sparkling with excitement. "Think of it, Malcolm. Our own orphanage!"

Malcolm opened his mouth, but nothing came out.

Chapter Eighteen

August 4, 1890

It was Saturday night, Gnarles and Paddy's off time: time of their own to do whatever they pleased, with no Betsy, no chores, no errands to run. It was a time to kick back and do what they did best – consume alcohol. Gnarles had talked Paddy out of the priesthood, and from that point falling back off the wagon was relatively easy.

Saturday afternoons they would load up with leftovers and whatever else Betsy could scrape together and head down to their little refuge in the scrub until Monday morning.

Down a white sand path that meandered through craggy pines and insolent saw palmetto was another clearing where they kept their still. Down another path was a third clearing. This was where they had planted their original garden, now overgrown by human-sized weeds and prickly pear cactus.

After they had returned from their glorious conquest of ginger ale and their near-death experiences, they had been sitting by the fire one night when Gnarles made a face. He reached into his pocket and pulled out the magic beans that *Señor* Salvatore had given him.

He had been about to toss them away when Paddy cried. "Dooon't thr-r-row them aweeey! They're magic!"

Gnarled had sneered.

"You really think these are magic beans?"

"Don't you?"

"No," he had mumbled, and he had tossed them at Paddy's feet. The next morning Paddy had gone out to the garden and planted them.

"They ain't gonna grow," Gnarles had told him. "Ain't nothin' grows in that sand, 'cept'n cactus and bayonets."

After that, Paddy went out to water them a couple of times, but when they didn't sprout right away, he had lost interest.

Now, two weeks later, Gnarles was teetering in front of the campfire, attempting to balance a cocoanut on his head when he heard Paddy's scream and he burst through the palmettos.

"Gnarles!" he gasped, trying to catch his breath.

Gnarles rolled his eyes.

"Gnarles! … Ya gotta see! … Ya gotta … see!!" Paddy fell to the ground, rolled onto his back, and gasped for air.

Concentrating on his balancing act, Gnarles said, "Whatever it is, just tell me after you get your breath back." Then he dropped the cocoanut on Paddy's head.

He was horrified.

"Paddy!" he cried, falling to his knees. "Are you all right?!" He grabbed the jug and poured some on Paddy's lips. "Paddy! Speak to me, old buddy! SPEAK TO ME!!" Looking heavenward, he sobbed, "What have I done?! Oh! What have I done?!" Then he looked down. Paddy was licking his lips.

"I think ya put toooo much cinnamon in this batch."

Sniffing back tears, Gnarles looked down at the pathetic form, and replied, "No! I didn't!" Then he dropped Paddy's head in the sand, stood, and dusted himself off.

Paddy dragged his plump form to a sitting position.

"Hey!" he exclaimed. "Did I already tell ya 'booot th' magic beans?"

"Yes," Gnarles replied. "Ya planted 'em; then didn't water 'em; now they're dead."

"Nooo!" Paddy howled. "They're growin'!"

"Well," Gnarles shook his head. "I wish 'em luck, 'cause they're gonna need it with all those giant weeds out there."

"Noooooo," Paddy replied. "Ya d'na understand!" He waved his arms high in the air. "They're all grown alr-r-ready! They're giants! Twice as tall as me" he cried.

"That cocoanut must 'a done some real damage," Gnarles mumbled. "Maybe we ought'a take you to see Sally on Monday."

"Nooooooo," Paddy cried. "They was all grown up b'fore ya hit me in the head with th' cooocoanut."

"I didn't hit you in the head," Gnarles pointed out. "You laid right under where I was droppin' it."

Paddy appeared deep in thought for a moment, then he ran off into the woods. A few minutes later he returned, out of breath again, and plopped down on the table bench.

"Here!" he said, throwing a branch on the ground.

Gnarles eyed it suspiciously.

"What's that?"

"That's one of the branches! Look!" he said. "It ain't nothin' like thooose weeds!"

Gnarles picked it up and studied it.

A moment later he said, "It stinks," and he threw it on the fire, causing a large plume of pungent black smoke to billow forth, enveloping the two men.

"Sure does," Paddy coughed.

"And there's three of 'em?" Gnarles asked, trying to wave the smoke away.

"Noooo," Paddy replied with a grand yawn. "There's a whole field of 'em!"

Gnarles felt suddenly very tired.

"A whole field of 'em?" he yawned. "From three little beans? Maybe we should take you to see Doc Sally right now." Yawning again, he sat down on the ground and leaned against his log. "I'm tired."

"Noooo!" Paddy urged, plopping down next to him. "Ya gotta come seeeee."

"All right, all right," Gnarles mumbled. "As soon as I take a little nap."

Paddy leaned against him.

"Aye," he said, yawning. "T'would be nice ta take a little nap."

And both fell fast asleep.

Later on, Gnarles had to admit it was a beautiful grove Paddy had planted. It was lush and green, as if it had sprung from a tropical rain forest instead of hot, barren, sugar sand. The plants themselves had broad, pointed leaves and gave off a pungent, not altogether unpleasant, odor.

Gnarles stepped back and studied the situation. When he looked down the side of the Magic Bean Patch, it only went as far as the edge of the clearing, but when he looked down each row: "Dang! It seems ta go on forever."

"Uh-huh," Paddy concurred. "Sooo, what should we dooo?" he asked. "Should we gooo for help?!"

"That's pretty stupid," Gnarles replied. "What are we gonna say? That our magic beans sprouted into giant plants in only a few days? And we need help doing … what?" Gnarles shook his head. "Shoot!" he snorted. "Ever'body'll just think we're crazy. They already think we're loco for the last one we told."

"Ya mean th' one about *Señor* Salvatore?"

Gnarles rolled his eyes.

"So what're we gonna doooo?"

Gnarles snorted again, then pulled up his trousers.

"Paddy," he declared. "We're gonna do what Charlie would do. We're goin' in."

"Huh?"

"We're goin' in," Gnarles repeated.

"Not me."

"Fine," Gnarles sneered, and he took another drink and stalked into the foreboding folds of greenery.

Tim Robinson

"But I d'na wanna goooo," Paddy said, following closely on Gnarles's heels.

"It's dark."

"Uh-huh."

"Sure is quiet."

They stopped to listen. Silence.

Paddy glanced around nervously.

"I'm scared," he said, and he turned to leave. Then he screamed. "Gnarles! I can'a see th' entrance anymore!"

Gnarles' first impulse was to trample Paddy and get the hell out of there. Instead, he slapped him in the head.

"Shhhh," he said, and pointed ahead. There appeared to be a light shining from the far end of the row. "Come on," he whispered.

Paddy grabbed hold of his shirttail and followed.

"What is that?" Gnarles said, growing ever closer to the strange luminosity. "It's so bright. I ain't never seen nothin' so bright. And white, too. It looks like some kind of … room."

Suddenly, they heard what sounded like distant thunder and the wind began to swirl around them, like they were in a tornado but with no sound. Paddy was clinging to Gnarles with all his might, then they were blinded by an all-consuming light and found themselves in a white room. From floor to ceiling, it was completely white, with lots of silver. They were desperately holding onto one another – and they were naked.

A green mist hung in the air.

From an opening in the wall, they could detect a bluish light flickering and a strange garbled noise coming from that direction. Then they heard approaching footsteps. Growing closer. And closer.

Paddy started to scream, but Gnarles put his hand to his mouth.

Then a little old lady in a floor-length, house dress stepped around the corner. In her hand was a fireplace poker.

They screamed.

The old lady screamed.

This went on for some time until the old lady realized she was in no danger and sticking her fingers in her ears, yelled, "SHUT UP!"

Gnarles and Paddy shut up, but continued to whimper, desperately clinging to each other like opposing halves of a peanut butter sandwich.

The old woman couldn't have been more than ninety-five pounds, but she wore a very serious expression. She shook the poker at them, then reached over to a little box on the wall, and said, "I'm calling the police. You two stay right where you are."

They watched with fear and fascination as she poked at the little handle-looking thing that was attached to the box with a curly rope. It made funny notes, like some kind of musical instrument.

Then she held it to her head and spoke into it: "I've got a couple of naked intruders in my house."

To which Gnarles responded, "Oh, we ain't intruders," but she shook the poker at him and made a face.

"Yes, ma'am," she said into the little handle thing, "This is Mrs. Scapolli, and I'm at 443 Port Avenue."

Gnarles and Paddy mouthed the words, "Port Avenue?"

"Yes, ma'am," she said. "No, they don't have any weapons that I can see. No, they don't look dangerous, but," she brandished the poker again, "I'd feel a lot better if you sent someone out." Then she said goodbye and set the handle thing back on the little box on the wall.

Taking the initiative, Gnarles spoke.

"We're sorry, ma'am. We don't really know how we got here. We was just walkin' through a field of –"

"Magic bean stalks," Paddy interjected.

Gnarles glared at him.

"And now here we are. We're real sorry, so if you could just let us go, we'll never come back again. We promise. Right, Paddy?"

Paddy nodded vigorously.

Mrs. Scapolli eyed them.

"What do you mean, you don't know how you got here? There's not any fields around here. We're in the middle of the city, for goodness sake! And," she nodded. "How come neither of you have any clothes on? You nudists or something?"

"Oh, no!" Gnarles protested. "We're not noogists."

Her brow wrinkled.

"Not noogists! Nudists! Don't you know what nudists are?"

The two men had yet to release each other.

"Not really," Gnarles replied.

"Hmmm," Mrs. Scapolli scowled. "What's wrong with you boys anyway? You act like you've just seen a ghost. It ought to be me who's scared. You're the ones that are breaking and entering."

"Oh," Gnarles said. "We didn't break and enter. We just … uhhh –"

She backed up and looked one direction, then the other.

"Now, how on earth did you two get in here anyway? I was sitting right in there watching *Wheel of Fortune*." She pondered a moment. "How did you two get past me? I was just in the kitchen a few minutes ago."

They both shrugged, then Paddy spoke, "We got here by magic."

Mrs. Scapolli shook her head.

"Magic, huh?"

"That's r-r-right," Paddy continued. "A little Spanish man saved us from drownin', then he gave us some magic beans, and I think he was an angel, but Gnarles says there's nooo such thing as angels but then the magic beans sprouted and grew big in only a few days, and we went into the Magic Bean Patch and suddenly we wer-r-re here!" He looked around, and added, "Wher-r-rever this is."

Mrs. Scapolli's eyes bore through the two men, then she turned to Gnarles, and said, "You don't believe in angels?"

"I might be startin' to."

"All right," she said. "If I put this poker down, will you two just leave and never come back?"

They nodded.

Backing up, she said, "Go on then, and get your clothes on." She looked around. "Where are your clothes anyway?"

They shrugged.

Shaking her head, she said, "Wait right there. My dear departed George's clothes should fit you fine," she said to Gnarles, "but you," she studied Paddy, "well, I'll find something."

The two men stood in the strange, white, shiny room, hands placed strategically, until she got back and handed them some clothes.

"Looks like the only thing I've got for you," she said to Paddy, "is one of my old house dresses."

When they were dressed, Paddy's outfit a tad tight, she showed them to the front door. As they passed through the house, they were awestruck. In some ways it looked like a regular house, but there were several strange objects that they could only guess the use of. The strange voices from the other room faded as they reached the door.

Then she opened it and pointed.

"Don't worry about the police. I'll just tell them there was a mix-up, is all."

Gnarles was about to step through the doorway when he heard a buzzing, like a giant bee, growing closer and louder. Then something big and yellow and shiny zipped past the house. He reflexively leaped backwards, knocking Paddy over.

"What was that?!" he cried, scrambling away from the door.

The old lady stared at him. "What was what?"

"That giant … bee!! It must have been goin' a thousand knots!"

"Bee?!" she said, studying the two men. "That was a VW Beetle, and it was probably going about forty miles an hour." She frowned, and added, "They need to do something about these people flying down this street. The speed limit is THIRTY!"

She looked at the two men huddled in the corner and closed the door. "Who are you two anyway?"

"I'm Gnarles and this here's Paddy." Gnarles got to his feet. "We work for Betsy down at the Port Starboard Hotel."

"Port Starboard Hotel? I've been living here all my life, and I've never heard of the Port Starboard Hotel. You mean the Port Starboard Hampton?"

"Uh-uh."

"Port Starboard Holiday Inn?"

"Uh-uh."

"Hmm. And where exactly is this Port Starboard Hotel?" she asked.

"On the lake front," Gnarles replied. "Right next to Booker T. Creek."

She thought a moment, then said, "That's not a hotel. The only thing there are condos, a marina, and the IHOP."

"The IHOP?"

Mrs. Scapolli was growing exasperated.

"Let me guess. You don't know what an IHOP is."

"When you jump around on one foot?"

She peered out the window. "Who are you two, anyway?"

"I'm Gnarles and this here's Paddy."

"I know that. I mean, where did you come from?"

Gnarles started to answer, but she waved her hand.

"I know. Port Starboard."

"Uh-huh."

She looked out the window again.

"There's the police."

"I d'na wanna goooo ta jail!" Paddy wailed.

Setting her hands on fragile hips, the old woman sighed, "All right, far be it from me to send someone guilty of nothing but idiocy off to jail. Come on," she said, leading them into a bedroom. "Wait here. I'll explain things to the police." As she closed the door behind her, they heard her mumble, "Children and fools."

* * *

At that exact moment, precisely one hundred years earlier, the Hackensaws and Humphreys were having their weekly sing-a-long. Every Saturday night, the Humphreys would come down to Sally and Bobby's house for dinner and a night of fun and merriment. Alfred always used the opportunity to ply Will with questions about sailing and navigation.

"Come on, you two!" Katie called from the music room. "We're going to start *Camptown Races* without you!"

"One more moment, dear," Alfred replied for the third time. Will was no doubt explaining the applications of plane and spherical trigonometry as it applies to the theory of navigation and nautical astronomy, and Alfred was almost to the point where he exclaimed, "Aaaah-haaa!!" It happened every time.

"Oh, good!" Katie giggled to those gathered around the piano. "They should be right in."

Those gathered included Katie and Annie (Benji was asleep on the sofa), Bonnie, and Malcolm. When they were in town, Booker T. and Maggie usually attended, sometimes Betsy and Sam, and Uncle Charlie and Molly came over every now and then. Mother Humphrey was there as well, but she didn't sing. Otherwise, it was the regular crew – including the newest member, Silas.

Never in his wildest dreams.

"Oh," Bonnie exclaimed. "That is so funny!" She looked to Malcolm. "Don't you think, sweetheart?"

Malcolm was staring across the sofa at the two men in the small study. "How long do you think, exactly?"

"Oh!" Annie replied, glancing at the grandfather clock from her perch on the extreme corner of the piano bench. "It won't be one-minute frommm now!"

Malcolm looked at Silas.

"What do you say Silas? Over a minute, or under? How about a small wager?" Silas appeared suddenly uncomfortable. "What do you say? A dollar?"

Every eye was on him.

"Um, sure," he replied, glancing at the two men huddled over a stack of charts and graphs.

"Splendid," Malcolm replied. "How much time left, Annie?"

"Forty-four seconds."

"All right," Malcolm said, "What do you say, my good man? Over or under?"

Following a short but tenuous pause, Silas mumbled, "Over?"

"Excellent!" Malcolm smiled, and he pulled Bonnie close.

Everything grew quiet as eyes darted between the clock and the two men. The only sound was that of Annie counting down, almost inaudibly.

"Six … five … four … three … two –"

"You, Will Dawson," Alfred's voice rang out, "are a veritable genius! Coming, dear!"

Silas immediately reached into his pocket, but Malcolm waved his hand.

"That's all right, old chap. We'll just call it even, for you transporting Bonnie back and forth and all."

Unsure what to do, Silas glanced at Bonnie, then timidly pulled his empty hand from his pocket.

"Sure," he mumbled. "That's fine."

Alfred wheeled Will through the parlor, around a snoring Mother Humphrey, and over to his spot between Bonnie and the piano.

"And it isn't I who is the family genius," Will was saying. "That would be my lovely niece here."

"Oh, Uncle Will," Sally replied. "Stop it."

"It's true, dear," he said. "But from what our lovely schoolmistress here says, you may be in for some competition." He winked at Annie.

"Oh, Uncle Will," Annie gushed, a big toothy grin. "Go on!"

Everyone laughed as Katie nudged Sally.

"Ready?"

Sally nodded and waited for the signal. "One and two and –"

Camptown Racetrack's five miles long, doo da, doo da ...

* * *

Hiding, Gnarles and Paddy spoke in hushed tones.

"It looks like that other door there leads outside." Gnarles was speaking.

"Should we run away?" Paddy queried.

"To where? Somewhere worse? We don't know *what's* out there."

It was a nice room, decorated in pastel pink and yellow stripes with a ceiling fan overhead. The fan was turning and a light beneath it was on.

"Got ee-lectricity," Gnarles mumbled. "Remember we saw a fan up at the train station at Titusville that time?"

"What's happened to us?" Paddy sniveled.

"It's those damned magic beans," Gnarles grumbled. "That smoke did somethin' to our heads. We're probably just dreamin'."

"Both of us? The same dream?"

"I don't know," Gnarles grouched, looking around. "What the hell is this place anyhow? And what the hell is that thing there?" He pointed at a large black box with a shiny front. He went over and studied it. "Some kind 'a mirror," he guessed, looking at his reflection.

"But," Paddy said. "There's a mirror right over here. And this one's a lot better than that one."

Gnarles didn't respond but walked over to the nightstand.

"And what the heck is this thing? Looks sort 'a like that thing she talked into on the wall." He picked it up, held it to his head, and quickly pulled it away.

"What?!" Paddy exclaimed.

Gnarles looked at it suspiciously, then held it to his ear again.

"It's buzzin'."

"Buzzin'?"

"Yep. Buzzin'. Ya wanna hear?"

"Uh-uh," Paddy replied, backing away.

"And look at this," he said. "It's got little lights with numbers and letters on 'em." He held it up for Paddy to see. Gnarles studied them a moment, then pushed one of the tiny buttons. It made a beeping noise, causing him to jump and drop it on the floor.

"Put it back!" Paddy pleaded. "It might be dangerous."

"It ain't dangerous," Gnarles sneered. "Didn't ya see that old lady usin' it?" He carefully picked it up and set it back on the little box. "Wonder what *this* is," he said, picking up a smaller black rectangular object sitting next to it.

"Dooon't touch it!" Paddy exclaimed. "Ya d'knooow what it is!"

"Hmph," Gnarles snorted, and he picked it up. "Lots 'a numbers and little words," he said. "And a big red button right here on the end." He pretended to push it.

"Dooon't push it!" Paddy cried.

"Shhhh," Gnarles said, walking over to the door and peering out. "The police are still here." He carefully closed the door and looked at the object in his hand. "Hmmm," he mumbled, a mischievous look in his eye.

"Dooon't push it!" Paddy repeated. "Ya d'knooow what it is!"

"What could it possibly do?" Gnarles replied. He closed his eyes and pushed the button. Suddenly, a loud beeping noise filled the room, sending Paddy, screaming, into Gnarles's arms.

The beeping abruptly stopped, and someone said in a loud voice, "Eight hundred dollars!" then another voice, "I'll take a 'P,' Pat!"

"Aaaiiieeah!" Paddy screamed, pointing at the black mirror. "It's the devil!"

Gnarles and Paddy wasted no time in climbing over each other to get away from the devil box; and just as Paddy was going for the door knob, Gnarles threw himself in front of him.

"No, Paddy!" he cried, pointing at the other door. "That way!"

* * *

Meanwhile, at the front door, the police officer said, "What was that?!"

"Oh!" Mrs. Scapolli answered, forcing herself not to eye the bedroom door. "That was just … uhh … my cats! Yep, that was old … uhh … Tabby! Oh, he's quite the wailer, you know." She laughed uneasily.

There was a pause, then Officer Biganski said, "You sure everything is okay?"

"Oh, yes! Perfectly fine!"

*　　*　　*

Later that evening, everyone was gathered on the front porch. There was a light breeze. Several smudges were going.

It was getting late, Will was growing tired, but he was in the middle of "The Tale of Don Pedro Gilbert; Fearsome Brigand of the Florida Straits." It was one of Annie's favorites, especially the part where Captain Gilbert got mad at his first mate and hit him over the head with his pirate hat.

It had happened back in the early thirties. The MacLeod family had been sailing down the coast from St. Augustine, and Gilbert had spotted them from his lair at the Bleach Yards, a section of high, sandy bluffs along the St. Lucie River. It was referred to as such because from out at sea the bluffs resembled sails laid out to dry. The family had been attacked and Nathan, Will's father-in-law, realizing they had no chance of out-running them, decided to ram them – or lead them to believe they would. It had taken what Nathan himself referred to as a "pair of cannon balls."

Will routinely left that part out when in mixed company.

"It worked perfectly," Will was saying. "That man, I swear, he wasn't well-educated, but he was a master mariner, and not by the numbers so much, but instinct. I've never known a man more attuned to the sea, wind, and tides than Nathan MacLeod." He chuckled. "You should have seen the looks on those rapscallions' faces when they realized we were bluffing and the plan had not been to ram them at all but to force them to show us their stern. For the plan to work, we had to get close enough for Uncle Johnny to shoot their rudder loose, and that's where Nathan displayed his true mettle. I could see it in his eyes," he sighed. "I'd have sailed with that man through the gates of Hades themselves." Will paused a moment, remembering people long gone, then said, "That Johnny. He was some kind of shot."

"Astonishing!" Malcolm exclaimed. "Circumnavigations? Shipwrecks? Pirates? Then a long, happy marriage?" He squeezed Bonnie. "You have lived a full life, Cousin Will. You're a lucky man."

"Yes," Will replied wistfully. "I am that."

"And buried treasure, to boot!" Malcolm added, tipping his glass.

"Yes," Will said, with a curious expression. "Well," he abruptly announced, "I think I'll be getting on to bed if you folks don't mind."

Alfred stood and stretched.

"I think it's time we all think about doing that as well," he said. "What do you say, honey?"

"I suppose," Katie replied with a big yawn. "We do have church in the morning."

One hundred years later

Gnarles and Paddy had burst out the door, eyes wide with fear; but then, simply being outside in the fresh air calmed them considerably. Following several minutes of discussion as to whether that had been the devil in the black mirror, they decided to simply go somewhere, lie down, and wait for morning. They were obviously dreaming.

"It's hot out here," Paddy commented.

"Sure is," Gnarles replied. "I wonder how she keeps it so nice and cool in there." Pulling up his too-big trousers, he grumbled, "Should'a got a belt."

Paddy adjusted his house coat.

It was growing dark, but they appeared to be in a fenced-in yard with a large mango tree. Directly behind the house was a small pond.

"What kind 'a pond is that?" Paddy asked.

"Hell if I know. But it looks like the water's movin'! How can that be?" They looked around curiously, then Paddy announced, "I gotta pee."

"Outhouse gotta be around here someplace."

"Maybe they got indoor plumbing," Paddy suggested, "like the Humphreys and Hackensaws."

"I s'pose," Gnarles replied. "They got ee-lectricity. They probably got runnin' water, too."

"But I gotta gooo," Paddy whined, "and I ain't goooin' back in there." He pointed, then walked out into the yard towards a tree.

"Ya can't pee in her yard!" Gnarles exclaimed.

"Then where do I gooo? I gotta gooo!"

Gnarles shrugged. "The pond, I s'pose."

That's what they were doing when a light came on and Mrs. Scapolli opened the back door.

She screamed.

They screamed.

Paddy was faster covering up because Gnarles couldn't figure out his zipper.

The old lady was livid.

"What in Heaven's name are you two doing?!!"

"Uhhhh."

"You're peeing in my pool!! What is wrong with you two?! You're peeing in my swimming pool!!"

Turning several shades of red, Gnarles finally said, "Swimming pool?"

"Don't tell me you don't know what a swimming pool is!"

"All right."

She stared at them for several seconds.

"You don't, do you?"

They shook their heads.

Stepping out onto her deck, she eyed the two men closely.

"What's wrong with you two anyway?" She stared at them for several moments, then sighed. "Are you hungry?"

As she shuffled them back into the house, she mumbled under her breath, "Children and fools. Lord help me."

One hundred years earlier

Silas was sailing Bonnie home. He couldn't help but notice how beautiful she was in the moonlight, the gentle radiance giving her the appearance of an angel. His mouth was dry, his tongue in knots.

"It's beautiful out, isn't it?" she said.

"Sure is."

"I really had fun tonight." Bonnie said. She lifted the hem of her skirt away from the bilge water sloshing at her feet.

"So did I."

Following a pause, she said, "You really have a wonderful voice, Silas. You should sing out more."

"Really?"

"Oh, yes," she said, dangling her fingers in the water. "You have real talent, you know."

"Really?!"

"Mm-hmm," she said absently. Then she giggled, "And with Bobby there, the louder you sing the better!"

Silas laughed, once again astonished at his good fortune.

"So," he ventured. "Did you happen to mention the orphanage to Malcolm?"

"Yes," she sighed, "but he wasn't as excited as I had hoped."

"Well, sometimes new ideas take a while to settle in."

"That's true, but he has his heart set on his resort. It *would* be nice, a place for the wealthy to spend their winters. There would be lots of activities and balls and things we can only dream about right now."

"It *would* be exciting," Silas agreed.

There was another long pause, and Bonnie said, "I hope you don't take this the wrong way, Silas, but Malcolm asked me to talk to you about selling him your homestead. Not the whole thing. Just the front part ... along the lakeshore. He'd give you free and clear access, of course."

"It's okay," he replied. "I know you're just asking for him. You are his fiancée, after all."

"So, what do you think? I mean, I don't want you to do anything you don't want to, but he would give you a fair price."

Silas could tell she hated being in this position, and he wanted only to ease her mind, but he had already fallen in love with his property; it was home, and the center of his dreams and ambitions.

"I don't know," he shrugged, uncertain what to say. Then he found himself blurting, "But if you were to convince him to start an orphanage instead, I'll *give* him whatever land he needs!"

"Really, Silas? You would actually do that?"

"Sure," he replied. "It is for the kids, after all."

"Yes," she said, looking off towards The Castle. "For the kids."

One hundred years later

It was almost midnight. Gnarles was sitting in the La-Z-Boy on the enclosed, air-conditioned porch, munching on popcorn and watching Nickelodeon. Next to him was a glass filled with ice cubes and ginger ale.

"Come on, Paddy!" he called out. "*Angry Beavers* is about to come on!"

He knew Paddy was in the bathroom, watching the toilet flush. There was a pause; then the toilet flushed once more. Then Paddy came out.

"Finally," Gnarles groused.

"Wait a minute," Paddy said, turning around. "I forgot to gooo."

"Dork," Gnarles mumbled, and he got up and went into the kitchen and Paddy heard him open the freezer. He leaned around the corner. "Hey, Paddy. You want some more ice cream?"

"Sure," he replied, curling up on the couch under an afghan. "Make it chocolate chip this time."

"Chocolate syrup or butterscotch?"

Paddy thought a moment, then said, "Boooth."

They hadn't yet figured out where they were, but they were enjoying it. Mrs. Scapolli had made what she said was her specialty: fried chicken with mashed potatoes and gravy, green beans, and corn on the cob. They had been amazed that most everything had come in a bag or container of some sort.

"Hmm," Gnarles had said, "mashed potatoes out of a bag?"

But were they good! After she had gone off to bed, they had discussed it and decided Maggie's were better, but if they had a microwave they'd be able to make them just as good as Mrs. Scapolli!

But it was just a dream.

A very nice dream.

"So," Paddy asked. "Do ya think beavers really have furniture and pictures of their mother on the wall of their dens?"

Gnarles shook his head.

"You're such a dweeb, Paddy. These are cartoons! Don't you get it? People draw these and then put 'em on the TV. It's not real. It's on TV!"

"But," Paddy said. "Mrs. Scapolli told us that other stuff was real."

"You mean the news?" Gnarles snorted. "Well, *Angry Beavers* is not the news. It's a cartoon."

It had been a tumultuous evening, the boys learning all the ins and outs of watching TV. In fact, the endless questions and asinine comments had been so trying on Mrs. Scapolli that she had developed a headache and gone to bed early.

"Turn everything off when you go to sleep," she had instructed.

Apparently, any reservations about her own personal safety had long since dissipated.

The first thing she had done was show them how to operate the TV, what Paddy had incessantly referred to as the "devil box" until Gnarles had finally clunked him in the head.

She had handed them the remote, which Gnarles had commandeered. He had yet to let it out of his possession. Then she had scurried off to the kitchen, occasionally peering around the corner, studying these strange little men who seemed to know nothing about so many things. Other items they were perfectly familiar with. They knew about canned green beans, for instance, but not frozen green beans.

Over and over she had heard them saying unbelievable comments as they "surfed" the channels.

"Channel surfin'," Gnarles mumbled to himself as he pushed buttons up, then down – mostly channel and volume. Mrs. Scapolli told them the other buttons were for geniuses and college professors, so Gnarles left them alone.

Channel surfin'.

He knew surfing was "cool" because he had seen a commercial for hair conditioner and another for Hawaii Five-O.

"Hawaii is a state?" he had yelled across the room.

"Yep," Mrs. Scapolli had yelled back.

"Where's Hawaii?"

"In the Pacific Ocean." Following a short pause, she had added, "It's an island."

"Oh."

They had gone at it great-guns at first, flipping the channels as fast as they could, soaking in mere glimpses of a world they could never have imagined.

"And now, CNN Headline News with Chuck Roberts –"

"No, Gilligan, you can't go in Wrongway's place –"

"BORN IN THE USA!! I WAS BORN IN THE USA!!"

"This just in! Two men were butchered by their roommate. The bodies were found in a dumpster outside of their apartment house this morning. This is Gale Storms for Eyewitness News, The One to Turn To."

Gnarles and Paddy had been horrified, but they couldn't turn it off.

"Mariel Boatlift! Castro unloads prisoners on U.S.!"

"Come on down!! You're the next contestant on the new Price is Right*!"*

"Jews are blowing up Palestinians!"

"Palestinians are blowing up Jews!"

"Nolan Ryan pitches a record sixth no hitter!"

"Tonight, the real story of Sammy Davis, Jr. Was he the real voice of Frank Sinatra? Did Frankie have him bumped off?"

Finally, they had settled on Nickelodeon – wall to wall cartoons.

"So, Gnarles," Paddy said as he slurped ice cream. "Do you think this is really a dream?"

"Of course, it is. Did you see that story on 20/20? Men on the moon? Come on! It's just all that talk about time travel, with Alfred's story of the time machine and all."

"Is that what you think? We're in the future?"

Gnarles shook his head. "Not *in* the future, man. Having a *dream* about the future, like the ones we had on the beach. I mean really, man. Think about it, a microwave oven that cooks in seconds? That's impossible. Airplanes? Dishwashers? NASCAR?! Come on, man. Just relax and enjoy the ride. It's the best dream I've ever had."

"Best I've ever had, too," Paddy replied, stirring his ice cream.

Suddenly a strange noise overshadowed the blare of the TV.

"What's that?" Paddy asked nervously.

"Dunno," Gnarles replied, turning down the volume.

They listened as the low grumbling stopped, then started again. Then before either could react, the door to the garage opened and in stumbled a young man with glassy, bloodshot eyes.

He stopped short and focused, wavering a little, and said, "Whoa! Like, who are you?!"

"We're Gnarles and Paddy."

He looked at them a moment, then said, "Cool, dude. Gnarles and Paddy." He laughed, a short, staccato snicker, and said, "So, which one is Gnarles?"

Gnarles raised his hand.

"That is one righteous name, dude. Gnarles," he repeated the name. "It's Gnarley. Get it? Gnarley Gnarles … dude."

Gnarles leaned towards Paddy, and said, "Just enjoy the dream." He looked at the young, scruffy looking man with a bushy mop of blonde curls and a surfboard earring, and said, "Who are you?"

"Du-u-u-ude. I live here with my grandma." Then he tottered forward and stretched out his hand. "I'm Jeff. Nice ta meet ya. So, like, what're you two doin' here?"

"Watchin' TV."

"Cool," Jeff said, then he staggered around the entertainment center, and exclaimed, "Whoa! I love *Angry Beavers*!"

Gnarles looked at the clock.

"It's almost over."

"That's okay," Jeff replied, sitting in the other La-Z-Boy. "What's on next?"

"*Cat Dog*."

"I love *Cat Dog*!"

"We dooo toooo!" Paddy said excitedly.

"Whoa!" Jeff exclaimed. "Where are you from, dude?"

"Port Starboard."

"No, dude," Gnarles replied to Paddy. "He means, where were you born."

"Ir-r-reland," Paddy said.

"Whoa! That is crankin', bro!"

"Yeah," Gnarles agreed. "You hear that, Paddy? Ireland is crankin', bro!"

"Aye," Paddy replied, swelling with pride, "Cr-r-rankin'."

Chapter Nineteen

Sunday, August 5, 1890

Will hated being an old man. He took it all in stride of course, and he never let on how it gnawed at him. But it did. Especially on Sunday mornings.

Getting to church was a chore.

It wasn't that far, just up the shore a quarter mile, but with the wheel chair, and the sand, well –

Up until a few months ago, he had been able to make the walk with several rest stops along the way. Following a bout with pneumonia, though, he simply wasn't able to stay on his feet for more than a few minutes at a time.

Thankfully, Bobby and Malcolm had volunteered to stay home with him on Sundays. Today was Malcolm's turn. He had confided in Will that he wasn't that much of a church-goer in the first place, and Will had told him with a sly smile that he never had been either.

"Of course," he had added. "If there had been one available to us on Biscayne Bay over the last fifty years, I have no doubt Elizabeth would have convinced me otherwise."

Sunday mornings they would go out on the front porch as everyone set off for church. They would relax, make their greetings to other church-goers passing along the Lake Trail, think about Sunday dinner, and watch the world go by. They talked mostly about generalities. Will's life was always a topic of choice. Malcolm enjoyed listening to his stories of the old days: sailing the seven seas or living on a desert island along the Great Florida Reef.

Will enjoyed reliving those times, but he was also curious about life back in England. He had returned only once, following the death of his mother, the news of which he didn't get until almost a month after she was deceased. He and Elizabeth had traveled there to pay their respects, and so she could see where the man she adored had spent his boyhood. Will recalled how much it had meant to her, to walk the streets and wharves from where he had gazed out to sea, dreaming of sailing the world.

He'd wished he had done it before.

"And," she had asked, "dreaming of the girl you would someday marry?"

"Absolutely," Will had replied, knowing in his heart that his dreams had indeed come true.

Whenever the subject turned to Malcolm, it most often centered on his plans for the resort. He could go on and on, talking about design and construction details, and the amenities they would provide, and the well-to-do clientele, and the advertisements that would run in northern newspapers, and, of course, the fabulous balls and parties he and Bonnie would host.

"I imagine Bonnie would be the perfect hostess," Will was saying. "She certainly has all the attributes for the job."

"No doubt," Malcolm replied.

"So," Will queried. "How are things with your investors?"

"Quite well, actually. Of course, I could always use more."

"Yes," Will replied, "I suppose that would be true, especially when building something on the scale you're describing. Tennis courts? A swimming pool? Electricity and running water in all the rooms? It is a grand plan."

"Yes," Malcolm proudly replied. "But I think it can be done. It's only a matter of time before the railroad comes through here, and when that happens this truly will become the Riviera of America."

Will took on a pained expression.

"Malcolm," he said. "There's something I've been wanting to speak with you about."

"You don't say."

"Yes," he said. "I've been struggling with something, and I need you to help me with it. It directly concerns you, and Bonnie for that matter."

The younger man's brow furrowed.

"Yes?"

"Well," Will said. "I suppose I might as well state it plainly. I don't know if you're aware, but I correspond regularly with my cousin on my father's side, Addison Palmer."

"Yes?" Malcolm replied, absently scratching his chin.

"Yes. And I received a letter from him earlier this week. I had told him about you and Bonnie in my last correspondence, how happy we were for you and what a perfect couple you seem to be."

"Mmm-hm. Go on."

"The fact is, Malcolm, he said some very disturbing things, and I wanted to ask you about them before accepting it at face value."

Will paused to see if Malcolm had anything to offer. He remained silent, staring out towards Pelican Island.

Will continued. "According to Addison, you got yourself into a difficult situation. He claims you were accused of stealing a large sum, including jewelry, from your father and step-mother." He paused. "Malcolm, he was quite adamant. He also said you were already married, and, as far as he knows, you were never divorced."

Malcolm remained silent, his strong Anglo jawline grinding feverishly.

"Malcolm," he said. "Addison swears that you were accused of running off with her dowry and leaving her near penniless. He also said, and he cannot confirm it, that the rumors are that you're a remittance man. Your family pays you an allowance to stay away."

Will was struggling to remain calm, but he had been holding it in for almost a week. He tried to breathe slowly, to calm his beating heart.

Malcolm stood and leaned heavily against the porch rail.

"It's not all true," he said. "I was only taking from my father what I was due." He grew silent again and turned to Will. "I suppose you'll have to tell Bonnie."

"I have no choice."

"No, I don't suppose you do."

Will could see it in his eyes, cold detachment, as if he were looking right through him. He instinctively tried to get up, but the younger man was much too fast. Much too strong. In an instant, Malcolm had the pillow from behind Will's head firmly pressed against his face. Will's feeble hands flailed.

* * *

At that moment, a thousand miles away, Charlie was with Molly, sitting in church with Maggie and Booker. They were singing along with the choir – clapping in time and feeling right at home in the all-black-except-for-them congregation – when an ominous feeling of dread settled over Charlie. So chilling it was that his leg started to shake, and he had to sit down. Molly, seeming to sense something was terribly wrong, sat beside him.

"Are you all right, Charlie?" She searched his eyes.

"I'm fine," he replied unconvincingly. "I think."

* * *

Will couldn't believe it was happening, and what reverberated loudest in his brain was Bonnie, that this miscreant might marry her. His mind frantically searched for some way to warn her. He tried to scratch him with his nails, desperately reaching backward for something, anything.

But he was losing strength. He couldn't breathe. The letter! It was on his desk, easy to find. Then his mind drifted.

It was dark, pitch black, and he was swimming.

Occasionally a monstrous swell, bigger than the rest, would rise from the deep, dropping tons of water on him, sending him sprawling head over feet. His senses and perceptions became distended flashes of reality, randomly mixed with distant memories and familiar faces. He had no idea which way was up, which way to swim for the surface, and each time he thought he could hold his breath no longer, he'd come up gasping for air just in time to see the ugly phosphorescence of another beast dropping out of the darkness. He was tired, his arms like lead, his lungs aflame. It would be so easy, he thought, to simply stop and take a deep breath of cold water, but he kept swimming, desperately following the waves towards shore. He didn't know how much longer he could keep it up.

Then his feet touched bottom. He tried to run, but only stumbled and fell as another wave propelled him face first into the hard-packed sand. He clawed desperately, dragging his beaten body forward, up and onto the beach, and into the relative safety of the mangroves.

As Will Dawson's brain ceased to function, he thought he heard voices.

"Don't move. I'll get you some water. Charlie! This one's still alive! Bring water! Hurry!!"

Will opened his eyes. He wondered if he was dreaming.

"Elizabeth?"

"Yes," the angel replied, tenderly holding his head in her lap. "I've been waiting for you."

Chapter Twenty

New York City

Following church, Charlie, Molly, Maggie, and Booker were walking down Madison Avenue, all dressed in their Sunday best – feathered hats for the ladies, bowlers for the men. They were window shopping, watching people.

It was an odd sight, even for New Yorkers: four people, two black, two white, one of them an old man sporting a mass of gray hair, a neatly-trimmed, flowing beard, an oversized silver earring, and a peg leg.

Maggie was going on about how strange it was, as if they had been living in two different worlds for the past months. On the one hand, she was a rising star of the theater, and while in that world she was treated as such. Sometimes it was almost as if she and Booker weren't black at all. They were accepted, even fawned over, by the various producers, bigwigs, and patrons, welcome to join them at restaurants, parties, other plays, or anywhere else they traveled.

If not within the bounds of the theater district, however, or in the company of these well-placed patrons, it could be as if they just stepped off the plantation: barred from certain restaurants and shops, and even some city streets.

Maggie was telling of their first day.

"Oh!" she said. "You should have seen the look on Booker T.'s face when we walked up to the front door of the theater, and they told us to go around back."

Booker chuckled. "And you should have seen her face when we went around back, and they put her to work in the kitchen."

"Really?" Molly asked. "They put you to work in the kitchen?"

"Sure did!" Booker exclaimed. "It was actually the restaurant next door, but they were waiting on a new cook, and they just assumed Maggie was her."

"And you actually started cooking?" Molly asked incredulously.

"What else could I do?" Maggie shrugged her plump shoulders. "They were desperate."

Booker laughed. "I had to go over to the theater and explain who we were and get someone to come over and drag her out of the kitchen. She didn't want to leave!"

Maggie smiled sheepishly. "I couldn't help it; I miss my own kitchen. Anyway, it was fun! They told me if I ever needed a job to come back."

They were coming up to Forty-Eighth Street, to their apartment.

"You see?" she said. "We, Booker T. and I, can just waltz into our own building like we own the place. But," she nodded across the street, "if we set foot in there, we'd be out on our cans in no time at all – or worse, arrested!"

"It is strange," Charlie said, "the way people are. The world is evolving though, slowly but surely. The fact that you're allowed in some of these places at all is a great leap from the way it was when I first came here back in '39." He looked skyward at the tall buildings. "Sure has changed since then. Sixteen stories some of these are."

"Quit looking up," Maggie advised. "Everyone will think you're a tourist."

"I *am* a tourist," Charlie replied.

"Well," Molly said. "You don't have to advertise it."

"Hey!" Charlie protested. "It's not like I don't stand out like a one-legged thumb as it is."

Port Starboard

Malcolm Geoffreys was in his element. A strong sense of the survival of the fittest had taken over. His entire life had been a game, a contest between the world and himself over who was most deserving; indeed, the man who had been that "special little boy."

As he worked, calmly and methodically, his mother's face remained in the forefront of his mind. He was pleased with himself. It was not something he had wanted to do or even imagined he might do. Yet he had pulled it off: no overturned furniture, no screams for help, no visible marks on the body – or on himself.

As Will had prattled on about things of which Malcolm was perfectly aware, he had concluded what must be done. By the time the old man had finished his litany of accusations, Malcolm had been fully prepared to put his plan into motion. In fact, he had already sprinted far ahead in his mind, considering what further steps must be taken.

There was just one damning piece of evidence.

It had not been difficult. He had found it on the desk, a letter addressed to Will Dawson, postmarked Southampton. He had taken it out the back door, burned it, and ground the ashes into the sand.

Returning to the front porch, he had carried Will's body into the house, laid him on the sofa, opened all the windows, lit several candles, and placed a Bible under Will's folded hands.

Perfect!

When everything was in place, he went down to the shore and sat in the shade of the chickee, gazing northward. There was little breeze, and it was hot. He appeared perfectly relaxed. His mind, however, was racing, going over everything, considering every possibility, one scenario after another.

He pulled out his watch; it was almost time.

A moment later, he saw someone wade out to a sailboat, then more people milling around the beach, all of them in their Sunday best, everyone conversing and fanning fans.

He stood and started northward, slowly. Some people were getting into their boats as fast as they could; others were in a duel to see who could hang on longest, perfectly content to be the last ones to leave. From experience, he knew Bobby would be one of those. Sally usually had to drag him away with a variety of threats, promises, and eye contortions.

Malcolm was prepared for anything, or anyone. Often, the Humphreys would come over for Sunday dinner, but he would have heard about that; it was never a spur-of-the-moment thing. As the Quimbys approached, he picked up his pace and assumed a grave visage.

"Good morning, Mr. Geoffreys!" Mr. Quimby said. Mrs. Quimby smiled and nodded.

"I'm sorry," Malcolm apologized. "I would so like to stop and chat, but I have troubling news for Sally."

"Oh, no!" Mrs. Quimby gasped. "It's not Mr. Dawson, is it?!"

"I'm afraid so."

Mr. Quimby shook his head.

"A good man."

"Yes," Malcolm agreed. "None better."

"Oh, you poor thing," Mrs. Quimby said, placing her hand on Malcolm's arm. "You must be beside yourself, having to tell Sally."

Malcolm brandished a stiff upper lip.

"Such a wonderful man," she sighed. "But we shouldn't hold you up." She looked up the beach at Sally. "That poor woman," she sighed, then she tugged at her husband's coat sleeve, and they continued down the beach.

Malcolm congratulated himself.

Everyone expressed a sad but not shocked expression. Sally took it the worst, and Malcolm was quick to console her. Then, just as deftly, he blamed himself. He had been responsible, but he had been in the kitchen, peeling potatoes – for Sally. When he had come back out to the front porch, he had thought him sleeping at first, but had soon discovered – to his horror – that the old man had died.

"Oh," Sally said, tears welling. "How could you have known, and what could you have done if you did?"

"I suppose you're right." He sighed grievously. "I believe he died quietly. His noble old heart appears to have just given out."

Chapter Twenty-One

Gnarles and Paddy awoke to the smell of coffee and frying bacon. Gnarles rolled over in his La-Z-Boy and stretched. Then he picked up the remote and pushed the red button.

Paddy yawned and stretched.

"Are we still dr-r-reamin'?"

"Looks like it."

Mrs. Scapolli walked out of the kitchen, wiping her hands on her apron.

"How do you boys like your eggs?"

"Sunny side up!" they harmonized.

Paddy sat up and fluffed his pillow.

"Are you sure this is a dream, Gnarles?"

"Of course, it is." He clicked away at the remote, stopping at a commercial for Fast Weight Loss Centers of America. A near naked girl was stepping out of a swimming pool. The two men stared. A near naked man stepped out of a swimming pool and Gnarles pushed the "channel up" button again.

A man appeared on the screen. He was dressed in a suit and talking to them.

"It's Sunday morning, August 5, 1990, and here's what's happening in the news."

Gnarles and Paddy looked at each other. L.E.D. bulbs were flashing on and off in their brains.

"Holy mackerel!" Gnarles exclaimed. "We're in the future! You see that, Paddy? That's why everything is so kooky! We're in the future!"

"Dooon't ya mean we're *dr-r-reamin'* we're in the fuuuture?"

Gnarles stared at the man on TV a moment longer, going on about some international crisis in a place called Kuwait, then he mumbled, "Oh, yeah. Right."

"A pretty long one," Paddy commented.

Mrs. Scapolli walked back out, and asked, "So, have you boys figured out where you're from yet?"

Gnarles shrugged. "I guess we're from the past."

"The past, huh?"

"Yep."

She rolled her eyes.

"All right. Whatever you say." Then she turned and walked back into the kitchen. "We'll talk about it after church today."

Gnarles and Paddy looked at each other.

"Church?"

She turned and put her hands on her hips.

"You are going to church, aren't you?"

Gnarles and Paddy hated church; the dream was falling apart.

Then Gnarles said, "We can't. Paddy ain't got nothin' ta wear."

Paddy nodded vigorously.

"Hmph," Mrs. Scapolli groused. "I suppose not."

A couple hours later, they were sprawled across their respective lounges, watching *Bevis and Butthead*.

"Bevis is an doofus," Gnarles was saying.

"No, he's not," Paddy responded. "He's just sensitive is all."

They were arguing their respective cases when into the room stumbled Jeff, his mop of bushy blonde hair hanging in his eyes. He was wearing nothing but a pair of tiny white shorts.

"Yo, dudes," he mumbled. "You still here?"

Gnarles and Paddy nodded.

He peeked around the corner of the kitchen.

"Cool," he said. "Breakfast."

"That's right," Gnarles replied. "Mrs. Scapolli said to tell you yours is in the microwave."

"Right," he said. Then there was lots of banging, clanking, and clunking – metallic humming for forty-five seconds – and he staggered past them out the back door, plate in hand.

Gnarles and Paddy looked at each other, then followed him out just in time to see him dive into the far end of the pool and swim towards them. He climbed out, dried off with the biggest, most colorful towel they had ever seen, and sat down in a long, low chair by the pool and put his plate between his legs.

"Have a seat, dudes," he said. Then he dug in.

Gnarles and Paddy watched with interest.

A few minutes passed, then Jeff said, "So, how long you dudes hangin' out?"

Gnarles shrugged. "'Til whenever we wake up, I guess."

"Whoa, dude! What do you mean, wake up?! Aren't we awake?!"

"No," Paddy said matter-of-factly. "We're havin' a dream, and when we wake up we'll be back hooome."

"Dude!" Jeff exclaimed. "You mean, I'm in your dream?!"

126

"Uh-huh."

"That is so freaking cool! So, am I dreamin' all this, too?!"

"Guess so."

"Whoa! But I remember gettin' out'a bed a few minutes ago!"

"Sure," Gnarles replied. "That's all part of the dream."

Jeff stared at his bite of gravy-saturated biscuit.

"Riiight," he said. "I get it. Whoa, you're pretty smart, dude!"

"No problemo," Gnarles replied.

"Riiight. So, where you dudes from when you're awake? I mean, like, you must be sleepin' somewhere right now. Right?"

Gnarles looked at Paddy and shrugged.

"We're not real sure, but it's in the past."

Jeff's brow furrowed.

"Wha'd'ya mean, the past? You mean like … yesterday?"

"Oh, nooo," Paddy replied, stretching out on a blue and white chaise lounge with a yellow duck pillow on it. "We're from a hundred years agooo."

"A HUNDRED YEARS AGO!!! Du-u-u-ude!"

"That's right," Gnarles said, leaning back in his own chair. "We're from a hundred years ago!"

"Du-u-u-ude! That is totally righteous!"

"Totally," Gnarles said, swirling his ice cubes in his glass of RC Cola. "Me and Paddy here's from 1890."

"So, how long ya gonna stay?"

Gnarles shrugged. "We don't know. Whenever."

"But," Paddy said, his voice shaking. "We gotta be home by tomorrow morning. If we d'na show up for work, Betsy's gonna be real mad." He bolted upright. "What if we're really in the fuuuture?!" he exclaimed. "What if we can'a get back to our ooown time?! What if we're trapped here in the fuuuture?!

Gnarles waved his hand.

"Don't worry, little buddy! We'll wake up and everything'll be just fine. Anyway," he looked around, swirling his straw, "I think I could get used to livin' here in the future."

Paddy was horrified.

"Just kidding," Gnarles said. "It's only a dream."

"Yeah, dude," Jeff said. "Don't you get it? It's only a dream. Man!" he said, sopping up some pancakes with syrupy gravy. "This is one cool freakin' dream, dude!"

Gnarles looked around.

"Houses sure are close together in the future. I can see like three, no, like four, five roofs from here."

"This is nothin', dude," Jeff advised. "I got a bud that's livin' in this condo, and he's got people livin' right over him! They're up all night havin' sex, though, so he don't mind too much." He snickered.

Gnarles and Paddy could do nothing but stare, wondering if they heard correctly.

"Anyway, dude, this is like livin' way out in the freakin' country compared to his digs. Like, I got it made, dude. I got this pool here, and all the cool nature," he pointed at a tiny lizard sitting on the fence, "and good old Grandma makes the best freakin' food ever!"

"You live here with your grandma?" Gnarles queried.

"Sure," Jeff replied, scraping his plate with the last bite of biscuit. "It's totally real, dude. Like, I used to live with my mom, but she's an astronaut –"

"Astronaut?" Gnarles asked. "I heard 'a them on *Nightline* with Ted Koppel. They really go off into space?"

"Sure."

"You mean, like, to the moon?"

"Sure. I mean, my mom hasn't been to the moon, but she's always in space somewhere."

"See?" Gnarles said. "It's all a dream."

Paddy's face contorted as little wheels turned.

"But, how does the dr-r-ream end? Dooon't we have to get back somehow? Even if we're dr-r-reamin'?"

"Yeah, dude," Jeff said. "Even if you guys are dreamin', don't you gotta have a way back?"

They looked at Gnarles, awaiting jewels of wisdom.

"Hmmm," he mused. "How do we get back? How do we get back? OUCH!" he abruptly sat up and rolled sideways. "What the heck is that?" He reached into his pocket, and when he opened his hand, both his and Paddy's mouths fell open.

Whoa!

"What is it?" Jeff asked.

Gnarles and Paddy stared in disbelief.

"What is it?!"

"They're ... magic beans."

"Whoa!!" Jeff exclaimed. "Magic beans?! Like in Jack and the Beanstalk?! Du-u-u-ude!!"

"Sort of," Gnarles replied. "That's how we got here, by planting these magic beans ... or different magic beans, just like them."

"And they just appeared in your pocket?"

Gnarles shrugged. "They're magic."

"So, all you gotta do is plant 'em, and then you can go back to the past?"

"I suppose."

"But," Paddy sniffed. "It took days for them to grow! We're gonna be late and Betsy's gonna be sooo mad!"

"Dude!" Jeff exclaimed. "No problem, dude!" He sprang from his lounge and ran over to a small cabinet under a metal flamingo with a background of sunset and cattails. He rummaged around a moment, then turned and held up a small green and yellow box. He pointed at the label.

"Look, dudes! Miracle Gro!!"

"Miracle Gro?"

"Sure!" Jeff declared. "Magic beans, magic dreams, and Miracle Gro!"

A few minutes later they were at the far corner of Grandma's back yard, digging a hole.

"Plant 'em just like you did last time," Gnarles instructed.

"I knooow!"

"Okay, dudes," Jeff said, reading the label. "It says one tablespoon for one gallon."

"Is that enough?" Gnarles asked. "We gotta be awake by tomorrow morning."

Jeff shrugged and dumped the whole thing in the watering can.

They let Paddy water it in since he insisted it had to be done just like last time.

They stared at the hole a while.

Then Jeff said, "It might take a few minutes to activate." They turned and headed back to the patio.

A few minutes later they heard a rumble and, as one, they turned.

In unison, they gaped.

Du-u-u-ude!!!

Without pause, Jeff leaped to his feet and ran over to the spectacle. He stood, frozen in place, gazing in wonder at the fully grown, magic bean patch.

Gnarles and Paddy could only stare as he broke the end off of one of the branches, ran back to his chair, filled a tiny, metal pipe with it, and smoked it.

Ahhhhh!

*   *   *

Gnarles and Paddy were quick to discover that Jeff spent most of his time relaxing. They were, at the moment, emulating him to a T: both of them were in brand new "tightee whitees," lounging by the pool, drinking a host of fun and interesting beverages – and "copping some rays."

"Yo, dude," Paddy said. "This Hot Pocket blooows my mind!"

"Which one you got?" Jeff queried.

"The 'Everything'."

"Cool."

Grandma Scapolli had arrived home from church later than usual. She said she had stopped off at K-Mart to pick up a few things, then gone over to Publix, and finally made one last stop at McDonald's.

Gnarles and Paddy had been amazed, astonished, and astounded. Of all the wonderful things they had discovered in this brave new world, nothing had come close to the heavenly bounty, the sacred manna from heaven that was The Double Quarter Pounder with Cheese!

Extra pickles.

"Everything all right out there, boys?"

Three sunburned faces wearing white, Wayfarer sunglasses turned and nodded.

"Told you, dudes. Grandma's the best!"

Yeah! Grandma's the best!!

"Oooo," Paddy said, looking down at his bulbous pink belly. "Ya better launch another-r-r round of Coppertone, dude!"

Jeff tossed the sunscreen.

"Whoa, dude!" He leaned on his elbow. "You're turnin' into a tomato!"

Gnarles sat up and laughed.

"Hey, Paddy! You look like a giant tomato!"

"Yeah," Jeff said. "And *you're* lookin' like a skinny one, or," he thought a moment, "more like a burnt raisin."

Paddy laughed. "Aye! Ya dooo!"

"I should probably move, too," Jeff said. So, followed by Gnarles and Paddy he dragged his chair into the shade of the porch. "That's better," he said. "Gotta cool down before we eat."

"Didn't we just eat?"

"Are you kidding? It's Sunday, dude. It's like, Grandma's favorite day!"

"You mean, because of church?"

"No, dudes! Because of Sunday dinner! That's why I stay home every Sunday – unless the waves are rockin'. I do it for Grandma. It's the least I can do. But today? With you two here?" he heaved a big sigh. "Man! I just know she's in there doin' it righteous!"

Gnarles and Paddy gazed at the kitchen window, and mumbled, "Yeah. Righteous."

Paddy, his mind spinning into high gear, said, "D'ya think she'll be makin' somethin' with frosting?"

"Are you kiddin'? Watch this. Hey, Grandma!"

"Yes?!"

"Are you making anything with frosting?"

A pause. "Maybe."

Gnarles started to say something, but Jeff put his finger to his lips then waited.

"Vanilla, chocolate … or cocoanut?"

Jeff looked to his cohorts.

"Can she make it half and half and half?" Gnarles asked.

"All three!" Jeff yelled. "Yep," he said, pulling his straw fedora over his eyes. "Grandma freakin' rocks!"

Yeah!! Grandma freakin' rocks!!

From their new vantage point they could see the other end of the backyard where there was an old koi pond, now a small pile of rocks engulfed by an overgrown white bird of paradise. Next to that was a large planter with a shriveled pony tail palm growing out of it, looking as if it had resigned itself to mere survival many years earlier.

"Holy bat guano!" Gnarles exclaimed.

The other two men ceased licking various appendages covered with cocoanut and other frostings.

"Holy guacamole!" Paddy exclaimed.

"What?!" Jeff said. "WHAT?!!" Then he followed them as they stalked like Zombies from the Beyond towards the back corner. He ran ahead of them, studying their faces. "Whoa!" he said. "Are you dudes okay?!" He waved his hands in front of their faces. "Dudes! What's wrong?!"

They stopped in front of the pony tail palm and stared at it.

"What?! WHAT?!!!"

"It's," Gnarles stammered, "our still." He uttered the words with awe and reverence.

"Still?" Jeff said curiously. "You mean for making –" And a big, wide, toothy, surfer-type grin engulfed his face.

"Du-u-u-ude!"

*   *   *

The first thing they had done was ask Grandma for permission to take the plant out of her planter.

"Planter? You mean that big kettle they dug up when they were building the house?"

Uh-huh!

"Oh, I don't know, boys. That tree was a gift from the church for all my years of service."

"But, Grandma," Jeff had said. "We gotta use the pot for a science experiment! Anyway, look at it. It's dying a slow, terrible death."

Mrs. Scapolli looked at it sorrowfully.

"It does look bad. Maybe you can save it."

"Sure we can!"

"Maybe you can plant it in the ground for me."

"No problemo!"

"Do you think you can get a good root ball with it?"

"Piece of cake!"

"All right, how about right over there by the bougainvillea?"

"Wherever you want."

As she stepped back into the house, she had yelled over her shoulder.

"It looks like it's time to weed whack out back again, Jeffie!"

He glanced at the Magic Bean Patch.

"Sure, Grandma!"

Now, almost two hours later, the three men – covered with dirt and grime, sweating profusely, and still in tightee whites – got the stubborn thing loose. Jeff held it up proudly. They looked at it – a sliver of something.

"I d'na see th' roooot ball," Paddy noted.

Jeff shrugged, then took it over to Grandma's selected location and stuck it in the ground.

"It'll grow a new one," he stated. Then he marched around the house followed by Gnarles and Paddy. "We just need to find some more of that Miracle Gro is all."

They returned a few minutes later.

"No problemo, dudes," Jeff was saying. "Grandma can pick some up tomorrow." Then they went over and watered the droopy, pulverized stick.

All of a sudden there was a big splash from next door.

Gnarles started to look through the fence boards, but Jeff stopped him.

"Whoa! Don't do that, dude! That's those two old biddies next door. They're always layin' around the pool topless. You'll burn your eyes out!"

Instantly, two faces were glued to the fence.

"I told you not to look," Jeff said, shaking his head, and he headed back to his lounge chair. He turned around. "Uh, dudes?" He walked back over. "What're you guys doin'?"

"Shhh." Gnarles waved his hand and watched a while longer, then he said, "I thought you said they was old."

"They are," Jeff replied. Curious, he squeezed in between the bougainvillea and the allamanda and peered through the boards. "Aughhh!" he cried, holding his hands over his eyes. He turned away, as if trying to erase the image from his brain.

He muttered something about old people having bad vision when a voice called out, "Is someone over there?"

Horrified, they all looked at each other.

Again: "Who's over there?"

Gnarles looked. "One of 'em's comin' this way!"

Jeff wasted no time.

Zoom!!

Gnarles and Paddy weren't so fast, and before they knew it they were staring through the fence at real, female breasts – up close! It was a first for both men, and more than they could have hoped for.

"Who is it, Gert?" a voice called out.

"Don't know, Mert."

Gertrude, who was not a "small woman," pressed herself against the fence and, peering over, said, "Looks like a couple of peeping Toms!"

There was a short pause, and Myrtle replied, "Well, invite 'em on over!"

Gnarles and Paddy looked at each other, then back at Jeff, who was hiding behind a fake ficus plant on the porch.

"What do you say, boys?" Gertrude said. "Want to have a little fun?"

Gnarles and Paddy bolted.

As the fake ficus bush trembled, they heard laughter, then a big splash.

*   *   *

Sunday dinner was leftovers from lunch, and there was plenty of that. The boys were gathered around the TV, watching a rerun of *Bonanza*. Grandma was in the kitchen, going on about the hussies next door.

"Oh, I wish those two never moved in! Every weekend it's the same thing, hooting and hollering, and running around half naked. And," she stuck her head around the corner, "I know for a fact they're drinking over there. I've seen the bottles out in their recycle bin: whiskey, gin, vodka, rum, wine, beer … anything you can think of."

Gnarles and Paddy looked at each other. The more Mrs. Scapolli went on about how decadent those two "floozies" were, the more they regretted their hasty retreat of earlier that day.

And now it was getting late.

They had gotten a lot done with the still: all cleaned up, bolted together, and set up on top of the Weber grill. Jeff had a list of things to get at Home Depot. They'd also had several discussions about how to go back in time, then get back to the future next week so they could get the still going. The plan was to re-create what they did last time: Jeff's idea.

At the exact moment they arrived the day before, about six o'clock – they didn't know for sure – Gnarles and Paddy would enter the patch together. They had asked Jeff if he wanted to come. He had asked if they had surfboards in the past. *No.* Or if they had TV. *No.* Or if they had radical wheels. *No.*

He had told them "No, thanks," saying he didn't want to risk being trapped in such a "bummer zone."

They said goodbye to Mrs. Scapolli, who patted their cheeks and rolled her eyes, telling them she expected them back for bedtime snacks.

They knew Grandma had been more than a little skeptical that they were from the past and that she still didn't believe it. In fact, she had been listening to WKNO, THE NEWS STATION!! more than usual; and when Jeff had asked her why, she had said she wanted to know if there had been any escapes from the mental institution.

Together, they walked out to the back yard.

"Ready, Paddy?"

"Ready, Gnarles."

They said goodbye to Jeff and walked hand in hand into the Magic Bean Patch, slowly, just like last time.

A few minutes later Jeff said, "I can still see you."

Gnarles and Paddy shuffled back out.

"We must be doin' somethin' different."

"Right, dude," Jeff replied. "But what?"

Gnarles contemplated the question.

"We walked in slowly. Paddy was crying and holding onto my shirttail."

They tried that. Nothing.

"Wait a minute, dudes!" Jeff exclaimed. "If you went in frontwards to come to the future, maybe you should go backwards to go to the past!"

Gnarles appeared deep in thought, then said, "Good one, dude!"

Once more they tried, edging backwards into the lush growth.

Suddenly, they heard what sounded like distant thunder and the wind began to swirl around them, like they were in a tornado but without sound. Then they were momentarily blinded by an all-consuming light. The next thing they knew they were home, standing only a few feet away from their still. A green mist hung in the air.

They stopped and listened. All was quiet except for the hoot of a distant owl. After getting the fire under the still re-kindled, they yawned, stretched, and went off to bed.

Some hours later Gnarles awoke to a pair of squirrels chattering.

"Paddy!" Gnarles exclaimed, leaping out of bed. He shook the snoring man. "Paddy!"

"Huh? What?"

"Did you dream we went into the future?"

Paddy abruptly sat up and looked around, then down at himself.

With a look of wonderment, he said, "Was it all a dream?"

Gnarles stared at him a minute: "I don't know. Is it Sunday? Or Monday?"

*   *   *

It had been a sad day for the citizens of Port Starboard. Will had been liked by all. Sally and Betsy took it the worst, of course. Alfred had sailed up to Juno, then taken the train to Jupiter where he sent a telegraph to Maggie and Charlie, informing them of Will's passing.

With the heat and humidity, and no undertaker available, they held services as soon as possible. By late afternoon, Bobby had a casket ready for Bonnie to line with white linen cloth.

Word spread quickly, and folks from all over the lake and as far away as Jupiter came for the funeral. He was, of course, buried next to his beloved Elizabeth, in the ancient oak hammock near the Port Starboard Community Church. It had been a favorite spot that Will had picked out himself following her death three years earlier.

Everyone gathered in the church yard. It was a beautiful evening, the sun casting long shadows over the lake beyond. A mocking bird was perched in a grand, shading oak tree, singing its happy song, oblivious to the subdued gathering below.

The Reverend Wickman presided, offering consolation and hope that all was not lost, that death was simply a door opening to another life that would last into eternity, a life in which Will and Elizabeth would stroll forever, hand in hand, he told them.

When he finished, he asked if anyone had anything they wished to say. Alfred, of course, got up and offered an uncharacteristically brief eulogy, and Bobby said several words of hope and encouragement, mostly directed to Sally and Betsy, before he choked up and had to sit back down. The reverend asked if anyone else had anything to say and was about to make his closing remarks when Malcolm stood up.

"Excuse me, Reverend," he said. "I do have a few words."

"By all means."

Malcolm squeezed Bonnie's hand, then walked up to the rostrum.

Before he started, he looked out over the gathered, making eye contact with several.

"I've only lived here a few months," he said. "For those who don't know me, I'm Will's cousin. Before I came here we had never met, but I feel as if I've known him forever. Our family spoke of him often. I remember growing up, whenever the subject of distant relatives, or America, or Florida, or simply men of adventure arose, Will Dawson's name was first on the list. He is legend amongst our clan back home. I ask, who could resist the telling of his amazing tale: shipwrecked on a desolate coast; the only survivor, rescued by a beautiful maiden; then how he married her and lived there in that tropical, uninhabited paradise for most of his life."

He sighed for effect.

"When I first arrived in the United States, I had no intention of coming to Florida, but one day I was speaking with some acquaintances at the stock exchange and the subject came up. I don't remember exactly how, but it was as if a light suddenly flickered to life. All those stories of adventure and the tropics finally came to bear, much like it must have for many of you. All of us here have that in common. We all left our comfortable, civilized surroundings up north and journeyed here, to the southern frontier.

"It was only when I arrived and saw for myself that I understood why you good people came, and why Will stayed. I will always owe him for that; otherwise I would have never come here myself, and," he added with a soft gaze for Bonnie, "I would have never been given the opportunity to spend my life as Will did, with the woman of my dreams at my side."

He paused and collected himself.

"I know in my heart that Will is looking down on us, a smile on his face, the kind and genuine smile we all knew and loved. I think I can say with surety that no better man has ever walked the earth. He was good to his core. I know it like I know the sun will rise tomorrow. And it will rise, and we will go on, just as Will would have wished for us.

"My only wish is that I had known him longer. I admit I have an ungrudging sense of envy for those of you who had him in your lives for so long a time, some of you all your lives." He looked at Betsy, then Sally. "Like you, I wish he was still with us, but I know in my heart he's happy to be with his dear, beloved Elizabeth again, and we should all take joy in that – that he has finally gone home to the loving arms of his wife and his Lord."

When Malcolm finished, there wasn't a dry eye to be found. He walked back to Bonnie's side and took her hand in his, knowing in his heart that he had pulled it off. His only regret was that he hadn't had more time to find out where Will's Spanish doubloons were buried, the true reason he had come south to look up his long-lost cousin.

Chapter Twenty-Two

Monday, August 6, 1890

"What on God's green earth happened to you two?!"

"Huh?"

"You look like a pair of pink raccoons! What happened to you?!"

Gnarles and Paddy looked at each other.

"Uhhhh."

"Never mind," Betsy said, moving a pot off the burner. She stopped and, wiping her hands on her apron, assumed a somber expression. "I've got some bad news," she said. Then she started to cry.

"We're sorry, Betsy," Gnarles said. "We overslept a little."

"It doesn't matter." She waved her hand, then sagged into a chair and dabbed at her eyes. "I'm afraid I have some awful news." She heaved a sigh. "Father died yesterday."

Gnarles and Paddy were stunned.

"Will?" Gnarles stammered. "He … died?"

Betsy knew they would take it badly. Neither man handled such things well. When Ben Hackensaw had died a few years back, they had gone into a horrible funk and started drinking – much more than usual. She sat up straight and took a deep breath.

"I don't know where you two were yesterday, and it doesn't really matter, but we had his funeral last night. He's laid to rest next to Mother."

Gnarles started to say something, but she cut him off.

"I want you two to listen to me," she said. "My father was very old, and he had a *wonderful* life." She paused and swallowed hard. "A fairytale life, in fact. Don't you agree?"

Paddy was sniffling and wiping at a steady stream of tears.

"Now, I don't want you two to feel bad. Whatever you were doing, it's fine; we don't necessarily want to know. But Silas said *Cocoa-Nuts* was at her berth, and you two were nowhere to be found. It's all right," she stressed. "You had no way of knowing. Will loved both of you, and he wouldn't want you to be sad. Like we all discussed last night, he would want us to celebrate his life, not sit around feeling sorry for him – or ourselves. Don't you agree?"

Betsy knew Gnarles and Paddy better than anyone. To them she was most like an overbearing mother, although she was a good twenty years younger than they were; and like a domineering but introspective mother, she knew precisely what they were thinking – most of time.

Wiping at tears, Gnarles said, "You mean, it's Monday?"

"Yes," she stammered, a curious expression on her face. "Of course, it's Monday." She studied them. "Are you two all right?"

Chapter Twenty-Three

August 9, 1890

It had been a difficult week for Gnarles and Paddy – a time of mixed feelings. They had concluded they had indeed gone into the future, and they were excited about the following weekend at Mrs. Scapolli's. On the other hand, they were devastated that not only had Will died, but they had not been there for his funeral.

Guilt weighed heavily.

And they were drinking more.

One moment they would be melancholy, the next excited; giddy even. The alcohol simply exacerbated either mood. Far into the night they would alternately celebrate and commiserate. At the moment, Paddy was crying.

"I d'knooow why he had ta die."

Gnarles, though sensitive to Paddy's feelings, was tired of answering the same question.

"Everyone has to die, Paddy, or else there'd be too many people in the world."

"I knooow," Paddy sighed, and he took another drink.

They were out in their tree fort, watching the moon rise. Lights from scattered houses along the far shore were becoming visible. The area around Palm Beach was growing every day, much more than any other community on the lake.

Gnarles took a pull from his jug.

"It sure is crowded in the future."

"Aye."

"Maybe that's why there's so many people in the future. People don't die anymore."

"Not accordin' to th' news," Paddy pointed out. "*Action Five News*! The leader in NEWS! says people are dyin' every day. One right after th' other."

"Yeah," Gnarles replied, "but those are mostly murders and car crashes. I don't remember hearin' anything about folks just dyin' of old age."

They sat with that a moment, sipping on their respective jugs, when they heard a voice call out.

"Hellooooo, the tree fort!"

"Come on up!" Gnarles said, scooting over.

"How are you, boys?" Silas said, climbing out to the precarious perch.

"Good," Gnarles answered. "How was your book club?"

"Ohhh, merely fantastic!" Silas replied. "We've been reading *The Picture of Dorian Gray* by Oscar Wilde. It's scary."

*   *   *

It was no accident that Silas had stopped by. Betsy had caught up with him at the schoolhouse and enlisted him to keep an eye on Gnarles and Paddy, then report back to her. It wasn't something Silas wanted to do, except he was a pushover. She had also instructed him to find out where they had been last weekend. She told him that over the previous three days she had queried and pressed, pried and interrogated, but to no avail. She thought if Silas stopped by at night on his way home, they might be drunk enough to spill some beans.

Everyone had noticed the change in their behavior – not to mention vocabulary. They had toned it down in the three days since, but sometimes they would say the darndest things.

"*The Picture of Dorian Gray* is the story of a man who has a painting made of himself. Then he doesn't age but the picture does," Silas explained.

Gnarles wiped a stream of Cocorum from his stubbly chin, and slurred, "Gnarley, dude."

Silas looked at him curiously.

"Yeah," he said, mimicking him. "It is gnarley … dude."

Paddy suddenly sat up straight, almost losing his balance. He wobbled a moment.

"Ya sayin' when he's young it's a picture of a young man, and when he gets old it's a picture of an old man, but *he* doesn't get old?"

"That's right … dude."

"Whoa! That blooows my mind, dude!"

"Me, too … dude," Silas replied.

He looked at the two men, still wearing vestiges of sunburn: big white eyes peering out of the darkness like a pair of drunken raccoons.

What on earth would make such marks on their faces?

He proceeded.

"So, I noticed you two weren't around last weekend."

Tact was not Silas's strong suit.

Acuity was not theirs.

"We went to the future," Gnarles replied.

"Aye," Paddy said excitedly. "At first, we thought we was dr-r-reamin', but then we woke up on Monday, so now we know we were really in the fuuuture! Right, Gnarles?!"

Gnarles took a long swig, then, stuffing the cork back in the jug, he said, "Yyyyep! A hundred years into the future! And back. Right, Paddy?"

"Damned straight! Into the freakin' fuuuture and back!"

Gnarles stared off into the settling dusk, and said, "You wouldn't believe it: cars, air conditioning, microwaves, TV –"

"Aye! And VCRs!"

"Right," Gnarles replied. "VCR's. And can openers and MTV."

Gnarles and Paddy looked at each other.

"Beastie Boys Rock!!"

A cavernous silence.

"Beastie ... Boys?"

"Yeah!"

You Gotta Fight, for Your Right, to Parrrr-ty!

"Oh."

Another excruciatingly long pause.

"So ... how did you get to the future?"

"Remember those magic beans we got from the angel that rescued us a few weeks back?"

"Yes. *Señor –*"

"Salvatore."

"Right."

"Well, Paddy planted 'em out in the old garden and they grew, like, ten feet in only a few days. So, me and Paddy walked into the Magic Bean Patch and a big wind come along and circled us, sort 'a like a tornado, and all of a sudden we seen a bright light and all of a sudden we was in Mrs. Scapolli's kitchen!"

"Mrs. Scapolli."

"Uh-huh. And we was naked as jay birds, but she run and got us some clothes, except she didn't have nothin' for Paddy so she gave him one of her old housecoats, and then we watched TV and ate popcorn out of little bags we cooked for three minutes on high in the microwave."

"I like the Movie Theater Super Extra Butter kind," Paddy interjected.

"Me, too," Gnarles agreed. "Then we met Jeff. He's a world-class surfer with a tattoo of a Hawaiian hula girl on his arm. He's cool."

Paddy took a big drink, and said, "Freakin' righteous, dude!"

"Totally," Gnarles concurred. "And then we was coppin' some rays by the pool and all of a sudden I found some magic beans that magically appeared in my pocket and we planted 'em. You wouldn't believe it, dude, but we put some Miracle Gro on 'em and they sprouted and grew big in like –"

"Seconds!" Paddy interjected.

"Yeah! Seconds!" Gnarles agreed. "Then we met some total babelicious babes who live next door and," he paused and lowered his voice, "they swim in the nude! That means naked. In the middle of the freakin' day! Hardly nothin' on!"

"Barely a stitch," Paddy said proudly. "And we saw 'em! Both of em!!"

"Yeah! Both of 'em! Anyway, it was gettin' late so we had to get back home so we could get up and go to work in the mornin'."

"Right," Silas mumbled. "Work."

"Right. So we had to try a couple of times before we figured out we had to *back* into the Future Magic Bean Patch to go into the past." He looked at Paddy, and together they bellowed, "Duhhh!!"

There was an extended moment.

Then Silas said, "So, do you think it's possible you just dreamed the whole thing?"

Gnarles waved his hand.

"Both of us? The same dream? Anyway," he explained. "It was Monday when we woke up."

Paddy nodded.

"Monday," Silas repeated. "And … the significance of that?"

"Because," Gnarles said. "If it was still Sunday we would'a got up and noticed that we was dreamin', but it was Monday so we must 'a really been in the future or else we would'a … uhhh … how did I say that worked?"

Paddy shrugged.

"Let's see," Gnarles contemplated. He took another drink. "If it was Sunday when we woke up, then … wait a minute."

"Maybe it really was a dream," Paddy suggested.

"No," Gnarles insisted. "Jeff said I explained it perfectly."

They were still trying to figure it out when Silas said his goodnights and quietly slipped away. As he headed down the Lake Trail, he worried about his two friends, telling himself that Betsy would to have to beat this one out of him.

Chapter Twenty-Four

August 10, 1890

It was Friday evening, reading night at the hotel. Alfred was in rare form, even for him.

Everyone was laughing.

With the long, difficult week behind them, he had asked Sally if she minded.

She had replied, "Uncle Will would expect nothing less."

So, in Will's honor Alfred had selected several humorous readings from Mark Twain. He was just finishing up his overly flamboyant rendition of "The Celebrated Jumping Frog of Calaveras County".

He was wearing an oversized mustache, his tiny chest swollen with pomposity, his voice reverberating with unaffected bombastry: "'Oh, hang Smiley and his afflicted cow!' I muttered good-naturedly, and, bidding the old gentleman good-day, I departed!'"

With the crowd in stitches, Alfred took several bows, ending with a deep, grandiose display for Betsy and Katie, the two women he most wished to impress – and for very different reasons. They were in the porch swing, applauding. He congratulated himself. Twain was one of his best routines.

"Thank you! Thank you!" he crowed over the applause. He glanced at the porch swing, then added, "And I believe this would be a good time for intermission." Getting the nod from Betsy, he bowed once again to his adoring fans.

"Katie," Betsy asked. "Would you get the coffee going? There's something I need to do."

"Sure," Katie replied.

Betsy pushed her way through the crowd, her eyes focused on a very average-looking man.

*   *   *

"Oh, Silas!"

His first impulse was to run away.

Instead, he turned to Gnarles, Paddy, and Eddie and said, "Would you excuse me?"

He met her half way; then she dragged him into the palm trees. It appeared as if she might actually beat it out of him.

"So?" she said. "What did you find out?"

"Not much, really," he stammered.

Betsy stared, her eyes reminding him of one of those many rattlesnakes he had shot since arriving here. He was aware that Betsy routinely killed them by hand with a garden hoe. The wall of her feed shed was plastered with their scaly hides.

"Go on," she rattled. "What the hell's wrong with those two lately?"

"Well –"

"Yesssssss?"

"All right! All right! I'll tell you!"

Betsy smiled.

Silas looked around.

"But you can't tell anyone."

"I'll decide that."

"All right," he gulped. "They were drunk, so, well, you know how they get."

"Yes," Betsy replied, glancing over at the porch. "Now, please, I have things to do."

"Right. So anyway, they were drunk and talking all peculiar again, you know, like they were on Monday?"

"Yes?"

"And I asked them where they were last weekend."

"And?"

"And they told me …"

A faint rattling sound.

"… they told me they went into the future."

"The … future."

"Yes. One hundred years into the future."

"One hundred years."

"Exactly."

Silas went on to recount every detail as best as he could recall.

"Whew," Betsy said when he had finished. "That is a good one."

"So," Silas asked. "What are you gonna do?"

She shook her head, and said, "I have absolutely no idea." Then she walked away, mumbling something about a wedding to plan and no time to worry about a pair of "doddering lunatics."

Chapter Twenty-Five

Saturday afternoon couldn't come soon enough. Gnarles and Paddy had finished their last chores of the day and week, cleaning out the hotel's upstairs outhouse and the downstairs receptacles.

They had hurried down to their little swimming hole, a sandy beach that was separated from their dockage by a clump of young mangrove trees. In addition to giving them privacy, these trees, with their long, spindly roots, provided an excellent place to tie up their boat.

They took a quick bath, then hurried down the path to their house. There was no sense in putting on any clothes so they checked the still one last time, stoked the fire, and hurried over to the Magic Bean Patch.

"Ready, Paddy?"

"Ready, Gnarles."

Next thing they knew, they were in Mrs. Scapolli's kitchen. She was waiting with their clothes. Jeff was standing nearby.

"Whoa! Gnarley, dude!"

Mrs. Scapolli was finally a believer. She had not been convinced, but she had made a big dinner just in case.

"You boys hungry?"

Yes, ma'am!

An hour later, they were in their favorite positions, watching *Miami Vice*.

"That Sonny Crockett is so cool."

"Aye. D'ya think he's r'lated ta Deevy Crockett?"

"Maybe," Jeff replied. "Could be his great, great, great grandfather."

"Yeah," Gnarles agreed. "Probably."

"Like," Jeff said. "What if Sonny went back in time? That would be cool if he could meet his own great, great, great grandfather."

"Aye," Paddy agreed. "Then he wouldn't be dead anymore."

"Yeah," Jeff said. "Like all your friends from the past."

Huh?!

Gnarles and Paddy appeared confused.

"You mean," Gnarles said, "all our friends from back home are … dead?"

"Sure. They died years ago. I mean, if this isn't a dream … again."

The revelation caught the two old men by surprise. Paddy immediately started crying; Gnarles's lower lip trembled.

"Whoa, dudes," Jeff said. "I thought you knew."

Gnarles shrugged. "I guess we never thought about it," he mumbled dolefully.

Although Jeff and Mrs. Scapolli did their best to cheer up their friends, the knowledge that all the people they loved were long dead and buried put a definite damper on the evening. Not enough, however, for them to pass up popcorn, ice cream, and *Angry Beavers*.

They were drowning their sorrows in microwavable decadence when the news came on. Gnarles was about to change the channel when Chandra Bill – the hottest news babe around, according to Jeff – announced: "It's been sixty-three years since the Port Starboard Strangler was captured, but questions remain. With the latest, here's Leslie Gayle. Leslie?"

"Whoa!" Jeff interjected. "She's hot, too!"

"Thank you, Chandra," Leslie said. "I'm here at the Port Starboard Marina, the site of the last murder committed by Malcolm Geoffreys, Jr. in 1927 –"

It instantly became the central conversation – whether the Port Starboard Strangler was the son of Malcolm and Bonnie. Gnarles and Paddy had told Mrs. Scapolli and Jeff all about them and the upcoming wedding. They were sitting around the enclosed porch; an old episode of *Gilligan's Island* was playing, no one really watching.

"Well, you have to tell her," Mrs. Scapolli was saying.

"But," Jeff replied. "What if that's not even their son?"

"How many Malcolm Geoffreys could there have been living in Port Starboard sixty years ago?"

"Ohhh nooo," Paddy cried. "What're we gonna doooo?"

Everyone shrugged.

It was an accepted premise in the house by this time that Gnarles and Paddy were indeed from the past. They had also concluded it was best they didn't tell anyone, just in case they were all crazy.

Jeff had told them he had seen a movie once in which some people who claimed to have seen aliens were put in a "booby hatch."

"You're not aliens, are you?" Jeff had laughed. Then he and Grandma had looked at each other funny.

Gnarles and Paddy had been pretty sure they were not aliens.

"Anyway," Grandma had said. "Aliens aren't real."

146

They had all agreed.

Gnarles glared at Paddy, and said, "I told you, we don't know what we're gonna do yet! That's what we're tryin' to figure out!"

"Don't get mad at Paddy," Mrs. Scapolli interjected. "He's just concerned is all." She reached over and patted his pudgy paw.

Paddy stuck his tongue out at Gnarles.

"You see that?!"

"What?"

"Never mind."

"It seems to me," Grandma said, "that you boys need to go to the library. Why, they have everything there: birth and death records, old newspapers, history books, genealogy books." She paused. "I ... saw a show about our local libraries on PBS."

"PBS," Paddy repeated. "Give. Today."

"Whoa!" Jeff said. "What if you can go back in time and stop the Port Starboard Strangler? That would be radical, dudes!"

"Yeah!" Gnarles and Paddy agreed. "Radical!"

"Think about it, dudes. You guys can go back and stop him ... ... somehow." He looked at the ceiling thoughtfully.

"But, how?" Gnarles asked. "He's not even born yet?!"

"I don't know, dudes. I guess you gotta wait until right before he kills his first victim, then call the police!"

Grandma shook her head.

"They can't do that, Jeffie. According to *The News Station*, he committed his first murder in 1918. The boys here would have to be ... over a hundred years old."

"Sooo, what're we gonna doooo?"

"You boys are just going to have to go to the library," Grandma stated. "I'm betting this *Señor* Salvatore is an angel, and he chose you two to become guardian angels for Bonnie. You have no choice now but to do all you can to save her. It's your God-given mission!"

"You're right," Gnarles said. "A mission from God. What do you say, Paddy? Library in the morning?"

"Oh, you boys can't go tomorrow. It's Sunday."

"Oh."

"You'll have to wait until Monday."

"But," Paddy sniveled. "We gotta be at the hotel on Monday! Or Betsy will kill us!"

"Whoa," Jeff said. "Why can't you just go back and ask her for the day off?"

"Because," Gnarles grumbled. "She's been askin' a lot of questions lately. I think she's on to us."

147

As Gilligan fell out of his hammock onto the Skipper, everyone stared blankly at the TV and wondered. Mrs. Scapolli got up and went into the kitchen.

"You boys want some strawberry shortcake?"

SURE!

"I know!" Jeff announced. "You can go to the library on Monday morning, then go in to work late. Just tell her you had a family emergency. I have a bro with a job, and he says he uses that one all the time."

"But we don't have a family."

Jeff shook his head.

"No, dude. You don't need a family. It's not really a family emergency. Don't you get it? It's just what you tell her."

"That's right, Paddy," Gnarles said. "That's just what we tell her."

"But isn't that lying?"

Jeff sighed. "It's a white lie, dude. It's meant to keep the peace, so it's a good lie. Okay, Grandma!" he yelled. "Gnarles and Paddy are staying over Sunday night!"

"Oh, good," she said, rounding the corner with what appeared to be three heaping plates of whipped cream. "That way we can watch reruns of *Lawrence Welk* together."

Gnarles and Paddy looked at Jeff, unaware why he would make a "puking" face by pretending to stick his finger down his throat.

"Sure," Gnarles replied. "Who's Lawrence Welk?"

Grandma pressed her hands to her chest and sighed.

Sunday morning

Gnarles and Paddy were home alone. Jeff was gone: he said that waves were cranking; there was a bodacious swell from the northeast with a light offshore breeze. Grandma would be late today; it was the third Sunday of the month, Ladies' Luncheon Day. She had asked if they wanted to go to church, but Jeff had already warned them to say that they didn't feel good.

They had spent the morning getting the still ready. Jeff had already picked up everything on the list at Home Depot, and Grandma was supposed to bring home as much molasses as she could find – for their "science experiment."

They were lounging by the pool: Jockeys, Wayfarers, Canada Dry, and Scooby Doo curly cue straws.

"This is the life, ain't it, Paddy?"

"Damned straight."

A big splash next door.

They looked at each other.

Breathing quickened.

"What dooo we dooo?"

"Shhh!" Gnarles nodded towards the fence. Then he stood up, hunched over, and ran towards the back of the yard.

Paddy was right behind.

Gnarles stopped at the old pond, the pile of rocks, then turned and ran along the croton hedge. He put his finger to his lips and peered through a hole in the bushes.

"Are they naked?" Paddy whispered.

"Shhh!"

Paddy waited, then said, "So? Are they naked?"

"SHHH!!"

Finally, Gnarles backed out of the way.

Paddy took a look, and his eyes nearly popped out of his big, round head.

They took turns.

One was lying in the pool in a floating chair. The other was smearing some kind of lotion all over her body. Each had a strange, pink drink with little palm trees sticking out of it, and both were wearing teeny weeny bikinis.

"Holy crap!"

The smaller, short-haired, petite one said, "I like Duke Ellington, don't you, Gertrude?"

The larger, buxom one said, "Yes!" and she sang along with the background music: "*It don't mean a thing if it ain't got that swing!*"

The petite one said, "I'm going in the house for a minute. You want anything?"

No, thanks, Myrtle."

Gnarles and Paddy continued to ogle.

Paddy was watching Gertrude when she abruptly tumbled out of her floating chair and started swimming up and down the length of the pool.

"Holy freaking crap!!"

"Let me see! Let me see!"

Paddy couldn't believe what he was seeing. Gertrude, tall and brunette, was swimming back and forth, back and forth. When he didn't think it could get any better, the little blonde one, Myrtle, came out of the house carrying a large piece of cake. It looked like carrot, or maybe red velvet, with chocolate frosting and what appeared to be at least two cherries on top of a cascade of whipped cream.

She was wearing a tiny red bikini and matching Wayfarer shades. She sat down at the table, crossed her legs enticingly, and then dug in.

Paddy was in love.

"What's goin' on?!" Gnarles griped.

"Shhh!"

"It's my turn!"

"Just wait a minute!!"

"No!!" Gnarles tugged furiously at Paddy's underpants. "It's my ... freaking –!"

"Hello! Is someone over there?"

*　　*　　*

Myrtle paused from her cake-eating.

"Are they still watching?" Gertrude asked, and she got back into the pool lounge and took a long sip of sloe gin fizz.

"Yyyyep. All I can see is eyeballs."

Gertrude laughed. "So, what do you think?"

Myrtle looked sideways through her Wayfarers. As if certain she had an audience, she slowly opened her mouth and inserted a bite. She chewed alluringly, then licked her rubicund lips.

"I can read the little round one's lips. He just said, 'Holy crap.'"

"So," Gertrude queried. "Which one do you want?"

"I don't know," Myrtle sighed. "The little round one sure is cute."

Gertrude shrugged. "I'll take the scrawny one. Looks like a little scrapper."

"He does that," Myrtle giggled. "Oh, wait! They're starting to argue again. Can you hear them?"

"Not what they're saying." Gertrude cocked her ear and shook her head. "So, what do you say, little sister? You up for some fun?"

"Always."

Grinning broadly, Gertrude called, "Hello! Is someone over there?!"

Nothing.

"Helloooo!" she sang, paddling towards them. "We know you're over there!"

Myrtle popped a cherry in her mouth.

"This is gonna be fun."

"Mm-hmm," Gertrude replied, then she tumbled out of her chair and waded over to the steps. "I'm not gonna let them get away so easy this time," she mumbled.

"Maybe you should put something on," Myrtle suggested. "You don't want to give the old geezers a heart attack."

"Right," Gertrude replied, throwing on a pink, Minnie Mouse, terry cloth robe but not tying it very well. "If there's a heart attack in the works, I'm envisioning different circumstances."

"Absolutely," Myrtle agreed. She reached behind her and grabbed a short, sheer, nearly useless, cover-up.

Gertrude strode over toward the fence.

Suddenly the bushes rustled, and through the fence boards she could see two pairs of tightee whitees flash by.

"Hellooooo!" she sang. "I can see you over there! Behind that fake ficus bush on the patio! It's quivering! In fact, it looks like it might shake all its leaves right off!"

When they didn't respond, Gertrude changed tactics. She crossed her arms.

"Now, I saw you two watching us, and I want you to come out right now! Right now! Chop, chop!"

She looked like she was trying not to laugh as they inched out from behind the bush, hands placed strategically.

"Come over here."

They shuffled over.

She shook her head, and asked, "What are you two hiding there?"

Gnarles and Paddy immediately pulled their hands away.

Nothin'.

"Ohhh," Gertrude said, "I see more than nothing."

They both looked down and blushed.

Myrtle walked up to the fence and stood on an overturned terracotta pot, the one she regularly used to spy on young, hard-body, surfer boy next door.

"Tsk, tsk, tsk," Myrtle said. "What a waste."

More blushing; squirming as well.

"Oh, stop it, Mert! You're embarrassing them." Cinching her robe, Gertrude smiled. "So, would you boys like to join us over here?"

Nothing.

Gertrude crossed her arms, flexing her breasts.

"Now, I don't know where you're from," she stated firmly, "but around here it's not polite to ignore someone's question."

"We're sorry, ma'am," Gnarles stammered.

"Ma'am?!" Gertrude exclaimed, setting one hand on a fully cocked hip. "Do we look like ma'ams to you?"

Myrtle giggled.

"N-no, ma'am."

She laughed. "Look, fellas. If we're gonna be friends, you're gonna have to refer to me as Gert, and my sister here as Mert." She paused. "You do want to be friends … don't you?"

They nodded enthusiastically.

"So, what shall we call you besides Peeping Tom and Peeping Tim?"

"Uhhh, I'm Gnarles Hawkins, and this here's Paddy O'Toole."

"Gnarles," Gertrude mused. "That's an unusual name."

"Uh-huh."

"Well," she suggested. "Why don't you two come on over? My sister and I could use some real, man-sized company for a change."

Suddenly, the door to the house opened and Grandma's voice called out: "Oh, boys! I brought Arby's! Come and get it before the curly fries get cold!"

"Uh, sorry, ma'am, uhh, ma'ams. We, uh … gotta go," Gnarles said, then they turned, bumped into each other, and hightailed it into the house.

Myrtle looked at Gertrude and, with confidence, declared, "Those two are goin' down."

Gertrude nodded complicitly, then she peeled off her robe, and yelled, "Last one in is an old maid!"

Chapter Twenty-Six

Monday, August 13, 1890, 7:05 A.M.

"Where are those two?!"

Betsy was beginning to repeat herself.

"I'll kill them!"

Mrs. Sebastian, who was bent over the stove stoking the fire, shrugged.

A small, plaintive woman with blaring evidence of her devotedness to taste-testing, Mrs. Sebastian had taken over for Maggie when she had departed for New York. She had done an excellent job, and Betsy was considering keeping her on during the busy winter months. Betsy figured the easier life was for Maggie, her partner and best friend, the less likely it would be that she would return to the city for next year's Broadway season.

The screen door slammed, and Bonnie entered the spacious kitchen. She set a basketful of eggs next to the sink and started pumping.

Without looking up from her work, she said, "No sign of them yet."

"This is the second Monday in a row! They know their … duties haven't been done since Saturday afternoon! I must have dumped a gallon of *Eau de Lilac* down that drain, but the smell is coming up from below." Betsy glared at the potato in her hand and grabbed the butcher's knife. "Someone," *Whap!!* "has to go in there."

Not a peep.

Bonnie rinsed and patted dry; Mrs. Sebastian was extremely busy doing something. It was as if both had magically lost their sense of hearing.

Betsy fumed.

"If there was something to salvage out there on the beach, you can bet they'd be up and at 'em by now! Shoot! They'd have been out that inlet before the sun came up!"

"Maybe something's wrong," Bonnie suggested.

Betsy whacked in earnest.

"There's nothin' wrong with those two! They just stayed up drinking too late. They know better than to tie one on Sunday night!"

"Do you want me to go check on them?"

Betsy finished maiming another helpless spud and took the bowl over to the sink.

"Would you mind?" she said to Bonnie. "Just make sure they haven't fallen into a bottomless pit or something."

"Sure, Betsy," Bonnie replied; and as she turned to go, she stopped at the sink and put her arms around Betsy. "I'm sorry about your father," she said.

Betsy nodded and pressed Bonnie's hands to her.

Then dabbing at the corner of her eye, she said, "Thank you, sweetheart."

*   *   *

As Bonnie navigated her way down the rutted and root-bound trail, she was grateful she had worn her lace-up boots. It was a good walk, nearly a mile there and back. Mostly, the meandering trail followed the waterfront, but in several places it veered into the darkness of heavily matted hammock.

She walked with her mosquito switch flailing, both for its primary purpose and to knock down any unseen spider webs. As she neared the swimming hole next to the "tree fort," she called their names. She stopped to listen, but hearing nothing she proceeded up the path to their house. A few minutes later she was there, in front of a small frame structure originally built for Callie Harper, who had lived with them at one time.

Bonnie called their names. Nothing. She proceeded cautiously, prepared to shield her eyes at a moment's notice, down the trail to the old place where they kept a campfire. The palmetto structure that had once served as their house was falling into ruin, though the makeshift, palmetto-covered kitchen remained in use. She called their names and went ahead with caution. She told herself not to go any further, but curiosity had taken hold.

When she came to where the path diverged, she took the trail leading further westward. A minute later she arrived at that fabled monument to revelry: The Still.

She couldn't help but laugh. It wasn't anything like she had imagined. Neither sinister nor grand, it looked more like an oversized Dutch oven with a tube coming out the top. She wondered at the spent fire. She had heard that it was important to keep the coals hot.

Bonnie looked around at the well-worn clearing: a few old chairs, a pile of cans and other garbage nearby, a small woodpile. She called their names, walked back to where the paths converged, and took the other fork. A minute later, she came into another clearing where a small plot of tall, strange-looking plants was growing. After seeing how Gnarled and Paddy "organized" everything else, she was surprised at the straight rows, like a company of soldiers standing at attention.

154

"I wonder what this is," she mumbled under her breath. She edged closer. The tall plants appeared to be flowering. She touched one of the leaves, then peered down the rows.

"That's strange. From here, it looks like it goes on forever. And … is that some kind of light at the end?"

She thought she might investigate.

Toot! Toooot!

"Oh, my Lord!" she exclaimed. "The *Lake Worth* is here. If I want breakfast, I'd better get going!"

She called out one last time, then hurried back down the path to the Lake Trail.

One hundred years later

Gnarles and Paddy were up early, preparing to embark on their mission. They were dressed in clothes Mrs. Scapolli had picked out for them at J. C. Penney, exactly what she told them she regularly purchased for Jeff but which they had never seen him wear: Polo shirts, Dockers, and Sperry Topsiders.

They were excited but anxious as well. It would be their first sojourn into this strange new world – and their first ride in a car, or more precisely, a cool, tricked out, former ice cream truck. When Jeff opened the garage door, Gnarles and Paddy were mesmerized: a big white box on wheels with colorful pictures of strange but delicious-looking things all over it. On the side it said in big letters, "Babelicious Mobile," and on the front was a small sign that read, "Gas, Grass, or Ass; Nobody Rides for Free."

Jeff noticed them looking at it, and said, "Don't worry about that, dudes. You ride for free."

Cool!

Grandma would have taken them, but she had a doctor's appointment. So, it was up to Jeff to get them the two blocks to the library.

"Can't we just walk?" Gnarles had asked.

"No way, dude. What if my bros saw me walkin' around town. They'd, like, rip me, dude."

"Oh."

A car zipped past, startling both men.

Another, then another.

Paddy looked around nervously.

"Maybe I'll just wait here," he said, and he started to back away.

Gnarles grabbed him by the collar.

"Oh, no ya don't, muttonhead. We're not runnin' away this time."

"Yeah," Jeff said. "I can't believe you dudes didn't jump on those babes when you had the chance."

"I thought you said they were old biddies."

Jeff shrugged. "Perspective, dude." He looked Gnarles and Paddy over. "And from your perspective, I recommend you dudes jump all over that."

After struggling with the lock, he slid back the squeaky, clanky door to reveal a super-cool, totally outrageous interior with lime green, shag carpeting from top to bottom. There was an old couch on the far wall, and peering inside, Gnarles and Paddy were impressed to see a bed with pillows and everything. Burnt orange, tie-dyed curtains covered the back windows.

Jeff clearly took pride.

"Rad, huh!"

"It's like a cool little houuuse," Paddy commented.

"That's right, dudes," he said. "They don't call me the babe magnet for nothin', you know."

"Babe magnet," Gnarles and Paddy repeated.

"So, dudes," Jeff said, climbing in and plopping on the couch. "It's too bad you didn't tell me about the chicks next door when I got home from the beach yesterday. I'd'a gotten you back in the game."

"We couldn't anyway," Gnarles grouched. "We had to wait for Grandma to go to bed."

"Aye," Paddy added, climbing in and falling backwards. "She'd flip her lid if she found out thooose two babes is our girlfriends."

"Dude," Jeff said, pulling an ice cream sandwich from the freezer. "Want one?" They nodded. "So anyway, dude. I don't think those are your girlfriends. You gotta, like, talk to 'em first. You know, get to know 'em a little. Then, when you got 'em fallin' all over you, you say, 'Whoa, babe! I gotta spread myself around a little!'"

Huh?

"Never mind." Jeff waved an ice cream sandwich. "What I'm tryin' to say is, you gotta get a little farther along than just sayin' your names and runnin' away. But don't worry, dudes! I'll be here next week, and I'll talk you through it."

"Talk us through it?"

"You know. Like that guy in real history with the big nose? I'll stand in the bushes and tell you what to say. You'll have those babe-apaloozas eating out of the palms of your hands. And a lot more than that, too," he added, popping the last bite into his mouth. "Yep," he said with confidence. "I'll get you two laid if it's the last thing I do."

It was a short but tumultuous ride to the library, Jeff constantly pumping the clutch and grinding the gears, Gnarles and Paddy in the back, cowering. Gnarles tried to be strong, sitting in the front, but the first time Jeff clipped a parked car, he joined Paddy under the covers.

"Don't worry, dudes," he said. "That hardly happens anymore."

"That music is looouuud," Paddy observed.

"Oh, you don't want Metallica? How about Queensryche?" Jeff reached over his shoulder and changed the constantly repeating song. Then he turned it up.

A police car put on its blue lights.

Jeff pulled over.

"Good morning, Officer Biganski."

"License and insurance."

"Yes, sir, Officer Biganski."

"I've told you about the music. It's too loud."

"Sorry, Officer Biganski. Like, I forgot."

"This is your last warning."

"Yes, sir, Officer Biganski."

When they pulled away again, Jeff mentioned it probably wouldn't be his last warning. None of the Port Starboard police officers gave Jeff tickets anymore. The one that did, Jeff had started dating his daughter, and though no one had ever been able to prove the two instances were related, none were willing to take the chance.

When they got to the library, Jeff parked far out in the near empty parking lot, then he opened the side window and told the string of kids following them to go away. He pulled out an ice cream sundae and crashed on the couch.

"See you dudes later."

"You're not … coming with us?"

"Sorry, dudes. I break out in hives if get too close to that many books."

Gnarles sighed. "Come on, Paddy," he said, tugging on his perma-press trousers. "Let's do this."

Paddy glanced around nervously, watching for cars to appear out of nowhere.

"Aye," he said. "'Tis for Bonnie."

Minutes later, they were staring at the big glass doors.

Finally, Gnarles mumbled, "Come on."

He stepped forward, then sprang backwards into Paddy, knocking him over. They scrambled to their feet.

"Would you look at that?!" Gnarles exclaimed. "The door knows we're here!"

They stared at the strange contrivance. Then Gnarles stepped forward again and the doors slid open. He stood back.

"Let me try!" Paddy exclaimed. "Let me try!"

They continued taking turns until a lady sitting at a table nearby whispered angrily, "You're letting the air out!"

They froze, then snickered, and proceeded inside.

It was their first foray into a library. And what a library!

"Whoa! There must be every book ever written in here!"

Several people were watching with interest, no doubt wondering what hospital they might have escaped from.

They stood there a while in their Polos, Dockers, and Topsiders. Then Gnarles noticed a tall, sophisticated lady standing behind a long counter. She was smiling pleasantly and waving him over.

Gnarles looked around, then pointed at himself.

Me?

She nodded.

"Come on," Gnarles said, nudging Paddy.

Paddy walked as if in a daze, eyes wide in wonder. Covering the walls were dozens of paintings. Some were of fields of flowers or waterfalls. Others were city scenes or portraits of important people. Then there were those that looked as if someone had spilled the can of paint. There was even a large sailfish on one wall, the biggest he had ever seen. He was mesmerized by the translucent hues and the big glassy eye.

As they approached the counter, the lady, who was peering over a pair of reading spectacles attached to a loop around her neck, smiled.

"Hi there," Gnarles said.

She pressed her finger to her lips.

"Shhh."

"Right," Gnarles whispered, glancing around nervously.

He was about to speak when she leaned forward, and said, "We should probably go over here and talk. Doris?" she said. "Could you watch the counter for a minute?" Then she turned and walked over to a table and chairs next to some strange machines that looked like TVs.

"How did you know?" she asked.

"Huh?"

"That you'd find me here?"

"Wha'd'ya mean?"

"Oh, don't be silly!" Then she turned to another lady pushing a cart of books past. "Look, Myrtle," she said. "The boys came to see us."

Myrtle stopped and peered at them over her glasses.

"Well, I'll be."

"Huh?"

Gnarles and Paddy remained clueless, something Gertrude clearly was just figuring out.

"Look at that, sis," she said. "They don't recognize us."

Myrtle laughed. "I don't think they were lookin' at our faces yesterday."

"Whoa!" Gnarles suddenly blurted. "It's you!"

"What?!" Paddy asked, still lost.

Myrtle glanced around, then hiked her skirt a little.

Paddy's eyes bulged as everything became clear.

"Looks like the cat's got their tongues, huh, Gert?"

"Uh," Gnarles stammered, trying to do as Jeff would. "You ladies sure do look a lot different … I mean … with your clothes on."

They giggled, though not like the day before. It was a more conservative, less intoxicated laugh.

Finally, Gnarles said, "So, you two are really librarians?"

"Yes," Gertrude replied, pointing at her name tag.

Gnarles and Paddy looked at it and mouthed the words, *Gertrude Maidenform; Head Librarian.*

Gertrude assumed a grim visage.

"Does it bother you that we're librarians?"

"Oh, no!" Gnarles protested. "We just, well … we didn't know."

"Hmmm," she said, tapping her foot sternly. "So, if you aren't here to see us –"

"Oh," Gnarles said, distracted by Myrtle who was sidling up perilously close to Paddy and causing him to quake. "We came here because we need a librarian."

"How about two?" Myrtle whispered. She inched closer to Paddy, who was backed up to one of the strange-looking TVs.

Gertrude took a moment to shoot her sister a look.

"Very well," she said. "What can we do for you gentlemen?"

"Well," he stammered. "We, me and Paddy, is lookin' for some information about someone."

"Yes?"

"Well," he scuffed his Sperry Topsider against the linoleum, "it's about the Port Starboard Strangler."

"Oh, yes. We've had some amount of interest in that since the latest body was discovered." Gertrude glared at Myrtle, who frowned and backed away from Paddy, who was dangerously close to knocking the entire row of machines over.

Gertrude continued. "Is there some aspect of the murders that you're most interested in? For instance, we have current newspapers, or we have old newspapers on the microfiche machines here."

"What kind 'a fish?"

She pointed. "These are microfiche machines. We can look at any edition of the Port Starboard News ever printed. There would be more information available in the old editions. When was that, Myrtle? The Twenties?"

"Late Twenties," she replied, scurrying off to pick up the relevant rolls of film while Gertrude got Gnarles settled into the chair and began going over the instructions.

A little while later, they had printed out several articles with a variety of information, from the first discoveries of female bodies to the arrest and conviction of Malcolm Geoffreys, Jr. He had been sentenced to electrocution at Raiford Prison in Starke, Florida in 1934.

"But," Gnarles said. "We need to find out about his childhood – who his mother was."

"His mother?"

"Aye," Paddy interjected. "We gotta see if his mother was Bonnie Blakely."

"Bonnie Blakely."

"Uh-huh."

Gertrude glared at Myrtle, who was rubbing up against Paddy.

"I suppose we could look in the birth records."

"Would he have been born here?" she asked.

They nodded.

"And that would have been when? Around the turn of the century?"

"Nooo," Paddy replied. "Abooot 1890. Right, Gnarles?"

"Oh!" Myrtle exclaimed. "I know what we should check first!"

Gertrude's eyes lit up.

"Of course!" she agreed. "1890 should be early enough."

As Myrtle hurried off, Gertrude asked, "Do you know when this Bonnie Blakely arrived here in South Florida?"

Gnarles shrugged. "In the late '80s. Right, Paddy?"

"Aye. She came when they ooopened th' schooool."

"The school?"

"Yep," Gnarles said. "Bonnie Blakely is our school teacher."

"I knew I heard that name before!" Gertrude said. "Bonnie Blakely was our first school teacher here in Port Starboard. I'm sure she's listed in here."

Myrtle laid a book on the table, a monstrously thick volume with a colorful shore scene on the cover.

"Look, Gnarles!" Paddy exclaimed. "'Tis Betsy's hooouse!"

They stared at the book cover.

"You recognize that house?"

"Aye," Paddy said excitedly. "'Tis Betsy's hooouse."

"Betsy?"

"Betsy Dawson."

The women looked at each other.

160

"You mean," Myrtle said, "Betsy Dawson? The owner of the Port Starboard Hotel?"

"You've heard of the Port Starboard Hotel?! And Betsy Dawson?!"

"Of course," Gertrude replied. "It's all in this book by Tim Robinson." She touched the cover and read, "*A Tropical Frontier: Pioneers and Settlers of Southeast Florida.* We use it all the time. It's the first thing we turn to for anything about our local pioneers. It's an amazing book." She scowled. "We've tried to get him to come speak for us, but he's some kind of hermit or something."

"So," she said, turning to *Blakely, Bonnie.* "How come you gentlemen know so much about our founders?"

Before Gnarles could stop him, Paddy blurted, "'Cause they're our neeeghbors!"

The women looked at him curiously, then turned to Gnarles, who said, "He means they live where we live now."

"You mean here in Port Starboard."

"Yep."

"Well, we all do," Gertrude replied. "Where exactly do you mean in Port Starboard?"

Gnarles and Paddy appeared stumped.

"All right," Gertrude said, holding her place in the book. "Let me ask you this. Where do you live now? The exact location."

They pointed to the east.

"Can you be more specific?"

"At 443 Port Avenue."

"So, you two live there with the Scapollis?"

"No. We're only there on weekends."

"Let me try," Myrtle suggested. "So," she queried. "When you two leave here today, are you going home?"

"Yes."

"Are you going to 443 Port Avenue?"

"Yes."

She gave her sister a look that was the essence of superiority and concluded, "And that's where you live."

"Not exactly."

Gnarles tried to explain, but growing frustrated he abruptly banged his fists on the table.

Gertrude took his hands and, in a very librarian fashion, said, "Shhhh!" She smiled sheepishly at several glaring patrons.

Staring at the soft, smooth hands holding his, Gnarles seemed to forget what he was saying. Then he remembered.

"Sorry, Paddy," he said. "But we're just gonna have to tell 'em."

"But we can't! Jeff said if they find ooout we're from the past, they might lock us up for experiments and turn us inta guinea pigs!"

Myrtle started to laugh, but Gertrude shushed her. She studied the two men.

"Okay," she said. "When you say the past, what exactly do you mean? Like, yesterday?"

"No," Gnarles said. "We're not supposed to tell anyone because people might think we're crazy." He looked around suspiciously and lowered his voice. "Ya see, me and Paddy are from a hundred years ago."

Big pause.

"Go on."

"Well, we was out wreckin' one day and we found a whole bunch 'a ginger ale in this wreck up the coast. We was real happy to find it, too, 'cause it's our favorite. Anyway, we lost track of time and a storm come up and we thought we was gonna die 'cause Paddy didn't tie off *Cocoa-Nuts* to the ship."

"T'wasn't me job!" Paddy protested.

"*Cocoa-Nuts*?" Myrtle asked.

"That's our boat. Anyways, we thought we was gonna die, and Paddy almost got ate by a shark except a little Spanish fella come along and saved us and the next day we woke up on the beach and he was gone and *Cocoa-Nuts* was pulled up on shore and the ginger ale from the ship was all piled up on the beach!"

Despite looking like they didn't believe a word, the women were mesmerized.

"So anyways, I forgot that he had given us some magic beans, and a few days later I found 'em in my pocket and Paddy planted 'em and like magic they come up in just a few days. Ten feet tall! Then me and Paddy walked in there and some kind 'a tornado come swirlin' 'round us and all of a sudden we was in Grandma's kitchen. A hundred years in the future!"

Another pause.

"Would you gentlemen excuse us?"

Gnarles and Paddy stared blankly as the two women got up, walked behind the counter and through a door that said "Employees Only." They closed it behind them.

*　　*　　*

"Okay," Myrtle stated. "These two broke out of somewhere."

"No question they're delusional," Gertrude nodded.

"No doubt there. So, what should we do? Call someone?"

"I don't know," Gertrude replied, opening the door a crack and peering out. They saw her and waved. "They're perfectly harmless," she said, closing the door.

"No doubt there either," Myrtle said. "So, what do we do?"

"Humor them, I guess. We don't need some kind of scene here. Anyway," she added, "My curiosity is piqued."

"All right, "Myrtle said, "but I'm keeping the phone handy and my thumb on 911."

Gertrude nodded, then opened the door.

Gnarles and Paddy were hunched over the book.

"Everything all right, gentlemen?" she asked, pulling out a chair.

"Look at this!" Gnarles exclaimed. "It says here Bonnie married Malcolm and they had a son named Malcolm Jr.!"

"Really?! So you think he's the same person as the Port Starboard Strangler?"

"He's gotta be! Go on, Paddy," he said. "What else does it say?"

Paddy started reading, very slowly, sounding out each word.

"Why don't you let me have a look," Gertrude said, gently pulling it to her. "Let's see, it says here that Malcolm Jr. ... oh, my God!"

"What?!!" Everyone, including Myrtle exclaimed.

She lowered her voice. "It says here that The Strangler was her son. Look!" she pointed. "Bonnie disappeared when Malcolm Jr. was only five years old. She was last seen at the orphanage she ran, then she just disappeared. No one ever saw her again."

Everyone looked at each other.

Gertrude continued: "It says here that her husband, Malcolm Sr., ended up closing the orphanage and turning it into a hotel called The Schooner Inn."

"I've heard of that," Myrtle said. "It burned down, I think."

"Yep. Says right here it burned down in 1901. I guess," she surmised, "Bonnie must have run away. That happens a lot more than people think, you know. A woman just gets fed up with it all and runs off – usually with another man."

"Noooo!" Paddy cried. "Miss Bonnie would never dooo that! She would never leave her son b'hind and run off with another man! Nooo matter what!"

"That's right," Gnarles agreed. "She'd never do that."

The women were surprised.

"You say that like you really knew her," Gertrude said.

"We did! I mean, we do!"

"Oh, right. You're from the past."

"Aye," Paddy replied. "I bet ther-r-re's lots 'a people we knooow in there."

"Really," Myrtle said, skeptically. "Like who, for instance?"

Gnarles shrugged. "Well," he said. "How about Booker T. Hooker? He was the first settler on Lake Worth. He'll be there."

"Of course, we've heard of him," Gertrude replied. "Booker T. Creek, Booker T. Rocks, Booker T. Boulevard, Booker T. Park. Everything's named for him around here." She flipped through pages. "There he is, Booker T. Hooker, married to –"

"Maggie!" both men chimed.

"Right!" she said. "You two really know your history! I'm sorry," she paused. "You know them personally."

"Uh-huh."

"And you know she was the –"

"Postmistress!" Paddy exclaimed as if he were a contestant on *Jeopardy*.

"And she owns the store!" Gnarles added.

"And she cooks at th' hotel!"

"The best cook ever!" Gnarles declared. "And she's a great singer, too! She even went off to sing on Broadway. In fact, she's there right now! I mean, right now a hundred years ago." He paused. "She's supposed to be back for Bonnie's wedding this weekend."

Gertrude flipped to *Blakely, Bonnie.*

"Married on August 18ᵗʰ," she said. "That's this Saturday; a hundred years ago."

"And Maggie's a great writer, too!" Paddy said.

Gertrude looked at Myrtle.

"They're batting a thousand."

"Yep." Gnarles agreed. "She can't sell her stories under her real name because she's a black woman, so she uses Charlie MacLeod's name."

"I've heard of him!" Myrtle said. "Wasn't he called the Old Sage?"

"Oh, he's called lots of things," Gnarles replied. Then he glanced at Paddy, and together they harmonized, "Just don't call me late for supper!"

"Shhh!"

The women glanced at each other. They were starting to wonder what was going on.

"So," Myrtle queried. "Who else do you know from back then?"

"You mean from a hundred years ago?" Gnarles looked perplexed. "Why, everyone, of course! We know the Humphreys, the Dawsons, the Hackensaws, the Reverend and Mrs., the Heysers, the Johnsons, the Milsaps, the Pierces, the Spencers, the Guildersleeves, the Potters, the –"

"Okay! Okay!" Gertrude said, writing as fast as she could. She started looking up names. "What do you know about the Humphreys?"

"Oh!" Gnarles said. "That's Alfred and Katie. They live north of the Hackensaws, Dr. Sally and Bobby, and they have two kids, Annie and Benji –"

"And Copernicus!" Paddy interjected.

"Right. Copernicus. That's their pet raccoon. And Alfred used to be an actor and he does readings every Friday night. Lately he's been reading Mark Twain."

"I love Mark Twain!" Paddy exclaimed, clapping his hands together.

"Shhh!"

"Sorry," Gnarles whispered. "And Katie is Billy Hackensaw's daughter. We've known her since she was a little girl up on Indian River."

Gertrude flipped to *Hackensaw, Billy*.

"Yep," she said.

There was amazement in her voice.

"That's right," Gnarles continued. "Billy is Abigail's brother. Her and her husband, Jimmy, lived right across from us up on Indian River. He's Betsy Dawson's brother."

She flipped back to Dawson.

"She's married to Sam Jesup."

"Yep. And he used to be a no-good hound dog, but Betsy finally … *trained him up!!*" both men said at once. "So, he don't run around no more. And one time he stoled all the gold that Will Dawson buried up at the St. Lucie Rocks that time back in the thirties and he run off with it, and me and Paddy chased him all over the U-nited States tryin' ta get it back."

"Aye," Paddy interjected again. "And we couldn't let 'im see who we was, sooo we had to dress up like ladies."

"Really?!"

"Yep," Gnarles replied. "But more men was checkin' me out than Paddy."

"Uh-uh!"

"Ya-huh!"

Gertrude raised her hand.

"I'm sure both of you made fine-looking women." She sighed heavily. "Let's just slow down a little. You boys have me winded, and I've done nothing but listen!"

"I have an idea," Myrtle said. "Why don't you look up Gnarles Hawkins and Paddy O'Toole?"

Gertrude turned to the O's.

"Let's see … Osborn, Otterstaeller … O'Toole. Paddy O'Toole," she said, her voice cracking with astonishment. "It says, see *Hawkins, Gnarles*."

"Du-u-u-ude!" both men cried. "It's us!"

A pause.

"Would you gentlemen excuse us?"

One hundred years earlier

"I don't know, lassie. Could ya be makin' too much of it?"

"Are you kidding me?" Betsy grouched. "They actually think they've been to the future!"

Charlie spread his arms wide.

165

"Come on! This is Gnarles and Paddy we're talkin' 'bout! They've always been a smidge off kilter."

"I'm just getting a little worried," she replied. "Bonnie said the coals were completely cold."

Charlie scratched his beard.

"That is strange," he said, "but I've seen them let the coals grow cold before, if they're off on a big wreck."

"Well, they're not off on a wreck, and anyway, this is different. They've been using all kinds of strange words, like dude, and gnarley, and freaking, and radical. Oh, my Lord!" she exclaimed. "The other day they told me to "Take a chill pill, babe!"

Charlie guffawed, his ears turning a bright red.

"Really?" he snickered. "Take a chill pill … babe?"

His hot-blooded niece crossed her arms.

"Yes!"

Chuckling to himself, Charlie mumbled, "That's a good one, huh, Salt." Then he added, "Maybe that's what you need, kiddo. A chill pill!"

"Chill pill!" Salty squawked.

Betsy glared.

"Come on!" he teased. "It's fun to say, 'chill pill.' As a matter of fact," he mused. "I'm gonna ask Sally if she has any chill pills in that little black bag of hers." He feigned a headache. "I don't feel good. I need a chill pill."

Betsy continued to glare, but with a little more umph.

They were sitting on the front porch, drinking coffee and nibbling on crumb cake. Charlie made it a habit of stopping over on Monday mornings, the weekend over, everybody back to their routine. He and Betsy would use the time to catch up, maybe gossip a little, and talk about old times on Biscayne Bay.

"Uncle Charlie," she said. "You really shouldn't feel guilty for not being here when Father died. How could you have known?"

"Oh, it ain't guilt I'm feelin'. I just wish I could'a given him a proper adios is all."

"I think we all feel that way. Like you said, it's just one of those things."

"One of many *things* we humans have no control over."

"So, Uncle Charlie," she ventured. "I know you don't really like to –"

"Yeeeees?"

"Well," she stammered, "concerning the boys. I know you don't like to –"

"Interfere?" he suggested.

Betsy shrugged sheepishly. It was a unique relationship between uncle and niece. He was the one person on earth who could make her feel like a little girl again, the larger-than-life character who had always gone his own way.

166

She always felt better after a few minutes with her blustery old uncle. Charlie's mere presence summoned up distant memories of her childhood, and, more specifically, her grandfather, Nathan MacLeod. It was his laugh. It invaded nearly all of her earliest memories: a hearty, eave-shaking roar that was by now hopelessly entangled with that of his son, Charlie.

"Only for you, m'darlin'," Charlie said.

"Oh, thank you, Uncle Charlie. They always listen to you."

"Well, I don't know about that, but I'll see what I can find out. I'm sure it's just some kind 'a game they're playin' between them." He squinted. "Looks like young Hempsted sailin' in. He's becomin' quite the sailor, ya know."

"Thanks to you."

"I just tossed him a few pointers is all."

"Well," Betsy replied. "Everyone around here with a dock thanks you." She laughed. "He's already better than Alfred."

"Alfred," Charlie shook his head. "For bein' so bloody smart, that man can do some real damage with that cranky old sloop of his. It's like this massive brain has no connection to the hands; one doesn't know what the other's doin'. Whoa!" he suddenly exclaimed, pointing. "Look at that!! Did you see that jibe?"

"Look at that!" Salty squawked.

"Yep," Charlie said. "Young Hempsted there's got it! He's been studyin' *Bowditch*, too. Why, before ya know it we'll have a real, Sally-round-the-Horn mariner on our hands."

They watched with fascination as Silas rounded up to the dock in a headwind. Charlie seemed to be on pins and needles.

"Oo! … Oo!! … Ahhh. Whew!" he sighed, and he sagged back in his chair. "Nice one," he said with a mentor's pride. "That one's gonna be a real salt, I tell ya!"

They watched as Silas tied off the boat with a double half-hitch on a bight, double-checked his spring line, made an adjustment, then retrieved a string of fish and headed up the dock.

"And quite the fisherman as well," Betsy noted.

Betsy had recently hired Silas to provide fresh fish for the hotel. In return, she fed him. Seafood was on the menu at the Port Starboard Hotel at least once every day. It was not just fish; he was learning to collect all manner of sea life. He had built lobster and crab traps and set them out around the lake; and he had sailed up to Hobe Sound to dig for oysters, which he was now growing in large chicken wire crates under his ever-expanding dock; and he regularly headed out to the inlet at low tide to wade around for conchs. In addition, he was building an extensive turtle kraal just inside the inlet near Charlie's beach hut. Whatever it took, he found out how to do it from the master seafarer himself, then went at it full bore.

Charlie commented that now, thirty-four years into it, it looked like Silas was finding his way in life. He wasn't an accountant, and he wasn't a bookkeeper; he wasn't a teacher, nor was he a farmer. Silas, it was clear, was born to be a man of the sea. With each passing day, saltwater seemed to seep into his Midwestern veins, transforming him into the man everyone yearns to be: someone at peace with himself.

"Howdy, folks," he sang as he strode up the path. "Took the cast net out and got a big mess of squid!"

"Ooooo!" Betsy was delighted.

"Is this gonna be enough?" he asked.

"Oh, plenty! Thank you, Silas!"

Silas grinned. "How you doin', Uncle Charlie?"

"Real good, son," he replied, studying his most recent protégé.

Silas set the fish down in the grass and stepped onto the porch.

Speaking to Salty, he said, "Hi there, Silas." He bobbed his head up and down.

Salty, bobbing back, said, "Hi there, Silas!"

"Do you mind?" Silas said.

"Go ahead," Charlie replied as Silas stuck out his finger so Salty could climb on board. "You, young fella, are becomin' quite the sailor."

"All thanks to you."

"And quite the fisherman as well."

"I'm learning," he shrugged. "You were right about those oyster bars up on Hobe Sound, though. It's best to anchor well out and wade over."

"*Well* out!" Charlie chuckled.

"So," Silas said, "I guess everyone's pretty excited about the wedding."

Betsy frowned.

"Ouch!" Charlie grinned. "You shouldn't have mentioned the 'W' word."

"Oops."

"It's all right," Betsy sighed. "I'll get through it, then I'll enjoy the memories."

"Of course, you will," Charlie said. "And Maggie should be here by –"

"Hopefully, Wednesday." Betsy scowled. "I hate to put her to work right away, but it looks like most of Lake Worth is gonna show up for this thing. Might be the biggest shindig ever!"

"I heard it's standing room only," Silas said.

"That's right, so if you boys want a good seat, you'd better get there early."

"But," Charlie queried, "family can come any time, right?"

"Yes, Uncle Charlie." Betsy replied with a melancholy smile. "You are the patriarch now."

The innocuous statement seemed to catch Charlie off guard.

"Yes," he mumbled. "I suppose I am."

Chapter Twenty-Seven

Inside the library's back room

"How can this be?!"

"It can't be!"

"It's impossible!"

"Completely!"

Gertrude sighed. "There's no way those two have memorized that book."

"Not the whole book. Just the parts about the people in Port Starboard."

"And most of those on Lake Worth."

"Yeah. And many of those on Indian River and Biscayne Bay. Did you hear them talking about William and Mary Brickell of Miami? And George Parsons? I feel like I know him myself!"

"I know," Gertrude said, sitting down at her desk. "No one, except for Tim Robinson himself, could know all that. But they talk like they *personally* know them! In the present!" She rolled her head back. "How can this be?!"

Myrtle shrugged. "Maybe they've got some kind of photographic memories."

"Both of them? Same memories?"

"Maybe they're part of a military science experiment."

"Science experiment." Gertrude rolled her eyes. "Oh, I know! Maybe they're aliens!"

"Oooo! Sex with aliens."

"Cut it out, sis. There's got to be an explanation." Gertrude paused. "Are they still out there?"

Myrtle looked. "Yeah." She waved and closed the door. "Maybe," she suggested, "they really are from the past."

"You've got to be kidding."

"We are devout agnostics, aren't we?"

Gertrude noticed the beginning of a hangnail and grabbed a nail file from the drawer.

"And what's that got to do with the price of platform pumps at Bloomingdale's?"

"Like you always say: 'Agnostics believe in all possibilities – even the ridiculous ones.'"

"I don't know if I meant time travel."

"Could be possible, though. A hundred years ago people said space travel was impossible, and before that electricity, and before that –"

"I get it," Gertrude said, unscrewing the lid of her subdued, earth-tone, nail polish. "But … time travel? By way of magic beans? And a funny little Spanish angel?" She pressed at her forehead, right over her eyes, with the palms of her hands. "And these two are the Chosen Ones?!"

"Why not?"

"You read way too much science fiction, little sister."

Myrtle shrugged. "Better than that romance pabulum you read."

"Most of those could be considered classics. They just tend towards sappy is all."

"I'm sure."

Gertrude scowled and studied her perfectly manicured nails.

"All right. What do you want to do?"

"I don't know," Myrtle replied. "They're both just so sweet, I want to gobble them right up." She paused. "I'm gonna jump the Pillsbury Doughboy's bones."

Following a long, drawn-out sigh, Gertrude said, "Fine." Then she stood and declared. "I suppose if we're going to do this, we might as well get to it."

Several minutes later: "So, are you boys coming by next Sunday? Maybe stay a while?"

"I don't know," Gnarles fidgeted. "We gotta be back by the time Grandma comes home from church."

"And why is that?" Gertrude asked.

"Oh," Gnarles replied. "We just don't think she'd like us, you know, hanging out over there."

Gertrude winked at her sister.

"Oh? And why is that?"

Gnarles glanced at Paddy, then lowered his voice.

"Because," he explained, staring eye-level at a fully clothed but still enticing chest. "You two run around," he lowered his voice, "you know, half-neked."

The girls couldn't help but giggle.

"Oh, is that all," Gertrude said. "She doesn't want you two hanging out over at our house because," she lowered her voice, "we lay around the pool topless?"

"I reckon," Gnarles shrugged and turned a deep crimson. "That and, you know, the liquor."

"Right. The liquor."

"And you don't go to church."

"Ohhh," they harmonized. "Chuuuurch."

"So," she said. "If we didn't drink and run around half-naked, and we went to church … what, semi-regular? She'd let you two come over on Sundays?"

"I s'pose," Gnarles mumbled, looking uneasily at Paddy.

Gertrude winked at her sister.

"How about best two out of three? After all," she added, "that is a *still* you two are running over there, isn't it?"

"A science experiment," Gnarles corrected.

Gertrude and Myrtle giggled. The more they talked to these strange little men, the more they liked them.

"What do you say, sis? Church next weekend? Followed by a pool party?"

One hundred years earlier

Betsy was growing concerned. They had never been this late. It would be time to start lunch soon – and the facilities still needed tending to. Much longer, and she would have to go in there herself. She considered asking Sam, then immediately dismissed the absurd image from her mind.

She peered over the rail towards the trail head.

Her thoughts bounded from, "I hope nothing happened to them," to "I'll strangle them," with little else in between. She, of course, would never admit it, but she adored the two "pipsqueaks."

She was convinced there were no purer hearts on earth, and not only that, she was beholden to them: it was they who had pulled her from the depths of addiction and depression several years earlier. She had always assumed she would be there to take care of them in their old age.

She just never realized they'd live so long.

She chuckled.

"What's that?" Silas asked. He was sitting on a bench under the cocoanuts, his bare toes buried in a cool tuft of Bermuda grass. He was mending a cast net, something else he had only recently learned. He was doing just as Charlie had instructed, using a shuttle to tie off perfect little sheet-bends.

"Oh, nothing," Betsy said.

Silas pulled on a string with his teeth.

"I'll get those fish cleaned and salted as soon as I get this done."

It had become part of his routine: fishing in the morning, lunch at the hotel, then head off to work on his farm, or go conching, or crabbing, or simply more fishing.

"Oh, no hurry," Betsy said. She looked towards the trail head again and continued snapping beans.

A few minutes later, Silas said, "Did you hear that?"

Betsy stopped her snapping and cocked her head.

It sounded like whistling.

"I'm gonna kill them."

The whistling abruptly ceased as Gnarles and Paddy came into the view of the occupant of the rocking chair.

Silas restrained a chuckle as they passed.

"Mornin', fellas!"

"Mornin', Silas."

By the time they reached the porch, Betsy was standing, towering over them, arms crossed menacingly.

"Where in God's creation have you two been?!"

"We had a ... family emergency."

"What?"

"We had a –"

"I heard you!"

Silence.

Finally, Betsy shook her head and mumbled, "Just go empty the buckets." As the screen door slammed, she mumbled, "I need a freaking chill pill."

*   *   *

The three men were out on the dock where they had just finished their lunches.

"So," Silas queried. "You say you had a family emergency?"

"Yeah," Gnarles said. "But it's personal business."

"Oh. So, where is it you fellows have been?"

Gnarles looked at him suspiciously.

"Did Betsy tell you to ask us that?"

Silas appeared baffled at this new, more cynical, outlook.

"Well," he said. "I don't know if she really *told* me."

Gnarles snorted. "She said she didn't want to hear it, so if she wants to hear it, she's gonna have to come ask us herself!"

This new perspective, this new attitude, was no coincidence. Before the girls had sent Gnarles and Paddy off, they had done something they had rarely done: lure unsuspecting men into the library's back room to show them their "stencil machine." The boys had been amazed, but not as much as when both women snuggled up close and accosted them, just a little, then kissed their respective victims.

Boom!

172

At that moment, something marvelous had happened. Not only did Gnarles and Paddy get their first kisses, but a tiny spark had been ignited in each man – a small, nearly imperceptible glimmer that would need only the faintest breeze to fan it into a smart flame.

The girls had released the two men, then led them like zombies to the door and gently nudged them through the sliding glass doors.

"Now," Gertrude had said. "Sunday. Church and a pool party, right?"

They had nodded.

It had been, without a doubt, Gnarles and Paddy's best day ever.

Gnarles, especially, was reaping the rewards of manhood.

"All right. You want the truth?!" he declared, recalling a line from a movie. "You think you can handle the truth?!"

"I … suppose," Silas timidly replied; and Gnarles went on to give him the entire story: from Arby's to poolside banter to Bonnie's son, The Strangler.

*   *   *

Silas swore to himself that he would not tell Betsy everything, at least not until after the wedding, but now he was spilling the beans – to the last bean.

Betsy sat stone-faced, her stoic countenance sagging with each syllable. Finally, he finished.

She sat there on her porch swing a long while, staring at nothing.

"I really cannot worry about this right now," she finally mumbled. "And Bonnie can *not* know. I can't have those two ruining her big day!" She sighed heavily. "We'll tell Sally, though. Maybe she can observe them at the wedding."

"But," Silas noted. "They seem perfectly fine otherwise. I mean, I don't think I've ever seen two happier people. Neither one of them will stop whistling … or singing that song about 'a whole lotta love'."

Chapter Twenty-Eight

Wednesday, August 15, 1890

Betsy and Sam were in bed. He was snoozing. She was staring at the telegraph Maggie had sent.

"It just seems strange," she said, "the wording. It says, 'Everything is on schedule. Should be back to work on Thursday.' Now, why wouldn't she have just said, 'Should be back on Thursday?'"

She nudged Sam.

"Huh?"

"This wording," she said. "You know what I think?'"

Nothing.

She nudged him.

"Huh?"

"I think she's already here." She scowled. "I bet they snuck in tonight so there wouldn't be some big to-do in the morning." She crossed her arms and grumbled. "She could have told me."

*   *   *

Up the shore, Maggie and Booker were lying in bed. No one knew they were home except for Alfred, who had come to pick them up at Juno.

"Oh, I feel just terrible about lying to Betsy."

"You didn't lie," Booker said, dismissively. "You just left out some information is all."

"Well, she's going to be furious."

"Ain't nothin' new. She likes bein' mad."

"Oh," Maggie said, rolling over on top of him. "You just stop it. Betsy does not like being mad. She just … well, so what if she does!" She giggled and bounced up and down. "I cannot believe how wonderful it is to be in our own bed again."

Booker sighed and gave her a couple of pats.

"Lord yes, girl," he said. "You can say that again."

"Mm-hmm," she replied. "And tomorrow you get to go out and play on your farm again."

"A dream come true," he said, "but it ain't gonna be pretty, all the work that's piled up."

"Oh, you'll have everything back to normal in no time, big fella."

"I'm just glad we were gone during summer. I'd hate to be gone during vegetable season."

"I know you would, honey, and now you never have to worry about leaving your farm again. Lord knows we've had our fun. I just want to get back to normal, to see all my friends, and get back to work, and," she smiled slyly, "see if this old bed still has the same old bounce."

Booker grinned from ear to ear.

*　　*　　*

Gnarles and Paddy were in the tree fort, freaking out.

The week was almost over, and they had yet to warn Bonnie. They had hoped Betsy would come to her senses and ask them to help tell Bonnie the horrible, awful truth, that her groom was going to kill her, and her unborn baby boy was going to become an infamous murderer. But Betsy just went about her business of being grumpy.

They were discussing telling Maggie when she got back.

"Maggie ain't gonna believe us, Paddy! No more'n anyone else will!"

"But why not?"

"Because, doofus, it's crazy talk! Nobody goes into the future! Don't you get it? Nobody's gonna believe we been to the future ... unless –"

"Unless what?"

"Never mind."

"Unless what?!!"

Gnarles lowered his voice.

"Unless we take 'em there."

"But," Paddy said. "Grandma and Jeff said that we don't know if other people can come or not, or if more than two can come or not."

"I know," Gnarles replied. "We could really mess things up, maybe get stuck in the future, or in a different future, or worse, one of us stuck in the future and one in the past."

"Oooo," Paddy said. "I wouldn't like that."

"Me neither," Gnarles said, "but we gotta do somethin'. And the only sure way to make Bonnie see that we're tellin' the truth is to take her there and show her."

"But," Paddy said thoughtfully, "she'll be naked."

"I know," Gnarles replied. "I already thought of that."

One hundred years later

Gertrude and Myrtle Maidenform were originally from Jefferson, Georgia, a rural farming community of good, God-fearing Southern Baptists. They had never formally abandoned the church but had ceased to go after swearing off men sometime in their early thirties. Since then, they had been more than happy to simply use them. One or two would show up for a while, maybe move in, start to feel at home, then one day they'd be out on their cans, piled on the curb like so many bags of refuse.

The problem wasn't that they despised men or couldn't trust them, it was more that they would eventually try to come between them.

From their earliest memories they had been a team. It had been forced on them, their mother a part-time nurse, part-time heroin addict, and their father a full-blown alcoholic and full-time loser. They had bounced around between other family members, then back to one or the other parent for a while, then split apart a few times. Finally, sometime during the Roosevelt administration, they had been sent to an orphanage in upstate New York where they had become inseparable.

They were discussing what they would wear to church for the first time in thirty years.

"Do they still wear hats?"

"I don't think so, and if they do it's not that kind."

"I love this hat!"

"It's fine with me," Gertrude said, "if you want to get shot by some squirrel hunter."

"It is *not* squirrel!"

"Whatever. Anyway, I think I'll wear my navy skirt suit."

"Didn't we give that to Goodwill?"

"No."

"I think we did."

Gertrude put her hands on her full and still shapely hips.

"Don't tell me you threw my satin suit away."

"All right. I won't tell you."

"You threw away my suit?!"

"Number one, I'm not telling you, and number two, I didn't *throw* it away. I *donated* it to Goodwill. And you knew about it. You were drunk at the time."

"I don't get drunk."

176

"You mean you don't *remember* getting drunk."

"At least I don't remember things that never happened."

"I don't do that." Myrtle crossed her arms.

"Really? What about your little 'moment' with Paul Newman?"

"That is *true*!!"

"Really! He gave you tongue when he kissed you in the reception line at the opening performance of Macbeth, The True Uncensored Story."

"Absolutely!"

Yes, there was no force on earth that could separate the devoted, mule-headed sisters. They were together; it was their plan; they were sticking to it.

"Do you think they could really be from the past?"

"No, Myrtle."

"But they know things about those people that no one could know, except for people who knew them."

Whenever the discussion turned to these possibilities, Gertrude became irritated.

"They could just be making all that up," she said.

"You mean, lying?"

She shook her head. "I actually don't think they have the capacity for it. I've never met anyone so ... honest. So –"

"Sincere?"

"Yes."

"You know," Myrtle said. "I can't stop thinking about my cute, little, Pillsbury Doughboy."

"Isn't it weird?" Gertrude agreed. "I can't either. You know," she said. "I bet we could mold those two into whatever we desire."

"I know what I desire," Myrtle stated.

Gertrude nodded slyly.

Myrtle pulled on a slinky dress she hadn't worn in twenty years, something from the age of Disco. She looked in the mirror and smiled.

"Not bad for a woman approaching her sixties."

Gertrude looked askance.

"Approaching?"

Myrtle scowled. "Anyway," she said. "That Buns of Steel gadget is incredible!" She studied her gluteus-maximus as she stood up and down on her toes. "You know what I think. I think they're telling the truth. You saw that big patch of ... weeds. What do you think that is? The way that old lady keeps her yard perfectly manicured? Something's going on over there."

"Could be some kind of crop."

"You know what I think," Myrtle said.

"Yes. And we're not breaking and entering to try out your theory."

"You afraid the old lady might catch us?"

"No. I'm afraid of being arrested for breaking and entering. I'm the head librarian, for God's sake! It won't look good with the City Commission."

Myrtle sat with that a while; then she mumbled, "Coward."

Chapter Twenty-Nine

Friday, August 17, 1890

Malcolm Geoffreys was not as well off as he let on. He was educated and perfectly well-spoken and "oh, so dashing." And he also did have several investors in his resort venture, but they were small, barely enough to cover the surveys and other preliminaries.

He had not been at it very long.

The day he hopped on a southbound train at Grand Central Station, the last thing on his mind were resorts and spas and the accommodations business. What he had in mind when he arrived on the shores of Lake Worth was nothing less than the proverbial pot of gold at the end of a rainbow.

And in a very literal sense.

It was Spanish gold doubloons, in fact – buried treasure that had lured him to this most out-of-the-way locale.

Even before he made his way to America several years back, Malcolm's daydreams had taken him directly to somewhere on Indian River. He recalled how small it looked on the map, and how big it turned out to be as he steamed southward in search of his long lost, dear cousin, Will Dawson.

It grated on him that he'd had to kill him. But everything had worked out well. Anyway, Malcolm told himself, he was old. He couldn't breathe. He had simply put him out of his misery, expedited the inevitable.

It was true. He did regret he hadn't located the gold – yet – but with a million dollars for a cushion, he could be patient. He couldn't help but be concerned about Bonnie's "obsession" with starting an orphanage, or worse, the most recent incarnation in which she thought it might be a good idea to start several orphanages – all over the South!

It didn't bother him terribly – he was certain she could be swayed – but it irked him that the little dirt farmer held such power over her. It was as if all he had to do was mention something, and she was all on board.

It didn't matter now, of course. Everything was working out splendidly, better even than he could have imagined, for his own pot of gold had arrived in the form of a blonde, buxom bombshell.

He kicked back in his rocker and, speaking from under his hat, mumbled, "I am a lucky man."

"You certainly are, young man."

Sam was sitting across from him on the front porch, reclining in a similar position.

Malcolm thought, *"Oh, no. He's the dad! It's time for the talk!"*

Samuel took an audible breath.

"You know," he said. "Theah's a virtual army of young men like yourself who would deahly love to be in your position."

"I do."

"And you, of course, know what a special young lady Bonnie is."

"Absolutely."

"Malcolm," he drawled. "I feel it my duty to ask if you fully realize the opportunity you are bein' given."

Malcolm pushed his hat back.

"So sorry. I was half dozing. And, yes, I do." He studied Sam, the old card shark. "As a matter of fact," he continued. "I know how you feel about Bonnie, and, as her father, you must be extremely concerned about her inheritance."

"I am, in fact," Sam replied.

"As you should be." Malcolm leaned forward, and speaking deliberately, said, "I don't want to lie to you and say I don't care about a veritable fortune. What I want you to know, however, is that I love Bonnie for herself. Even if she were penniless, I would want to spend my life with her at my side."

Sam smiled, and said, "I appreciate that, young man, and I hope with every fiber you are bein' sincere."

The two men watched as a flock of ibis flew past.

"You know," Sam declared. "I do believe what we need is some sort of celebratory pastry or pie."

"Hear, hear," Malcolm agreed.

*　　*　　*

Reading Night. Everyone was there. Alfred, however, was being upstaged by the local lovebirds.

He had been prepared for such a development and had brought with him a few choice excerpts from a variety of poems, plays, and novels, all with a decided slant towards unabashed mush and shameless sentimentality: Browning, Wilde, Bronte, Shakespeare: including *Romeo and Juliet, A Midsummer Night's Dream*, and *Othello*.

He had planned to keep that one short, a solitary verse from near the end – a profession of Othello's love before he strangles the life out of Desdemona. But, once he got started he hadn't been able to stop.

Finally, Katie shouted, "That ought to do it, Alfred!!"

He looked up, startled, first at his wife, then the gathered, all with shock written across their faces.

"Oh! Yes," he said. "Maybe I'll save that one for later."

Everyone laughed, with one notable exception.

Betsy was barely aware Alfred was on the "stage" at all. Her mind and eyes were focused on three targets: Gnarles and Paddy; Bonnie and Malcolm; and Sam. She had set her husband on a mission: to keep the first target from coming in contact with the second one.

She had made it clear to Gnarles that she did not want him telling Bonnie about his "little fantasy" and had been surprised at his response, he declaring in no uncertain terms that it was his and Paddy's "God-given mission!" to rescue her from Malcolm.

Betsy had told Sam earlier that day that she would be in need of his services.

"Oh, really," he had drawled, a sly smirk on his lips. "I've been waiting some time for those words. Shall we do it now? Here?" He had pointed at the porch swing.

"We've tried the swing before, Sam. It doesn't work." He scowled. "However," she had added. "If you do me this little favor, I'll do that … 'special thing.'"

Sam took a long drag on his stogie and gazed off at the puffy clouds forming beyond the inlet.

"Tonight?"

"I don't know, Sam. Things are pretty hectic right –"

A disappointed face.

"Fine," Betsy had grumbled.

"And tomorrow night?"

"*And* tomorrow night?!"

Sam had made a crafty smile.

"It would be after the wedding." He had raised an eyebrow. "You know how weddings affect you, my deah."

Betsy had heaved a sigh.

"Fine. Tonight *and* tomorrow night."

"With enthusiasm?"

"With enthusiasm."

Sam had smiled, as if pleased with his negotiating skills.

Now, she could see he was on his mission, throwing himself between opposing forces. Betsy didn't really expect Gnarles and Paddy would try anything with so many people around, but she feared if they got to Bonnie, they might convince her to step aside for a more private conversation.

"Well!" Alfred announced from his dais. "This looks like a good place for intermission. When we return, we'll delve into what Homer had to say about love, marriage, and the Power of Nuptials!"

Betsy and Maggie were sitting in the porch swing.

"Oh, Maggie," Betsy said. "Would you mind supervising the coffee? I have something important to take care of."

"Sure, Betsy," Maggie replied, and she leaned into her. "It's so good to be back home."

It had been a grand homecoming. As word spread, people had gathered at Maggie's store where she gave an abbreviated version of her and Booker T.'s great adventure – more to come at a later date. Everyone had begged Booker to put on his fancy dinner jacket and button-down spats, but he had declined. It was obvious to one and all that he wanted nothing more than to get back to his beloved fields of toil and sweat.

Of course, no one was happier to see Maggie than Eddie. When he first saw her, it appeared as if he might cry. Then, when she told him he was officially relieved of duty, he did, burying his face in her plump shoulder and sobbing uncontrollably.

Annie had giggled and cheered, telling Maggie that Eddie held down that stool without a problem the entire time. Eddie had laughed and dragged his little cousin into the ever-swelling group hug. Truly, it had been a glorious day in Port Starboard.

And if it weren't for Gnarles and Paddy, everything would be fine!

Betsy's eyes didn't stop moving, darting between Target One and Target Two. *Where's Sam?* She spotted him over by the crumpets at the other end of the porch.

"Oh, Sam!"

He looked over and held up his finger. He indicated that he needed cream for his coffee.

Betsy fumed. Her eyes darted. She was beginning to perspire.

She had hoped Gnarles and Paddy would use the intermission to go out for a couple of drinks. No such luck. They were out near the dock, talking to Charlie, Eddie, and Silas, but preparing to make their way to the refreshment table. Her eyes darted to Bonnie and Malcolm. They were in line, almost to the table. She perceived a bottleneck at the porch steps.

"Oh, Sam!"

She could, of course, take care of it herself, but she didn't like this new attitude from the boys, especially Gnarles. She feared a big scene in which they would spout their ridiculous scenario for all to hear. It was the last thing she needed. There was a wedding, for Heaven's sake!

Betsy had not informed Sam of why she wanted them kept apart for fear he might spill the beans, or worse, alert Bonnie himself.

"But, deah Betsy," he had said. "What possible reason could there be for keepin' them apart?"

"Don't worry about it, Sam," she had replied. Then she had casually adjusted her voluminous bosom.

Sam had winked. "Whatever you say, my deah."

He wolfed down his crumpet, and, taking his coffee, he edged to the middle of the expansive porch steps. Target One was approaching with Eddie and Silas. He noticed Gnarles had his eyes fixed on Bonnie.

Suddenly, an opening.

Sam had little time to react. Gnarles abruptly split from the group and pushed through some other people towards Bonnie. Betsy's eyes grew wide. They were only feet apart and closing fast when Sam shoved Mrs. Milsap out of the way – *Excuse me, madam* – and stretched his long arm past Mr. Pierson, almost knocking his glasses off – *Pardon me, suh* – and, nearly falling over himself, he grabbed Gnarles by the shirt collar, nearly yanking him off his feet.

"Well, hello theah, little buddy!" Sam sang, pulling him close. "How have you been lately?"

"Huh?" Gnarles said, straining to peer over a throng of taller people.

"I said," Sam continued, pulling the smaller man into a hug. "How are you … pal?"

Gnarles tried to poke his head higher.

"Fine," he replied. "I just gotta talk to Bonnie."

"Oh, theah's plenty of time for that," Sam said. He looked down at a thinning pate. "Hey!" he exclaimed. "I've never noticed that you have an extraordinary head!"

Gnarles pushed himself away.

"What are you talkin' about?"

"Oh, nothing. It's just … uh … I've been taking a correspondence course in skull-ology."

"Skull-ology?"

"Oh, yes," Sam said. "It's the newest thing, and by the looks of yours, you could be a bona-fide genius."

"Really?!"

"Oh, yes!"

As Sam delved into the very new science of skull-ology, Betsy caught Sally's eye and motioned her over.

"Hi, Aunt Betsy!" Sally said. "How are you?" She sat down in the swing. "Push?" she asked.

"Sure."

"So," Katie said. "I imagine you'll be happy to see the wedding done and over."

"Lord, yes," Betsy sighed, then she leaned in, and said, "Have you had a chance to observe the boys yet?"

"Not really, but from what I've seen, they look perfectly fine. In fact, I noticed they didn't even go back for a drink tonight." She patted Betsy's hand. "I'm sure it's just some sort of game they're playing in which they go off into the future. I wouldn't worry about it, probably just a way for them to feel important. You know, people need to feel needed."

Betsy looked askance at her niece.

"Are you trying to tell me something?"

Sally shrugged. "I don't know. I mean, no one loves those two more than you, but maybe you could just, you know, shower them with a little more … praise?"

"You want me to *shower* them with praise," Betsy repeated.

"Couldn't hurt," Sally replied as she hopped up and hurried over to where a crowd was gathering down by the dock to hear Charlie tell the tale of *Bamboo, the Spanish Saint of Shipwrecked Sailors*. It was a legend he had heard as a child and had perpetuated as a man, ever since he himself had been rescued by the apparition at Jupiter Inlet many years earlier.

Betsy looked at Sam, towering over Gnarles, explaining something in depth.

Maybe Sally's right, she thought. Maybe I am too hard on them. She noticed Gnarles extricate himself from Sam.

He looked at her.

She motioned for him to pursue.

Everyone was gathering near the foot of the dock. Betsy had heard the tale many times and had a pretty good idea what Charlie was saying:

"Yep, we were dumbstruck, both me *and* Salty, and we remained in that sad state as the little man came bounding across the deck towards us! He was spry, no doubt! It seemed to us that the little fellow flew over the broken, canted surface; and before we knew it, he was standin' right in front of us.

"'*Buenos dias*,' he said with a grand smile, and he removed his oversized straw hat and bowed, like he was one of the Three Musketeers come to life. I remember his black eyes sparkled and, though I don't think he looked more than thirty years old, his eyes told me he was well beyond that mark. It was very strange. Well, he finished his long, deep bow, and then he stood erect, tucked his hat under his arm, and declared, 'It is a beautiful day, *sí, mi amigo*?'

"And with that, he clapped his hands, and said, 'My name is Bamboo!'"

As Charlie went on, telling his tale to a rapt audience, Gnarles and Paddy looked at each other, their eyes wide.

Betsy frowned, wondering if this had something to do with their time traveling notions. *Didn't Bamboo sound a lot like their Señor Salvatore?*

Betsy sat bolt upright.

*   *   *

Reading Night, and Alfred was standing on his stage, waiting patiently. He understood the value of great storytelling – and Charlie was a master. It was just him, Betsy, Katie, and Maggie on the porch. Everyone else, including the children, especially the children, were gathered around the Old Salt and the Son of a Sea Dog himself. At the moment, it was actually Salty who was doing most of the entertaining. Charlie was in the throes of cajoling him into quoting the Golden Rule, the only words Charlie said his mother, Mary Ann, had been able to impart to her "little green seafarer."

Salty had been with Charlie from near the beginning, having been found by his father, Nathan, after a day of wrecking. The bird had washed ashore with the same storm that had delivered one Will Dawson to the MacLeod family. As for his tendency towards foul language, Salty had spent his formative years with the ship's cook – enough said.

Everyone present with children understood: Charlie had little control over what Salty said.

No control, actually.

"Oops!" Charlie said, trying to hold his hand over Salty's beak. Everyone howled; mothers held hands over little ears. "No, Salty," he instructed. "It sort of rhymes with that, though." Charlie glanced up at the porch.

"Uh-oh!" he said, "I think Salty's havin' a little *too* much fun. Charlie held Salty to his ear. "Huh? … "Oh, I see … Yes, I understand."

He turned to everyone, and announced, "I'm sorry. Salty's tired."

Boooo! Hissss!

"Sorry," Charlie shrugged. "Anyway," he said, nodding to Alfred. "It's time to hear Homer's views on the Power of Nuptials!"

As grumblings subsided everyone wandered off to their places, all except for the little flock of hecklers in the back, the regulars: Charlie, Eddie, Silas, Gnarles, Paddy, and little Annie Humphrey.

Charlie handed over Salty.

"There ya go, Sweetpea!" Patting Annie on the head, he said, "He sure does love you, kiddo."

185

She scratched him behind the ears. "And I love you, too. Don't I, Salty Walty? Yes, I do."

Charlie was hoping to get a moment with Gnarles and Paddy before he left, except with all the people, he was beginning to wonder if he should put it off. But, the wedding was less than a day away. Betsy was counting on him. He looked at the two diminutive figures leaning against a palm tree nearby, absorbed in the performance.

Leaning over, he told Annie he'd be right back then tapped Gnarles on the shoulder and motioned them to follow.

One hundred years later

Gertrude and Myrtle were scheming, making big plans.

"Myrtle," Gertrude said. "You can't actually *believe* we're going into the past."

"Probably not," she replied, "but if we do, I am not going unprepared. Let's see," she said, rummaging through a large beach bag. "Sunscreen, hand lotion, body lotion, Off, more Off, toothpaste, toothbrush, deodorant, extra socks, running shoes –"

"Running shoes?"

"Bears. Panthers. Rattlesnakes."

Gertrude put a pair in her bag.

"I hope no one sees us," she said. "Or arrests us. We're gonna look pretty stupid, standing there in that weed patch loaded down with all this stuff and dressed up in replica dresses from 1890."

"Oh!" Myrtle said. "I didn't tell you. The museum only had samples from the 1860s and the turn of the century, 1900 or so. There was nothing from 1890."

"Great," Gertrude said. "People are going to think we're from Mars or something."

"Are you kidding? These are gonna be cutting edge designs in 1890."

"More like undreamed of designs."

"Better than being out of style."

"I suppose," Gertrude replied, looking in the mirror. "I can't believe what I'm saying. We are *not* going into the past. But," she sighed. "I really do love these dresses! They make me feel so feminine, so, I don't know … romantic? It's like I've already stepped back in time." Another drawn-out sigh. "It was a beautiful time, you know. I love movies set in this period." She pulled at the waist. "I think I'm going to take this in a little more."

"Not too much," Myrtle, the eternal stick, replied.

"Don't worry about me, little sister. You just make sure you don't expose too much skin. It's another time and place … well, same place, different time. Anyway, we don't want them thinking we're some kind of hussies or something."

"Speak for yourself."

"I can't believe what I'm saying. We are NOT going into the past!"

"Only one way to find out," Myrtle countered.

"I know," Gertrude droned. "The Agnostic's Creed: anything is possible." She turned. "Unbutton, please?"

As Myrtle started the tedious job, she mumbled, "Thank God for Gideon Sundback!"

"Thank God," Gertrude nodded.

One hundred years earlier

They didn't go far, just beyond the edge of the hammock to where Gnarles and Paddy had set up their little "Pub in the Woods."

John Highsmith shuffled in behind them.

"Y'all openin' up shop?"

"Later," Charlie said.

Sheriff Highsmith frowned, then ambled away.

"All rightee," Charlie said, leaning against the bar. "Maybe I'll take a short glass."

Gnarles poured out three shots. He and Paddy downed theirs.

"So," Gnarles said. "Is that all you wanted, a drink?"

Charlie smacked his lips approvingly.

"I swear, boys. This stuff gets better with every batch."

"Same recipe we been usin' for years."

Charlie wet his lips again.

"Maybe it's just me."

They nodded, clearly wondering what Charlie wanted to talk to them about.

"You know," Charlie finally said. "It can be tough growin' old."

"I s'pose."

"It ain't for sissies," he added.

"Nope."

"You know," he sighed. "I think it could be said that we, all three of us, had good lives."

"Uh-huh."

Charlie decided on a more direct tact.

"So," he said. "Betsy says you boys have been to the future."

"Uh, yeah," Gnarles stammered. "That's right."

Charlie studied them. He had noticed throughout the evening that they were using a different language, or more precisely, adding to the English language. Not words necessarily, mostly different meanings for words currently used.

"Yeah." That was the word they used most often. He found he liked it, though not as much as "chill pill."

Molly already hated that particular phrase. She said it seemed every few minutes that either she or Charlie needed a "chill pill" for some reason or another.

Charlie had been keeping count. There was "dude", of course, and "man", and "gnarley", and "radical", and "awesome", and "check it out", and most perplexing of all "bad!" which apparently meant good.

"Yes," he said. "As you know, Betsy confides in me at times."

Garnering no response, he continued. "Well, the fact is she asked me to talk to you fellas about, you know, time travel." He paused. "Now the first thing I want you to know is that I don't think you're crazy."

"So, you believe us?!" Gnarles blurted.

Charlie sat down on a barrel that served as a barstool, and said, "Why don't you just tell me the entire story?" He peered through the bushes at Alfred, who looked as if he had at least another hour in him. "From the very beginning," he added. Then he got comfortable and signaled Paddy for a refill.

"Well, it all started right after that hurricane. Remember?"

Charlie nodded.

"You were already gone to New York when we got back, so you never heard."

"Go on."

Gnarles went on to tell about how they had found the ginger ale, and how Paddy had forgotten to tie off *Cocoa-Nuts*, and how they had drifted for hours waiting for the ship to sink, and then how they had hung onto a keg for several hours more, and how a little Spanish fellow saved them at the very last minute.

Charlie took a deep breath. It was strange, no doubt, but Gnarles and Paddy had heard his story of Bamboo many times over the years, a story which may have exaggerated a little. They probably knew it better than he did. Charlie wondered: could they both have had the same dream?

Gnarles continued all the way to the end of the story where the "two *babes* copped a feel."

"Copped a feel," Charlie had repeated. "That's a good one."

Charlie was in a state of wonder. It was an astonishing tale, and the amount of detail was incredible. In fact, a fleeting thought occurred that they should tell it to Maggie – it could be a best seller.

He pushed such extraneous thoughts away.

Gnarles and Paddy waited for the verdict.

Are we crazy or not?

"Well," Charlie said. "That is some story." He looked at them, their eyes clinging to his. "I'll say this, though. I believe you two believe it."

They looked confused.

Charlie sighed. "Look, fellas. Here's the deal. Betsy and everyone else here have a wedding to get through. Now, I know you two feel the need to tell Bonnie before she gets married, and I'm not here to say you can't. But you have to think about the ramifications before you tell someone something like that on the night before her wedding." He took a deep breath. "Listen, I know you want to tell her, but even if you did, do you think she would believe you?"

"No," Gnarles said. "That's why we gotta take her with us, so she can see for herself!"

"I know, but it's just not the right time. You fellas are just gonna have to accept that she's very busy right now. She won't be going into your Magic Bean Patch tonight or tomorrow." He paused. "Look, by saying anything now, all you'll do is upset her. You don't want that, do you?"

"No."

"Good," Charlie said. "Anyway," he added, nodding towards the gathering, "Betsy would absolutely kill the both of you; and the rest of us would have to spend the rest of our lives staring at your hides pinned to the side of her feed shed."

The image seemed to hit the mark.

"Now, come on, boys!" he said. "Let's have another round!"

While they waited for the performance to end, Charlie studied the two men. There was no question, they were truly distressed.

He stuck around until after the performance was over, talking about old times, sharing memories.

Then as folks started wandering into the "pub," he slapped Gnarles and Paddy on the back, and said, "Thanks, boys! Never a better drink *or* conversation." And he hobbled away.

"Bar's open!" he said as he passed the sheriff going in. He stopped and waved at Silas, Eddie, Christiane, and Annie, all of them staring down the trail at him, obviously wondering what was going on.

Suddenly, several kids flew by, followed by a smaller one yelling, "Gimme back my freakin' hat, dudes!" To which one mother declared to another, "Are they allowed to say that?!"

Unable to contain himself as he passed by, Charlie said, "Yo! Take a chill pill, babe!"

That night Charlie slept fitfully. He couldn't stop thinking about Gnarles and Paddy. No one, he thought, could make up such intricate details, unless they were delusional – but the same delusion? He wanted to speak to Sally about it, to ask if it was normal for old folks to have such strange and vivid imaginations.

He tossed and turned, going over their story, searching out inconsistencies, noting blaring consistencies, and telling himself he was crazy for even considering such a thing, that they had indeed gone into the future. But he always returned to the one piece of evidence he found indisputable, that he himself had experienced something unexplainable years earlier, also involving a diminutive Spanish sailor.

He recalled that evening, weeks earlier, shortly after the hurricane had passed: he had been sitting on the beach with Molly, and a little boat had sailed past. He recalled how he had commented that it looked familiar. Charlie stared at the shadows on the ceiling and told himself that this could not be.

As the sun rose next morning, he couldn't shake the thought that the boat he had seen heading north that night was indeed that of his own guardian angel, the little Bamboo. Over the years, he had told the story countless times: how Bamboo had shown up out of nowhere and disappeared just as mysteriously. And never had he failed to spice it up a little, maybe add a few "facts" here and there; but now, as time had passed, he wondered if he had simply begun to believe his own embellishments.

Did it really happen as I remember, he wondered. Could this *Señor* Salvatore actually be Bamboo?

He racked his brain. Gnarles and Paddy would not lie – and a perfectly cohesive and consistent lie at that.

He rolled over and stared out the window at the graying sky.

Taking care not to disturb Molly, he got up and started a pot of coffee. Then he walked out onto the beach and sat on a large timber. He set Salty down and tossed a stick for Floppy, the normal routine.

Staring at the sunrise, his eyes followed a shower forming out over the Gulf Stream.

As it drifted towards shore, he wondered, *Could it be possible?*

Chapter Thirty

Saturday, August 18, 1990

Gertrude's alarm clock went off: *I'm crazy for cryin', crazy for lyin', and I'm crazy for lovin' you ...* Then it went silent.

In the next room, a second alarm clock went off: *If you want my body, and you think I'm sexy ...* Myrtle cranked it up, then lay back in bed and stretched. Bopping with the beat, she swung her legs over and stared at herself in the mirror. A phosphorescent, night-cream mask stared back. She smiled, then hopped out of bed, prepared to meet the day.

There was nothing Myrtle Maidenform liked better than a good adventure. She was prepared for anything. It excited her to think about sneaking into the yard next door, or even getting caught in the act – or even arrested! Nothing, however, excited her like the thought of actually going into the past. Of course, in the back of her mind, she understood nothing would happen. They'd walk into the tall weeds, stand there a minute, and come out. Gertrude would bitch about spiders and whatever.

But, she wondered, what if they actually did go into the past? Anything is possible, she told herself. She wanted to be prepared, and she wanted to make sure she kept a good record. So, in order to gather accurate notes, she had packed her mini cassette recorder with extra tapes and batteries.

It was something to which she had always aspired, to be a real journalist – not someone who logs and organizes the information after the fact, a mere conduit of knowledge, pointing people to the card catalog or interminably stuffing books onto shelves. Unlike her sister, Myrtle could not see the intrinsic value of the position of librarian.

Gertrude, on the other hand, could not imagine a loftier goal; "Keeper of the Flame!" is how she put it.

The library thing was supposed to have been temporary, but one year ran into another; and before Myrtle knew it, she as a career librarian.

It was all Gertrude's fault. It was she who had suggested little sister come to work at the library. It had been 1969, a tumultuous era: men were landing on the moon; war was raging in Southeast Asia; Jets were the Super Bowl champs; Helter Skelter was a song *and* a murder scene; Butch and Sundance died better this time; "*Here's the story of a man named Brady . . .*"; there was Mi Lai; Walmart; Wendy's; John Lennon made a point; the Black Panthers rioted; Chicago cops cracked heads; and, of course, Woodstock.

Sex, Drugs, Rock and Roll ... and mud.

It had been the height of her existence, a defining moment. It was her, Myrtle Maidenform, in the second most famous picture of two people kissing in the mud pit with her bikini top coming off. The picture still hung on the living room wall and remained a point of contention between the sisters.

"You can't even see anything!"

"That's because there's nothing there to see."

Regardless, it had been Woodstock that indirectly led Myrtle into the library business. The judge had been prepared to throw the book at her when Gertrude had stepped forward and offered her errant sister a job. With resources tight in upstate New York at the time, the judge was obliged to put her on probation.

After all these years, Myrtle continued to claim her innocence: *The drugs weren't mine! They belonged to my big-mouthed boyfriend!*

He had written from prison, but she had never replied. To this day she carried a grudge. It was all his fault, and Gert's, that she was a librarian.

Of course, Gertrude told her daily that she was welcome to go find another job.

"Maybe as a drug dealer!" Her sister was prone to suggest.

Myrtle would sneer.

But now she was on the verge of becoming famous, a world class journalist! She thought she might like a job on NPR, or maybe her own show on PBS: "A Serious Look at Time Travel in the Twentieth Century." She thought "Back to the Future and Back" might be a good title. Gertrude had pointed out that "Future to the Past and Back" would be more accurate, but it just didn't have the same ring.

Myrtle always did have a vivid imagination, and a long-suppressed sense of adventure. True adventure. Not their yearly sojourn to the Caribbean to admire young, hard-bodied, olive-skinned men, and seduce old, beer-bellied, white ones; or going on a cruise; or taking an airboat ride.

Again, unlike her big sister, Myrtle had often considered finding a man and settling down. Like her sister, on the other hand, she had concluded that men sucked.

They spoke of it often.

Is it us? Why is it they grate on us? We love them ... except we hate them. If only they weren't such bastards!

But they saw other women who seemed to truly like their men. They were everywhere! At the mall, at the beach, at the grocery store. Everywhere! *Are they faking it?*

They couldn't help but ask: *Is it us?*

When these feelings occasionally bubbled forth – not often, usually following a sappy tear jerker or when the library cleaning lady celebrated *another* fabulous anniversary – the sisters would drink too much, hug and cry, then sing old melodies and proclaim to the world: *Men? We don' need no stinkin' men!*

But then, it would be nice to have one.

One hundred years earlier

His morning swim was a constant of Charlie's life. Rarely had a day passed that he did not take the time to peel off his peg leg and enjoy the healing effects of Mother Ocean. He adored her, having been brought up by his father, who had instilled in him an abiding love and respect, instructing him in her many secrets and passions.

"Ahhh," he would say. "She's a fickle lover ta be sure, but a more passionate one you'll never know."

"Of course," Charlie snickered. "Pa never met Molly Blue."

He wondered what his father, the consummate man of the sea, would say about him marrying an ex-madam. He was certain, on the other hand, what his mother would say.

He snickered as he hopped up the beach to where he had left "Ole Peg." Floppy ran up and dropped a dog-spit laden stick, then sat down and panted happily.

"Good girl," he said, and, taking the stick, he flung it into the sea.

After drying off, he strapped on his leg and pulled on his mid-calf trousers. Then, using the driftwood staff, he struggled to his feet.

He went in and got Molly's coffee started. A little while later he tip-toed into the bedroom and sat in bed next to her.

She rolled over.

"Mornin', sunshine." Charlie kissed her on the forehead.

"Hi there, lover boy," she said, rubbing her eyes. She scooted up a little then reached over for the cup of coffee. "Mmmm," she said. "You're a master coffee maker, Charlie MacLeod."

"Only because you inspire me, m'darlin'."

She smiled. "Oh! I am so excited about the wedding!"

"As am I, m'darlin'."

A minute later, he said, "I think I'll sail over to see Gnarles and Paddy this morning?"

"As long as you get back in time to get ready for the wedding."

"Not a problem, lass," Charlie replied. "I won't be gone long."

One hundred years later

"This stupid thing won't work!"

"Did you charge the battery?"

"Yes, I charged the battery! The screws are too rusty!"

Gertrude sighed. "I'm already hot. Do we have to do this?"

They were standing at the back corner of their yard, dressed in clothes from the turn of the century, two suitcases, two travel bags, and two purses.

"Yes! If we don't, we may never know!"

"Right," Gertrude grumbled. "Then let me try. You're such a weakling." Taking the screw gun from her sister, she said, "You see? You have to put some muscle into it. It's not magic. You … gotta … push!"

Whizzz!

"See?! All it takes is a little effort."

Myrtle stood by and watched. She checked her nails.

"Well, hurry up then!" she said. "We gotta be out of here before Studley McSurfbum comes out for his morning dip."

"Just hold on," Gertrude replied, squinting at the next screw. *Whizzzz!* "What do you think? Two boards?"

Eyes went to Gertrude's chest.

"Better make it three."

"Make it four."

A few minutes later, they were through and making their way across the yard, eyes peeled, hoping the old lady wasn't looking out the back window. They stopped halfway across and hid behind the mango tree. They peered around either side of the trunk.

"Okay," Gertrude said. "Keep low."

"Right!"

Gertrude sprinted – suitcase, travel bag, purse; Myrtle was right behind.

Myrtle stopped short at the wall of weeds.

"So, this is the Magic Bean Patch."

"Get in here!"

Once within the confines, they looked around.

"These aren't bad-looking plants, actually."

Gertrude felt a leaf.

"Yes, you're right. Smells like something –"

"Hmm," Myrtle replied. "Kind of looks familiar, too."

"All right," Gertrude said. "Let's do this right. I don't want to spend all day out here. We'll give it a couple of tries."

"Oh, more than a couple."

194

"What do you mean?"

"What do you mean, what do I mean? I mean, we need to try every position possible."

"Right. That's backwards and frontwards."

"No. There's sideways left and sideways right; and backwards stooping, frontwards stooping; and frontwards sidling, backwards sidling; you on left –"

"All right!" Gertrude snipped. "We'll try it … ten ways."

"Twelve."

"Fine."

The women gazed down the center row.

It looked a lot deeper than it did from the outside.

"Some kind of optical illusion," Gertrude mumbled.

"Yeah," Myrtle agreed. "A damned good one."

"And what in the world is that?" Gertrude said, squinting.

"Looks like some kind of … white light."

"Right," Gertrude said, her voice cracking. "A white light, just like the boys said."

Myrtle's eyes were wide, peering over her sister's shoulder.

"Yeah, a white light … I think I've changed my mind."

Gertrude grabbed her by the collar.

"Not a chance, sissy!"

"I'm not a sissy," Myrtle mumbled, staring at the strange sight.

"All right," Gertrude stated. "We hold hands and walk backwards, together."

Myrtle looked at her sister.

"You're kidding. You really want to do this?!"

"It was your idea!"

"Yeah, but what if it's not a time machine at all, but a portal to hell?!"

"So you get there a few years ahead of time. It's an eternity! You won't even notice after a couple of epochs."

"You don't think it's going to work, do you?" Myrtle said.

"No."

Myrtle glared at her sister, then putting her purse over one shoulder, her traveling bag over the other, and taking the handle of her suitcase, she turned, took her sister's hand, and said, "Whenever you're ready, sis."

Slowly they went, hands clasped tightly, one step at a time they backed in. They heard what sounded like distant thunder and the wind began to swirl around them, like they were in a tornado but with no sound. Then they were blinded by an all-consuming light and suddenly found themselves standing in the piney scrub – naked as a pair of Florida jaybirds.

No suitcase; no travel bag; no purse.

No Off.

"Ouch!"

Smack!

"Holy crap!"

"Holy crap!"

The girls gazed in awe, stubby spruce and scrub oak all around, the sound of two mourning doves calling to each other. Otherwise, it was quiet.

Finally, Gertrude spoke. "This is the same exact spot, a hundred years ago."

A more subdued, "Holy crap."

"And look," Gertrude pointed. "It's their still."

"Holy crap!"

Gertrude looked at her sister, standing naked in a clearing in the woods next to a still, and said, "Can you say something else?"

"I think I want to go home now."

"Look," Gertrude said. "What's the worst that can happen? We get stuck back in time?"

"STUCK BACK IN TIME?!!!"

Myrtle was about to lose it, so Gertrude grabbed her by the shoulders and shook.

"Look, sis, this was your idea! Now, what we're gonna do is make the best of it. Understand? The first thing we'll do is find the other Magic Patch. It's got to be around here somewhere. Then we'll take a look around."

Myrtle stared at the woods surrounding them.

"Maybe we should just go back now."

"Not a chance," Gertrude said, striding forward. "The first thing we'll do is find their house and get something to wear."

Myrtle followed behind, keeping her eyes peeled for bears, panthers, or rattlesnakes.

"I can't believe those two didn't mention the naked thing. I wouldn't have come."

*   *   *

Charlie and Salty sat in their little boat, *Dolly Varden*, across the lake, watching, until Gnarles and Paddy had loaded their pub equipment into *Cocoa-Nuts* and headed up to the hotel. When the coast was clear, Charlie set sail.

He not only felt concern for his friends; a gnawing curiosity had taken hold.

He knew the trail well. He was no stranger to their place, having gone there often for a night of unfettered male fun and frivolity. It was a unique relationship between him and the old sots. During his years of living the life of a hermit, he had not allowed anyone near him, physically, emotionally, or socially; anyone, that is, except for Gnarles and Paddy. With them, it had been different. There was no ulterior motive, no desire to improve him or his situation. All they ever wanted was to visit, knock back a few, and talk about nothing.

Now, he felt an obligation to make sure they were all right – and satisfy an underlying need to ascertain that Bonnie was not in any danger.

It was a relatively straight trail, at one with nature's design, nearly invisible except for the well-worn earth beneath one's feet.

The tiny, two-room house wasn't far; it was close enough to the coast for an ocean breeze. Much of the jungle here had been cleared by order of young Callie Harper during her short but welcome stay. Since she had married and moved away, it was becoming overgrown again.

As Charlie passed the house, he stopped short and cocked his ear.

"Hmph," he mumbled, shaking his head, "What's next?" and he tottered on down the trail.

*   *   *

Inside the cabin, Gertrude was holding her hand over Myrtle's mouth.

"Shut ... up!"

Myrtle pushed the hand away.

"But it's Charlie MacLeod!" she whispered. "And Salty!!"

"I know, all right?! But we can't let anyone know we're here!!"

Myrtle could barely contain herself.

"I can't believe it! Charlie MacLeod!" she cried. "The Old Sage! Look!" she exclaimed, pointing at the old man teetering down the trail. "And the old Son of a Sea Dog himself, Salty!!!" She clasped her hands to her chest and fell back on the bed.

"I wouldn't sit there," Gertrude said.

Myrtle looked around and sprang to her feet.

"They need a maid service."

"Look in here," Gertrude said. "Clean clothes."

"We have to wear those?"

"Unless you got a fig leaf."

The women started going through the clothes. They were all the same: trousers and shirts for a short fat man and a short skinny one. Myrtle's fit pretty well; Gertrude's, well –

"You look ridiculous."

Gertrude studied herself in the mirror.

"Yes. I suppose I do. Oh, good!" she remarked. "Clean socks!"

"Thank God," Myrtle replied, glancing at the two pairs of shoes by the door. "So," she said, growing excited at the prospects. "What's the plan?" She rubbed her hands together.

"Well, the first thing is to avoid people."

"I really don't see why."

"We've discussed this. Did you or did you not see *Back to the Future*?"

"It's only a movie."

"Yes, but as you know, the main tenet of any time travel movie, or book, is that you cannot change things in the past. It can lead to a whole different future."

"That hasn't been proven."

Gertrude rolled her eyes.

"I know. That's because no one's ever gone to the past."

"As far as we know."

"Right."

"Right."

"Anyway," Gertrude sighed. "Let's try not to mingle, at least not yet."

Myrtle rolled her shoulders.

"Whatever."

"Now," Gertrude said. "According to the boys, everyone will be up at the church from about two until four, then they'll head down to the hotel, which, if I remember correctly, should be five or six blocks north of here."

"There are no blocks yet."

"I know. Anyway," Gertrude sighed, "I cannot *wait* to see the hotel. And Betsy Dawson's house. Oh, my God!" she exclaimed. "I can't believe this is happening! Are we dreaming all this?!"

"At this point? I have no idea."

Gertrude was giggling like a schoolgirl.

"I cannot believe it! We might actually be able to see all the people we've been reading about all these years!"

Myrtle checked the mirror and tucked in her shirt.

Then she gazed out the window and said dreamily, "What I want is a gander at that big hunk of a man, Booker T. Hooker."

* * *

The trail abruptly changed several hundred feet back from the lake, from hammock jungle to pine scrub. Almost instantly, it transformed from rich, loamy soil to sugar sand – white and hot, unceasingly reflecting the sun's broiling, blinding rays. The dominant but sparse Florida spruce and scrub oak that grew here provided little in the way of shade. Otherwise, it was saw palmetto, Spanish bayonets, and prickly pear cactus.

Not all that inviting.

Charlie fully expected to find a big clump of weeds in the old garden, nothing else. He was, however, stunned.

A patch of tall, green plants was laid out in perfect rows – just like they had said, and it appeared as if they might be flowering soon by the purple-reddish hue at the ends of the branches.

"What do you think about that, Salt?"

Salty made a gurgling sound.

"You don't like this Magic Bean Patch, do ya, buddy?"

Salty hunkered down.

Charlie walked around to the end and peered down the middle.

"Well, I'll be!"

He stared a long while at the faint, almost indiscernible, white light at the end. He squeezed his eyes shut several times, then tried one eye at a time.

"I don't believe it," he mumbled.

Standing back, he took a deep breath and looked around.

"What do you think, old buddy? Shall we give 'er a try?"

*   *   *

KAAAAAPHLUMP!!!OOOOF!!!AARRAAAAAAAAK!!!SONOFA ...

Mrs. Scapolli called out, "Be right there, boys!"

When she came around the corner, she looked shocked.

"Charlie MacLeod?!"

"Yes, ma'am," Charlie replied from a crumpled position next to a big white, cold box made of metal. It hummed; he wondered what it was. He was missing Ole Peg, still back in the Magic Bean Patch. He squirmed into a better position and, casually covering up with one hand, said, "Mrs. Scapolli, I presume?"

"Are you all right, young man?"

"I think so."

"I'll be right back," she said, and she hurried off.

Charlie heard some banging, then some voices, then running footsteps.

Jeff barreled around the corner.

"Whoa! Dude!! It's Charlie Freaking MacLeod!! AND SALTY!!!"

Charlie extended his hand.

"You must be Jeffrey – a truly righteous dude."

"Damned straight!" Jeff replied, grasping Charlie's hand and cocking it into the "Right-on" position. "One righteous dude to another! And SALTY!" he howled. "Son of a Freaking Sea Dog! This totally freaking rocks!!"

Mrs. Scapolli came around the corner holding a robe.

"Don't say that, Jeffie," she said. "Now bring a chair for Mr. MacLeod, then go get those old crutches out of the garage."

A few minutes later, Charlie was resting in the La-Z-Boy, staring at *The Young and Restless*. It was almost too much to absorb: Nicky was drinking again, and Jack was about to lose Jabot to The Black Knight, Victor Newman – again.

"Let me turn that off," Mrs. Scapolli said. "It can be distracting." Charlie watched with fascination as she picked up a tiny black box and pushed a button. The "thing" went dark.

"What *is* that?" he asked, as if in a daze.

"Oh, that's the TV. If you stick around, you'll get addicted to it."

Charlie tried to focus. The old lady and the kid were staring at him, waiting for him to speak. His eyes were taking in everything, but his brain was processing almost none of it.

How can this be?!

Mrs. Scapolli went into the kitchen and came back with a cracker.

"Salty want a cracker? Can I hold him?" she asked.

"Sure."

They waited.

"So," Charlie finally said. "This is August 18, 1990?"

"Yes."

"And we're in Port Starboard."

"Uh-huh."

"On Lake Worth."

"Right."

"And Gnarles and Paddy come here on weekends."

"That's right, dude! Those guys rock!!"

"Right. Rock. And in your backyard there's a Magic Bean Patch?"

"Uh-huh."

"And they just come and go as they please."

"Oh, yes," Mrs. Scapolli said. "They land right here in my kitchen every Saturday. That's why I thought you were them, except they usually don't show up until late afternoon. But," she added, "they said they might be a little late tonight because of the wedding. Oh!" she exclaimed. "Is that why you're here? To help save Bonnie?"

Charlie had a sinking feeling in his gut.

"Yes,' he replied. "That's why I'm here."

One hundred years earlier

"Oh, my God!"

"Holy crap!"

The girls had made it to the end of the path. They were not really paying attention when a shimmer of light caught their eyes. It was the sparkle of rippling water.

"It's freaking ... magnificent!" Gertrude exclaimed. She ran up to the small white sand beach and took in the view. It was a swimming hole: wet, hard-packed loam bordering a sandy crescent and enveloped within the draping folds of several ancient oak trees. Though hidden from view, they could clearly see beyond the curtain of greenery.

A sailboat was pulling up to the far shore.

Neither woman could contain herself. Both gazed and sighed, holding hands to their chests.

"It's ... beautiful!"

"Like a painting, but ... better!"

"Much better," Myrtle replied. "And look!" she said. "It's Singer Island; not one condo and only one house."

The women stood in awe.

"I can't believe it," Gertrude said. "And we think it's beautiful now? I mean, in the future?"

"No comparison," Myrtle snorted. "All of a sudden, *our* Lake Worth looks kind of crappy."

"Yeah. Real crappy," Gertrude stated. "Look how blue the water is. And LOOK! Oh, my gosh! Dolphins!"

They froze. Someone was speaking. Before they could react, a small boat sailed nearby, not more than a hundred feet out. The women watched with fascination. A little girl at the tiller was speaking to a raccoon.

"Wow," Myrtle said as they passed out of sight. "I wonder if she knows how good she has it, living here in this ... paradise. A REAL paradise," she added.

"That's not just any little girl," Gertrude stated. "That's got to be Annie Humphrey."

"Of course!" Myrtle exclaimed. "The one with the raccoon!"

"That would be Copernicus."

"Right. The former mayor – Annie, I mean."

"Imagine," Myrtle said. "She has no idea she's going to grow up to become a doctor and later on the first woman mayor of Port Starboard. The first woman mayor in the state! Wow," she said, growing suddenly somber. "I can't believe this is really happening. Are we dreaming?" Myrtle shook her head. "I just wish I had my recorder, better yet, a camcorder. Oh, this is going to make us rich, big sister. We have to write a book about all this. We'll blow Tim Robinson right out of the water! In fact, when we get back, we have to write everything down, right away!"

"I'll leave that to you, sis," Gertrude replied. She looked north, then south, then up. "The Lake Trail," she sighed, staring at the hammock canopy towering over them. "Come on," she said, and they started up the trail.

A few minutes later: "Oh, my God! It looks just like the book cover!"

The sisters were standing inside the edge of the hammock along the Lake Trail, gazing at Betsy's house. Through some palm trees beyond was the hotel.

"This is even better than I imagined!"

"I know," Myrtle replied. "Look!" she pointed. "I think I can see the schoolhouse! Way up there!"

Gertrude squinted. "It's red. That's got to be it. There's Booker T. Point on the other side of the creek. See? A picnic table in the cocoanut trees?"

Never had the sisters been so excited, not even when Frank Sinatra blew them a kiss – along with several thousand other women.

They stared a while, then Myrtle said, "So, what do we do now?"

"I don't know. I wish I knew what time it is."

"I think I can tell by the sun," Myrtle said. "Let's see." She held up her hand and looked at the shadow on the ground. "I think it's somewhere around ten … or eleven. Definitely between nine and twelve … do they have daylight savings time?"

Gertrude rolled her eyes, folded her arms, and sighed again, taking it all in, figuring out what to do next.

"Well," she said. "The wedding is at three, so everyone will be making their way up there by two at the latest. That gives us a couple of hours or so. "Oh, my God!" she exclaimed, pointing. "It's her! Betsy Dawson!"

A statuesque woman with red hair walked out on the front porch of the hotel. She was yelling at someone.

"And look! It's the boys!"

Myrtle raised her hand and started to call out.

"Shhhh!" Gertrude yanked it down. "We don't want them to know we're here! Do we?"

"I don't know. I haven't really thought about it."

They watched as Gnarles and Paddy got up from their relaxed positions down by the dock and walked around back of the hotel.

"Now's our chance," Myrtle said. She started forward, but Gertrude yanked her back.

"No! We're simply here as observers. We have to follow protocol; no mingling with the natives."

"But we already know them."

"I know, but I just don't think it's a good idea. You saw *Back to the Future*. There's no telling what might happen."

"But, isn't that what the boys are doing, trying to change the future by rescuing Bonnie?"

"Yes, but that doesn't mean we have to add to it. We'll just stay right here and observe. Come on," she said, slipping down by the water and sitting on a low-lying branch. She took her too-small shoes off and dipped her toes in the water. "I can't believe we're here," she said, staring off towards Munyon Island. "That's called Pitt's Island now."

"Mm-hmm. And look at that. No Australian pines."

"I do love the Australian pines."

"Yeah. Me, too."

One hundred years later

"This book is amazing!"

"Oh!" Mrs. Scapolli remarked. "We haven't been able to put it down!"

"This fella, Tim Robinson, put a lot of work into this thing."

Charlie couldn't stop turning pages. *Hey, I know him!; So, Flagler really is extending the railroad! A new inlet? Way down there?! Hey, how did he know that? Uh-oh, wait a minute.*

"Well," Charlie said, shaking his head. "I suppose the guy can't get everything right. It is a hundred years ago, for Pete's sake."

Even under such disconcerting circumstances, Charlie was having fun.

He was sitting at the table, a large compendium open in front of him. When they first showed him the book, he had gone straight to *Geoffreys, Bonnie Blakely*. His first inclination was that of a skeptic, so he had started checking facts, one after the other, flipping from the P's to the B's to the H's to the K's. On and on he had poured over the words, but always he returned to the G's, for Geoffreys, to the words that proclaimed a horrifying reality for someone he held dear.

It must be true, he told himself. Within the biography were quotes from newspapers of the day and various legal documents. It appeared indisputable.

He was at once enraged and horrified, all the while wondering if this was some sort of crazy dream. His mind reeled: would Bonnie's yet-to-be-born child actually grow up to become a serial killer?

It was an unfamiliar term. It scared him, witnessing this sad, disturbing future.

He needed time to think, but there was none. As one side of his brain checked facts and reminisced about people who were still alive in another time, the other continued to grapple with the larger question: *What the hell do I do?*

Never had he been so ill equipped to deal with a crisis. All his life it had come easy: the tighter the situation, the more he and Salty liked it. This was different, however. It wasn't about him this time. This time he might very well be deciding someone else's fate.

Not only that: in addition to the stress of coming to grips with time travel, he was realizing there are things better left unknown.

He had been barreling ahead, reading short biographies of people he knew, adding his own commentary, when it hit him like a ton of bricks. He had just turned to *Hackensaw, Dr. Sally MacLeod*, and off the page leapt her date of birth – and death. His little girl. Dead. He knew both when and how. It was emblazoned in his brain.

He crumbled inside.

He slammed the book shut and pushed it away, staring at it as if it were evil incarnate. His entire body trembled.

Mrs. Scapolli put her hand on his broad shoulder.

"Are you all right, Charlie?"

"Yeah, dude. Are you okay?"

Charlie stared at his hands, then choked, "I … there's just too many things in there I don't need to know. Things I got no business knowin'."

"I understand," Mrs. Scapolli said. "More Gatorade?" And she went into the kitchen.

"So," Jeff laughed nervously. "It must be tough goin' into the future, all this new stuff. That's why you won't see me goin' into the past. It's way too freaky, dude. Like, what if I got stuck there? I don't know what I'd do, dude. Gnarles and Paddy say you don't even have surfboards. Is that true?"

"Surfboards?" Charlie tried to imagine what a surfboard might be. "You mean, for riding the waves?"

"Yeah, dude! For shreddin' 'em and tearin' 'em to tiny, pulverized pieces, dude!"

"No," Charlie said, thinking how Jeff's passion reminded him of his dear old friend, Little Ricky. "We don't have surfboards, but I can see how that would be a good idea. I've had to surf boats over sandbars into inlets before, but only as a last resort." He laughed. "We hate doin' it, but afterwards we're always –"

"Stoked!! Right, dude?!!"

"Yes," Charlie said reflectively. "Stoked. Good word."

"Damned straight!"

"Watch your mouth, Jeffie."

"Sorry."

"You know," Charlie said. "I can see how much fun it would be to surf the waves on a board."

"It's freakin' gnarley, dude! Rippin' the curl!! Shootin' the barrel!!" Jeff's eyes grew wide, and he dashed out to the garage.

"Oh, don't bring that in here!" Grandma yelled, but he was back in a flash, holding his pride and joy.

"Ain't she totally hot?" he said, caressing it.

Charlie stared at the strange object a moment, and said, "I gotta tell ya, that ain't exactly what I expected when you said surf *board*. But by jolly it is a pretty thing."

"Yeah," Jeff stated with pride. Me and this baby, we totally freaking shred the waves! The guys down at the beach call me Shredder, you know."

"Shredder," Charlie repeated. "Nice moniker."

"Whoa!" Jeff exclaimed. "And you've surfed sailboats?! That freakin' rocks!!"

"Well," Charlie replied. "It's not somethin' we set out ta do, but sometimes it's best ta run for shelter and hope ya don't get clobbered in the process."

"Righteous, dude."

Jeff stared at the old man, as if trying to imagine him young.

Mrs. Scapolli set a glass in front of Charlie and, resting her hand on his shoulder, said, "I can only imagine what it's like to go into the future. Everything must be so different and scary."

Charlie nodded. "That's for sure, eh, Salty?"

Salty grumbled something.

"But the future's not for us, is it old bird?" he said, standing up. "So me and Salty here best get goin'." He glanced at the clock. "We got a weddin' ta stop, ya know."

"Oh," Mrs. Scapolli sighed, "I wish you could stay longer. I'd love to hear more stories about the old days. I wish I had the nerve to go back in time. Oh, I would simply love to see Bonnie in her wedding gown. From what the boys say, she's the most beautiful woman on earth!"

Charlie chuckled. "She is somethin' ta see, especially for an old salt like me, but I tell ya that girl's got a heart ta match." He frowned. "I can't believe this son of a sea slug, how he's been able to pull the wool over everyone's eyes. Even Salty!" He looked down at the little green bird sitting on Mrs. Scapolli's finger. "Hey!" he said. "You're supposed to warn me about such folks."

Salty shrugged.

"I so wish you could stay longer," Mrs. Scapolli said. "I just love hearing stories from the old days. You know, our next door neighbor grew up around here, and I imagine he must have been born before the turn of the century. Jeffrey?" she said. "How old do you think he is?"

Jeff shrugged. "About a thousand?"

"Oh, don't be silly. Let's see," she pondered. "Doc Potter must be close to one hundred now."

Charlie looked up.

"Doc Potter, you say?"

He had to meet him

Dr. Potter was old. He was in fact the oldest person Charlie had ever known. It took several minutes for him to make it in the door, another few to get him situated in a chair at the table. Mrs. Scapolli set his walker next to him.

"There you go, Frank."

"What?"

"THERE YOU GO!"

"Thanks."

Mrs. Scapolli made introductions.

"Anything you want, Frank?" she said loudly.

"That looks mighty fine," he said, eyeing Charlie's Gatorade. He was small and hunched over, but Charlie liked the way he looked at him. His eyes remained bright and piercing.

"So, Doc," Charlie said. "You related to the Doc Potter who lived with his brother George down at Figilus back in the 1800s?"

"Yep," Doc drawled. "George is my father and Doc's my uncle."

Charlie was riveted. Here, sitting in front of him was a living connection to the past.

"When were you born?" he asked.

"Long before you came along, sonny," he replied. "I was born in 1889."

"I remember!" Charlie exclaimed. "Ella May had a baby last year!"

Doc Potter scrutinized the one-legged man in a pink bathrobe with a parrot on his shoulder.

"I mean," Charlie said. "I read it in that book there."

Doc Potter looked at the thick book and shook his head.

"Drivel," he grouched. "Hardly says a word about Mama."

"Well," Mrs. Scapolli said. "It looks like the man was running out of room as it is. That book could be classified as a deadly weapon, you know."

Doc shot her a look and was about to respond when Charlie said, "So, you must remember the Port Starboard Strangler."

"Sure. Knew him all his life." He shook his head. "We couldn't believe it was Malcolm Jr. that did it, but considering his upbringing people came to believe it after all."

"What do you mean?"

"We never knew for sure, the rest of us, but we always thought that kid was tortured. If not physically, mentally and emotionally. That bastard father of his was some kind of sicko himself. His wife disappeared way back – I was still a kid – everyone said he murdered her and tossed her remains in a gator hole up Booker T. Creek. You know, that creek used to have several tributaries that went way out into the sawgrass." The old man looked off in the distance. "Yep, I remember when you could walk over that ridge there and see nothing but sawgrass and cypress slough for miles. This was long before they put in all these ditches and canals. There was nary a road beyond the Dixie Highway. Anyway, he never let Malcolm come with us when we went off fishing or hunting – made him stay at home." He lowered his voice. "In fact, folks used to say he was sexually abused by his father and tortured in all sorts of ungodly ways. I remember he came to school several times with red marks on his arms and neck, but nobody did anything." He snickered. "I remember that lying bastard, his dad. My father didn't like him one bit. Said he had a tongue as smooth as silk; said he could talk his way out of a nest of rattlesnakes if he had to."

Charlie's Scottish blood boiled.

One hundred years earlier

"I'm hungry."

"Me, too."

Tantalizing odors wafted from Betsy's house and the Port Starboard Hotel. Both kitchens were going full steam. A young black girl, in her twenties, was scurrying back and forth between the houses.

"I wonder who that is."

"Oh, I wish we had the book with us."

"I bet it's Callie Harper," Gertrude said. "Remember? She married Maggie's son, Isaac – I think that's his name. Maybe it's Isaiah. Oh, I wish I had studied up more."

"I'm starving," Myrtle groaned, holding her stomach.

"Me, too."

A few minutes later, Myrtle said. "Next time Carrie –"

"Callie."

"– goes over to the hotel, I'm gonna sneak in and get something."

"No, you're not."

"I have to! I smell pumpkin pie! Pumpkin pie, Gert!!"

"I know," Gertrude sighed. She studied the house, her own stomach grumbling. "And we haven't seen anyone else go in or out. Only Callie."

"Right."

"We can't be ruining any dishes."

"Not at all."

"We might not get exactly what we want."

"Whatever we can find."

"Just a few bites."

"Right."

Gertrude took a deep breath.

"Okay, we'll go in the back door. Cautiously. No big hurry."

"Except we don't want to get caught."

"Right."

"So, we need to hurry."

The women scurried along the edge of the hammock, in and out between the bordering trees, then dashed across the open space to the rear of the chicken coop.

"Something stinks."

"Oh, it's disgusting! Come on!" Gertrude took off for the house.

"You look ridiculous running in those clothes."

"So do you."

They hid under a window next to the chimney and scanned the area. Gertrude pointed to the back, then, stooping, ran along the house. She peered around the corner. Across the way was the pig sty and directly behind the hotel beyond was a sandy path leading to another building.

"Okay," Gertrude said. "The coast is clear." She giggled. "I've always wanted to say that."

"I've always wanted to say, 'I'm full.'"

Looking around one last time, Gertrude said, "Let's go!"

Eyes peeled, they ran around a bougainvillea bush and over to the porch steps. The wide porch extended the full length of the house, and on the far end was an open window with four pies sitting on the sill. A blue, checkered curtain fluttered in the breeze.

They froze.

Finally, Myrtle spoke.

"It's freaking Mayberry!" She bolted, but Gertrude grabbed her by the collar. "What do you think you're doing?"

"I can carry two; you can carry two."

Gertrude yanked her back.

"No!"

"All right, I'll take one, you take one. I'm taking the pumpkin."

Gertrude yanked again.

"One is enough!" she said. "Now lower your voice!" She looked around. "Oh! Hi there."

"Who are you?"

Gertrude and Myrtle looked at each other.

The sandy-haired boy stared.

Myrtle finally spoke.

"We're the … Pie Fairies."

Gertrude glared at her sister, then, seeing no other option, she added, "Yes. We take sample pies to the, uh –"

"Great Pie-man in the sky," Myrtle offered.

He stared a moment more.

"Then how come you're wearing Gnarles and Paddy's clothes?"

"What makes you think these are Gnarles and Paddy's?"

"Because I thought you were them."

"Oh," Gertrude said. "That's because we're also the, uh –"

"Old Clothes Fairies," Myrtle interjected. "We pick up old ones and leave new ones." She looked at her sister and shrugged.

The boy studied the women.

Finally, he said, "I find that very difficult to believe."

The women almost laughed.

"If you're really hungry," he said, "Mrs. Dawson won't mind."

"Really?" Myrtle said.

"Uh-uh," the boy, who couldn't have been more than seven or eight, replied. "If you shared."

A few minutes later, they were all sitting on the back-porch steps, forks in hand, eating pie right out of the pan.

"So," Gertrude queried. "What's your name?"

"Benji," he replied, swallowing a big mouthful. "Benji Humphrey."

"Benji Humphrey," Gertrude repeated. "You must be Alfred and Katie's kid."

"You know them?" he asked. "Because I've never seen you two around before, and I know everyone in Port Starboard."

"Oh, we don't really know them – we haven't been introduced – but we know about them."

"How?"

"We told you," Myrtle said. "We're fairies. We know everything."

"Suuuure," he said. "Anyway, I'm too old to believe in fairies."

"Well," Gertrude replied. "Just because you don't believe in us, doesn't mean we don't exist."

"You sound like my pa." He reached over with one of three forks he had retrieved from the kitchen and scooped up another bite. "He says there's a lot we don't know, and just because we don't know it doesn't mean it isn't real."

"So," Myrtle said. "Aren't you afraid you'll get in trouble if someone finds out a pie is missing?"

"Not really," he said. "Miss Callie won't tell. We've been eating all morning. She said that since it's Bonnie's big day, we all get to eat all we want."

"Sounds like solid logic to me," Gertrude stated.

"Me, too," Myrtle said, taking another bite. "Mm-mmm, this has to be the best pie I've ever eaten."

"Mmmm. Me, too," Gertrude agreed.

"Benji!" Someone called.

"Oops," he said. "I gotta go." He sprang to his feet and grabbed another pie off the window sill. "Mrs. Hooker sent me over for one of these," he said. "She's celebrating, too."

"Oh, by the way," Gertrude said as he darted around the corner. "You don't have to mention you saw us. It's a surprise."

"I know!" he yelled back. "For Gnarles and Paddy!"

Chapter Thirty-One

"Ouch! Dammit!" Betsy glanced across the hotel kitchen. Benji stared at her. "Excuse my French," she said. Then they both giggled.

Betsy was Benji's bawdy aunt – bawdy *old* aunt was how his father put it. Betsy told Benji his father was full of hooey.

Benji was sitting at the table, licking a bowl of icing. It was turned upward, his head completely inside – like he was wearing a helmet on his face.

"I think you missed a spot," Betsy said. She was standing over the sink, scrubbing something.

"Thanmph yumph."

Callie walked in the door.

"Oh, my Lord, that breeze feels good out front!"

Benji pulled the bowl from his face and their eyes locked.

She mouthed the words, "You ate a whole pie?"

He shrugged. They giggled.

"What are you two laughing about over there?" Betsy asked.

"Nothing."

Pretty Callie Hooker was Maggie and Booker's daughter-in-law. They were only here for the wedding as Isaiah was still attending the State Normal College for Colored Students in Tallahassee. She, like most every female in Port Starboard, was madly in love with one Benji Humphrey.

He couldn't walk out of a room without a female voice saying something pertaining to cute: cute as a button; cute as a cupcake; cute as a bug's ear. Every female, that was, except his sister, Annie. She thought he was a big pain in the *derrière,* as Christiane Dawson, the sultry French maiden, might put it.

"Oooo-wee!" Christiane exclaimed as she walked in. "It is a nice breeze out front. No?"

"Yes."

"So," she said, sitting down at the table with a basket of freshly snapped beans. "What is next?"

"Well," Betsy said. "Maggie should be back in a little while with some more sweet potatoes. Booker T. was out pulling them, so until then," she paused and peeked in the oven, "I suppose we can take a little break."

"Oh, Hallelujah!" Callie said. "I have got to get out of this kitchen."

As if on cue the three women lifted their aprons, searched out a clean spot on the backside, and dabbed their foreheads. As they headed out to the front porch, Betsy said, "How's Bonnie doing out there?"

"Going crazy."

* * *

Bonnie was sitting on the front porch – by appearances, perfectly calm.

Betsy and Maggie had insisted that she not help in the kitchen today, so she had been banished to the front porch. She wasn't lacking for company. People had been coming and going, preparing for her big day. They all had a snappy comment or two, most centering on how beautiful she was, even though she hadn't yet begun "the process." She didn't want to start too soon. She wanted to time things so she'd be slipping into her dress just before they headed up to the church.

Eddie would be transporting her there, and the Count Contraire, Christiane's father, would be bringing her back. There had been some to-do over who would be performing the all-important task of transporting the bride, the Count insisting that it should be he, since his vessel, the magnificent *Au Revoir*, was the finest vessel on the lake and thus deserved to be utilized for the much-heralded event.

Eddie had been incensed; but it was his father-in-law. He was sitting with Bonnie, munching on a carrot.

"That man is a big pain in the neck."

"Oh, you love him," Bonnie replied.

"Sure, I do." He rolled his eyes. "Like I love palmetto bugs, or red bugs, or being interim postmaster. I swear, I have never experienced such boredom! It was like being in prison. By the very minute, every shred of life was being sucked from my marrow! Unload boxes, stack shelves, write it down. Sort mail, hand it out, write it down. Sweep the floor."

"Why, Eddie," a voice declared. "I had no idea."

"Oh! Maggie! I, uh, didn't see you there."

"I know."

She was standing at the entrance to the trail leading through the orange grove, hands on hips, a grin etched on her round, cheery face.

"I'm sorry," he said. "I didn't really mean it. I'm just griping is all."

She strolled over, as if allowing him a moment to stew in his own juices, and slowly ascended the porch steps. Then she reached out and pinched an already red, embarrassed cheek.

"It's all right, Eddie," she said. "I'm sorry I left you holding the bag, and because of that I'm going to give you free food for life!"

"Thanks, Maggie," he replied, looking relieved she wasn't mad at him. Then he cocked his head. "Wait a minute. I've always had free food – all my life!"

Eddie turned red while Maggie and Bonnie giggled.

The screen door opened, and three more women emerged, all of them emitting the same, satisfied *Ahhhhhhhhh!*

They scattered to their regular places.

Lots of wedding talk.

Sporadic torturing of Eddie.

Grins and giggles.

Only one topic off limits: time travel.

Under-the-breath mumblings about said topic.

Betsy glared at the offenders.

Bonnie knew about the "time travel" issue, of course. It hadn't taken long for that to get out, but Gnarles and Paddy had remained curiously mum on the subject of her own future, saying that the Old Sage would handle everything, whatever that meant.

The time travelers had just returned from the church, where they had been delivering flowers from Mrs. Oxar's garden to the decorating committee and picking up a kettle from Sally. A call had gone out for one. Apparently, three wasn't enough.

They finished tying off *Cocoa-Nuts* and headed up the dock, hefting a large cast-iron pot between them.

Betsy scowled, her mind obviously working feverishly.

Their feet hadn't hit the steps when she said, "Oh, thank you, boys! Now, would you mind going over to Uncle Charlie's and check on them? See if there's anything they need."

"Do you think we can put this away first?"

Everyone stared with blank faces at Gnarles's new, more assertive attitude.

Christiane held the door while the two men passed.

When they were gone, muffled laughter, sideways looks, then Callie said, "And all this started a few weeks ago?"

Betsy bristled.

"That's right," Bonnie said. "Oh, you should hear some of the things they've come up with, like –"

"Blows my mind?" Maggie suggested.

"Yes," Callie agreed. "Or how about 'Rock on?'"

"Oh, there's lots with the word 'rock.'"

"Yes," Christiane added. "And sometimes they make a fist and shake it and say "Right on, dude!"

"Oh!" Bonnie exclaimed. "It's like they can't say a sentence without the word 'dude.'"

Christiane giggled. "And, oh! It was so funny when Betsy shook her fist at Gnarles, and said, "'Eef you call me dude one more time, I will use thees to knock your head so far down that you must remove your socks to see!'"

Eddie had been quiet up to now, and remained so.

Gnarles called from the kitchen, "Can we have a piece of pie?"

From her perch on the swing, Betsy motioned to Eddie, who was sitting nearest the door.

"Tell them yes, but only the one that's already started."

Eddie started to yell through the screen, then he looked around at all the smiling, female faces and abruptly stood up.

"Maybe I'll tell them in person. How much is left in there, anyway?"

Betsy sighed. "Go ahead and start another one." Then, sagging into her breezy seat, she moaned, "I hope we have at least one pie left for the reception."

Benji suddenly darted around the corner and through the door.

"Can I have some?!" He didn't wait for a response. The door slammed.

"Oooo," Bonnie giggled, "I bet that little scamp was over there listening to every word we said!"

"I don't know how he does it," Betsy sighed, "but that child is everywhere."

* * *

Four eyes observed from the cover of a cape honeysuckle bush in Betsy's front yard.

"That kid has those women wrapped around his little finger."

"He's a cutie, that's for sure."

"No doubt," Myrtle replied. "You know these people have no idea how good they've got it living here."

"In this place or this time?"

"Both."

"Well," Gertrude replied. "They have none of our conveniences, remember. Life is a lot more difficult here, especially for women. No washing machines or self-cleaning ovens – not to mention running water."

"Didn't Gnarles and Paddy say there's some houses with running water? And generators?"

"Maybe a few. Only for the wealthy at this point, I'm sure."

"Right," Myrtle said thoughtfully. "We'd need money."

Gertrude looked at her sister.

"We're not staying here."

"I know."

"In fact," Gertrude said. "We should probably head back soon."

"But I wanted to see Bonnie in her dress … and the reception! Everyone's going to be here!"

"Exactly. We don't need to get caught, especially with so many people around. Can you imagine the questions?"

"We can at least stay until Bonnie comes out in her dress."

"That could take couple of hours," Gertrude grumbled. "I'm not sitting in these bushes much longer."

They looked around. Betsy's front porch looked mighty inviting.

*   *   *

In the hotel kitchen, forks and plates were singing. There not much conversation; primarily moans and groans of ecstasy.

"Mmmmm."

"Goooood."

One at a time, forks rested.

"That was good."

"Mm-hmm."

"Bodacious, dude."

"Blows my mind, bro."

They were all leaning back in their chairs, holding their bellies.

Benji eyed Gnarles and Paddy – their clothes.

"What?" Gnarles asked, looking to see if he had dripped any mango filling.

"Oh, nothing," Benji replied. A moment later, he said, "Can you fellas keep a secret?"

"Sure!"

"Go ahead," Eddie said. "We won't say a word."

Benji lowered his voice

"Well, I was over at Aunt Betsy's, and there were two ladies over there dressed in clothes just like Mr. Gnarles and Mr. Paddy's. I even thought it was them for a minute, but it wasn't."

"Two women?" Eddie said.

"Uh-huh. And they said they were the Pie Fairies." He shook his head. "I didn't believe them, though. There's no such thing as fairies."

"Pie Fairies?!" Eddie laughed. "That's the craziest thing I've ever heard." He glanced at Gnarles and Paddy. "I think young Humph's had too much pie today. He's hallucinating."

"No, I'm not," Benji protested. "I saw them, and I ate a pumpkin pie with them and everything!"

The men were snickering, eyeing each other, when Benji added, "One of them called the other Gert."

And Gnarles and Paddy were out the door.

*   *   *

A little while later, Gertrude and Myrtle were comfortably ensconced on Betsy's front porch.

"See?" Myrtle said. "We can see everything, but no one can see us through this latticework.

"Sure, as long as no one uses the front door."

"No one's used the front door all day," Myrtle replied with confidence.

The front door opened.

Chapter Thirty-Two

1990

"Well, I grew up in the Northwood section of West Palm Beach."

"*West* Palm Beach?"

"You know," Doc Potter said. "The big city south of here?"

Charlie was confused.

"Oh. Right. West Palm Beach. And you've lived up in this neck of the woods for how long?"

"Oh, going on sixty years now. This is where Margie and I raised our family. I had several job offers over the years, but Margie held firm. We had some real spats over it at the time, but now I'm glad we stayed. This is home. This is where I belong."

"I miss Margie," Mrs. Scapolli said. "She was the salt of the earth, that woman."

"She was that," Doc replied.

"So," Charlie said, glancing at the clock. "Are there lots of folks like you around? I mean, over a hundred years old?"

"Why, yes," Doc replied. "You remind me of some of us, with your speech patterns and inflections – you have an understated innocence about you, like some of us do, left over from the era of our youth. That – or it's as if you've arrived here from a distant planet! Do you have a home near here?"

Charlie laughed.

"Yes," he said. "My home is very near here, as a matter of fact."

"Oh, I see. Well, yes, we're seeing more and more people eclipsing the century mark. Why, I'd bet just in our town of Port Starboard we've got a half dozen or more centenarians." He paused and concentrated. "I wonder if Ben Humphrey is still around."

You could have heard a book drop.

"OUCH!"

It landed on Charlie's toe.

"That thing's dangerous," Doc Potter remarked.

"Yeah, dude," Jeff replied, scooping it off the floor. He hefted it. "Whoa! That's way too much writing for me. This guy," he looked at the cover, "must be like, anal, dude. Look at all the words!!"

"Very important words," Mrs. Scapolli corrected, taking it from him and wiping off the cover.

"So," Charlie stammered. "You think Benji Humphrey –"

Doc snickered. "I haven't heard him called that since I was in grade school."

"But you think he might still be alive?"

Doc scratched his clean-shaven chin.

"I sure don't recall hearing that he died. He's been the oldest resident of Port Starboard for several years now, since his sister, Annie, died."

Daggers plunged through Charlie's heart.

Sweetpea.

He suddenly wanted nothing more than to rid himself of this place, to get up and get back into that cursed bean patch and go home.

But it was Benji. He had just seen the tyke Friday night showing off his official Texas Ranger badge from the Montgomery Ward Catalog.

"How old is he now?"

"Oh, he's got to be a hundred and eight or nine, I'd guess. Maybe more."

Charlie looked at the clock and wondered if there was time to get back, time enough to whisk Bonnie away to here, the future, so she could learn about her destiny and the destiny of her child with Malcolm.

One hundred years earlier

"You see, Eddie?! There they are!"

Gert and Mert felt like a couple of deer caught with their pants down. They quickly sat up and looked nonchalant.

"I told you, Eddie!" Benji exclaimed. "It's the Pie Fairies!"

Myrtle was first to recover.

"You weren't supposed to tell anyone!"

Benji shrugged angelically, and Myrtle's heart melted.

"Hello," Eddie stammered, letting the screen door close. "I'm ... Eddie Dawson."

Gertrude and Myrtle looked at each other and mouthed the words, *Eddie Dawson.*

"Hello," Gertrude said, adjusting her Paddy outfit.

"Soooo, are you friends of Betsy?"

"Sort of."

Eddie stared, focusing on their clothes.

218

"So," he ventured. "Are you friends of Gnarles and Paddy?"

"What?" Myrtle mumbled. "Are these things uniforms?"

"Kind of," Eddie shrugged. "So ... you know them?"

"Yes," Gertrude said, getting to her feet. She reached out and shook his hand. "We're *good* friends of Gnarles and Paddy. Right, sis?"

"I ... suppose."

"So, you're sisters."

"Yes. I'm Gertrude and this is Myrtle. We've known Gnarles and Paddy for years. We just recently arrived from Albany."

"But how did you get here?"

"Oh, we came by sailboat ... last night. Late."

"That's right," Myrtle said. "Very late. Then they sailed away."

"Oh. Well ... welcome to Port Starboard!"

"Why, thank you, Eddie Dawson!"

Benji apparently couldn't stand the burning question any longer.

"So, you're not the Pie Fairies?"

"No, we're not, dear," Gertrude said kindly. "We were just teasing."

"That's okay," he replied. "I thought it was kind of dumb that the Pie Fairy would take a pie instead of leave one."

Riiiight.

Since Eddie had apparently lost his sense of curiosity, Benji persisted.

"So, how come you're wearing their clothes? Don't you have any of your own?"

"Of course, we do," Myrtle replied, growing tired of his third degree. "We just ... like to wear these when we're here."

"You've been here before?"

"Well, no."

"Then why did you say –"

Eddie grabbed Benji and covered his mouth.

"Sorry. He's curious."

"Well," Gertrude said. "It's good for a boy to be curious."

"See?" Benji said, struggling to extricate himself.

Once again, Gertrude took charge.

"We should be going now," she said. "But it was very nice meeting you, Eddie and Benji. And, oh," she added as they hurried down the steps. "Could you two not tell anyone? It's a surprise."

*　　*　　*

Bonnie was once again alone on the porch, listening to the muted sounds of an active kitchen. She sighed, taking in the day, imagining how her life would be changing in only a few short hours. Random thoughts and latent perceptions wafted over her like the cool, salty breeze.

Of everything, she was most nervous about her wedding night. It had been difficult remaining pure; she had come so close so many times. But it had been worth it. Malcolm was everything she had dreamed of since she was a little girl, with fantasies of a handsome prince sweeping her off her feet and onto the withers of his gallant stallion.

She had never been so sure, and this time everyone agreed.

Malcolm is a wonderful man, a man of sound judgment and character.

That was the main thing: character. More than anything, Bonnie wanted a man she could count on through thick and thin, for better or worse.

She waved at the little boat pulling up to the dock and smiled.

"Hi, Silas!" she shouted as he walked up the sandy path, a box of something in his arms.

She knew he had spent the day moving things, running errands for anyone who needed them done.

"Whoo!" Silas said, setting the box on one chair and sitting down in the one next to her. "Katie says that's every vase that isn't already crammed with flowers."

"Oh, Betsy is going to be so happy," she sighed. "I think every available flower in Port Starboard has been picked."

"Close to it, I'd say."

"Thank you so much for helping today, Silas."

"Oh, it's nothing. "I can't think of anyone who deserves to be happy more than you."

"And I am, Silas. I truly am. You know," she said, absently thumbing the pages of the book in her lap. "This might sound strange, and I hope you don't take it wrong, but if you were a woman, I'd want you as one of my bridesmaids. You know, I don't have a better friend." She reached out and took his hand. "I just hope we can remain friends forever."

"Oh, you don't have to worry about that."

Bonnie squeezed his hand and sat back in her chair.

"I have to tell you, Silas. I'll be glad when this is all over. It's been kind of stressful."

"I hear that's pretty common, thus the phrase, 'wedding jitters.' Before you know it, you'll find a routine, and everything will settle down."

"You always know what I'm feeling," she said. "That's exactly what I'm worried about, finding my new routine. I really want to keep on teaching, you know. I'll miss the children so."

"But you'll have your own before you know it."

"Oh!" Bonnie's eyes brightened. "I simply cannot wait!"

"You'll make a great mother, you're so wonderful with children. So," he ventured. "What's going on with the orphanage? Do you think that's what you'll be doing, or –"

"Oh, I don't know right now. I hate to say it, but that's the last thing on my mind lately. I haven't given up on Malcolm, though." She scowled. "He doesn't really like the idea, you know, with me having babies and all."

"I don't know why you couldn't do both. It's not like you would need to be there all the time. You'll have staff to take care of the day-to-day things, right?"

"I suppose," she sighed.

"I'm sorry," Silas said. "I shouldn't have brought it up. It's your day. Hey!" he said, noticing her empty glass. "What if I get you something to drink?"

"Oh, would you, Silas? You know, they won't let me step foot in that kitchen."

"And you shouldn't," he replied. "You should just relax and enjoy it."

"Yes, I should," Bonnie agreed with a sigh.

*   *   *

Gnarles and Paddy were freaking out.

"They'r-r-re really here!"

"I know that, mo-ron!"

They had searched everywhere: the swimming hole; the house; the Magic Bean Patch; and the still.

"They wer-r-re naked! R-r-right here!" Paddy had exclaimed.

They were standing at the landing, staring at *Dolly Varden*.

"And Charlie is in th' fuuuture."

"Yes, Paddy. Charlie's in the future."

"So, what're we gonna dooo?"

"We gotta find 'em."

"R-r-right. We gotta find 'em … why do we gotta find 'em?"

"Because we don't want them telling Bonnie anything."

"R-r-right. But … dooon't we want her ta knooow?"

"No, knucklehead. It might ruin her wedding."

"But, if she's not gettin' married, ther-r-re wooon't be a wedding."

Gnarles had to think about that one.

Time Rummers

One hundred years later

"See you later, Doc!" Mrs. Scapolli called as Jeff helped the old man down the driveway.

Salty was sitting on Mrs. Scapolli's shoulder, enjoying the female company. Charlie was reclining in the La-Z-Boy on the enclosed, air-conditioned porch, staring at a commercial for a new sitcom called "Seinfeld" – a show about nothing.

He wondered what the world was coming to.

Mrs. Scapolli caught Charlie's eye.

"What's Molly like?" she asked.

"Oh," Charlie replied. "She's a fine lass, to be sure."

"I bet she's a real pistol."

"More like a cannon!" Charlie snorted. "But never has there been a better spirit to walk this earth. Not in a million years has there been another Molly girl, and not in a million years will there be another."

"Molly girl," Mrs. Scapolli repeated. "Is that what you call her?"

"Among other things," the old salt said with a sly grin.

"Oh, you are a devil, Charlie MacLeod."

"Just tryin' to live up to me own heritage."

"Yes, I was reading about your father. He was quite the character. Nathan, I believe?"

"Yep, toughest, saltiest strip of leather to ever bend a tiller, but with a heart as big as the Seven Seas themselves. You know, the reason we still have old Salt here today is because of Pa. We had left for St. Augustine at the start of the Seminole War, and somehow in all the confusion we forgot Salty. Well, Pa wouldn't have it any other way. We went back there to get him and were jumped by four Seminole braves. Pa killed three of 'em, but one of those Indian arrows killed him." He paused, then said, "He might have lived a long time, seen a lot of things. But," he said wistfully. "He saved my good buddy here. The best friend a guy could ask for."

Mrs. Scapolli handed the little green bird to Charlie and ran into the kitchen, saying something about a tissue.

The front door opened.

"Yo, dudes. That was the slowest I've ever walked."

The door closed, and Jeff shuffled into the room.

"All rightee," Charlie said. "I suppose I better get going. And if things go well, I might be back in a little while with Bonnie."

"WHOA! DUDE!! I can't believe this! Bonnie Blakely –" He looked dreamily towards the fake banana tree in the corner. "She is *so* hot!"

"Stop that, Jeffrey. It's in bad taste. And you're not going to see her naked."

"Whoa!! I can't help it if I'm standin' around, and some totally hot babe pops in the kitchen wearing nothin' but a smile!"

"Well, I'm putting a sheet up over the pass-through, and I'm going to have a nice bathrobe right there waiting for her."

"But, what if I'm, like, getting a glass of water … or somethin'. You know? Dude?"

"Jeffrey," Mrs. Scapolli said. "I've been meaning to say something about that."

"About what?"

"I don't want you to call me that anymore."

"Dude?"

"Yes."

"Sorry."

"Excuse me," Charlie said. "But I really gotta get goin', and I've been thinkin', and there might be a little problem, you know, backin' into the magic patch." He looked down at the spot where a leg should be.

"That's right," Grandma said. "You could fall down."

They looked at Jeff.

"Oh, no, you don't!" he exclaimed, slowly backing away. "I'm not goin' into the past. What if I get stuck there?!"

Charlie shrugged. "You ain't gotta go with me, kid. Just help me back in and get situated and all."

"I suppose I could do that," Jeff mumbled.

One hundred years earlier

Gert and Mert had fallen madly in love with Gnarles and Paddy – as "masters of the distillery," that is.

After they got away from Eddie and Benji, they had run off, down the Lake Trail, back to the landing, laughing all the way. They regrouped.

"It's gonna take at least, what, two hours for her to get ready? And she was just going in when we last saw her, before that little brat showed up."

"He is a cutie."

"Ain't no doubt," Myrtle agreed.

They had decided to do some exploring and had walked south a ways to where they came upon another house, a shack was more like it, with a distinct lean to it, as if it might fall over at any minute. There were the very beginnings of a farm, not much land cleared, a small garden behind a high, chicken-wire fence. There was a rickety outhouse.

"I couldn't live here without indoor plumbing," Myrtle sighed. "Maybe without electricity, but not plumbing."

"We're not staying."

"I know."

On their way back, Gertrude stopped and looked around.

"I cannot believe this is how Port Starboard used to look. It's like a jungle. A tropical jungle! And look!" She swept her arm. "It's beautiful! The lake and the inlet. I just cannot believe it!"

"Me either."

"You know, sis."

"Yes?"

"We need to relax. We just need to slow down and relax. We've been going at this like we're on a mission. What do you say we just kick back and enjoy the ride? We're in a tropical paradise, for God's sake! Let's have some fun!"

With that, Gertrude unbuttoned her shirt and pranced down the path.

An hour and a half later they were perched on the highest point of the coastal ridge, white hot sand reflecting the sun's rays, sitting under a spindly spruce singing "What Do You Do with a Drunken Sailor?"

One hundred years later

"Ya ready, youngster?"

"Let's rock and roll, dude-ster."

Slowly, Jeff assisted Charlie backwards into the Magic Bean Patch, one step at a time, making sure he placed his crutches properly. It was a tight fit, and Salty was letting his angst be known.

"Yo, dude, I'm surprised you're not deaf in that ear."

"What?" Charlie replied. "I can't hear too good out'a that ear."

Salty squawked again.

"Whoa, dude! How can you stand that?!"

"I went deaf in that ear."

"Oh. Right." He glanced around nervously. "So, you're not scared?"

"Maybe a little. But this contraption worked just as Gnarles and Paddy said it would on the way here, so I'm pretty comfortable with it."

As they neared the end of the row, the air began to swirl around them, and Jeff bolted.

Charlie could see Jeff and Grandma peering at them from the end, but they seemed to be shrinking, growing fuzzy. The swirling grew more pronounced, and he thought he heard thunder in the distance. Then they were gone.

"Any time now," Charlie mumbled. "I'll just appear at Gnarles and Paddy's distillery. Any time now," he repeated. "Any … time … now."

Suddenly he was there, in the woods, the still only a couple feet away, the hurricane hut nearby. Everything was as it should be, except –

"Hmmm," he said, steadying himself on the still.

All was quiet but for the hum of cicadas under a full moon, high overhead.

It was the middle of the night.

"That's weird."

Chapter Thirty-Three

"Now, stop it! You're not helping!"

Sally was assisting the groom with his tie.

"What is wrong with this thing?" she said. "Why does it droop on the left side, no matter which way we tie it?"

They were standing on the wide, airy, front porch, overlooking the lake and Pelican Island.

"You see?" he said. "It's simply defective."

"How can a tie be defective?" Sally giggled, untying it. "One more try," she said, "then we'll starch it again."

Sally had the most fetching green eyes and, though beyond her prime, remained a striking woman. The confidence of her Scottish lineage blended perfectly with a soft, gentle side that served her well. She liked people and had a knack for making them feel comfortable. This desirable trait was illustrated by a clientele that actually included men. She had a beautiful smile.

"Sally, I wish to express once more my gratitude for your generous hospitality, allowing me, a total stranger, the use of your home these many months."

"Oh, you weren't a stranger, Malcolm. You're family."

"And a more marvelous family I cannot imagine. Why, the best thing I've ever done was to come here, to this unrivaled retreat. Just look," he swept his arm at the view stretching before them. "Absolutely breath-taking," he sighed, "very much like my beautiful hostess." He waited until she looked up, and with a twinkle in his eye, he said, "Maybe we should starch it again."

"All right," Sally sighed. "One more time."

She didn't notice his eyes following her every movement as she walked back into the house.

* * *

Katie Humphrey was in charge of getting the church ready. She and Annie had been going great guns since five o'clock that morning. Alfred was nearby, prepared to "spring into action" at a moment's notice. Booker and Isaiah were ready as well, so Katie had several strong backs to assist her if needed.

There had been a continuing discourse between the two camps – cooking and setting-up – most of the day: *Should we have the wedding in the building as planned? Or in the church yard so everyone who wants to attend, can?* It would be cooler outside. It was a beautiful day.

The churchyard was a charming location. The entire hammock surrounding the building had been cleared except for several ancient, live oak trees. On some of them, their massive, gnarled, orchid- and lichen-encrusted branches drooped to within inches of the ground. A festooning of Spanish moss gave the impression of an enchanted forest.

The area immediately around this little chantry in the oaks received just enough sun to foster a cheery patch of greenery around the edges: puffy tufts of Bermuda grass and colorful crotons and ixora hedges.

A small boat approached the sandy beach where several other sailboats were moored or pulled on shore. The red-haired girl at the tiller expertly dropped the sail and nosed the tiny vessel shoreward. As it neared the beach, a fat little raccoon clapped his human-like hands and chattered excitedly.

Annie answered, informing him that she was fully aware of the tides.

Just as *Miss Kitty* touched sand, Copernicus leaped off the prow and scampered over to the table most likely to have crumbs below. A lady shooed him away.

Annie tied off the boat and ran to the church.

"Hi, Mrs. Milsap! Hi, Mrs. Johnson! Hi, Mrs. Guildersleeve!"

"You shouldn't run with that bowl in your hands, dear!"

"Yes, ma'am," Annie replied, and she slowed to a fast walk. When Mrs. Guildersleeve looked away, she made a face. Mrs. Milsap laughed.

"What's so funny?"

"Nothing."

Annie burst through the door.

"Momma!" she yelled. Katie was up front, sitting at the piano, looking over music. "Momma," she repeated, breathing hard. "Everyone said yes, we'll … have it outside. They'll … put out the word for chairs."

Katie scowled.

"Oh, I really don't want to do it outside because the piano sounds better in the church, and I do hate last minute changes. But – "she smiled fondly at Annie, whom so many people said was the miniature image of herself – "All rightee, then. I suppose we should get busy." She looked at the piano. "Could you round up Booker T. and anyone else?"

Chapter Thirty-Four

Gnarles and Paddy glanced around uneasily. They looked good, both decked out in tuxedos – top hats and tails – standing at the rear of a sea of non-matching chairs.

Bonnie was walking down the aisle, her proud father, Sam Jesup, at her side. Music was playing. Everyone's eyes were on Bonnie, with occasional glances towards the groom and his best man, Bobby. Standing up for Bonnie were Christiane and Callie.

The Reverend appeared pleased.

All grew quiet and the Reverend spoke.

"Welcome," he said, extending his arms wide. "I suppose it's a good thing everyone doesn't come to church regular or we'd need a much bigger building."

Following a burbling of mixed laughter, and a few knowing looks, he continued.

"Dearly Beloved, we are gathered here in the presence of God and of this company so this couple, Malcolm Geoffreys and Bonnie Blakely, may be united in holy matrimony."

Paddy nudged Gnarles.

"Where's Charlie?"

"Shhh! You know as much as I do!" He glanced at Betsy, who was standing a few feet away, her eyes shifting between them and the ceremony.

"We are here to celebrate and share in the glorious act that God is about to perform – the act by which he converts their love for one another into the holy and sacred estate of marriage –"

"Oh, nooo," Paddy said uneasily. "Here it comes."

"I know!" Gnarles looked around, expecting Charlie to pop out of the woodwork at any moment.

Is that a sail? No.

"He said he'd take care of everything."

"I know!!"

Paddy put his hands over his eyes.

"Oh, nooo! Oh, nooo!"

"Shhh!"

"From the beginning of the Creation, God made them male and female. For this cause shall a man leave his Father and Mother and cleave to his Wife. And they shall become one flesh, so they are not separate but one –"

"Oh, nooo! Oh, nooo!"

"So, what God hath joined together, let no man put asunder."

Paddy shut his eyes and stuck his fingers in his ears.

"If there be any here who believe that these two should not be united in holy matrimony, speak now ... or forever hold your peace."

Gnarles looked over his shoulder once more. *No Charlie.* It was up to him. His eyes went to the preacher, then Betsy. She was glaring.

He raised his hand.

Betsy made her move.

*   *   *

Gertrude and Myrtle never recalled having so much fun. They had gotten hot up on the hill and had trudged the near mile back to the still, a much longer trek than they had recalled on the way there. After topping off the jug, they headed down to the waterfront.

They were splashing and playing in the swimming hole.

"This is so much better than a swimming pool."

"You think?" Gertrude replied. "The water's not quite as clear or blue."

"No, it's better! No chlorine, just salt and minerals. Saltwater is good for the skin, you know."

"So I've heard."

"And unlike the lake water back home – or back in the future, whatever – this is perfectly pristine. No pollution. Not a drop!"

Gertrude crawled up on the bank and took another slug of Coco-rum. "Ahhh," she said. "This is some amazing stuff."

"Sure is," Myrtle said, sitting down beside her. "We could make a fortune off this recipe in the future."

"Probably do just as well right here in the past. Good liquor is good liquor, no matter when or where."

"Sure is," Myrtle replied, leaning back on her elbows. "Those two are just too nice. They give most of it away. Can you imagine?"

"Nope."

"They said their still back home, in the future, is already producing. They need more molasses, I suppose."

"Mm-hmm."

"Are you thinking what I'm thinking?"

"If you're thinking we're gonna be rich, you are."

"Mm-hmm."

Gertrude raised the jug.

"To the Rum Queens!"

"The Rum Queens!"

They drank to themselves

"You know what?" said Gertrude. "I'm hungry again."

"Me, too."

"Everybody should be gone to the wedding by now."

"Okay. Let's go."

A few minutes later they were scanning the area. No sign of life. They dashed across the lawn for Betsy's house and up to the front porch. They paused, looked around, then slowly and cautiously Gertrude opened the door a crack.

"Helloooo! Anybody home?"

"No one's home," Myrtle said, and she pushed her sister through. They closed the door and looked around.

"Nice."

"It is."

"I don't know what I was expecting, but this is really, really nice."

"Oh, thank God," Myrtle gasped. "Something soft!" And she flopped onto a fully-padded sofa. "Mmmmm, velvet," she sighed.

Gertrude draped herself across a matching loveseat.

"Ahhhh." She motioned for Myrtle to pass the jug.

They sat there a while.

"Oh, my gosh!" Myrtle suddenly blurted. "Do you know what we could get for this furniture in the future? They're all antiques! Brand new antiques!"

"I don't know," Gertrude shrugged. "I think some of this stuff is old now, in this time. Look at that roll top desk."

Myrtle stretched out.

"I wish we could take this sofa back with us. It's simply fabulous."

They sat there a while.

"I wonder what's in the kitchen."

A few minutes later they were sampling a variety of pies, cakes, and cookies.

Through a stuffed mouth, Myrtle mumbled, "Someone's gonna be mad about all this."

"They'll just blame it on the Pie Fairies," Gertrude replied. "We'll clean up good before we leave."

"This lime pie is amazing."

"Mm. I know."

230

Once they were contentedly stuffed to the gills, Myrtle abruptly stood up.

"You know," she said, taking another slash. "I got the impression Callie and Isaiah are staying here with Betsy."

"So?"

"So, I bet she's about my size."

Gertrude raised an eyebrow.

"Betsy's pretty close to my size."

Grabbing the jug, they went in search of bedrooms.

"I was right!" Myrtle called out. "They're staying here! Oh, my God! Look at this dress!"

In the other bedroom Gertrude had already found the one she wanted – a lavender silk gown with a fitted bodice and elaborate beaded fringe. She was in the process of changing.

"Mine's a little tight!"

"Mine's a little big!" Myrtle yelled from the other room. She appeared at the door to Betsy's room. "Oh, Gert!" she cried. "It's beautiful!"

"I know!" Gertrude giggled. She turned around. "Finish buttoning me?"

As Myrtle buttoned, she said, "Buttons."

"They are a pain," Gertrude agreed. She ran her hands along the folds and gazed in the full-length mirror. "I feel so ... pretty!" She spun around.

"I know," Myrtle said. "How do I look?" Her dress was pale yellow chiffon, low cut, with puffy, elbow-length sleeves and a ribbon bow at the waist.

With her signature bad Cockney accent, Gertrude said, "Ya loike loike a real loidy!"

Myrtle tugged at the sides of the garment.

"I need a couple of safety pins," she said, and she went over to rummage through Betsy's dressing table.

"Do they have safety pins now?" Gertrude wondered out loud. "I mean, they don't have zippers. Maybe they haven't invented them yet."

"Yes, they ha-ave," Myrtle sang, holding one up. She found another one, then handed them to Gertrude and turned, examining herself in the mirror.

Gertrude studied them.

"They haven't changed much in a hundred years, have they?"

"I guess sometimes they get it right the first time," Myrtle said, holding the side panels of the dress. "Not too tight," she said.

"How's that?"

"Tighter."

"Good?"

"Good."

Myrtle spun around.

"Perfect! Oh!" she sighed. "I feel *so* beautiful! I cannot believe how ... *feminine* I feel! What is it about these dresses? Why don't we wear stuff like this anymore?"

"You got me, sis. Of course, we aren't really doin' it like the natives. You know, all those petticoats."

"Hmph," Myrtle said, "I can do without all that. Come on. Let's go see what's goin' on outside."

"Hold on, sis," Gertrude said. "There's one more thing. You know, to top it all off?"

"Oh, right! How could I forget?!"

A few minutes later they were both fully decked, head to toe, including floppy, plumy hats and shoes.

"Mine are too big."

"Mine are too small."

They were looking in the mirror.

"Damn, we look good!"

"Damned straight, we do!"

An hour later they were celebrating, prancing around the house, pretending to be "past people," speaking properly and "having tea" – actually, Cocorum in tiny tea cups.

"Oh," Gertrude said. "I'm so glad we got back in time to get a look at Bonnie before she left. Wasn't she ... stunning?!"

"Gorgeous!" Myrtle abruptly scowled. "I just wish she wasn't marrying that deadbeat. You know he did it."

"Did what?'

"You know. Killed her. You know he did it. That bastard killed her and buried her body somewhere in the swamp west of here." Myrtle pounded down another teacup of rum, and said, "I wonder if the boys put the kibosh on it."

Gertrude shook her head.

"I hope so. I mean, you know how I love weddings, but just the thought of that sleazeball marrying her sends a shiver down my spine."

"Me, too," Myrtle replied, skipping the teacup and drinking straight from the jug. She set it down.

"What was that?!"

They listened.

"Sounds like wedding bells!"

"Wedding bells," Myrtle sighed, then she frowned. "That bastard."

* * *

232

Gnarles and Paddy were setting up their pub in the woods, south of Betsy's house.

"I told you Betsy's right. We need to wait for Charlie. He said to let him take care of everything."

"I'm worried abooout Charlie," Paddy said. "He should'a been back by now."

"Molly's pretty worried, too," Gnarles said. "It didn't seem to help none neither, us tellin' her we found his clothes and Ole Peg."

"Nooo," Paddy replied. "I d'na think we ought ta tooold her that."

"But we told her he's probably fine."

"Aye."

Following a pause, Gnarles said, "She didn't seem real mad, did she?"

"Uh-uh."

Everyone was wondering where the Old Sage was. Most didn't know much, just that he couldn't make it.

"There'll be no more talk of time travel," Betsy had advised Gnarles and Paddy following the wedding. "Wherever Uncle Charlie is, it is *not* in the future. I don't know what you two have gotten into down there, some kind of Indian Voodoo elixir or magical fairy dust, but you just need to get a grip on yourselves." Her brow furrowed. "What's really happening down there?" she asked. "Is Uncle Charlie passed out? Did you two get him drunk this morning, testing out one of your new … concoctions?"

Betsy had looked around nervously, then taking a deep breath she lowered her voice.

"Look," she had said as gently as possible. "Whatever is going on, Uncle Charlie said he'd take care of it, right?"

They had nodded.

"And you say he's in the future. Correct?"

"Uh-huh."

"So, if he's still in the future, doing whatever it is he's doing there, then we should just wait on him. Right?"

"I s'pose."

"Good," she had sighed. "We'll just wait for Uncle Charlie. In fact, why don't you two go on down and check on him when we're finished here?"

They nodded.

"By the way," she had added. "What is it exactly he's supposed to be doing?"

"We don't know. He didn't tell us he was goin'. We just found his clothes and Ole Peg layin' there in the Magic Bean Patch."

That's when Betsy had given them the rest of the day off, abruptly turned, and wandered off into the comforting mist of wedding fun.

*   *   *

Peering through the window, the girls could see the entire lakeshore in front of the house and hotel, all the way up to Booker T. Point. People were milling around in and amongst the cocoanut palms, socializing. Children were running about, chasing each other. A group of three girls were studying something in the water down by the dock. One was carrying a jar.

The men were dressed mostly in white, many of them wearing Panama hats. The women were in white or pastels, and all had splendid hats of every shape and size, some quite extravagant.

"Sure is a lot of white."

"It is cooler that way," Gertrude replied. "And some of those women have got to be wearing two or three petticoats underneath."

"You'd never get me into one of those things."

"You got that right, sister." Gertrude shook her head. "With no air conditioning? I don't know how they do it. Oh, look! There's Betsy and Katie Humphrey!"

"How do you know that's Katie?"

"Because she has the same red hair as Annie. Anyway, I saw Benji run up to her and ask something. It's got to be her."

"She's pretty."

"Uh-huh. But," Myrtle leaned back and sighed. "Did you see Christiane? She could be on the cover of *Vogue*!"

"When I first saw her, I thought I was staring at Scarlett O'Hara herself."

"She'd make a perfect Scarlett O'Hara, but I was picturing her as Cat Woman."

"Cat Woman?!" Gertrude howled. "Where did you come up with that?"

"I don't know," Myrtle shrugged. "It's just what popped in my mind."

"We really have got to get you checked out one of these days."

"That's such a romantic story," Myrtle sighed. "Girl of European nobility marries regular American Guy and Girl's Father challenges him to a duel."

"I know," Gertrude giggled. "A duel of sail! Can you imagine?"

"Oh, look, it's him! Count Contraire! A real Italian count!"

"I thought he was French."

"Whatever."

Gertrude took a long drink, then, wiping her mouth, said, "I just wish we could have brought 'The Book' with us."

"Oh, my gosh! Look! There she is!"

The two women watched, awestruck, as the bride stepped off the magnificent vessel, *Au Revoir*. Assisting her ashore was the groom.

"Oh, my God! He's ... gorgeous!"

"Bastard!"

234

*   *   *

Betsy had told Gnarles and Paddy they could take the rest of the day off as soon as the bride and groom arrived from the photography session. She had felt kind of bad about putting Gnarles in a headlock and threatening to "crush his boney skull like a rotten egg."

Alfred had brought all of his photographic equipment along and had insisted that the entire wedding party stay afterwards. There had been moans and groans, but he advised everyone that it would someday be a common practice for newlyweds to have a series of pictures made directly after the wedding.

Bonnie had been excited.

Afterward, Alfred had enlisted Gnarles and Paddy to transport the bulky equipment to the reception party down the lake and help him set it all up. Now, everyone was gathered at the foot of the dock, waiting for the newlyweds to disembark the magnificent vessel, *Au Revoir*.

"All right," Alfred announced. "Everyone out of the picture except the bride and groom." A moment later, he said, "You, too, Count."

"But," the small, dapper Frenchman, declared, twisting his funny little mustache with his fingers, "I am zee cap-i-tan of theese magnificent vessel that has transported theese couple from zee place of nuptials to zee place of temporary reseedence! I should be een zee picture weeth zee magnificent vessel, *Au Revoir*, the finest vessel to ever sail zee waters of zee Lake Worth."

"Fine," Alfred sighed. "But this time don't make that ridiculous face."

"What ridiculous face?"

"The one you made last time, right before I photographed you and Bonnie and Malcolm getting on board."

"I deed not make zee face. I smiled."

Christiane, who was standing nearby with Eddie, said, "It is true. I have seen my father smile before. It is, how do you say, not pretty."

"Maybe I can fix it later," Alfred mumbled, then he called out, "All right, just try not to smile too big."

The Count shrugged, then smiled grandly.

*   *   *

"So, what are they doing?" Myrtle asked. She was splayed across the sofa with her jug.

"They're taking a picture of Bonnie and Malcolm and the Count."

"Oh?" She got up and looked through the window. She squinted. "What's wrong with the Count?"

"Don't know," Gertrude replied. "But it looks like he's in pain."

"Agony is more like it."

"Look how happy Bonnie is," Gertrude sighed.

"For now," Myrtle griped. "She'll be dead and buried in just a few years, then that bastard turns their son into a serial killer." She was starting to slur her words.

"Do you see the boys?"

"Uh-uh."

"Someone needs to stop him,"

"Yep."

"Doesn't look like the boys are gonna do it."

"Nope." Following a pause, Myrtle grumbled, "Someone's gotta stop that son of a bitch!" She glared at him through the window.

"Now, don't get any ideas, sis."

Too late.

By the time Gertrude realized it, Myrtle was halfway out the door, jug in hand, eyes riveted.

"Crap."

Gertrude caught up with her halfway to the dock, but there was no stopping her. Myrtle was on a mission. All Gertrude could do was tag along in the hopes of averting disaster – and to see what her sister was going to do to that unsuspecting bastard.

Everyone saw them coming and parted.

A mumble passed through the crowd.

Who could they be? Have you ever seen them before? Maybe they're guests at the hotel. Is that my dress? Is that my dress? All right! What the hell is going on around here?! I think that's my dress!

Myrtle strode up to Malcolm, Gertrude close behind. Myrtle was just about to lay into him when she paused to gaze upon Bonnie. She couldn't help herself.

"Oh, Bonnie," she slurred. "You are so beautiful." Tears came to her eyes. "You are so … freaking … beautiful!" Her misty eyes grew suddenly pointed. "You really deserve better than this!" she said, then she glared at Malcolm with disgust dripping from her eyes.

Everyone was uniformly flabbergasted, unable to speak.

Meanwhile, Alfred was behind his camera, underneath the black covering, muttering something about the inadequacies of modern technology.

"Hold on, everyone!" he said. But no one was listening. They were all focused on the two strange, inebriated women confronting the bride and groom.

Myrtle glared at Malcolm.

"How dare you?! Taking advantage of a sweet girl like Bonnie! How –" She paused and made a strange face. "How –"

A horrified Betsy finally made her move.

"What the hell's going on around here?!" she said, stepping forward, hands on her hips. "And," she looked curiously at Gertrude. "Is that my dress?!"

*   *   *

Gnarles and Paddy were coming to Betsy's rescue.

When they heard her screams, they bolted. Storming out of the woods, they noticed some sort of commotion on the dock.

"Whooo's that?" Paddy asked, out of breath.

"I don't know," Gnarles yelled over his shoulder. Then his eyes grew wide. "Oh, no! Paddy!" he cried. "It's the girls! They're talkin' ta Bonnie! They're talkin' ta Bonnie!!"

"Oh, nooo!" Paddy gasped, trying to keep up.

Gnarles was almost there. He worked his way through the crowd. Myrtle was yelling something at Malcolm, jabbing her finger in his face; and just as he got there, Myrtle abruptly stopped in mid-sentence.

"Uh-oh," she swallowed hard, then everyone watched, stunned, as she threw up all over Malcolm, just as Alfred said, "Say cheese!"

A flash went off.

Betsy screamed, focusing on Gnarles and Paddy.

"Do you know these … women?!"

"It's all right," Gnarles said reassuringly. "No problemo." Then he turned to Gertrude, and said, "Maybe we should go now."

"Yes," Gertrude replied, and she grabbed Myrtle by the arm. As they led her away, Myrtle moaned, "It must have been that black and white cookie."

Chapter Thirty-Five

As they walked up the path to the house, the girls told Gnarles and Paddy everything, how they had snuck into Mrs. Scapolli's yard, and how they had met Benji and Eddie, and how beautiful Bonnie was.

Gnarles and Paddy didn't say much: lots of nodding, yeps, and uh-huhs.

"It doesn't look like you stopped the wedding," Myrtle said, snuggling up close to Paddy, who turned as red as her nose.

"No," Gnarles replied. "Charlie told us to wait."

"And," Paddy added. "Betsy almost cr-r-racked your head ooopen."

Gnarles glared. "She's got a good grip."

"She does look like she could be intimidating," Gertrude said.

"And she's got a good grip," Gnarles reiterated.

"I do too-oo," Myrtle sang, pulling Paddy close.

Paddy's impulse was to run, but something held him back. He felt really good, and really, really scared – but a very good kind of scared.

"We saw Charlie this morning," Gertrude said, "but that was hours ago."

"Uh-huh," Gnarles replied. "We think he went into the future to find a way to save Bonnie from Malcolm."

"I *hate* him," Paddy said, trying to ignore Myrtle's hand slithering into his pants. It was getting hard to concentrate.

"Oooo. We hate him, too," Myrtle whispered in his ear.

"Well," Gertrude declared. "I cannot imagine Charlie would miss Bonnie's wedding."

"Uh-huh, and we had to take Molly over."

"So, is this like Charlie?"

"Oh, no. Not Charlie. If he could'a been here, he would'a."

"I wonder if something went wrong with the time machine."

"Ooooh, nooo!" Paddy cried. "What if somethin' happened t'th' time machine!"

"Oh, no!" Myrtle cried. "What if we can't get back?!"

Panic was setting in.

One hundred years later

The sound of distant thunder.

"Be right there, boys!" Mrs. Scapolli called from the porch. "You're early!"

"It's not just us!" Gnarles yelled. "We brought someone else!"

"Oh!" Mrs. Scapolli could be heard rummaging through another part of the house. "Is Bonnie here?!" The sound of sudden commotion and a door slamming. "No, Jeffrey! You are not going over there!"

"Come on, Grandma!! Please!!"

"It's not Bonnie!" Gnarles yelled. "But it's women, so they need somethin' ta wear."

Women? Hmmm.

"Okay, Grandma," Jeff yawned. "I guess I'll just go back in my room now."

"Good boy."

There was more door-slamming, then all four of the time travelers watched as a young, unsuspecting face slowly rose in the kitchen window.

It clearly wasn't what Jeffrey had expected.

Myrtle got a chance to blow him a kiss before he realized what he was seeing and ran away like his hair was on fire.

Mrs. Scapolli came around the corner, "Oh, we're so excited to have visi...tors."

Eyes locked.

"Oh. It's you."

"Yyyyyyep," Myrtle declared. "The naked neighbors! The weekend wenches! The downtown trollops!"

Gertrude glanced sideways.

"Downtown trollops?"

"It just came out."

"Oh, Mrs. Scapolli," Gertrude slurred. "We're so sorry about showing up unannounced. If you could just," she pointed at the bathrobes in her hand, "hand us those, we'll be on our way."

The old lady stared.

Gertrude looked around.

"Oh, I just love your kitchen. I guess we've never been here before. It's very nice and ... clean." Her eyes scoured the kitchen. "I mean really ... clean."

"Fine!" Myrtle blurted. "Who needs a robe anyway?!" Then she waved her hands and sashayed right past Mrs. Scapolli and out the back door. "Toodle loo!"

Before the door slammed, Mrs. Scapolli yelled, "You'd better fix my fence boards!"

"I'm sorry," Gertrude stammered. "We will. She's kind of … like that. Anyway, thanks for the use of your kitchen." Then she leaned over and kissed Gnarles on the cheek. "See you later, big boy," she said, and she hurried out the door. "And don't worry, Mrs. Scapolli! We'll fix your fence!"

Mrs. Scapolli scowled, then turned. Gnarles and Paddy were waiting for their robes.

She glared.

They shriveled.

"I don't know what you boys see in those two."

Chapter Thirty-Six

Sunday, August 19, 1890

The moon cast a pale glow over the far shoreline. Charlie could hear waves crashing on the ocean beach. He didn't know exactly what time it was, but by the position of the moon, it was about three in the morning. Of course, he really had no way of knowing if it was even Saturday: it could be Sunday or Monday or even Friday – the night before. He studied the shoreline. Everything appeared normal. He could see Eddie's *Hasta La Vista* docked at Maggie's, and there was a faint light on at Betsy's.

The winds had long since died so he was rowing, making slow time of it, wondering how he was going to explain everything to Molly. He chastised himself for leaving her to attend the wedding on her own, but what could he do? When he had arrived at Gnarles and Paddy's that morning, he never had expected the Magic Bean Patch to actually work. Never in his wildest imaginations did he think he would be spending the day a hundred years in the future.

It caused his mind to reel. He studied his hands, clutching at the oars, and knew it had not been a dream. Old, familiar scars were visible even in the moonlight, all reminding him of who and what he was. They were the same hands that had earlier that day grasped the hand of an old man – an old man who at this moment was sleeping in a crib fifteen miles to the south, "probably with a diaper full of crap."

He looked at Salty.

"Did it really happen, old bird? Were we really there?"

Salty seemed as unsure as he.

Pulling steadily, Charlie checked his heading.

"It really happened, didn't it, little buddy?"

* * *

Molly Blue understood Charlie MacLeod.

She knew who and what he was. If it had been possible for him to be there with her, he would have been. She was worried sick, of course, having heard some crazy story from Gnarles and Paddy about him going into the future to rescue Bonnie, but she knew her husband. He would have been there if he could.

Charlie had once told her he didn't trust anyone more with the truth than Gnarles and Paddy – and they had insisted he was fine.

She was lying on the bed of the screened porch, listening to the waves lapping on shore, extracting every nuance of breeze from the still, balmy night. Her mind ran rampant, but she forced worry away and concentrated on the greatest moment of her life.

Charlie had been a seasoned sailor when they first met some forty odd years earlier. Though barely more than a girl at the time, she had known many men like him: bold, blustery, vagabonds of the sea; windswept mariners who lived for nothing more than a good drunk, a warm body, and a day to sleep it off. Most of these men cared not a whit for any woman beyond Momma and Mother Ocean, and they carried bilge stones enough to proposition any young lady they happened to meet, regardless of where they were or who might overhear.

Charlie MacLeod, however, was no cad. He was, in fact, built more along the lines of a gentleman, but with an earthy, bawdy side that he had no intention of shedding.

Molly had seen it in him right away, the man of her dreams, a man who could rabble-rouse with the worst of 'em while at the same time make any woman, even someone in her profession, feel like a real lady.

She had met him while working in Key West at a friendly, waterfront, den of iniquity called the Happy Clam. She had been barely more than a girl.

Those were wild days back then, the island town isolated and distant from any semblance of "civilized society." It seemed a country of its own, mostly a mix of expatriate Bahamians, black and white, Americans, Cubans, and a smattering of others from a wide sampling of Caribbean islands.

She had been entertaining a table of horny shrimpers when a deafening cacophony shook the entire bar. The tumbler in front of her rattled. She had stared at the glass, listening, watching it dance on the table each time the thunder and tremors erupted. She thought it not unlike the roar of a lion.

A very happy lion.

Finally, she turned her attentions from the fishermen, and, peering through the smoke-filled bar, she had spotted the brawny, barrel-chested source of such belly-busting merriment. His bushy face glowed and his eyes sparkled. To top it off, a little, drunk, green parrot weaved back and forth on his shoulder.

He had been telling a story, his face and body animated, people hanging on every word. Then he would burst into laughter, spurring the entire table and others surrounding to laugh along and raise their glasses high.

From that moment, the formerly cynical Molly Blue had come to believe in love at first sight. It was a moment she treasured.

But there was another.

That moment had come many years later, long after she had given up imagining he might return to her. She had heard he had become a hermit, a crazy old man who lived with his bird and dog along the beaches of the lower east coast. She had even fantasized about searching him out, how that might be, but it never went beyond that.

Time passed, and one day she received a letter from her stockbroker informing her that she was rich, and not only rich but old money, European nobility rich. She soon after moved to New Orleans where she took up a quiet, placid life of rest, reflection, and regret.

She was having dinner at the Hotel Provincial, at her regular dining time, a young, male companion seated across from her, when she heard it.

The blood drained had from her face.

"Are you all right?" her young companion asked.

Her entire body trembling, she turned to lay eyes upon a ghost: the bold, blustery, Old Salt himself, sitting at a table with some other men, all of them laughing and drinking. This time, however, his happy eyes were waiting for hers. He raised a toast, and with a crafty wink he mumbled something to a little green bird perched on his shoulder; and, as in a fantastical, magical fairy tale, the little bird dutifully puffed up and squawked, "How are ya, m'darlin'?!"

It had been Molly's moment in time.

*   *   *

By the time Charlie pulled up to The Mansion dock, the sky was graying over the ocean. A breeze had yet to rise. Climbing out of the tiny craft, he stretched. He had not rowed a boat that far in years.

"I'll be feelin' that tomorrow," he said to Salty, and they headed up the cottage path.

He went out to the beachside, screened porch to find Molly sleeping peacefully. He set Salty on his perch, then went into the kitchen and put on a pot. When he returned, she was sitting up, her eyes bright, happy – and relieved.

"Hi, sweetie."

"I didn't want to wake you," he said.

"I know."

"I don't suppose you got much sleep last night."

She stretched. "I did all right." Taking his hand in hers, she said, "I dreamed you were sailing home to me."

He chuckled. "I was. Rowing actually."

"All the way from Gnarles and Paddy's?" She smiled. "You're gonna be sore tomorrow, old man."

"It's already tomorrow," he replied, sitting down next to her. "I'm guessin' this is Sunday?"

Molly nodded, then looking beyond the palm trees at the lightening sky, said, "Thank you for loving me, Charlie. And thank you for bringing me here."

Gazing seaward, Charlie replied, "'Tis a lovely thing, aye m'darlin'?" A moment later, he said, "I'm sorry I didn't get back for the wedding."

"Oh, don't worry," she said. "I just told everyone you were 'indisposed,' and left it at that." She giggled. "Nobody questions 'indisposed.' It's a wonderful word."

Charlie shook his head.

"That's my Molly girl."

"That's me," she replied. "Your Molly girl."

Charlie told her everything.

*   *   *

All Molly had known before he left was that he was going over to inspect Gnarles and Paddy's "Time Machine." They had laughed.

Now, she was hearing this fantastic tale about stepping into another world, instantaneously traveling to an unknown plane: here, but not here.

Her first impulse was to dismiss it.

But it was Charlie.

It was just another of his incongruities: the master prevaricator who never "lies." All it ever takes is to question the storyteller – but that would ruin the tale.

Following her initial disbelief, Molly accepted every word as fact, and within minutes she was herself speaking of these strange future people as if she knew them.

"Oh, Charlie!" she exclaimed. "This is the best thing to possibly happen!" She held her hands to her heart. "Oh, thank you for going, and being so curious, and wanting to help, and just … being you! Don't you see, Charlie? Life goes on! There are real … *people* living in the future. Just like us, Charlie! Don't you see? Life goes on! Times change, but people remain the same!"

Charlie looked tired, but he looked like he was getting epiphany.

"It's true, Molly. But along with lots of amazing and wondrous things in the future, there's an awful lot of bad, especially the things they showed and talked about on the Midday News Hour."

"Yes," she said. "Some of it sound absolutely horrifying. But bad things happen here and now, too. You know that. And here we are, drinking coffee together on a lovely morning, and –" Her voice trailed off.

"Yes," Charlie sighed. "Steaming hot coffee. It's one of God's wonders, now and in the future."

She couldn't get enough of Mrs. Scapolli and Jeff, but what struck her most was the two women, the scantily clad neighbors, the librarians who might or might not be interested in Gnarles and Paddy. She giggled with delight as Charlie went on about how in love Gnarles and Paddy were with the two women: Gert and Mert.

"Gert and Mert?!" Molly howled. "And you think they might actually be attracted to the boys?!"

Charlie wagged his shaggy head.

"You know how they can think sometimes."

"Gnarles and Paddy?" Molly queried. "Or women?"

Charlie shrugged. "Both, I suppose."

Soon the sun was the color of a ripe orange, but glowing, only a crescent now and rising, unmasking and putting its routine glory on display.

Another day.

Molly was thankful. She remained Molly, however:

"Oooooo! I could just … strangle him!"

"I know."

She seethed

"How could he do that to Bonnie?! Our Bonnie!!"

Charlie shrugged, but his eyes were livid with life.

"So, my big, savory, sailor boy," she said. "Just what do you plan to do about it?"

Charlie shook his head. Through the cocoanut trees they could see a ghost crab scurry from one hole to another, snatching a morsel of something dead along the way. A seagull flying overhead took notice.

"What can I do?" he said as they watched the crab come back out of the hole and get swept into oblivion. "I can't just say: 'Oh, I've been to the future and your husband is going to kill you and turn your son into a serial killer.'" He sat back in his chair and started packing his pipe. "It would all be on my word, and I can't even say for sure that I really went into the future … although I'd bet my last five toes on it. Then again, maybe it's something in the air at their place, some kind of Voodoo dust or something, like Betsy said."

"And now," he sighed. "It looks like the time machine – I cannot believe I'm saying the words – is starting to break down." He shook his head. "I think it has something to do with the flowering of the plants. I'd go back if I thought I could discover some fact or something that might convince her. The last thing I need to be doing is filling her head with questions, all based on what three old men have to say. I mean, come on. Three old men? One of 'em known for spinning tall yarns? No, I need something solid, some sort of evidence, *proof* that her life is going to turn out like it will."

Molly could see how Charlie had once again taken the weight of the world upon his broad shoulders. She brushed her fingers along his hairy arms.

"You know," she said. "Maybe you just need to look at it a little differently."

"What do you mean?"

"Well, instead of trying to come up with proof that Geoffrey is a slug, maybe you just need to come up with some proof that you actually went into the future. It seems to me if you can prove that, then she would be more inclined to believe anything else you say."

Charlie gazed at the sun, now climbing into a bank of cumulus clouds, a distant morning shower heading towards shore.

"Yes," he said, excitement rising in his voice. "By the Great Horned Spoon, I think you've got it! Why, I've married a bloody, freaking genius!" With that he leaned over, pulled his bride close, and gave her a dose of the old Seafarer's Special.

When they finally came up for air, Molly studied the weathered old visage staring back at her and, with a twinkle in her eye, said, "You know, big boy. We haven't consummated that wedding ceremony I witnessed yesterday."

Charlie grinned broadly and took a whole lot of Molly in his arms.

Chapter Thirty-Seven

1990

The air conditioner was going full blast.

The glass door slid open.

Myrtle staggered out. She was perspiring heavily. Making her way across the deck, she reached the edge of the pool, turned, spread her arms wide, and fell backwards. She draped herself across a floating lounge.

A minute and a half later, the other sliding glass door opened. Gertrude, also perspiring, staggered over to the pool, turned, spread her arms wide and fell backwards. She flopped across a Budweiser raft.

A minute passed. The waves subsided.

"Holy crap."

"Amazing."

"I had to stop."

"Me, too."

"That's never happened."

"Me neither."

A short, fat figure stepped out the door, tightee whitees, cool shades, hands on hips.

A short, skinny figured stepped out the other door, tightee whitees, cool shades, hands on hips.

Gnarles and Paddy looked at each other with Romanesque expressions, then they high-fived and swaggered out to the pool deck and plopped down in the lounge chairs.

"Hey, Gert," Gnarles said. "How's about a beer?"

Gert and Mert looked at each other.

"Sure, honey. Green bottle or brown?"

"Surprise me, baby."

*   *   *

A green mist dissipated as Charlie's eyes focused on the stove clock.

"Good," he said to himself. He was balancing on one leg. He looked to the left to see a pair of crutches and robe next to the refrigerator. "Good old Mrs. Scapolli."

He looked out the kitchen window and smiled. As he was passing through the enclosed porch, he noticed a preacher on TV: "Please, be generous!"

"Some things never change," he mumbled as he opened the back door.

"Yo, dude-ster!" Jeff exclaimed. "You need some help, dude?"

"I'm all right, young fella," Charlie replied, making his way over to the table and chairs by the pool.

"So," Jeff said. "What's happenin'?"

"Not sure really," Charlie replied. "I came back to get some more information."

"To save Bonnie Blakely?"

"Yep."

"So, I guess she's not coming?"

"Afraid not, young fella."

"You gotta tell me, dude-ster. Is she really as hot as everyone says?"

"No," Charlie replied. "She's *hotter* than everyone says." He cocked his head in thought, then added: "A totally babelicious, blonde bombshell!"

"Bombshell," Jeff repeated with reverence.

"And as beautiful inside as out," Charlie added.

"Huh?"

A splash from next door.

Charlie nodded. "Sounds like the pool party has started."

"Yeah. They went over as soon as Grandma headed off to church. Haven't heard anything for a long time, though."

They looked at each other and nodded.

Another bigger splash.

Another approving nod.

Soon they were in Jeff's van, headed to their destination. Charlie kept his eyes closed most of the way over, only a few short blocks away. Cars flying past at speeds of forty miles an hour was something he didn't think he could ever get used to. He did notice, however, that the other vehicles on the road made a point of staying out of Jeff's way.

Charlie was sucking on a grape popsicle.

"I could make a habit out'a these," he mumbled as they pulled up to the 1920s era, stucco-frame house. It was painted an attractive lime green.

"This is it, dude. 506 Evergreen."

"That's some kind of green," Charlie commented.

"It's blowing my freaking mind, man," Jeff replied as he backed up the asphalt driveway.

Beep. Beep. Beep. Beep. Beep.

It was an old neighborhood, Jeff told Charlie. Many of the houses were constructed during the waning years of the Great Florida Land Boom, just prior to the bubble's bursting in 1925. The neighborhood had held lots of shattered dreams.

In the small front yard were several palm trees and down the driveway, running along the side of the house, was a small garage apartment. The heavy branches of a large mango tree extended beyond the boundary of driveway and yard. The roof was the original metal shingles with many years of silver paint protecting them, and on the gable end was a decorative vent in the shape of a bent, windswept palm tree. The front porch was like so many built during those days, with metal jalousies designed to let the breeze in but keep hurricanes out.

"I gotta tell you, I don't know if I'd'a gone with the green," Charlie commented.

"I don't know, dude. It like, reminds me of this trip I had once."

"To where?"

"Huh? Oh. Never mind."

Charlie nodded at the brass door knocker, and Jeff banged it three times.

"Cool."

A moment later, a little old lady came to the door. She cranked open the jalousies and, over reading glasses, peered through the screen.

"Yes?"

"Good afternoon, ma'am," Charlie said with a sailor's grin. "Would you be Mrs. Humphrey?"

"Yes? How can I help you?"

"Well, my name is Charlie MacLeod, and this is my friend, Jeffrey."

The old lady squinted then looked away, at some pictures on the wall. Opening the jalousies some more, she scrutinized Charlie and Salty, then looked back to the pictures on the wall.

"Charlie MacLeod?" she asked.

"Yes. We hate to be a bother, ma'am, but we were hoping to speak to Mr. Humphrey. Benjamin Humphrey?"

She looked at him suspiciously.

"Are you friends of his?"

Charlie was taken aback at the question.

"Why, yes. I am. A very old friend."

"Oh! Did you serve with him in the war?"

The war? Charlie thought. "Uh, no. It was before that."

"Oh, a childhood friend. And where are my manners?" She opened the porch door. "Please, come in." She scrutinized Charlie, glancing between him and the picture on the wall again. She was opening the door into the house when suddenly his feet became as if glued to the floor. A lump rose in his throat as he scanned the pictures; two in particular, both yellowed with time. He squinted through Mrs. Scapolli's reading glasses. One was of the wedding party. It was strange seeing it now, a hundred years later, all of those people he had seen just the other day, long gone, all except one. His eyes focused on a little, tow-headed boy standing next to the bride, wrapped in the folds of her dress.

Then there was the other photo. It was him and Molly standing on Alfred and Katie's dock, preparing to go to New York. Molly was gorgeous.

"Is this your ... father?" Mrs. Humphrey asked Jeff, glancing at Charlie's missing leg.

"Oh," Jeff said matter-of-factly. "He has Ole Peg for that back at home."

"That's ... nice," Mrs. Humphrey said, obviously puzzled at this extremely odd couple.

Jeff could almost read her mind: *Scammers! Don't let them distract you and split up so one can rifle through the drawers! If one goes to the bathroom, keep an eye on the hallway and ... wait a minute! Did I flush?!*

The small, cozy, living room led straight back through the dining room then to the kitchen. Charlie could see a dog with pointy ears peering through the kitchen door jalousies.

"Come on," she said, and she led them through the kitchen. "He spends most of his days out on the back patio. Ben?" she said as she opened the door. "There's someone here to see you."

They walked out into the shaded back yard, fenced, with dirt paths where the dog ran back and forth, chasing squirrels and neighborhood cats.

"This is Jasmine," she said. "She won't bite."

"Good dog," Charlie said. Salty wasn't so sure, the way Jasmine was eyeing him.

"Ben?" Mrs. Humphrey said louder. "There's someone here to see you. An old friend." Mrs. Humphrey, who was a good ten or fifteen years younger than the old man turned his wheelchair around.

He was a withered old soul, looking every bit of his one hundred and eight years. He was hunched over, and one eye had a decided droop to it. On his bald head was a baseball cap: Miami Dolphins.

Charlie was about to speak, but the recognition was instant.

The old man sat up, eyes growing wide, and stated plainly, "Charlie MacLeod." He grasped the wheels and inched the chair forward. "And Salty." His eyes became suddenly piercing as he looked down at Charlie's missing leg; but then something distracted him, out of the corner of his eye. "Hey!" he said to Jeff. "Aren't you the kid that thinks my knee-wall out front is some kind of skateboard park?"

"Oh," Jeff stammered. "Not lately."

The old man glared, then turned.

"You're Charlie MacLeod," he stated.

"Yes. I am."

"Are you a ghost?"

"Not yet, as far as I can tell."

Ben glanced at his wife, as if seeking assurance that he wasn't losing it.

"How can this be?" he asked.

"I can't really say," Charlie replied, shaking his head. "I don't know how it happened, or why, but we've found a way into the future. Exactly one hundred years to be exact."

"We?" Ben said.

"That's right," Charlie sighed. "To make a long story short," he said, "it was Gnarles and Paddy got these magic beans from a little fellow who saved them from drownin'. They planted 'em, and a Magic Bean Patch – that's what they call it – sprung up and, well, here we are."

The old man was incredulous.

"I recall rumors, stories, that they had gone into the future. And they're here? Right now?"

"Couple blocks over."

Jeff sat down in a lounge chair and started tossing a ball for Jasmine.

"Please have a seat, Mr. MacLeod," Mrs. Humphrey said. "Can I get you something to drink? Water? Lemonade? Soda?"

"You got Snapple?" Jeff queried.

"Of course. And you, Mr. MacLeod?"

"Oh, sure. I'll have one of those Snapple things, thanks."

Ben was clearly trying to sort it all out.

"I can't believe this. I'm sitting here with Charlie MacLeod and Salty."

"Son of a Sea Dog!" Salty squawked, prompting Jasmine to run around and bark.

"Hush up!" the old man said. He studied Charlie. "All right. I'm gonna believe this is happening; but if it is a dream, it sure as hell's a good one. And," he shifted in his chair, "dreams are about the biggest fun I have these days."

"I'm with you," Charlie said. "We had trouble accepting the whole crazy thing ourselves. You get used to it, though." He paused a moment. "It's great to see you again, though you look a little older than I remember."

Ben laughed. "I bet I do. You look the same, though, except for Ole Peg."

Charlie shrugged. "He couldn't make it."

"I understand. Laws of time travel and all?"

"Exactly."

251

The old man scratched his head.

"You look exactly as I remember." He searched his memory. "I remember the last time I saw you, in fact."

Charlie stopped him.

"I'm sorry, Ben," he said. "But it's best I know as little about my own future as possible. You wouldn't believe how troublesome it can be to know your own fate."

"I can imagine," the old man nodded thoughtfully. "So, Charlie MacLeod, my old friend, how can I help you?"

"Well, it's not really about me, young fella. It's about Bonnie Blakely."

The blood drained from the old man's face.

*   *   *

Later on, Charlie was sitting at the table with Mrs. Scapolli, watching the Dolphins get creamed. Jeff wasn't there; surf was up.

"This football match isn't bad," he said, looking up from the *Reader's Digest Encyclopedia of World History*. "I asked Ben what the difference was between a Miami Dolphin and a regular dolphin, and he said regular dolphins have a reason for living."

"Oh, they used to be much better," Mrs. Scapolli said. "Best team ever, the '72 Dolphins."

"Really," he said, putting his nose back in the book. He made a notation on a pad.

"That's right. The only team to ever go undefeated."

As Charlie flipped pages and made notes, she continued, anger rising in her voice.

"I don't think I've ever been so mad at Coach Shula! That poor Earl Morrall – he was the second-string quarterback, the one who *took* that team to the Superbowl! Then at the last minute, for the *biggest* game of the century, Shula put Bob Griese back in! It should have been Earl there!!" She crossed her arms and made a sour face. "They said he was too old. Well, he sure wasn't too old to get them there!"

"Mm-hm," Charlie replied absently, scribbling something down. "That ought'a be enough," he said, closing the book, "Now I just gotta remember what I wrote." He picked up the piece of paper and studied it. "Okay. Headlines for December 29, 1890: Army massacres 150 Indians at Wounded Knee; and Mrs. Polly Dickey of Belfast, Maine turns one hundred years old." Charlie shook his head. "If this doesn't convince her we traveled into the future, nothin' will."

"Oh," Mrs. Scapolli said. "With what Mr. Humphrey told you? I don't even think you'll even need that information. After your talk with old Ben, it should be obvious to Bonnie and everyone else that she's better off without that low-life."

"Well, I've got it if I need it."

"If you can remember it."

"Right."

Mrs. Scapolli reached out and patted his hand.

"I really enjoyed meeting you, Charlie MacLeod."

"Right back at you," he replied. "Now don't forget. After I've been gone a while, go ahead and check that history book, see if it actually worked. Of course, you won't be able to relay the information to me, but ... I don't know. Either it works or it don't."

"Oh, it will, Charlie. I can feel it in my bones."

He heaved a sigh.

"Well, old bird," he said, extending his finger for Salty. "I suppose we should get goin'." He looked out the window towards next door. "I gotta stop and talk to the boys before I go."

Mrs. Scapolli made a sour face.

"You know," Charlie said. "Everyone deserves someone to love."

"I know," Mrs. Scapolli pouted. "But those two?"

"They seem to make 'em happy."

"I suppose. But you haven't met them yet."

"Well," Charlie said, grabbing his crutches and climbing to his foot, "I'm about to *real* soon."

Chapter Thirty-Eight

SPLASH!!!

The pool party was on.

"A little to th' left ther-r-re. Aye. That's it. Ahhhhh."

Paddy liked having a girlfriend. It was a lot easier than he thought, and much more fun than he ever imagined. Myrtle, as she had explained, was a master tantric masseuse. Paddy wasn't sure exactly what that meant, but he was sure he liked it.

"Hey!" Gnarles yelled from his perch on Gertrude's shoulders. "Watch me stuff this basket, guys!"

Swoosh!!

Gert submerged herself and came up with Gnarles in her arms.

"To your throne, Sire?"

"To the throne!"

Obviously, Gnarles was enjoying himself as well.

"What to drink, sweetie?" Gertrude asked.

"How about one of those Molson's. That's some good stuff."

"Aye!" Paddy called out. "How abooot a Mooolson for-r-r me, toooo."

"Anything, sis?"

"I'm good," Myrtle replied, lying back in her chaise lounge. "As long as I have my Little Irish Dynamo here. Go ahead," she said. "Say, 'It won't be long now, my darlin'.'"

Paddy swelled and sang, "I wooon't b' loooong noooow, m'daaarlin'."

"Oh," she sighed. "I just love your accent!" She reached over and gave him a friendly squeeze.

Paddy put his hands behind his head and grinned.

"Hey!"

Everyone was startled.

"Who's that usin' me own *'m'darlin's'* over there?"

A cheery face peered over the fence.

"Oh!" Myrtle screamed. "Charlie MacLeod!" and she grabbed a cover-up and ran into the house.

Just then, Gertrude came out the door wearing only a bikini bottom. "Oh!" she screamed. "Charlie MacLeod!" and she ran back into the house.

Charlie grinned. "Should I ask how you boys are doin'?"

Gnarles and Paddy sat motionless, as if they had been caught doing something they shouldn't.

"Gotta say, you boys look good in those dark spectacles and those tight, white shorts."

"They're called shades," Gnarles said. "Wayfarers."

"Well, ya look good. And you're havin' fun, I presume?"

They nodded.

Charlie looked around at the back yard.

"Now this is something I could get used to," he said. "I've never seen such clear water. Scantily clad women are always a draw as well." He shook his head. "I gotta say, it looks like you boys struck gold here."

Myrtle came out, dressed and coifed, followed by Gertrude.

Adoring fans.

"Oh!" Gertrude gushed. "Hello." She glanced at Myrtle. "Aren't you going to introduce us to your friend? Boys?"

"Uh, yeah," Gnarles said, getting up from his chaise lounge. "Girls," he said, "this here is Charlie MacLeod. Charlie? These are the girls, uh, Gertrude and Myrtle."

"Well, well," Charlie replied. "It's a mighty big pleasure to meet you young ladies."

"Oh!" Gertrude continued to gush. "We've read all about you, Mr. MacLeod!"

Charlie seemed taken aback.

"Is that so?"

"Oh, yes. Not only in Tim Robinson's wonderful book, but in Debi Murray's, and Marty Baum's, and Sandra Thurlow's."

"That's right," Myrtle interjected. "It's like you were everywhere. From Biscayne Bay to Indian River. Your name is mentioned in local histories from all up and down the coast. You're an icon!" she exclaimed.

Charlie looked at the girls, then the boys, and asked, "Why is it you kids aren't married yet?"

They all looked at each other.

"I am a sea captain, ya know. I could marry you kids."

They all gave him blank stares.

He laughed.

"I'm just kiddin'. But before I go, I thought it might be nice ta visit a while."

"Oh!" Gertrude exclaimed. "I'm so sorry. Please, Mr. MacLeod –"

"Charlie."

"Charlie," she gushed some more. "Just come around the fence there, and we'll get the gate for you. Oh, lover boy! Would you mind getting the gate for Charlie while I go in and get him something to drink?"

"Sure thing, hot mama," Gnarles replied, grabbing a bathrobe hanging on a chair. "Oh!" he shouted. "Why don't you grab him one of them Molson's, baby?"

He turned to see Charlie's grinning face.

"Baby, huh?"

The women fell in love with Salty, passing him between themselves, testing his sailor vocabulary.

"He does have a mouth on him," Myrtle said.

"He does that," Charlie replied.

"So, you think it's all true?" Gnarles asked.

"Looks like it to me. This egghead Robinson seems to have most of his facts straight elsewhere. And I don't want to get your hopes up, but I just went over to see old Ben Humphrey."

Gnarles and Paddy's eyes grew wide.

"Now I know what you're thinkin', but believe me, you don't want to go over there. Anyway, I got some information that might just take care of everything for us – and Bonnie." He held up his hand. "I don't want to go into it right now. You'll just have to trust me on that. Now," he said. "I want to thank you boys for takin' me Molly girl to the wedding yesterday. You two are good friends."

"Aw, it weren't nothin'," Gnarles replied.

"Well, I just want you to know it's appreciated; and I've never had better friends. Now," Charlie said, sipping on his Molson. "I gotta get home and check on that lovely lass of mine." He paused. "I'm sorry I didn't believe you boys."

"Oh, that's all right," Gnarles replied. "We know it all sounds crazy. Heck, you were the only one that believed us enough to come over and see for yourself. According to Gert here, that means you're an ag-nostril."

"I think it's agnostic."

"Right. They believe in all possibilities."

Charlie glanced at Gertrude, and said, "I reckon that's a good way 'a puttin' it."

They were sitting around the table, in the shade of the porch. Myrtle was perched on Paddy's lap, wiggling and distracting him. All four were living in the moment, oblivious and uninterested in their next move.

"I noticed the Past Time Machine still works fine." Charlie was blunt: "I'm concerned about the Future Patch, though." He pointed over the fence. "Have you two noticed anything different about the Future Patch and the Past Patch?"

They shook their heads.

"Well, I did. The Future Patch is flowering way ahead of the Past Patch. I find that mighty strange, don't you?"

"Oh," Gnarles said. "That must be because of the Miracle Gro."

"Miracle Gro?"

"Yeah. We put some on the Future Patch to get it to grow faster. And did it! Right, Paddy?"'

"Aye. It did."

"Well," Charlie said, "I've got a sneakin' suspicion that this Miracle Gro has sped up the process for the Future Patch, and by doin' that it's not as accurate at landin' us where we ought'a be." He sighed and took a drink. "I gotta tell you, boys. You might want to get used to the idea that this is all temporary. At some point this time machine will completely fail. I'm guessin' when the plants finish flowerin' or sometime thereabouts."

The full weight of the situation settled over them.

You mean –

"That's exactly what I mean. I ain't sayin' you shouldn't go back there, but if you do, you gotta accept the fact that you might not be able to make it back here."

Paddy's lower lip began to quiver.

"Look," Charlie said. "I really don't want to get you two all worked up, but you got a decision to make."

The pool partiers looked at each other. They knew it was true. They had blocked it from their minds.

"Seems to me it's decision time," Charlie said. "I'm leavin' right away myself. Now, I don't want to alarm you folks, but it seems to me the sooner we leave, the better chance we got of landin' in the right time." He looked from one to the other. "Have you kids thought about this? Gnarles," he said. "If you want to go back, you have to do it soon. Real soon."

Gnarles looked helplessly at Gertrude, who reached out and touched his cheek. "Mert," she said. "We have to decide. Now."

"But you said we weren't going back."

"I know, but … if it's our only chance." She sighed and looked at the roofs of the surrounding houses. "It's so nice back then," she sighed. "A beautiful, unscathed, pristine world." She looked at her sister, who had stopped wiggling and distracting. "We'd have to go now: no packing; no preparing; no goodbyes."

"Goodbye to who? The library staff?" Myrtle said. "Just leave 'em a note. Tell 'em we were swept away by a couple of rum barons."

"Are you serious?" Gertrude said. "You really want to go back? To stay? Forever?"

Myrtle shrugged. "Are you kiddin'? This place sucks."

"But," Gertrude said, glancing nervously at the boys. "We'd need a place to stay, you know, a *real* house. And what would we do for money? We can't be scrubbing on a washboard, and we don't know how to cook if it doesn't come in a bag that says 'three minutes in microwave on high.'"

"Ahem," Charlie said. "If I may assist?"

"Really?"

"Well," Charlie said. "I don't know if the boys told you, but I have a pretty nice 'saving's account,' buried up on Indian River."

"Oh, no!" Gnarles exclaimed. "You can't give us your buried treasure."

"Buried treasure?!" Both women gasped.

"That's right," Charlie said. "And I wouldn't be giving it to you. It'll just be payment for all these years that you supplied me with the finest rum known to man. Lord knows I've tried, but you've never let me pay you one red cent over all these years."

"That's 'cause you're our friend."

"That's right, "Charlie said. "And as a friend, I've decided I should finally pay my bill, for forty some odd years of happy days and sloshy nights. In fact, if you won't accept payment, I'd take it kind of personal."

Gnarles sighed. "O-kay."

"Good," Charlie said. "Now, it's not enough to keep you gals in furs and diamonds, but it's enough to keep you comfortable."

"Oh!" Myrtle exclaimed. "We wouldn't need much, right, Gert? You know," she nodded towards the yard next door. "The still?"

"Riiight," Gertrude said. She squeezed Gnarles' knee. "You know, sweetie. I was going to bring that up. You two really need a middle man, a manager, someone who can up production and push that sweet nectar you call Cocorum. Hoo!" she sighed. "You boys could make a bundle!"

"I've been tellin' 'em that for years," Charlie said. "They're the ones sittin' on buried treasure, by Jiminy! Why, I been around the world and back a few times, and I've never tasted anything like what comes out of that little rum kettle over there."

They all looked through the fence slats at the still on top of the Weber grill, going steadily, dripping its nectar into a milk jug. It was clear Jeff was learning his craft well.

"So," Charlie said. "I guess it's settled. I'm headin' home, and you all should be clearin' out soon."

Everyone looked at him as if he were from a galaxy far, far away.

You mean ... now?

"Just one thing left," Charlie said. "Right, Salty?"

"Right, Salty," Salty squawked.

Wondering faces.

"Well," Charlie explained. "It seems to me you can't be takin' Gnarles and Paddy back in this condition."

Huh?

"Oh, no," he went on. "They departed the past as pure as the driven snow. They should return as properly married men."

Everyone looked at each other.

"I am a sea captain, ya know." He pointed. "And that," he indicated the pool, "is a body of water." He paused and looked around, as if sizing up the situation. "So," he announced with authority. "Everybody in the pool. I'm goin' next door for a Bible – and a very reluctant witness."

Chapter Thirty-Nine

1890

As a green mist dissipated, Charlie smiled. His clothes and Ole Peg were lying nearby on a chair.

"Good old Gnarles and Paddy," he said, balancing himself against the still. "Must 'a found these in the Magic Bean Patch last time they were here." He carefully hopped over and sat down.

He looked up through the craggy pines. He couldn't see exactly where the sun was, but it was sometime in the afternoon. What day, he had no idea. He dressed as quickly as he could, and he and Salty hurried down the trail.

"What do you think, old bird? Everything looked pretty normal back there. I don't think we're too far off the mark."

When he got to the lakefront, *Dolly Varden* was still tied where he had left her. He noticed *Cocoa-nuts* was not in her berth. He tried to make sense of it, but, realizing there was no point, he climbed in the fat little boat and pushed offshore, out from under the mangroves and onto the lake.

As he expertly set the sails, he looked northward, and what he saw astounded him.

"Well, I'll be a son a –"

"Aarrak! Son of a Sea Dog!" Salty squawked.

A mighty grin enveloped Charlie's face as he got the boat moving. He'd be there in in a matter of minutes.

The closer he came, the bigger he grinned. It had been a topic of conversation mere minutes ago – plus one hundred years. He had laughed, big powerful guffaws when the "kids" had told him how Myrtle tossed pie and cookies all over Malcolm, and from what he could see he might actually make it in time to witness it for himself.

He pushed his little craft harder.

"Look at that, Salty!" he howled. "That Bamboo – or *Señor* Salvatore, whatever that Puerto Rican angel's name is – has got one wicked sense of humor!"

"Wicked humor!!" Salty squawked.

When he got to shore, Charlie took special care getting out of the boat, then he hurried up the path. No one seemed to notice his arrival with the spectacle unfolding before them. Then he remembered something. A small detail had not escaped him, and he hurriedly pushed his way through the crowd.

"Excuse me. Yes, thank you. Nice to see you. Thank you. Pardon me."

A murmur coursed through the assemblage.

Gertrude stepped aside, obviously aware of who he was but just as obviously unaware she had just met him a little while earlier, one hundred years later.

Charlie could not believe his luck. The timing could not have been better. He caught Bonnie's eye and sidled up next to her, as if he were posing for the photo, then he concentrated on Myrtle's changing expression. Timing it perfectly, he pulled Bonnie to safety just as a slimy barrage splashed across Malcolm's chest.

Charlie had recalled Gertrude's future words to Myrtle: "It's too bad you got spew all over Bonnie's dress."

As everyone stood in stark, stunned silence, Charlie's unrestrained guffaws reverberated across the shores of old Port Starboard.

And when Charlie MacLeod laughed, everyone laughed.

Malcolm was horrified, as was Bonnie, but her dress remained perfectly spotless.

"Oh, Charlie!" Mrs. Milsap exclaimed. "You saved Bonnie's dress!"

"How did you know?!" someone shouted.

Charlie simply grinned, and said, "Salty here! He's been to the future!"

Betsy's ears were turning red.

"What the hell's goin' on around here?!" she bellowed. "Oh, I see! You were in on it the whole time, Charlie! You were in on Gnarles and Paddy's plan to ruin my wedding! My wedding! Oh, it all makes perfect sense now!"

As Gnarles and Paddy quivered, Charlie took Gertrude and Myrtle, one under each arm, and said, very conciliatorily, "Sorry, Betsy. We were just going. Come along, girls!"

Myrtle grimaced as they led her away.

"It must have been that black and white cookie."

Everyone then watched as the strange spectacle hurried down the Lake Trail into the woods – and not once did any of them look back.

A few minutes later returned up the lake trail.

"Hey, Uncle Charlie!"

It was Annie. She ran to meet him.

"Uncle Charlie, I don't know what to think! Who are those women? Do Gnarles and Paddy really have girlfriends? They look really pretty. That was what everyone was saying." She sighed heavily and frowned. "They said they looked much too good for Gnarles and Paddy, but I don't think so. I think they look perfect for them."

"Ya know, kiddo?" he said, handing off Salty. "I do, too."

"Are you all right, Uncle Charlie?" Annie asked, concern in her voice.

"Fine and dandy, Sweetpea!"

"We missed you at the wedding."

"I know ya did. I just couldn't make it is all." He paused and took a breath. "I'm fine, though. Just had some things ta tidy up is all."

"So, is everything okay?"

"Well, yes. I hope so." He took a deep breath. "Look, kiddo. Someday I'll tell you everything that's happened the last few days. It's crazy, though. I'm still tryin' ta sort it out in me own head. You'll just have to trust me about it right now. But," he said, "I do need to talk with your ma."

"Momma? But –"

"Nothin' to worry about, kiddo. It has nothin' to do with you, right, Salty?"

"Aarrraak! Not likely, dude!"

"I just need to talk to Katie is all," Charlie said. He could see Annie was crushed. They were best friends. That's what best friends do. She wanted to help.

"I'm sorry, kiddo."

She sighed. "It's all right, Uncle Charlie." Then she giggled. "I'll get it all out of Momma later on!"

Charlie grinned. "There's my Sweetpea. Just like her old Uncle Charlie."

"Gnarles and Paddy took Molly home after the wedding," Annie said.

"I know."

"How did you know?"

"Oh, well, I mean, I noticed she wasn't here and just … assumed. Look, kiddo," he said, "I'm goin' up to Betsy's porch. Would you ask your ma to come on up?"

Annie looked at him curiously, then shrugged. "Okay!" And off she went.

As Charlie got comfortable on the porch, he watched Annie get Katie's attention. She looked at him, perplexed, then excused herself and hurried across the lawn and up to the porch. As she made her way over, Charlie focused on Bonnie.

"She really is a beautiful girl," he said to himself, "inside and out."

He hated what he had to do. The thought that he would be ruining Bonnie's day, the day she had dreamed about since she was a little girl, made him ill to his stomach.

He would have to tread lightly – and Charlie wasn't known for his delicate touch.

"Hi, Uncle Charlie," Katie said.

"And how is m'darlin' lass?" he said. He stood and gave her a hug.

Charlie looked at Annie.

"I'm sorry, Sweetpea. Do you mind?"

"No," Annie sighed, and she shuffled away.

Katie was concerned. "What is it, Uncle Charlie? Is everything all right?"

"I'm not sure, lass, but I'm gonna need your help." He paused. "Now, I know this is gonna sound crazy, but ya gotta trust me. I'm not sure myself exactly what the end point is, but I'm certain there's no harm that can come from it." He paused. "What I want is for you to let me talk to Benji, with you here, of course."

Katie put her hand to her chest.

"Benji?"

"You just gotta trust me on this."

She studied her uncle's weathered face a moment, then called out, "Benji? Would you come up here a minute? Not you, dear! Just Benji!"

Annie scowled.

"Benji," Katie said. "Uncle Charlie wants to talk to you. Okay?"

Benji shrugged as only a seven-year-old boy can.

"Benji," Charlie said, leaning forward and tousling his hair, "I'm gonna ask you a couple 'a questions, all right?

"Sure."

"Do you remember the day Uncle Will died?"

Benji looked at the ground.

He continued. "Now, Benji, I want you to listen to me. You've done nothin' wrong. You are not in any trouble. Isn't that so, Katie?"

"Why … yes," she replied, shock written across her face. "Benji, no matter what it is, you can tell us. You won't be in any trouble."

"Not even from Poppa?"

"Not even a bit."

He scuffed his shoe on the ground.

"Or Grandmama?"

"Well … no. Not with Mother Humphrey either."

"Or … God?"

"Heavens, no!" she exclaimed. "God loves you! Whatever it is you think you've done, God … and Mommy, still love you!"

"Benji," Charlie said. "You don't have to worry. God knows you snuck out of church that day, and he has already forgiven you." Benji's eyes grew wide. "Why," Charlie continued. "I've missed so much church, I'm surprised the Big Guy hasn't … uh, never mind. The point is, God is more concerned with what's in your heart. Right, lassie?"

"Oh, absolutely!"

"Now," Charlie said. "What I want you to do is tell your ma and me what you saw that day. Down at Sally's house."

Without lifting his head, Benji mumbled, "Mr. Geoffreys put a pillow over Uncle Will's face. I couldn't see real good, but I saw him hold Uncle Will's pillow over his face and then Uncle Will went to sleep."

Katie couldn't contain a gasp.

Suddenly Benji burst into tears and buried his face in her lap.

"I'm sorry, Momma," he sobbed. "I didn't know, and Grandmama told me about a boy who snuck out of church one day when she was a little girl and he got lost in the woods and was eaten by a wolf because God was punishing him! I'm sorry, Momma. I didn't know Uncle Will was gonna die!"

Katie couldn't believe what she was hearing. She looked at Charlie.

"How ... did you know?"

"It's a long story, lass. Now, Benji," he said, "I just need you to answer one more question, then we'll be all done."

He wiped clumsily at his eyes. "All right."

"Benji," he said. "Do you think you could tell Miss Bonnie and Judge Heyser the same thing you just told us?"

Chapter Forty

Revealing the truth to Bonnie was one of the most difficult things Charlie ever had to do. At the same time, it was one of the most exhilarating and rewarding. His emotions had run the gamut over the past hour and a half.

It had been a slow, agonizing process. After Benji told Katie what happened, they had called Bonnie over. It was a moment Charlie never wanted to relive, the moment he pulled the rug out from under her entire life, her life dream, her entire future, gone.

He thought she had handled it as well as could be expected, the initial shock. She had sobbed uncontrollably and had been nearly inconsolable. Katie and Betsy had taken her inside so she wouldn't have to witness the proceedings: Sheriff Highsmith leading her husband off to the Juno Courthouse. There was little question of his guilt.

They were in the hotel dining room, Bonnie and all her closest friends, Maggie, of course, Christiane, Callie, Annie, and Silas.

Most of the guests had remained. Betsy had instructed them to go ahead and enjoy the giant table of food and drink; Bonnie had asked that she do so. Bonnie had calmed down to some extent, though she looked horrible, eyes red and puffy and a runny nose.

Charlie went outside and waited. He had instructed Annie to let him know when Bonnie was ready for a short discussion. She came out to the front porch and tapped him on the shoulder.

"Momma says she's calming down now."

"Good." Charlie got up and led Annie around the side of the hotel. "All right, kiddo," he said, lowering his voice. "Here's what we're gonna do."

As he laid out his plan, Annie could barely contain her glee.

No one was in the kitchen. Charlie sat down at the table.

"All right," he nodded. "Go ahead." Then he waited. A moment later, Bonnie walked in.

"You wanted to see me, Uncle Charlie?"

He could see she needed a hug, so he obliged. She sobbed for several minutes as he told her he was sorry.

"It's all right," she choked. "I know you did it because you love me."

"I do that, lass," he replied. He motioned her to sit down.

Taking smooth, alabaster hands in aged, gnarled ones, he said, "There's one more thing, but don't worry, ya hear? It's nothin' bad."

Bonnie nodded and dabbed at her swollen nose.

Charlie stared into beautiful, blue, bloodshot eyes, and said, "You know, I've been around."

Bonnie nodded.

"And I like to think I know people."

"Yes?"

"Well," he said. "I got one question, and I want you to think before you answer, all right?"

"Okay."

Charlie squeezed her hands, and said, "What I want is for you to tell me what you're lookin' for in a man, the perfect man for Bonnie Blakely."

"Well," she sniffed, taking time to think. "First of all, he would have to be honest." Saying the word caused her to grimace, but she kept on. "And he'd have to be kind. And gentle, and generous, and forgiving," she choked up again and took a deep breath. "And funny." She faintly smiled and almost started to cry again. "I'd want him to make me laugh."

"Young lady," Charlie said. "I hope I'm not bein' too presumptuous here, but I got just one more question."

She nodded and dabbed at her nose.

Charlie cleared his throat, and gazing deep into iridescent orbs of sapphire, he said, "Bonnie Blakely, would you do me the honor –" he paused and gestured with his hand towards the kitchen door – "of marrying my good friend here, Silas Hempsted?'

Bonnie looked at her best friend, suddenly standing there, and surprise – on both sides – transformed to comprehension, then to astonishment as if she realized she was indeed looking into the eyes of the perfect man. It was as if in one glorious instant, Bonnie knew exactly what she wanted – in a man, out of life, everything!

Her eyes frantically searched those of Silas.

"Really, Silas?"

Silas looked like he was having trouble concentrating.

He glanced at Charlie, then mumbled, "Well, yes. I mean, yes! Yes!! Of course, I do!!"

He appeared unable to move, however, so Charlie said, "So? Are ya gonna kiss your fiancée or am I gonna have to do that for ya, too?!"

Even with that, Annie had to nudge Silas forward. Then she giggled and squirmed with delight as the best friends suddenly and unalterably became much, much more than that.

Chapter Forty-One

After everything settled, Katie and Betsy put Bonnie to bed. Then they headed out to celebrate. Everyone had concluded that it was not a bad thing. In fact, it was the very best possible thing! They had sung *For He is a Jolly Good Fellow* to Charlie as he departed in his fat, little boat.

It had been a trying day for Bonnie, a horrible day, but by the time she went to bed she was feeling much better. Much, much better. There had been only one possible cure for Bonnie's ill, and that turned out to be none other than Silas Hempsted.

He had handled the situation perfectly, holding her hand and telling her to take all the time she wanted, even that he would not hold her to her promise. He understood; she was under a lot of pressure. But Bonnie had been adamant; she wanted to marry him, and as soon as possible!

"Except," she sighed. "What will people think?"

"Think?"

They had sat alone in the smoking lounge, sitting on a sofa, facing each other. Everything felt strange, and awkward.

"Silas," she said. "I truly, truly love you. I don't know how I could not have seen it! It was right in front of me all the time. I do love you!" She took his plain face in her hands and held it, taking the time to gaze deeper into his eyes than she ever had before. "Silas," she said. "I am looking at everything I have ever wanted. Everything!" She paused. "All my life I've let myself get swept off my feet, when all I ever needed was someone to help me keep my feet planted firmly on the ground."

Silas appeared to be pretty much in a coma. He was trying to act normal, muttering something about being with his best friend and jabbering about books and pirates and sea cucumbers.

Bonnie leaned forward, and asked him again, "What about what people think, Silas?"

Silas stared, then he sputtered, "What do you mean 'What people think?'"

Taking his hands in hers, she said, "Silas, people will think I married you just so I could inherit my family's fortune."

"Oh, that," he said dismissively, even with relief in his voice.

Bonnie smiled affectionately, waiting, until finally, Silas said, "Well, if you still want to marry me –"

"Silas," she stopped him. "Please don't say that. I *do* want to marry you. I've never wanted anything more!"

"Then," he stammered. "Maybe we should wait until the benefit date has expired."

Bonnie's eyes grew wide.

"Really? You'd give up all that money, just like that?"

"Of course," he replied. "You are not your money, Bonnie. I hope you don't mind my saying so, but you are so much more than that. In fact, your inheritance is the very least of you. Less than your eyes or your nose or your elbow. Infinitely less even than the toenail on your pinky toe!"

Bonnie smiled adoringly and once again she cried, but this time with tears of joy.

"But," she sniffed. "If we do get married before the cutoff date, we could start that orphanage."

Silas smiled at her, not as a friend but the man who would swim through shark-infested waters to bring her a lemonade, and said, "Well, then, who cares what people say?" He paused, then said, "It's for the kids."

"Yes," Bonnie sighed. "For the kids." Then she took Silas's plain face in her exquisite hands and kissed him, not as a friend, however, but as a lover, the man she would adore until the day she died.

Chapter Forty-Two

Charlie was pretty full of himself.

"Yep! One damsel in distress rescued. Check!"

He and Molly were sitting out on the back porch, watching the tiny waves. The seas were almost flat, and several pelicans were bobbing around on the water. The sun was beginning to cast shadows as it sank into the clouds.

"And they really sang 'For He's a Jolly Good Fellow'?"

"Yep." Charlie rested his foot on her lap.

"Oh," Molly said. "And now I suppose the hero of the day needs his foot rubbed?"

"Now, that's not why I put it there, m'darlin'. You know that. I just want to feel close to you."

Molly gave him a look, then brushed some sand off and started rubbing.

"Oh, you deserve it," she said. "Shoot, you deserve a freaking medal!"

Charlie looked sideways.

"Freaking?"

Molly shrugged. "It's a good word … dude!" She giggled.

"There's a few of 'em," he said. "Ya know? Hot momma?!"

Just a few minutes later, Charlie was lost in thought.

"What's goin' on up there?" Molly asked.

"Oh, just thinkin' about Silas."

Molly giggled. "I wonder if he's still out there."

Charlie grinned. "Oh, I don't think he's goin' anywhere until they get back. I told him he had to see it, a once in a lifetime opportunity."

"I cannot believe you told him to go stand out there in the dark and wait for them to get back."

"If they get back."

"All right, big fella," Molly sighed. "You're not gonna be happy until you know, so go on and get in your little boat and get over there before it gets dark. You're not gonna get wink of sleep thinkin' about it, so get on over there and sit with Silas."

"Really?" Charlie said. "You're sure you don't mind?"

"Well," she said, pushing his foot to the floor. "As long as I can be assured that there's no more travelin' to the future, and," she added with a sly smile, "I've got a foot rub comin' when you get home."

"Oh, you'll be gettin' a lot more than that," Charlie said, and, kissing his bride, he set Salty on his shoulder and hobbled off.

Several hours later

Charlie was sitting next to Silas in front of the still, staring. He had placed the chairs for an optimum view; then he had gathered up everyone's clothes and laid them out on a third chair.

He was concerned but not worried; not yet anyway. Of course, he had no idea if they even planned on coming back, but he had decided he would give it until morning, then he'd head home. He wondered if he would ever see his old friends again, and if he did, if they would return with the girls. It's one thing to say you'll leave everything you know behind, quite another to actually do it.

He had told Silas it was something he would not want to miss, a once in a lifetime opportunity to witness someone arriving from another time. While they waited, Charlie filled Silas with endless tales of the sea.

By the wee hours, they were both having trouble staying focused and were starting to nod off.

Charlie's eyelids grew heavy. He was dreaming of New York City, the sounds of cobblestone streets and horses' hooves, children playing and people talking.

Someone was speaking.

"Oh, look. They're both sound asleep."

"And look, they laid out our clothes for us. How sweet."

Charlie was slowly coming around when he heard someone else exclaim, "Oh, my Lord!!"

His eyes popped open. A green haze hung in the air.

Surprise!!

Four naked old people.

Charlie sat up and looked over at Silas. He was making a strange gurgling sound, like he was choking on his own words. The sight seemed almost too much to bear, but he couldn't look away.

Charlie laughed, and, slapping Silas on the back, he said, "Surprise, young fella!"

"Surprise!" Salty squawked.

The women modestly covered up with their hands and giggled.

"Sorry ya had ta see that, young fella!" Charlie boomed. "But that's life! Ya got your ups, and ya got your downs!"

After turning several shades of red, Silas dragged his eyes away, and mumbled, "I'll just wait for you all over there," and he hurried down the trail.

Before the quartet had departed the past, eleven hours earlier – or forty-three seconds, depending which end you were measuring from – the newlyweds had celebrated their passage and built up their courage with an enthusiastic sampling of "Capt. Jeff's Infamous Cocoanut Spiced Rum; est. 1990; Port Starboard, Florida." Jeff had already made up several prototype bottles with hand-drawn labels.

"Aw, you scared him, Gert!"

"How d'ya know it was me?"

"'Cause of those, of course." She pointed. "Those things can be scary to a tenderfoot like that."

"You think?" Gertrude pouted, holding them up. "I wouldn't call them scary. Would you, boys?"

The three men stared a moment, then Charlie said, "Yes. But in a *very* good way."

After everyone was dressed, they called Silas then headed down the trail.

"Ya can't tell anyone," Charlie explained. "The fewer people that know, the better."

"That's right," Gnarles said. "First of all, people will think you're crazy, and second of all, uh –"

"Secon' of all," Myrtle slurred, "ya haven' seen *Back to the Future*."

"Right." Everyone agreed.

As they neared Gnarles and Paddy's house, that particular subject came up.

"Oh," Myrtle said. "I want to put the house as close to the water as possible."

"Yes!" Gertrude replied. "With a deck that goes right out over the lake!"

"And a diving board!"

"Oooooo," Paddy clapped. "A diving board!"

This went on for some time until they reached the swimming hole, and Charlie said, "You kids might want to think about more pressing matters right now."

"You're right," Gertrude said. "I'm just SO excited! I cannot believe this is happening!" She twirled around like a teenage girl, staring skyward at the blue speckled canopy overhead. "It's like a dream come true! A dream come true!!" She pulled Gnarles close and kissed him on the forehead. "And it's all thanks to my little sledge-hammer here."

Gnarles pulled up his trousers with a smug smirk.

"Nothin' to it, baby."

"So," Gertrude said, looking to Charlie. "What do we do? We need a place to stay, I mean, I love you, Sledge, but your place, well –"

"I think the boys understand," Charlie said, "don't you, boys? The girls don't want to stay in that radical bachelor pad. They're girls, for Pete's sake!"

"No problem, babe," Gnarles replied. "We'll just put you up in the hotel, right, Charlie?"

"That's a good idea, Gnarles. A great idea, in fact!" Charlie grinned. "Just tell Betsy I got it covered."

"Oh, Charlie," Gertrude said. "I don't know how we can ever repay you."

"Just take good care of my two buddies here is all I ask. Ya won't find a better pair, now or in the future."

"That's for sure," Myrtle cooed in Paddy's ear. "I don't think I'll ever find a better pair."

"We're discovering that more and more all the time," Gertrude replied, and she kissed Gnarles on the head.

"Thanks, baby."

"And I'm discovering more all the time, too," Myrtle added, squeezing Paddy's rear.

As they went on, discussing their new, exciting future, Charlie's mind wandered to Betsy's reaction to the news.

"Oh, this is gonna be good," he mumbled under his breath.

"Gonna be good!" Salty squawked.

Epilogue

Mrs. Scapolli got dinner started and went out to the enclosed porch. Lying on the table was the big book. She closed her eyes a moment and made a wish, then she flipped through the pages until she got to the "B's." She ran her finger down the page.

"Blakely, Bonnie," she mumbled under her breath. Her eyes lit up. "See Hempsted, Bonnie Blakely. Oh!!" she exclaimed, jumping up and down. "Jeffie!" she yelled. "Hurry!!"

Jeff bowled out of the room, looking like he'd just awakened from a deep sleep, or a very good buzz.

"What?!" he cried, then he ran into the corner of the piano. "Shi-i ... i-DAMMIT!!"

He lurched around the corner, a very red face and tears in his eyes.

"Did you run into the piano again, Jeffie?" Grandma called from the other room.

Jeff sat down in the nearest chair and held his pinky toe.

"I thought ... something was ... wrong!"

"Oh, I'm sorry, but look!" she exclaimed. "This is so exciting! Look! It's all different! Everything is different! See?! Bonnie marries Silas. And look! That lowlife goes to jail!!"

"For life?"

"No, just thirty years. It says he got out and became a Fuller Brush salesman. But look! There is no Malcolm, Jr. at all. And look! Their two kids are named Charlie (Charles) and Molly Hempsted. Oh," she said, holding her hands to her chest. "That is so sweet. And look, young Charlie graduates early and goes to college and becomes an engineer, then he joins the navy and later becomes an admiral! An admiral, Jeffie!"

"That's nice."

"And when his parents, Bonnie and Silas," she giggled, "got old, he and his wife took over the orphanage and kept it going for another thirty years!" Mrs. Scapolli scowled. "I bet that's that giant, ugly condominium they made that big fuss over. Remember, Jeffie?" Jeff was studying his little toe, as if wondering if he'd ever surf again. "The government took the land from him," Grandma continued, "then sold it to some developers who built that hideous monstrosity. Oh!" she said. "Let's look up Gnarles and Paddy!"

"Can we celebrate with a chocolate soufflé?"

Mrs. Scapolli didn't hear him.

"Oh, look!"

The doorbell rang, and Jeff hobbled over to answer it. It was a tall man with a suit and little round glasses.

"Yo, dude."

"Yes, my name is Frederick Fratterman, and I would like to speak to a Mrs. Wanda Scapolli. Do I have the correct address?" He glanced at the Babelicious Mobile.

"That's my grandma, dude. Hold on."

"Just let him in, silly!" said Mrs. Scapolli.

"Come on in," Jeff said.

Following several pleasantries, something to drink and a place to sit, Mr. Fratterman said, "Mrs. Scapolli, we at Fratterman and Associates represent a trust originally set up by, let's see, a Gnarleston and Gertrude Hawkins and a Patrick and Myrtle O'Toole back in, let's see, 1898. This trust was created to maintain an escrow account funded by proceeds from, let's see, Cocoa Rico Rum Distillers International."

"Cool! Don't they make Parrot Cove Cocoanut Spiced Rum?"

"I'm ... not sure."

"So," Jeff snickered. "How much we talkin' here? Millions?"

"Not quite," Mr. Fratterman replied. "It's, let's see, one point two three billion in total assets and interest in several thousand acres of land in Puerto Rico, Barbados, and Jamaica."

Mrs. Scapolli and Jeff looked at each other. Then Jeff fainted dead away into his grandmother's arms.

After Mr. Fratterman helped her get him onto the sofa, he said, "There was also a message from the last survivor of the trust, that would be, let's see, Gertrude Hawkins. She died in ... 1923. He peered through his reading glasses. "It says, 'Sorry we didn't fix the fence.'"

* * *

Molly awakened from a deep sleep and realized the bed was shaking. She sat up and stared at Charlie. A smile creased her lips. She watched a little longer, then she giggled and sank back into the covers, pulled the pillow over her head, and mumbled, "Leave it to you, Charlie MacLeod, to have such entertaining dreams."

Postscript

March 12, 1938; Linz, Austria

A man sits alone in an empty office, staring out a window overlooking the town square. He is wearing a soldier's uniform. In the corner the previous owner lay lifeless, his trachea crushed.

He is a tall man, curly blonde hair and good-looking with a strong, square jawline and piercing blue eyes. He is smoking a Camel cigarette and watching the proceedings below where tens of thousands of people are gathered in the square, their attentions singularly focused on a solitary man in a military uniform. He is speaking from a hotel balcony, forcefully and with passion. Surrounding him is a phalanx of soldiers, all at rigid attention, listening attentively to their vaunted leader.

The man looks at his watch.

Though the man at the window speaks fluent German, he pays little attention to what the speaker is saying. He is absently reading a letter, now worn and frayed and coming apart at the folds. He has read it so many times that he has it memorized, but it isn't the words that compel him. It is the handwriting, the scratched-out, misspelled words, the humanity it represents, his last and only connection to a world very far away.

He wonders if he will ever see home again.

The speaker pauses, the crowd thunders applause, then he continues:

> "The fact that Providence has summoned me forth from this city to the leadership of the Reich was a special assignment! The assignment of restoring my cherished home, Austria, to the German Reich! I have believed in this assignment! I have lived and fought for it! And I believe I have now fulfilled it!!"

"*Seig Heil! Sieg Heil! Sieg Heil!*" The throng chants.

The man returns to his reading, imprinting it to memory: "Little Timmy wants me to tell you that he got a dime from the Tooth Fairy," the letter states, "and Daisy Marie does *not* want you to know she has a boyfriend (Don't worry, honey, I have a firm handle on things). Your mom and dad are fine, just saw them the other day. Your mother is recovering nicely from the operation; no complications at all you'll be happy to know. I don't think your father has left her side for more than twenty seconds in the past two months. I so hope we're like them when we get old. Oh, darling, we all miss you terribly and pray for your safe return, morning, noon, and night. I'm sorry. You'll have to let me go now, your oldest is screaming something about her new curlers melting her hair. I love you sweetheart and hope you are safe and well. Kisses, your adoring wife, Audrey."

The man displays no emotion as he glances up at the proceedings.

> "May you all witness and vouch for this! I do not know when you yourselves will be summoned! I hope the time is not far off! Then you will be asked to stand up to your own pledge! The outcome must then prove to the world that any attempt to tear this people asunder will be in vain!!"

The man takes a long drag on his cigarette and checks his watch, then he pulls the lighter from his pocket and lights the letter on fire. He watches it burn until it is nothing but ash. It is the last vestige of evidence identifying him as an officer in the U.S. Navy.

> "Just as you will then be under an obligation to make your contribution to this German future, the whole of Germany will likewise make its contribution to you! And this it is doing today!! May you see it in the German soldiers who are marching here this hour from all the Reich! Fighters willing and prepared to make sacrifices for the unity of the great German people as a whole, and for the power and the glory and the splendor of our Reich! Now and forever!! *Deutschland!! Sieg Heil*!!"

The crowd is in a frenzy.
"Seig Heil! Sieg Heil! Sieg Heil!"
The man in the room shakes his head.
"Sheep," he mutters under his breath, then he crushes his cigarette under his boot heel and picks up his Mauser rifle. The irony does not escape him. Kneeling in front of the window, he releases the safety, raises the scope to his eye and pauses.

"Providence, my ass," he mumbles, and Cmdr. Charles Hempsted, USN, squeezes the trigger.

It is an easy shot.

From The Hermit, *by Tim Robinson*

February 1881

Jedediah Stranahan wasn't aware of the screaming until it abruptly stopped. He ceased what he was doing, his eyes fixed on the small metal rod in his hand. He waited a moment, listening. The sound of a baby's first cry. He continued with his task.

He was in his workroom, a small building attached to the barn, and though it was cold outside, it was snug in the tiny, well-built structure. A potbelly stove radiated a steady stream of warmth, and a large window over the workbench bathed the room with morning light, made brighter by the reflection of fresh fallen snow. The window panes were frosted.

Focused on his work, he didn't hear the distinct sound of snow crunching under foot as someone approached, or the stomping on the doorstep. He was filing a rod to fit a small hole he had drilled in a bracket. He ignored the girl, his youngest daughter, standing in the doorway. Finally, he said, "Close that door; you're letting the cold in." He didn't look up.

Emily closed the door and stared at her father.

"What is it?" he finally asked.

She didn't respond. Finally, Jedediah looked up from his work and peered over the rim of his spectacles. She was crying.

He removed his glasses and studied her face.

"She's dead, Pa."

He showed no reaction.

"She's dead, Pa," she repeated, her voice shaking. The melting snow on her face blended with her tears. She stared at him, her eyes red with sorrow and rage. "It's all your fault," she said, emotion rising in her voice. When he didn't respond, she screamed at him. "She's dead, Pa! Gracie's dead! And it's all your fault!" She glared at him, then she ran out the door, slamming it behind her.

Jedediah listened to her footsteps fade away, then the door to the house bang shut. He stared at the empty space for several minutes before turning back to his task.

It was the cold.

That's what he told himself as he gazed at the object in his hand. If only it hadn't snowed last night. If only the temperature hadn't dropped below zero. If only his leg wasn't bothering him. If only the doctor didn't live so far away.

If only it wasn't so damned cold!

*   *   *

April 7, 1881

Dearest Mother,

If you are reading this, I am gone, never to walk our good Lord's green pastures again. Please forgive me if this is written badly, for I pen it at the helm of my sweet "Calliope." I am currently making my way northward to the home of the only doctor on the river, one hundred miles away. If you are reading this, Mother, you will know that I am no more.

You were correct, Mother, in warning me of the inherent and real dangers of such an undertaking. Indeed, it was one of these unlikely situations that you yourself brought to the fore that has now befallen your devoted son. It was a rattlesnake, Mother. Yes, the dreaded serpent assaulted me this morning, just as I was preparing to start work on the new cabin I am building. I heard his baleful rattle and leaped out of the way. But, as all woodsmen know in these parts, that was not the proper tact to take: the traveler is instructed to stand perfectly still until the devilish beast slithers away. He was large, even as these vipers go, his body as thick around as my own thigh. Never have I been hit with such force. It was as if a burly dockworker hit me square on the calf with a large, stiff board. I haven't the words to describe the pain, but rest assured, dearest Mother, my first thoughts were of you. Your kind, smiling face calmed and reassured me as I hurried back to my humble abode. You will be pleased to hear I had onions growing in my garden and quickly made a poultice of these, as you have taught me, to extract the poison, then I packed my grip, and though racked with pain and delirium I pushed off in my sweet "Calliope" with little more than a beggar's hope and a sinner's prayer.

Dearest Mother, I fear I may not be long for this cold, cruel world as it has been some time since the horrendous attack. At present, I remain in a coherent state though I am feeling light-headed and it is increasingly difficult to breathe. I loathe that I must disclose such unsavory details, but I've no doubt that you would want more than anything to know what became of me. I grow weary now and fear I must stop, but I will persevere. Mother, please count on this as I make my way northward towards civilization and competent, humane assistance.

As Always, Love and Gratitude, Your Devoted Son, Dexter.

Port Starboard and Upper Lake Worth

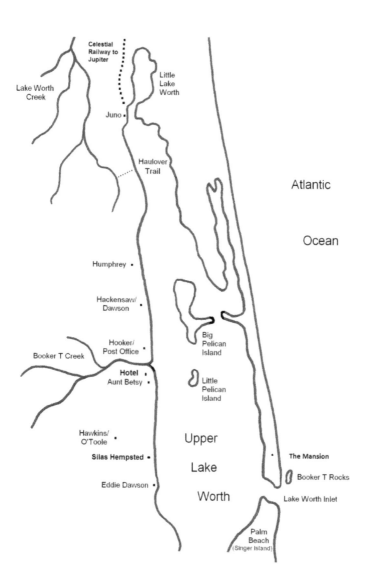

Celestial
Railway to
Jupiter

Little
Lake
Worth

Lake Worth
Creek

Juno •

Haulover
Trail

Atlantic

Ocean

Humphrey •

Hackensaw/
Dawson •

Hooker/
Post Office •

Big
Pelican
Island

Booker T Creek

Hotel •
Aunt Betsy •

Little
Pelican
Island

Hawkins/
O'Toole •

Upper

Silas Hempsted •

Lake

The Mansion

Eddie Dawson •

Booker T Rocks

Worth

Lake Worth Inlet

Palm
Beach
(Singer Island)

CPSIA information can be obtained
at www.ICGtesting.com
Printed in the USA
LVHW040018261118
598237LV00002B/499/P